COMPOSERS OF THE
TWENTIETH CENTURY
ALLEN FORTE, General Editor

THE MUSIC OF
EDGARD VARESE

JONATHAN W. BERNARD

Yale University Press
New Haven and London

Published with the assistance of the Frederick W. Hilles Publication Fund of Yale University.

The works of Edgard Varèse are copyright of Colfranc Music Publishing Corporation of New York and are reproduced by permission of E. C. Kerby Ltd., Toronto, General Agent. Examples from the following works have been reproduced in this book: *Amériques,* copyright © 1929 and 1973; *Density 21.5,* copyright © 1946; *Ecuatorial,* copyright © 1961; *Ionisation,* copyright © 1934; *Nocturnal,* copyright © 1969; *Octandre,* copyright © 1924 and 1980; *Offrandes,* copyright © 1927.

Designed by James J. Johnson and set in Baskerville & Optima types. Typeset by Keystone Typesetting, Orwigsburg, Penn. Printed in the United States of America by Halliday Lithograph, West Hanover, Mass.

Library of Congress Cataloging-in-Publication Data

Bernard, Jonathan W., 1951–
  The music of Edgard Varèse.

  (Composers of the twentieth century)
  Bibliography: p.
  Includes index.
  1. Varèse, Edgard, 1883–1965—Criticism and
interpretation. I. Title. II. Series.
ML410.V27B5 1987   780'.92'4   86–22431
ISBN 0–300–03515–2 (alk. paper)

10 9 8 7 6 5 4 3 2 1

To my parents

The goal of a theoretic investigation is

1. to find the living,
2. to make its pulsation perceptible, and
3. to determine wherein the living conforms to law.

Living facts—as isolated phenomena and in their interrelationships—can be gathered in such a manner. It is the task of philosophy to draw conclusions from this material, and it is a work of synthesis of the highest order.

—WASSILY KANDINSKY, *Point and Line to Plane* (1926)

CONTENTS

PREFACE

For many of the examples in this book, a mode of graphic representation has been devised. In the grid of each graphically notated example, the total available range from lowest to highest pitch (or whatever portion of that range is occupied at the point where the example occurs) is calibrated on the vertical axis, from lowest at the bottom to highest at the top. Each square equals one semitone. Numbers in the left margin of the grid mark the locations of C from the lowest octave, 1 (corresponding to the lowest C on the piano) to the highest, 8. Time is represented along the horizontal axis and elapses from left to right; on this axis the calibrations have no constant value. Measure numbers are given along the upper edge of the graph.

In the text, each pitch is identified by its letter name and a numerical suffix; each such expression is called a *pitch/registral name*. The number denotes the octave in which the pitch is located. Numbering in each octave begins with C; thus middle C is C4, and the B one semitone below is B3. Enharmonic equivalence is reflected in these designations, with two exceptions in each octave; for example, B♯3 is equivalent to C4, and C♭4 is equivalent to B3. Pitches lower than C1 bear the number 0.

Pitch collections in the text appear as concatenations of pitch/registral names separated by dashes: for example, B♭1–D2–C♯3. A configuration such as (D–E–F)5 abbreviates, for the sake of convenience, D5–E5–F5. The parentheses serve only a distributive function; they do not imply in themselves an association between the pitches that they enclose.

Numbers in square brackets, both in the graphs and in the text, refer to vertical distances between two pitches, expressed in numbers of semitones. These numbers are also combined with certain other terms: *[6]-span*, for example, means an interval of six semitones; *[6]-chain* refers to a series of two or more vertically adjacent [6]-spans (example: A3–(D♯–A)4–E♭5). A series of bracketed numbers always refers to a vertical arrangement of adjacent intervals. Expressions such as [6][7] refer to trichordal forms distinguished on the basis of spatial disposition; these are explained fully in chapter 3.

The various closed curves, dotted lines, solid lines, brackets, arrows, and so

ix

forth employed in the graphs have no fixed meanings but serve simply as pictorial devices to explicate analytical points in the text.

The reader should be aware that several musical examples have been reproduced directly from the published scores or have been copied in open score. In the following examples the conventions of transposed score are observed: 3.20, 3.37, 4.12, 4.27, 4.33, 4.35, 5.4, and 5.19. In examples 4.9 and 4.21 all instruments sound as written except for piccolo (one octave above).

In the endnotes, the first reference to each work cited is followed by a tag indicating in which section of the bibliography it may be found (for example: bibl. IA).

ACKNOWLEDGMENTS

I am grateful to those who have lent their assistance, material or spiritual, to the completion of this study. My heartfelt thanks to William Gaver, Music Director at Mt. Greylock Regional High School in Williamstown, Mass., during my student years there, to whom I owe my first exposure, at the age of thirteen, to the music of Varèse; to Bo Alphonce, Robert Moore, and Greg Sandell, whose evaluations of all or part of my dissertation have made this a better book; to Christopher Hasty and Jeannette Swent, whose careful reading of portions of the manuscript led to certain crucial and much-needed changes; to Chou Wen-chung, whose responses to my many questions about the Varèse musical and literary estate were very helpful; to Robert L. Parker, for letting me see his copies of Varèse's correspondence with Carlos Chávez (from the Archives of the University of Mexico Library); to Claude Palisca, Michael McGerr, and Raphael Atlas, whose word-processing expertise saved me a great deal of trouble at various stages in the production of the manuscript; to Pieter van den Toorn, reader for Yale University Press, who made several useful suggestions that have been incorporated into the present book; to Edward Tripp, editor-at-large at Yale Press, who saw this project through its various last-minute crises with his customary aplomb and good humor; to Nancy Woodington, my manuscript editor, whose fine ear for language and fine eye for detail have produced a much more consistent and readable text; and to Dorothy Robinson, General Counsel for Yale University, for assistance in copyright questions.

I wish also to acknowledge the support provided by Yale University, in the form of a Morse Fellowship during 1982 and 1983, when the greater part of this book was written; the access permitted me to the facilities of the Library of Congress, the New York Public Library, and the Houghton Library at Harvard University; the assistance provided by the staff of Inter-Library Loan at Yale University, particularly Victoria Johnson; and the Frederick W. Hilles Publications Fund at Yale University, for supporting the considerable cost of preparing the illustrations.

To Allen Forte I owe a greater debt than I could ever repay. From him I have learned what music theory is, what it may aspire to, and where its limits lie. He took an interest in my theoretical ideas about Varèse's music from their inception; as my dissertation advisor, then as my editor, colleague, and friend, he has been a never-failing source of encouragement and guidance throughout the many metamorphoses that my work has undergone during the past twelve years. This book may not much resemble his own work, but his influence has shaped it in ways that are all the more significant for not being obvious.

Last but certainly not least, I would like to thank my wife Molly, who saw to what degree Varèse had become my alter ego and who married me anyway, and without whose loving and patient support this book would still be very far from completion.

INTRODUCTION

This is a book about the music of Varèse, the first full-length study of his works. It is not a biography; although the definitive biography of Varèse has yet to be written, the task of chronicling Varèse's life has been carried out, with a certain measure of success, by those who knew him personally.[1] This is also not a book which attempts to be comprehensive in the usual manner of a chronological survey, either by mentioning every single work (no matter how cursorily), or by focusing upon a few "representative" works, or by some combination of the two. Of course, it is possible to say something of value even in brief comments about a piece, but analysis under such conditions usually sinks rapidly to the level of record-jacket notes. The kind of landscape description in which a piece is run through and its prominent features mentioned for the benefit of those who know the piece only slightly or not at all is nearly useless in a serious book.[2]

Those who are familiar with the Varèse oeuvre may be surprised that no attempt has been made here to cover every single work, since there are so few. But that Varèse, over a career of forty-seven years, produced but twelve completed compositions is a monumental obstacle to chronological, work-by-work treatment. What does the history of such a career mean for the music composed?

Varèse's life as a composer was anything but normal, and there is a great deal that we will likely never know about it. At least nine substantial works from the years before 1915—almost his entire production to that date—have been either lost or destroyed. Surviving sketches from *Amériques* (1918–21) onward are mostly sparse, where they exist at all.[3] A great quantity of material—from the so-called silent years (1936–54)—that never coalesced into completed works was thrown out and lost in Varèse's lifetime.[4] Except during the 1920s, when Varèse produced steadily, there were always projects among the materials in his studio which were at various stages of progress but which for one reason or another remained unfinished. The resulting lacunae in the record of his career will probably never be filled.

Lack of continuity, or what would customarily be called lack of continuity, is one reason why dealing with Varèse's music in terms of the usual stylistic "development" or succession of "periods" is practically impossible. Every work is scored for a unique combination of instruments, and none is cast in any even remotely recognizable version of a classical form. Indeed, the very expression "cast in a form" is inappropriate to Varèse's music. There are no Symphonies Nos. 1, 2, and 3; there is no series of string quartets. On the face of it, there is no reassuring regularity of any kind. The complete Varèse catalogue for the 1930s, for example, consists of the following: a work of 91 measures for 40 percussion instruments and 13 performers (*Ionisation*); a work of 256 measures set to a Spanish translation of a Central American Indian text and scored for bass voice, two Ondes Martenot, organ, piano, trumpets and trombones, and six percussionists (*Ecuatorial*); and a work of 61 measures for solo flute (*Density 21.5*). The variety is bewildering, the dearth of information frustrating. Under the circumstances, each work must bear a tremendous freight of significance, but how can these significances be assessed? How is it possible to draw correspondences where there are, apparently, so few grounds for comparison?

To resolve this difficulty, one must recognize that—paradoxically—there *is* a kind of continuity to Varèse's work after all. It is not the traditional sort of continuity discussed above. But Varèse's output makes no sense until it is understood as the product, not of a tendency to skip aimlessly from one medium to another, but of a compositional approach that, once settled upon and brought to a mature state, underwent little if any real development. This does not mean that nothing of importance distinguishes one work from another apart from differences in scoring and length. But it does suggest a consistency of conception and technique that makes questions of chronology largely irrelevant. Although we cannot be certain, it does seem likely that the music written before *Amériques* was in large part derivative, substantially influenced by the contemporary music to which Varèse had been exposed in France and Germany. With the exception of the one little song that has survived, all seem to have been written for large orchestra; some included additional choral forces, and one, never finished, was an opera.[5] One possible hypothesis is that the consistent choice of the large ensemble as medium was a reflection, in Varèse's case, of a not yet completely developed compositional sense.[6] After 1918, however, Varèse wrote only twice for orchestra. Once he had reached maturity, he was free to accomplish his aims with practically any combination of instruments and voices. The vestiges of earlier musical styles (impressionism, for instance) audible at points in *Amériques* and *Offrandes* are probably signs of a less-than-perfect focus, of a palpable, even if slight, diffusion of purpose. But certainly from *Hyperprism* on the Varèsian sound is completely and confidently established.

This will hardly be news to those who know even a few of the works. And to practically everyone who has ever written about Varèse it has long been clear that there is some constant quality which all of his works have in common. Thus any analytical study of Varèse's music should aim to express the nature of that constant quality in as precise terms as possible. To do this properly it is necessary to perform some sort of reductive analysis. This prospect will, I realize, seem unfortunate to some and perhaps even unacceptable to others. It has been asserted in the past, not infrequently, that Varèse is so much of a piece that it is impossible to speak of one domain—pitch, say, or rhythm—without engaging all the others simultaneously, and that it is just this quality which has made and will continue to make Varèse's music impervious to reductive analysis. While to some extent I can understand the listener's response which induces this attitude, I cannot accept its validity. My reasons will become evident to the reader further on, but there are a few things that I can say now as a preface.

If musical analysis has any value at all, then presumably it can explain not only structures of individual pieces but also relationships between pieces that are written by the same composer or that belong together for other reasons, such as their place within the same tradition or stylistic period. As the formulation of theories and the analytical techniques drawn from them has become increasingly sophisticated, most educated musicians have come to acknowledge the power of theoretical inquiry not only to fulfill these functions, but further, to provide orderly explanations of all sorts of evolutions in compositional practice, no matter how amazing. Confidence in the power of theory has grown, however, only slowly—especially with regard to its evolutional application. It is only natural that some riddles remain, and that there are still those who are convinced for one reason or another that no theorist will ever solve them.

If the claim concerning the inutility of reductive analysis to Varèse's work could be substantiated, it would signify that Varèse's music stood entirely outside the evolutionary continuum of Western music: that Varèse had made such a radical departure in approach as to overthrow all previously held assumptions about musical structure. However, a composer who managed such an achievement—a real *tabula rasa*—would probably also be writing music that no one else would recognize *as* music. Judging from the critical reception accorded Varèse's work in many quarters during the 1920s, it must have seemed to some ears that he had done just that. Nevertheless, most of those whom he had provoked to the point of hostility eventually came around, leading one to conclude that only at first did Varèse appear inaccessible from the vantage point of Western musical tradition. It is this initial, erroneous (although widely held) opinion, attributable to a lack of perspective which the passage of time has helped to alleviate, that Milton Babbitt has contradicted: "Varèse's music engages the same issues, represents the same kind of stage in the mainstream of musical development as that of Schoenberg, Stravinsky, Webern, and Berg, and . . . its eventual originality is thus most fruitfully and justly gauged in the light of its shared connections, as 'competitive' rather than as insular."[7] Varèse was an innovator, but one who worked with a firm grounding in the musical past and with an informed grasp of the limitations imposed by his heritage. He was not, therefore, "an isolated freebooter," as Boulez once called him, nor was he part of any fringe movement of the kind whose adherents wrote experimental or even open-ended works.

We should not leave this discussion of Varèse's place in the twentieth-century continuum without noting that his considerable influence on music written in the last thirty to forty years is already an essential part of the history of serious composition. This is not the sort of influence exerted by Schoenberg and Hindemith, the two principal composer-pedagogues of this century, who wrote textbooks and propounded their compositional principles in terms that, ostensibly at least, were accessible even to the modestly talented. Nor is it that of Stravinsky, composer of practically the only first-rate music that has gained immediate, widespread acceptance since 1920—music that reached the ears of so many fledgling composers through the teaching of Nadia Boulanger. Rather, Varèse's influence at first glance appears to be no influence at all, for it has depended upon neither large numbers of pupils nor an identifiable school, or ideology, of composition. Varèse taught, it is known, only reluctantly, and the music of André Jolivet, William Grant Still, and Chou Wen-chung—all widely disparate in style, and none like Varèse—is enough to demonstrate that whatever went on in the lessons he gave, Varèse certainly did not insist that his students learn to write as he did. "He never explained why he suggested anything," Marc Wilkinson, another former pupil, has recalled—which is not to say that Varèse's criticisms were arbitrary, but that they forced the student to decide how to respond to them (for example, whether or not to agree with them in the first place) and thus served as an impetus for the student to attack compositional problems with tools of his own devising.[8] Varèse set an example of great originality, and for those with the courage and the ability to follow it must have been an inspiring experience to study with him.

But if Varèse's influence were limited to the few who actually had this kind of personal contact, then it would be of paltry dimensions indeed. In fact, a great many composers have mentioned Varèse as a significant formative influence upon their work. Often cited, for example, have been his pioneering efforts in the alteration of tape-recorded sounds, his path-breaking achievements with percussion, and his truly radical uses of sonority in general. Much of this influence may well have been absorbed intuitively, but the specific characteristics of Varèse's music must have had something to do with the extent of his impact upon other composers. If these characteristics could be defined, they would go a long way toward explaining what Varèse means, and has meant, to contemporary music.

Even more indirectly, Varèse has served as a role model, as Morton Feldman's tribute attests: "What would my life have been without Varèse? For in my most secret and devious self I am an imitator. It is not his music, his 'style,' that I imitate; it is his stance, his way of living in the world."[9] It might be argued that this sort of influence cannot be traced in analysis, since by definition it encourages diversity of technique. But such influence may not be entirely untraceable. Artistic revolutions do not take place all at once; what seems at first to be a complete break with the past may turn out to have more in common with preceding practice than not.

As for Varèse's heirs, then, so for Varèse. But it is possible to agree with Babbitt's assessment quoted above (p. xv) without feeling compelled to apply the same specific techniques of analysis to Varèse's music as to that of his contemporaries. After all, Babbitt has also said of Varèse that "His mind's ear changed not only the sonic surface but the very anatomy of musical structure."[10] What distinguishes Varèse from his fellows is the *degree* to which he found it necessary to innovate. Varèse set himself formidable tasks, and they demanded a great deal of him. Much had to be invented from scratch, and the process had to be repeated in large part each time a new work was begun. Worse, even the expenditure of enormous effort could not guarantee entirely satisfactory results, for everything he wrote was constrained by the extant means of sound production—conventional instruments. It seems that Varèse felt increasingly in need of new kinds of instruments as time went on, especially after about 1930, and that as his attempts to interest foundations, sound studios, and other commercial enterprises in subsidizing research into and construction of such instruments were repeatedly rebuffed, he sank into a state of discouragement which led eventually to creative paralysis. He still composed, but "would tear up at night what I had written during the day and vice versa."[11] As a result, almost nineteen years elapsed between the premiere of *Density 21.5* and that of *Déserts*.[12]

However, even discounting these years of silence Varèse fell far short of producing even one complete work per year from 1922, the date of the premiere of *Offrandes,* to his death in 1965. It is a curious aspect of his career that the earliest years were also the most prolific; while his compositional objectives may have crystallized around 1920, clearly they did not bring with them a fluent technique, or one that became more fluent with use. What might be the nature of such a technique?

If there was one word which was anathema to Varèse above all others, it was "system." For him the word connoted an inability to think for oneself, an excuse for "lying down in other men's thoughts," as Romain Rolland put it so memorably in his novel *Jean-Christophe,* which Varèse quoted in his lectures. The tendency to systematize was something Varèse inveighed against all his life. Perhaps this is an indication that he was, in his younger years, lured into a derivative style (or one which seemed to him, in retrospect, derivative), and that he had had to learn how to extricate himself from its influence. To the category of "systematic" Varèse relegated both neoclassic tendencies and the twelve-tone school. The first of these he attributed to Stravinsky in large part, and as early as 1934 he was already saying, "I think that Stravinsky is finished"—a statement which only begins to reveal the depths of his antipathy.[13] Dodecaphony, of course, was Schoenberg's fault, and while Varèse directed his most withering contempt at neoclassicism, he reserved a few barbs for the twelve-tone approach, calling it "hardening of the arteries" and referring to its practitioners as *"les pompiers de douze sons."*[14] He considered it a great tragedy that Schoenberg, having freed music from tonality, subsequently sought refuge in a system.

We learn from this that Varèse saw the willingness of composers to adopt approaches devised by others as tantamount to confession of a failure of imagination—but also that *inventing a system oneself* was hardly any better. Unless we assume that Varèse was a hypocrite, we must conclude that he saw no value in this sort of invention for his own purposes and based none of his compositions on anything resembling one. This refusal to impose certain limitations on what could be done in a composition, for the sake of greater technical facility, may explain why Varèse completed so few works. But to say this is not to deny the possibility that there is something *methodical* about Varèse's compositional procedure. Granted, it is difficult to be sure what qualified by Varèse's lights as methodical, what as systematic. Nevertheless, I hypothesize that he did draw the line between the two somewhere, and that he would not have objected to characterization of his compositional procedure as methodical.

That method has something to do with Varèse's work must in fact be allowed if serious theoretical inquiry is to go forward. However, while we must expect that a viable theory for Varèse will be held to the same standards of rigor that have shaped successful theories of other music, the actual details will bear little relation to any theory previously formulated. Quite a few attempts have been made to solve the unusual theoretical problems that Varèse's music poses; that most have met, at best, with very limited success can be attributed in large part to a preoccupation with *object* rather than *process*. As those who have launched investigations have quickly discovered, the variety of Varèse's pitch, rhythmic, timbral, and dynamic structures is staggering. No attempt simply to classify these as a repertoire of possibilities available for deployment once introduced in a given work will get very far, for such a repertoire grows before long to unmanageable proportions. What it means to focus on process instead of object will be demonstrated in the core chapters.

The actual devising of a theory, and from it an analytic method, must remain an exercise based largely upon conjecture. The available hard evidence of Varèse's compositional procedures is very skimpy, principally because Varèse did not think that it was anyone else's business how he composed. He was no hermit—by all accounts he was warm and gregarious by nature—but when asked to talk about his own music he invariably became cryptic and indirect. This is reflected in his lecture texts (not extensive), in his writings for publication (even fewer), and in his statements for the press and in other interview situations. The disinclination to talk shop may also have had something to do with the fact that Varèse numbered very few composers among his close friends and on the whole preferred the company of people from the other arts, notably painters and sculptors. During his student years in Paris he had already begun to gravitate toward artistic circles where innovation and change were held in the highest esteem. To a far greater extent than his formal musical education, the ideas he encountered as a result of these associations must be assessed as the principal forces that formed his aesthetic. By tracing the origins of this aesthetic in the documents of early twentieth-century painting and sculpture, one comes to appreciate the extremely unusual point of view, for a composer, that Varèse brought to questions of musical structure. The correspondences between his descriptions of his work and the language of contemporaneous artists and critics suggest that Varèse's compositional method not only challenged assumptions that were then nearly universally held but actually managed as well to neutralize and replace many of them.

There certainly are risks involved in relying upon Varèse's recorded statements as the primary basis for a theory of his work. Fernand Ouellette's observation that Varèse "would play wicked tricks on interviewers who did not know him" and that "it was necessary to have known him a long time to be able to tell *when* in his replies he was telling the truth" has left the impression that those who never knew him at all will never be able to sift the truth from the lies, be the latter calculated or whimsical.[15] But there is no need to be as despairing as that. Varèse's life was marked by a passionate, absolutely unswerving commitment to what he called "the liberation of sound"—a modernization that would give composers the same freedom as their counterparts in the other arts—and by a fierce desire both to educate and to convert the public to his view. This evangelical spirit was most evident during the twenties, the years of the International Composers' Guild, and was nearly in eclipse during the time of his great discouragement (most of the forties). But it never completely disappeared, and came back in force during his last, "rediscovered" years. Certain readily identifiable themes arise again and again in his lectures, articles, and statements to interviewers. Unless one postulates some sort of lifelong plan to deceive everyone, surely these common themes must be taken at face value. Varèse wanted very much to be believed. Thus it seems unlikely that he responded evasively or misleadingly to questions about his music which he could answer *in general terms*.

What Varèse did shy away from was the more specific kind of discussion usually called "analysis." He preferred to speak analogically, not analytically, of his music, often with reference to physical phenomena. The analogy to crystallization, of crucial importance both to his aesthetic and to the invention of specific theoretical tools for his music, is a good example. Attempts to involve him in more narrowly defined, "analytical" discussions made him uneasy. Varèse's years as a student, both at the Schola Cantorum and the Paris Conservatoire, had left him with an almost entirely negative impression of pedagogy; his encounters with musical analysis there had convinced him that most people who taught it were stuck firmly in the past and were inclined to use analysis as a weapon against innovation. Varèse more than once related an anecdote about Vincent d'Indy, who, in the course of discussing a passage from *Parsifal* one day, noted, "Here Wagner failed to modulate in time."[16] Small wonder that Varèse, later remembering his exposure to such pedantry, bitterly proclaimed: "By its very definition analysis is sterile. To explain by means of it is to decompose, to mutilate the spirit of a work."[17]

Even years later this attitude persisted, as is demonstrated by one bit of evidence preserved in print. In a forum that could reasonably be described as sympathetic, in which Varèse was asked to respond to questions put by a number of other composers, the following exchange took place:

MILTON BABBITT: It is customary to conceive of a complex of tones, predefined functionally with regard to one another, as the motivating unit whose internal implications generate a musical structure. You, however, have stated that you consider the individual tone a "complex entity" capable of fulfilling a generative function. Does this mean that in your music the structure of the individual tone functions in a manner comparable to that of the triad in so-called "tonal" music, and the tone-set in twelve-tone music?

EDGARD VARESE: Your question gravitates around a statement that the individual tone is a complex entity capable of fulfilling a generative function, and you attribute this statement to me. I should like to know where you found this misquotation? I don't even know what "I" mean. Consequently I am sorry to say that I cannot answer your question, which, moreover, would seem, if the glimmer I get of your meaning is correct, to involve a more thorough investigation of my music than could be undertaken here.[18]

It is possible, of course, that Varèse genuinely was at a loss to engage the question. Certainly there is no written trace of the statement attributed to him by Babbitt. Perhaps Babbitt was remembering something that Varèse had been quoted as saying about expanded timbral possibilities that new instruments might afford the composer through control of overtones. Varèse might have responded with some comment along these lines if the direction of the question had not been so specifically and uncompromisingly analytical.

Other problems of interpretation arise because Varèse was prone to occasional exaggeration for the sake of making a point more forcefully. Further, he was never as comfortable in English as he was in French, and even with Louise by his side to help it is probable that his slightly awkward replies to questions, combined with the typical reporter's ability to garble even the most straightforward of responses, now and then produced seeming contradictions between one interview or article and another. Armed with a thorough acquaintance with Varèse's manner of expression, however, it is usually possible to resolve such contradictions. For example, consider Varèse's use of the word *atonal*. In a 1930 interview, Varèse characterized his music as "naturally atonal," with the qualification that "certain tones" served as "axes around which the sound masses seem to converge." But four years later, in conversation with Michael Sperling, Varèse applied the word pejoratively to Schoenberg's then new approach: "This 'system' of atonality simply does not exist; it is a fallacy of thought, for we feel a tonality whether or not we deny its presence."[19] On which of these two occasions did he say what he really thought about atonality? It is probably best to conclude that Varèse meant the word in two different senses: in the case of his own music, to describe its lack of "tonality" in the old sense (and therefore also in the neoclassical sense); in the case of twelve-tone music, to debunk the notion that it is possible to give every note a meaning absolutely equal to that of every other (a notion, the reader will observe, specifically excluded from Varèse's own practice in the earlier statement).[20] It is important to understand this, for from the last phrase of the Sperling quotation, taken out of context, might be inferred—mistakenly—the presence of some kind of secret tonality in Varèse's music.

Varèse's statements about his work *Déserts* at the time of its composition and its premiere afford another interesting comparison. In a letter to the composer Luigi Dallapiccola, Varèse denounced "the intellectualism of the interval" and promised that it would play no part in his new piece.[21] Does this indicate that a study of the intervallic content of the work, of the relative sizes involved and their interplay, is irrelevant? Apparently not; the program note for the first performance states that "movement is produced by the exactly calculated intensities and tensions which function in opposition to one another" and that the word *tension* refers to "the size of the interval employed."[22] By the time Varèse wrote to Dallapiccola he had been to Darmstadt and had encountered the rigors and rigidities of post-Webernian serialism. If he had disliked Schoenberg's twelve-tone "system," one can imagine how much more repelled he must have been by the "mathematically" involved varieties of dodecaphony that the European avant-garde then was so avidly pursuing. Hence his phrase "those clever-clever fellows who need crutches," from the same letter. Again, there is a great danger in interpreting statements out of context. Phrases such as "the intellectualism of the interval" should not be used to justify the idea that only vaguely defined, intuitive approaches to Varèse can tell us anything worth knowing about the music.

Not everything Varèse said is unambiguous, and not everything was of unrelievedly serious intent. Toward the end of his life Varèse seems to have fallen prey occasionally to the temptation to embellish the details of his personal history. One can scarcely believe what he told Georges Charbonnier in 1955: that even his earliest compositional efforts had nothing to do with other musical activity in Paris, simply because he associated with artists and writers rather than with musicians.[23] We listen somewhat skeptically, too, to the claim that when he was studying with Charles Widor at the Conservatory he "even became the star of the class owing to the ease and dexterity with which I juggled the subtleties of counterpoint"—as if to say that he could have beaten the neoclassicists at their own game had he been so inclined.[24] If other reports are to be believed, Varèse may have been better known to his classmates as "one who appeared each week with one or two new measures of music and a new fascinating description of what he intended to write but never completed anything."[25] But clearly such trivial instances of self-indulgence do not bespeak a larger intention on Varèse's part to misrepresent himself.

Varèse was not always the most patient of men, either, when confronted by interviewers. If they took care not to ask him stupid questions, then he was perfectly cooperative, even forthcoming; otherwise, he was easily provoked. To a reporter from the Philadelphia *Evening Bulletin* who asked him, after a performance of *Amériques,* why he had used all those unusual sounds, he responded: "I do that to avoid monotony."[26] Or witness his testy behavior at a press conference which he and André Malraux had called to announce a collaboration on one of the several metamorphoses of *Espace*—promptly dubbed the "Red Symphony" by reporters—and at which, to judge by the tone of the newspaper article about it, he must have been questioned somewhat derisively:

Mr. Varèse will call upon new electrical instruments, he said, and will have sections
of the orchestra and chorus wired to amplifiers in different sections of the au-
ditorium so that the music will at times "hit the hearer on the back of the neck."
"Why?" he was asked.
"Because I want to," he replied.[27]

It would certainly be unwise to conclude from these responses that there were no
other reasons for what Varèse did.

As for the specific details of Varèse's working methods, so little is known about
them that we must resist the temptation to draw more conclusions than are
warranted from the amount of information available. But at least a few interesting
facts have survived. The recollections of several people who saw Varèse's studio
while he was alive are in close agreement about the appearance of work in
progress. For example, in a diary entry dated October 1941 Anaïs Nin, friend of
the Varèses over a period of many years, provided the following description:

> On the music stand there is always a piece of musical notations. They are in a state of
> revision, resembling a collage: all fragments, which he arranges, rearranges, dis-
> places, cuts, glues, reglues, pins, and clips until they achieve a towering con-
> struction. I always look at these fragments, which are also tacked on a board above
> his worktable and on the walls, because they express the essence of his work and
> character. They are in a state of flux, mobility, flexibility, always ready to fly into a
> new metamorphosis, free, obeying no monotonous sequence or order, except his
> own.[28]

Chou Wen-chung also mentions the sketches hanging in "a long line—on the wall
in front of his desk—that he called his 'laundry line.' "[29] Although Nin was not a
musically trained observer, still the apparent *physical* aspect of Varèse's approach
to compositional assembly that she has described is fascinating: actual, physically
distinct fragments that could be moved around. What does this have to do with the
dichotomy of process and object mentioned earlier? Possibly it affirms his involvement with process rather than result—that is, in his search for the best way to
express a particular process, he composed, juxtaposed, and rearranged fragments
that were simply the means to that end. These fragments, nominally remaining
the same while they were being moved about, would in a new configuration
actually be fundamentally altered because their function in process was being
changed. Indeed, it could be argued that unless their primary significance was as
stages in a process, rather than as objects in themselves, their meaning could not
have survived shifts in location. Otherwise one would be forced to assert that order
of events has no relevance at all—surely an untenable position, at least until much
later in the history of composition.

Contributing to and strengthening this hypothesis is the fact that Varèse
"borrowed" on occasion from both finished and unfinished works of his own as he
composed new ones. There are a few well-known instances of such borrowing.
Measures 21–29 of "La croix du sud," the second of the two *Offrandes* of 1921, is a

conflation and abridgment of mm. 34–42 and mm. 120–124 of *Amériques*, begun
in 1918. Stravinsky has mentioned that the vocal line of *Ecuatorial*, mm. 80–81,
reappears in *Density 21.5* (mm. 32–35).[30] This, however, is a much less specific
correspondence than the first, as is the resemblance between the figure in *Intégrales* first given in the E♭ clarinet in m. 1 and the passage in *Arcana* beginning at m.
98. Except for the *Offrandes-Amériques* link, these connections seem hardly at all
like quotations, whose quality might reflect a certain fascination with the material
itself, divorced from its contextual function, but much more like echoes, so
changed over time and distance of transmission as to be just barely recognizable.
As for the incomplete works, Chou has attested to the resurfacing of ideas originally composed for *Espace* in *Poème electronique* and *Nocturnal*, although his impressions about this may in large part be based upon what he can remember of the
sketches for *Espace* that were hung on the "laundry line," many of which have not
been preserved.[31]

   The nonsystematic nature of Varèse's approach inevitably raises questions of
consistency. Varèse's secretive attitude about the technical aspects of his work
should not be taken to imply that there is some hidden key, some all-encompassing
principle to which every detail of every piece can be subjugated. The analyst must
expect the occasional anomaly. Chou Wen-chung has revealed that Varèse did
indeed draw up all-inclusive designs when he began work on new projects but then
constantly revised these designs as he composed. Thus the results often differed
considerably from what had initially been envisioned.[32] That Varèse may have felt
a certain ambivalence about this piecemeal approach, and perhaps even a nagging
dissatisfaction with the results, is expressed very well in his aphorism: "No matter
how consummate a work of art may seem, it is only an approximation of the
original conception. It is the artist's consciousness of this discrepancy between his
conception and the realization that assures his progress."[33] Alterations in the basic
plan made while executing the work would form new structural connections while
dissolving others. Those created might well be more indirect than those originally
conceived; and in some cases, connections of any kind might completely disappear. Extensive recomposition carried out in this fashion would no doubt destroy
the original order, but more modest changes, putting only a few details out of
place, would leave the larger intentions intact.

   Conceptually, this study takes as its province all the works of Varèse. In
practice, a few have been given far less extensive treatment than others, and some
have been omitted from consideration entirely.[34] Treatment of the pieces that can
be regarded as the core of Varèse's work (*Offrandes*, 1921; *Hyperprism*, 1923;
Octandre, 1924; *Intégrales*, 1925; *Arcana*, 1927; *Ecuatorial*, 1934; *Density 21.5*, 1936;
Déserts, 1954; *Nocturnal*, 1961) is subject to limits as well. If one cannot provide a
verbal equivalent for a musical work—or for any work of art, for that matter—
then the "complete analysis" is a chimera, and attempts to *depict* a work by
translating all of its contents into manipulable symbols are simply futile. The
analyst can only hope to identify what he finds most significant about his subject
and explain as best he is able the evidence that attests to that significance. He must

aim to illuminate, realizing as he does so that only selective illumination is possible. The choices involved must be made with great care, for they will affect the entire analysis. But these *analytical* choices ultimately depend upon prior *theoretical* choices, which one either inherits or makes oneself. For the music of Varèse there is nothing to inherit; whether one's theoretical choices are appropriate or not thus becomes an absolutely crucial matter.

Varèse's time was long in coming, but he has made it into history at last. Stravinsky's comment that "Varèse's music will endure," that "we know this now because it has dated in the right way," which once seemed such a left-handed, even patronizing compliment, actually makes this very point.[35] Has the time now come as well for his theoreticians? Some plainly wish that this advent could be postponed indefinitely (Morton Feldman [1966]: "Do we think Varèse is now something to dissect? Are we making ready the test tubes?"[36]) On a less ominous note, Chou has said (1977): "I am not sure we can find all the answers. I don't think one can really do that with Varèse's music at this time. We will need perhaps a little more hindsight."[37] Perhaps the passage of years has changed Chou's assessment—but even if not, there seems little point in hanging back any longer, despite the formidable size of the task confronting us.

"I have already seen," said the author of the first truly theoretical article on Varèse, "too many reviews either berating his music without showing the reason why, or praising without telling wherein its excellence lies."[38] Henry Cowell in 1928 saw very clearly what lay ahead of him and others who would attempt to understand Varèse's music. Some important steps toward that understanding have been taken in the nearly sixty years since the publication of Cowell's article; the past ten years, in fact, have witnessed an accelerated pace. The matter of hindsight is important, but exactly how much is sufficient is largely a matter of opinion. Furthermore, hindsight does not simply accumulate as times goes by. If nothing is learned in the interim, then the most likely effect of the passage of time will be to throw the subject into greater obscurity.

Not all the answers to the perplexing questions posed by order and structure in Varèse's music are to be found in this book. But the set of theoretical constructs developed here and used as a basis for extensive analysis of the oeuvre does represent a breakthrough, for it arises directly from those features of Varèse's aesthetic and method which most clearly distinguish him from his contemporaries. For the musician who is sufficiently acquainted with Varèse's music to recognize its distinctive and powerful character, and who is intrigued enough to seek its underlying principles, this book offers a path to understanding what Varèse meant by "the corporealization of the intelligence that is in sound," and a way to emulate him in his aspiration "to be *in* the music, part of the acoustical vibration."[39]

ONE
VARESE'S AESTHETIC BACKGROUND

Avant [19]14, c'était une merveille. Avant 14, c'était fantastique.
C'était une montée en flèche, la vie en 14. Il n'y a qu'à voir ce qu'on
donnait en peinture. Le mouvement qui s'affirmait ici et en
Allemagne. C'était quelque chose d'inimaginable.[1]

As a composer, it is clear, Varèse felt himself to be very much on his own. Although a few close and lasting friendships, with Carl Ruggles for example, are a matter of record, Varèse belonged to no circle like Les Six in Paris, or even like the group of Boulanger alumni in the United States. His steadfast and lifelong resistance to chumminess with other composers stemmed from several factors: for one, his dislike for schools of thought, such as neoclassicism or dodecaphony; for another, his conviction that most composers of his day were unable, by virtue of disposition or training, to think in really new or original ways. Musical composition, in Varèse's view, had been held back for some time in its progress by the failure of musicians to see the necessity of developing new instruments and new means of sound production in general, and by academic conservatism, which perpetuated old forms and formulas.

By contrast, the visual arts had undergone fundamental and liberating changes: "It is many years now since painting freed itself from the constraints of pure representation and description and from academic rules. Painters responded to the world—the completely different world—in which they found themselves, while music was still fitting itself into arbitrary patterns called forms, and following obsolete rules."[2] Varèse's preference for the company of painters and sculptors developed, according to his own account, rather early. Responding to one interviewer in 1955, Varèse recalled his student years in Paris and mentioned that he had been more attracted to painters (as well as to writers and scientists) than to musicians.[3] In her biography of Varèse, Louise Varèse mentions La Belle Edition, a small publishing concern, which brought out several short-lived magazines devoted to the arts, and L'Abbaye de Créteil, an experimental commune of artists and writers, as places which Varèse frequented and where he got to know many artists and writers about art. The names of Guillaume Apollinaire ("un animateur de génie," as Varèse called him), Albert Gleizes, André Salmon, Jean Cocteau, and Henri Barzun are readily recognizable today as influential figures.[4] Other friends

1

and acquaintances of the Paris years included Fernand Léger, André Derain, Manolo, Modigliani, Robert Delaunay, Raoul Dufy, Max Jacob, and André Lhote.[5] Undeniably Varèse met many composers and other musicians during this period of his life as well. Yet it is some measure of the importance of the painters and poets to Varèse that he seems to have remembered them much better: their personalities shine through much more strongly in the colorful anecdotes and quotations transmitted by his biographer.[6] Of the composers, only Satie (and, to a lesser extent, Debussy) show the same vitality.

After 1916, when Varèse arrived in the United States, he also gravitated toward the company of artists, most notably the members of the "291" group (Stieglitz's Photo-Secession), and Walter Arensberg's salon. Again there is a long list of artists connected in some way with Varèse, ranging from casual acquaintances to enduring friendships.[7]

By the late 1910s, of course, Varèse was already a composer of considerable experience, having written at least nine substantial works. Unfortunately we will never have more than a vague notion of what these works, now lost, were like.[8] Given the unusual circumstances, Varèse may be regarded as a composer whose career began in his thirty-ninth year, with the premiere of *Offrandes* in 1922, for this is the Varèse known to the world, the Varèse who has left his indelible mark on the music of this century. Consequently, his associations with artists up to that time may plausibly be assessed as formative influences.

Bram Dijkstra has written, in his book on William Carlos Williams: "Because even the inventors must be followers first, it is of primary importance for the understanding of an innovative artist's work and intentions to know how the artist's predominant interests were shaped by his immediate intellectual milieu."[9] That this applies to Varèse too is quite clear. The contacts made in those years are, conceivably, as important to Varèse's development as the books that he mentioned so often as his sources of information and inspiration—Helmholtz's *On the Sensations of Tone,* Durutte's *Technie Harmonique,* and Busoni's *Sketch of a New Aesthetic of Music.* But since we will never have transcripts of the conversations, and since nearly everyone who could have recalled even approximately what was said has long since passed away, how can we discover what, if anything, was actually transmitted?

One possibly fruitful approach would be to examine contemporary art theory and criticism—accounts of the nature and aims of the new painting and sculpture of the time written by the artists themselves and by other informed and sympathetic writers and critics. There can be little doubt that much of what was being written then was also being said informally in many settings. Ideas that one finds surfacing and resurfacing in writings of the time were evidently in the air. Any attempt to pick out the ones which might have stuck with a young, revolutionarily inclined composer, and which might, in some transmuted form, have been incorporated into his artistic credo (general) and approach to his material (specific), is ultimately speculative, but it is certainly an attempt worth making:

The real developments, the innovations, in art and life, whether in literature or
painting, depend on the manner in which the elements of one medium are translated to the conditions of another. Thus, if an artist's work is strikingly different
from that of his predecessors or contemporaries, one may well look for the source of
his originality to those of his interests which fall outside the proper sphere of his own
medium.[10]

Varèse probably never even read, much less studied, most of the documents
considered here. No reliable indication of Varèse's reading habits exists; we do
know that he was familiar with Marinetti's writings on futurism,[11] but no one is in
a position to say whether he ever saw Apollinaire's book on the cubist painters, for
example, or even any of the other futurist writings, some of which seem even
closer to Varèse in spirit than Marinetti's. At least some of the ideas that Apollinaire put forth in his 1912 book would very likely have been on his mind several
years earlier, and his friends and acquaintances would have heard about them.

By now everyone knows how unreliable these contemporary documents are for
present-day study of art. The value that they have as eyewitness accounts, as
chronicles of the rapid changes that artistic expression was then undergoing and
of the immediate, often vivid attempts of artists and their friends to put these into
words, is offset by the authors' lack of perspective on these developments (certainly unavoidable), by their mistaking trivial issues for great ones and vice versa,
by their separation of works into nonexistent subgenres, and, conversely, by their
failure to mark important differences between types of art that now seem to bear
only a superficial resemblance to one another. Nevertheless, it would be misleading for our purposes to read the manifestos and commentaries of 1907–1920
(approximately) in light of the understanding of the art of this era which has
accumulated since then.[12] With very few exceptions, I will avoid clouding the
waters with insights not available to anyone at the time, even to those most
intimately involved with artistic creation.

This restriction does not mean, however, that Varèse necessarily belongs in any
one of the categories that were customarily delineated in those days. Varèse was a
man of eclectic sensibilities, and he would have found only encouragement in this
tendency among the New York artists of the time, who in their response to the
melting-pot effect of America were not much inclined to maintain the distinctions
held in Europe. Furthermore, Varèse never adopted anyone's opinions wholesale;
he never simply and uncritically absorbed ideas about visual art to apply them to
music. Traces there are, and in abundance, but whatever he borrowed became
uniquely his own.

Thus it is not possible to develop a series of fixed, one-to-one correspondences
between this visual idea and that musical idea. For one thing, even the analogies
that Varèse himself explicitly made are mutually contradictory on a number of
points. For another, some of the most hotly debated issues of the time in the art
world—issues which received a disproportionate amount of attention—either

lack convincing analogues in music or have at best only trivial meanings there. Finally, every analogy, taken far enough, eventually breaks down. We must be content to discover what connections do exist, employing them as Varèse did to draw analogies and to liberate the mind from restrictive ways of thinking about musical structure. The history of ideas assembled in this way will show that Varèse, though he did not simply make others' ideas his own, clearly did not develop in a vacuum either.

To provide some kind of workable organization for the following discussion, the currents of artistic thought have been divided into three main channels, fairly well defined at the time along national lines and still recognized as historically valid: cubism, futurism, and expressionism (the blaue Reiter group). But these currents continually touched and crossed, even if they ran for the most part separately. Cubism and futurism, for instance, were often confused at first (the terms seemed initially to serve as national identifications for the new art of France and Italy respectively). And while many artists professed similar aims, the means actually employed to achieve them were often radically different. Thus cross-referencing will frequently be necessary. In the process certain lesser, related movements, such as purism, will be mentioned, and certain ideas important to Varèse that were held in common (though understood in divergent ways), such as simultaneity, will also be covered.

CUBISM

The earliest documents in our study date from 1907, the year traditionally—then as now—identified as the time when cubism first burst upon the scene.[13] Born in France, this movement was bound to have a certain cultural immediacy for Varèse, and thus it makes sense to start here.

In the cubist writings, one finds a large range of ideas, some peculiar to cubism, others (of more general interest and application) which reappear, if not precisely in the same form, in writings associated with other movements. In the latter category there are several recurrent themes which have clear correspondences in Varèse's recorded statements. The idea of newness for its own sake as a measure of worth of a work of art is quite important. In his earliest extended article Varèse quoted approvingly from two authors on the subject:

"Genius . . . is above morality: for its only duty is to create and consequently to live. What is called its probity is its gift to men of a beautiful newness." . . . "Beauty in art is a relative result obtained from a mixture of different elements, often the most unexpected. One only of all these elements is stable and permanent and must be present in any combination: this is novelty. A work of art must be new and may be recognized as new if it gives one a sensation never before experienced." The same author demands for art: "Freedom of conception, the renunciation of taught formulas, a tendency toward all that is new, even at the risk of seeming eccentric."[14]

The value placed on newness in art is evident, for example, in Apollinaire's comments on Braque's work: "This painter composes his pictures in absolute devotion to complete newness, complete truth . . . each work becomes a new universe with its own laws."[15] William Carlos Williams, too, has been quoted on this subject: "The only way man differed from every other creature was in his ability to improvise novelty and, since the pictorial artist was under discussion, anything in paint that is truly new, truly a fresh creation, is good art."[16]

In the quotation from Apollinaire, and in de Gourmont's renunciation of taught formulas, we find the idea of emancipation from old rules and the attendant formulation of new ones particular to each newly created work of art. Indeed, the exaltation of newness practically demanded that the artist not be bound by pre-existing notions of what art ought to be. From his own, musical past, Varèse supplied Debussy's famous aphorism, "Rules do not make a work of art," and a similar sentiment from Busoni: "The role of the creative artist is to make new laws, not to follow those already made."[17] He also insisted that he did not follow anyone else's rules, as when he said of his work *Déserts* (1950–1954) that it was "not based on any fixed set of intervals such as a scale, a series, or any existing principle of musical measurement" but rather that the materials used were "decided by the exigencies of this particular work."[18] This kind of thinking was already a part of the cubist aesthetic by early in the second decade of the century. We read in Albert Gleizes and Jean Metzinger's book *Du Cubisme*: "Cubism, whch has been accused of being a system, condemns all systems. . . . Let us grant that it is a method, but let us not permit the confusion of method with system." Anything that might compromise individuality was shunned: "The artist who abstains from any concessions, who does not explain himself and who tells nothing, builds up an internal strength whose radiance shines all around."[19] To do otherwise was to risk another kind of codification, precisely what the cubists sought to escape from. Varèse agreed. His well-known statement against analysis has the same bristling, almost superstitious quality.[20]

The disinclination to over-intellectualize one's art, however, did not imply an avoidance of thought or logic. Indeed, the ability to think was seen as a sine qua non for the creation of real art. In Picasso's words: "Art is not the application of beauty but what the instinct and the brain can conceive beyond any canon."[21] The cubists' attitude on this issue can to an extent be attributed to a disdain for the impressionists, who professed not to know how their work came about. For instance: "Let us turn to the defense of [the new, constructive movement in art] against that romantic view which would forbid the creative artist all thought and speculation and would see him simply as an inspired dreamer whose left hand knoweth not what his right hand doeth."[22] In general, as Kozloff has observed, "the typical metaphor of Cubist doctrine . . . was not of mystical emergence, but of ordered comparison and judgment."[23] Again the correspondence to Varèse's beliefs is clear. We have it from Louise Varèse that he detested the word "inspiration," and from a newspaper interview that he sought "new technical mediums which can lend themselves to thought and can keep up with thought."[24] That he called music an "art-science" is also revealing; he often reminded his readers and listeners that in the Middle Ages music was numbered among the sciences, with important consequences for its historical development.[25]

Following logically from the rejection of received truth is the idea that a work of art takes itself as its subject and not the objects or scene supposedly represented. Léonce Rosenberg, for example saw the artist drawing "by synthesis . . . from some object the *elements*—form and color—necessary to the assembling of the subject," thereby creating a work that has not a comparative, but rather a purely instrinsic, value: "beautiful in itself."[26] Similarly Gleizes and Metzinger: "The beauty of a work resides expressly in the work, and not in what is only its pretext."[27] Varèse, for his part, was adamant about the absence of programmatic or anecdotal content from his music: "Don't connect my music with anything external or objective. Don't try to discover a descriptive program for it. Regard it, please, in the abstract. Think of it as existing independently of literary or pictorial associations."[28] And Louise Varèse quotes from Varèse's own program note for the premiere of *Intégrales:* "The music is not a story, is not a picture, is not [a] psychological nor a philosophical abstraction. It is simply my music. . . . Music being a special form of thought can, I believe, express nothing but itself."[29]

Even though in music there is seldom any question of actual depiction of images from the "real world," it is still possible to see why Varèse would have been impressed by the cubists' attempt to distinguish between subject and object. His statement, "Form is a resultant—the result of a process,"[30] and the analogy to crystallization (discussed below, pp. 16–18), correspond closely to the quotations from Rosenberg and Gleizes and Metzinger above. That is, the *objects* in a Varèse work, be they called themes, chord patterns, or—to use his own terminology— planes, masses, and volumes, have no importance in themselves; it is only their interaction over time that establishes the form of the composition. Even clearer in relation to Varèse's words is the following passage: "The subject is the result of the use of the means of creation one has acquired: it is the picture itself. Since the object comes in only as an element, it will be evident that what has to be done is not to reproduce its appearance but to extract from it—in the service of the picture— what is external and constant (for example, the round form of a glass, etc.) and exclude the rest."[31] Just how this process of extraction might be translated into temporal terms and implemented in music will be seen in later chapters.

Cubist Methods and Varèse's Aesthetic

The aim was . . . to create space in a convincing way and therefore a new reality.

SPATIAL THINKING. The depiction and use of space in a painting was hardly a new concern in the twentieth century, but in many respects the means chosen for the purpose were an enormous departure from the past.[32] First of all, the focus on space itself as an element in a painting, and a conscious re-evaluation of its conventional treatment, produced radical changes in the use of perspective and viewpoint. Kahnweiler said: "These painters distinguish between primary and secondary qualities. They endeavor to represent the primary, or most important qualities, as exactly as possible. In painting these are: the object's form, and its position in space."[33] But space has a dual nature: while elements are placed within it, defined by their position within it, they also define the space themselves. Raynal saw the composition as an assemblage of spaces: "Objects must no longer be considered as haphazard representations, but as agglomerations of forces and as aggregates of distinct parts governed by mathematical laws. These objects will henceforward be volumes—volumes, in the strict sense of the word, that is, spaces filled and occupied by aggregates of bodies."[34]

For Varèse, too, space could be considered in two ways, internally and externally. He often spoke of his idea of "music as spatial—as bodies of intelligent sounds moving freely in space," an idea which seems to locate the spatial quality *in* the music, since this formulation existed in Varèse's mind long before the availability of electronic methods and thus referred to music for ensembles of conventional instruments which did not move during performance.[35] In an even earlier lecture Varèse described "movement of sound masses" and their collisions, and projections of movements onto "other planes, moving at different speeds and at different angles."[36] Since one of Varèse's musical dimensions—arguably the most important—is the vertical, it should come as no surprise that Varèse looked forward to the day when new musical apparatus would allow the composer access to the "limits of the lowest and highest registers" and the "unsuspected range," meant in the spatial sense, thereby opened to him.[37]

One of the most detailed accounts that Varèse ever provided of structure in his own compositions concerns *Intégrales* (1924–25). In a radio interview, Varèse asked his listeners to

> visualize the changing projection of a geometrical figure on a plane, with both plane and figure moving in space, but each with its own arbitrary and varying speeds of translation and rotation. The instantaneous form of the projection is determined by the relative orientation between the figure and the plane at the moment. By allowing both the figure and the plane to have motions of their own, one is enabled to paint a highly complex and seemingly unpredictable picture with the projection. In addition, these qualities can be further enhanced by letting the form of the geometrical figure vary as well as its speeds.[38]

The description leaves little doubt as to the inherently spatial quality of *Intégrales*. However, it is also true that Varèse had intended his composition for realization by "certain acoustical media that were not then in existence, but that I knew could be built and would be available sooner or later."[39] What sorts of media might he have had in mind? Contemporary accounts of the planning stages of *Espace* provide a few hints, in their mention of amplified sound designed to reach the audience from different directions.[40] This suggests an intent to externalize spatial considerations beyond their existence within the score itself.

Further, corroborating evidence is available in another newspaper interview from the year before:

> Mr. Varèse's particular interest is in composing rhythms in space as well as rhythms in time. No startling achievements toward this end can be realized until means are developed for transmitting musical sounds electrically from the instruments to different sections of the auditorium, he said. Were this possible, the symphony could be broken down into its component patterns and then reblended through diversely situated amplifiers, thus relating rhythms of space to the rhythms of time and pitch, he explained.[41]

The reporter's paraphrase may be somewhat garbled, but the intent behind Varèse's words is reasonably clear. Finally, in the lecture entitled "Spatial Music," Varèse noted the parabolic and hyperbolic effects of the sirens used in *Amériques* (1918–21) and *Ionisation* (1931) and the tendency of critics to speak of "sound masses molded as though in space" when describing his music. "Of course," Varèse added, "it was still only a *trompe d'oreille*, an aural illusion, so to speak, and not yet literally true." The first literal realization of spatial projection in his music, he said, came with the production of the *Poème électronique,* the collaboration with Le Corbusier for the Philips Pavilion at the 1958 World's Fair in Brussels, in which 425 loudspeakers mounted at various locations in the building were arranged and combined by numerous amplifiers to present "sound routes" for Varèse's taped music. This allowed "various effects such as that of the music running around the pavilion, as well as coming from different directions, reverberations, etc."[42] For Varèse, then, space is something which both expresses and is expressed by music.

The idea that a painting might employ spatial means as an integral feature of expression is certainly rooted solidly in cubist thinking. Gleizes and Metzinger focused upon the division of the canvas as a principal concern, and outlined two methods of approaching the problem:

> According to the first, all the parts are connected by a rhythmic artifice which is determined by one of them. This one—its position on the canvas matters little—gives the painting a center from which or toward which the gradations of color tend, according as the maximum or minimum of intensity resides there. According to the second, . . . the properties of each portion must be left independent, and the plastic continuity must be broken into a thousand surprises of light and shade.[43]

The first of these methods appeared in analogous form in a remark of Varèse's quoted by José André: "Varèse once explained that while his language was naturally atonal, certain tones, repeated in the manner of tonics, functioned as axes around which the sound masses seemed to converge."[44] As for the second, it bears a close affinity to Varèse's ideal of independently moving sound masses and the "sensation of non-blending" which he sought to achieve.[45]

AVOIDANCE OF REPETITION. For Gleizes and Metzinger, spatial considerations entailed certain conditions for proper realization. One is "the inequality of parts," which in the same passage is taken as a granted condition. The reconciliation of the two approaches outlined above—an imperative for the cubists—produces "that superior disequilibrium without which we cannot achieve lyricism."[46] How could "inequality of parts" be guaranteed? The answer involved avoidance of repetition, which thus emerged in a position of overriding importance. Gleizes and Metzinger explained this as well: "Taste immediately dictates a rule: we must paint so that no two portions of the same extent ever meet in the picture. Common sense approves and explains: let one portion repeat another, and the whole becomes measurable. The art which ceases to be a fixation of our personality (unmeasurable, in which nothing is ever repeated), fails to do what we expect of it."[47] "Balance" or "equilibrium," apparently, did not mean the same thing for everyone. For some, the word *equilibrium* seemed to connote a condition of blandness or lack of tension; for others it incorporated tension—stability without weakness. Apollinaire subscribed to the latter meaning in his prediction that "the new painters will provide their admirers with artistic sensations by concentrating exclusively on the problem of creating harmony with unequal lights."[48] For Varèse, no less, the concepts of balance and stability were compatible with inequality of parts. Even in his earliest works, Varèse said, he "wanted to find a way to project in music the concept of calculated or controlled gravitation, how one element pushing on the other stabilizes the total structure, thus using the material elements at the same time in opposition to and in support of one another."[49]

This brings us to an issue that had important ramifications for both the cubists and Varèse, that of the role of rhythm in the delineation of form. The word itself is potentially deceptive, for its use with reference to both painting and music may be only a coincidence: rhythm in music is bound up inextricably with the passage of time, a phenomenon which a painting can probably only suggest. Yet there do seem to be grounds for comparison. Recall, for example, Varèse's stated intention of creating rhythms in space as well as in time. Moreover, he disliked exact repetition as a compositional device and focused much of this dislike on rhythmic and metric matters. Varèse professed to find jazz, for example, essentially uninteresting because its dependence upon "fixed patterns of rhythm" and "reiterated schemes of syncopation" suggested the practice of earlier times, the same failing for which he castigated the proponents of neoclassicism.[50] Besides, this aspect of rhythm was only a distraction:

> Rhythm is too often confused with metrics. Cadence or the regular succession of beats and accents has little to do with the rhythm of a composition. Rhythm is the element in music that gives life to the work and holds it together. It is the element of stability, the generator of form. In my own works, for instance, rhythm derives from the simultaneous interplay of unrelated elements that intervene at calculated, but not regular, time-lapses. This corresponds more nearly to the definition of rhythm

in physics and philosophy as "a succession of alternative and opposite or correlative states."[51]

Note the connection made between stability and irregularity here. Juxtaposition of this statement with the following strongly suggests an analogous procedure in visual art: "These are painters aware of the miracle that is achieved when the surface of a picture produces space, and as soon as line threatens to take on a descriptive or decorative importance they break it. Elements of light and shade, so distributed that the one engenders the others, justify these breaks in plastic terms; the arrangement of the breaks creates the Rhythm."[52]

THE ESCAPE FROM ILLUSIONIST PERSPECTIVE. This was probably the most controversial aspect of cubist work, at least initially, and most writers, whether artists themselves or sympathetic onlookers, felt obliged to say something about it. Kahnweiler, for example, spoke of the problems that Picasso had grappled with in *Les Demoiselles d'Avignon:* "These problems were the basic tasks of painting: to represent three dimensions and color on a flat surface, and to comprehend them in the unity of that surface. 'Representation,' however, and 'comprehension' in the strictest and highest sense. Not the simulation of form by chiaroscuro, but the depiction of the three dimensional through drawing on a flat surface."[53] "Simulation" is the key word here. The new painters were attempting, not simple imitation of optical "reality," but depiction of reality in a more direct way: "In representing conceptualized reality or creative reality, the painter can give the effect of three dimensions. He can to a certain extent cube. But not by simply rendering reality as seen, unless he indulges in *trompe-l'oeil,* in foreshortening, or in perspective, thus distorting the quality of the forms conceived or created."[54] Attitude toward perspective had shifted radically. No longer was it regarded as an eternal verity; instead, it had become simply another convention, to be done away with because it obstructed new artistic development: "The convergence which perspective teaches us to simulate cannot evoke the idea of depth."[55]

But what was to be installed in its place? Before considering this question, we might ask another: how the demise of perspective could possibly interest a composer. In music it would not seem that the issue of simulation or depiction of "reality" could ever arise. This is no doubt true, but for Varèse the efforts being made by artists in this direction were evidently a source of encouragement. The safe, accepted ideas about proper depiction of a subject that were the stock in trade of academies must have seemed to Varèse all too depressingly similar to the instruction in harmony, counterpoint, and form which he received at the Schola Cantorum and the Conservatoire in Paris, and against which he eventually rebelled. For him the escape from perspective in visual art was probably analogous to the escape from tonality in musical art. Such an analogy would certainly help to explain why Varèse hated so bitterly the trend toward neoclassicism that flourished from the 1920s onward, and why he so frequently denounced the work that it produced as "music written in the manner of another century."

THE USE OF COLOR AND SHADOW AS AGENTS OF CONTRAST. Such contrast was necessary to the representation of distances between objects. Jacques Rivière began by eliminating the customary treatment of light: in place of employing a single source of light, the painter must "divide up between all the surfaces the shade that formerly accumulated on some; . . . use the small portion of shading allotted to each one by placing it against the nearest edge of some other lit surface, in order to mark the respective inclination and divergence of the parts of the object."[56] Continuing along these lines, Rivière exposed at some length the workings of the new method. The key to the right approach lay in painting depth "as if it were a material thing." The edges of objects would be delimited by "gentle planes of shadow" receding, as if flowing, toward the background, "as the waters of a river fall regularly from a dam." Finally, "this procedure will have the advantage over perspective of marking the connection as well as the distinction between objects; for the planes which keep them apart will also form a transition between them. These planes will at one and the same time repel and bring closer the more distant objects."[57]

Color was used for similar purposes. The painter Fernand Léger quite explicitly outlined its uses:

> Composition by multiplying contrast. . . . You compose a picture so that groups of similar forms are set against other, contrary groups. If you distribute your colors in the same way—that is, by coloring each of the formal groupings in a combination of similar tones which contrast with the tones of another equivalent grouping, you obtain collective sources of tones, lines, and colors acting against other, contrary, and dissonant sources. Contrast = dissonance, and hence a maximum of expressive effect.[58]

Some commentators went even further, as did Julio Gonzales, speaking of Picasso's cubist paintings of 1908: "These paintings—all you would have to do is cut them apart, the colors being only indications of different perspectives, of inclined planes from one side or the other. Then you could assemble them according to the indications given by the color and find yourself in the presence of 'sculpture.'"[59]

The new functions ascribed to color and shadow represented a tremendous change from, and a certain hostility toward, the practice of earlier eras. One author identified, as the "shared ideal" of the new group of painters, the desire "*to react with violence against the notation of the instant, the insidious anecdotalism and all the other surrogates that pass under the name of impressionism . . . to exclude . . . the bric-a-brac of false literature and pseudoclassicism.*"[60]

Varèse's position with respect to the role of a closely analogous domain in music—timbre, or what is often called "color"—was fully in accord with the painters' revision: "The role of color or timbre would be completely changed from being incidental, anecdotal, sensual, or picturesque; it would become an agent of delineation, like the different colors on a map separating the different areas, and an integral part of form. These zones would be felt as isolated." Further, "these zones would be differentiated by various timbres or colors and different loud-nesses" and "would appear of different colors and of different magnitude."[61] This attitude goes hand in hand with his rejection of programmatic content, mentioned earlier (p. 6). Speaking for himself, and for others of like mind, Varèse once told an interviewer that: "We should write today, I presume, in a telegraphic style. We should not hint at situations and emotions; we should do nothing by round-about means; we should discard, as far as we can, material which is not purely musical and should try for expression in the simplest way."[62] As far as his own working methods were concerned, Varèse's special attitude toward timbre was reflected in his complete opposition to the idea of writing a piece and then orchestrating it. For him, the two processes had to be carried out at the same time, "for orchestration is the response to the musical content of the work."[63]

THE ADOPTION OF MULTIPLE VIEWPOINTS. This aspect of cubism was also widely commented upon at the time. Descriptions of the technique are markedly similar from treatise to treatise; their differences seem largely to be variations in the degree of emphasis assigned to one or another purpose of the technique. Gleizes and Metzinger, for example, spoke of "moving around an object to seize from it several successive appearances, which, fused into a single image, recon-stitute it in time."[64] Metzinger extended this a bit: "The men known as cubists . . . have allowed themselves to move round the object, in order to give, under the control of intelligence, a concrete representation of it, made up of several succes-sive aspects. Formerly a picture took possession of space, now it reigns also in time."[65] Thus it was possible to go beyond the mere fact of seeing and bridge the gap between sight and conception: "Conception makes us aware of the object in all its forms, and even makes us aware of objects we would not be able to see. 'I cannot *see* a chiliagon [a thousand-sided figure],' said Bossuet, 'but I can conceive it perfectly well.' "[66]

SIMULTANEITY. At least some of the cubists came to think of the possibility of displaying multiple viewpoints of the same object in one painting in terms of the general concept of simultaneity. Simultaneity or simultaneism (the terms are used synonymously here), in present-day histories of art, tends to be dismissed as "a rather naive idea"[67]—presumably because it takes a mere byproduct of the tech-nique (as that technique is interpreted now) and elevates it to the status of intent. However, there can be little doubt that in those days it was taken seriously, and there can be no doubt at all that Varèse seized upon the idea and made it forever his own. From Apollinaire: "Representing planes to denote volumes, Picasso gives an enumeration so complete and so decisive of the various elements which make up the object, that these do not take the shape of the object, thanks to the effort of the spectator, who is forced to see all the elements simultaneously just because of the way they have been arranged."[68] Louise Varèse has explained the specific means of transmission of the concept to Varèse in her biography, recounting the frequent occasions on which Varèse met Apollinaire and Robert Delaunay at the Delaunays', where Apollinaire and Delaunay "formulated the doctrine of simultaneism": "While poets were juggling words on a page and painters were producing curious juxtapositions of noses, ears, eyes, and breasts in the name of simultaneism, Varèse was beginning to wonder how it might be obtained musically. He believed that, given the means, simultaneism was literally possible in music."[69]

In Delaunay's own writings there is a great deal on the subject of simultaneity, most of it having to do with the increased importance of color. The period when Varèse had regular contact with Delaunay was probably just before the artist's (self-identified) cubist period (1909–1912). A few of Delaunay's surviving writings date from this period, such as his letter to August Macke (1912) setting forth the gist of his views: "What is of great importance to me is the observation of the movement of colors. Only in this way have I found the laws of complementary and simultaneous contrasts of colors which sustain the very rhythm of my vision. In this movement of colors I find the essence, which does not arise from a system, or an *a priori* theory."[70] This bears a certain resemblance to Léger's statements a few years later, quoted above, about the use of color for the purposes of contrast.[71] Note as well the repudiation of system that characterized the cubist aesthetic.

In a short essay, "Light," also dating from 1912, Delaunay delved in more detail into the meaning of "movement of colors":

> Movement [of colors] is produced by the rapport of *odd elements*, of the contrasts of colors between themselves which constitutes *Reality*.
> This reality is endowed with *Vastness* . . . and it then becomes *Rhythmic Simultaneity*.
> Simultaneity in light is *harmony, the rhythm of colors* which creates the *Vision of Man*.[72]

Color, in other words, came first, and from the interaction of colors came the form of the work, for both harmony and rhythm were expressed in terms of color. The designation of color as the prime mover represents a far more extreme position than is found in strictly cubist writings, but Varèse's exposure to Delaunay's ideas on this subject may have encouraged him to think in analogous terms for musical composition. For Delaunay, simultaneity also meant depth, as he explained in a letter to Franz Marc at around this same time; thus Delaunay's concept of simultaneity lent itself well to Varèse's simultaneity of sound-masses in space.[73]

Certain other ideas that Delaunay put forth are likely to have been of interest to Varèse:

> In order that Art attain the limit of sublimity, it must draw upon our harmonic vision: *Clarity*. Clarity will be color, proportion; these proportions are composed of diverse elements, simultaneously involved in an action. This action must be the representative harmony, the *synchronous movement* (simultaneity) *of light* which is *the only reality*. . . . This synchronous action will then be the Subject, which is the representative harmony.[74]

The definition of simultaneity as an action and the idea that such an action would be the real subject of the painting are in clear correspondence to Varèse's own emphasis upon the importance of process in his music. For his part, Apollinaire agreed that Delaunay had accomplished something new. Commenting on the latter's *L'équipe Cardiff, troisième représentation* (1913), he said: "There is nothing successive in this painting, which not only vibrates with the contrast of complementary colors discovered by Seurat, but in which every shade calls forth and is illuminated by all the other colors of the prism. This is simultaneity."[75]

In his famous quadripartite classification of the cubist painters, Apollinaire placed Delaunay among the adherents to orphism. Delaunay did not agree that he belonged in that company, but at least it is clear that others shared his interest in simultaneity, including Henri Barzun, who published a book in 1912 entitled *Voix, chant et rythme simultané* and whose claim to have coined the term *orphism* competed with Apollinaire's.[76] Barzun's involvement with simultaneity was primarily literary, but his works of this period were called "orchestral poetry" and were meant to be performed. He was also one of the founding members of L'Abbaye de Créteil, and Varèse seems to have encountered him there.[77] Later descriptions of the orchestral poetry of Barzun and his followers, and printed versions of the poems themselves, leave little doubt that Varèse knew of this genre and retained lifelong memories of it. Allan Reginald Brown wrote:

> By spacing, and by vertical as well as horizontal harmonization on the page, words uttered synchronously are represented as being heard together. When the poem is read, the voices actually speak simultaneously. Thus the voices and sounds of a crowd, for instance, can be reproduced with the most exact fidelity to reality. The various voices are heard speaking together where the facts require it, while the sounds of the mob, the clash of weapons or implements, the press of bodies, and the like, are represented at the same time. By the combination of voices every effect of shading or emphasis can be secured.[78]

The same author provided an account of a performance of Barzun's *Panharmonie Orphique:* "Eighteen voices were required. The speakers did not appear on the stage but spoke behind masks which formed part of a specially designed cubistic stage setting. Great care was taken to realize in the performance the exact relation of the various voices as indicated by the author's manuscript. The director's copy looked like an ordinary orchestral score."[79] Example 1.1 reproduces the first two pages of Barzun's *L'universel poème, troisième épisode: Terre des pionniers.*

The author of another, contemporaneous account entitled "The art of orchestral poetry / Simultaneism = a means of expression which perhaps will permit great things" posed a serious question: "There is only one objection that might be made to this: Can we hear it? Is it possible to distinguish the meaning of the words in this vocal mass?" To which he answered: "This comes down to a question of *savoir-faire,* of 'craft,' if you will. And one must admit that simultaneism is a snare for the novice, just as much as musical composition. Experience has shown that, when the instrument is well handled, *we hear.*"[80]

Varèse himself never completed any works employing voices in the manner of orchestral poetry, but from what we know of his plans for *Espace,* the disposition of the vocal parts would probably have borne a resemblance to the techniques that Barzun pioneered. Varèse's own evocative description of *Espace* as he conceived it,

euueurssss

huuuuu   drr   ouwhoo ah

hohoeere   ssssll1   thou   houooo

heho eh hooo haaa whou de toutes les splendeurs hiou eeopll dss

heho   uh haaall   whou O m'abolir en Toi Mère   oooo ohio thoo ooorrr haaaaa

heho   whououou   oooo   hioououo   ih haaa   u haaohi   ihoo   sssssserssss

he hooooo oh   e eh   o oh   u uh   i ih   hihooooo ih

héhooo eoeoe   ahouou ououo   ehuuuo uotououo   hiuuui iiiuiui   ihoo

hooooo   houoouo   whou houououo   whou houououo   hiooooo

whoo   whou   O Séductrice   whou   whoo

ou whou ou   O Nature

o ooo ooooo   oooooooooaaauuuu oou

oo   oooo

Example 1.1

a work which was to be broadcast simultaneously from numerous different points on the globe so that all the world could hear it at once, reads in part:

> Voices in the sky, as though magic, invisible hands were turning on and off the knobs of fantastic radios, filling all space, criss-crossing, overlapping, penetrating each other, splitting up, superimposing, repulsing each other, colliding, crashing. Phrases, slogans, utterances, chants, proclamations . . . snatches of phrases of American, French, Russian, Chinese, Spanish, German revolutions like shooting stars, also recurring words poundingly repeated like hammer blows or throbbing in an underground ostinato, stubborn and ritualistic.[81]

In Varèse's hands, simultaneity employed two techniques for presenting sound masses independently of one another: one, a high degree of timbral differentiation; the other, rhythmic patterns that resisted the listener's attempt to mesh them. These were always integral to Varèse's music but apparently fell short, in realization, of completely satisfactory results because, for him, working solely with conventional instruments was always an exercise in compromise. When, near the end of his life, electronic techniques finally became available, he was willing to say that they had "made possible the simultaneity of unrelated elements."[82]

But this may not be the whole story. Recall Varèse's statement that rhythm in his works "derives from the simultaneous interplay of unrelated elements that intervene at calculated, but not regular, time-lapses," and that rhythm is also "an element of stability, the generator of form." Implicit in this calculation is balance (stability) through irregularity. Varèse was once asked whether his "architectonic" preoccupation with volumes of sound was the progenitor of "the special kind of static continuity in your music, and its use of repetition and near-repetition of the same elements in constantly new juxtapositions and successions." Varèse provided no detailed response to this, but he did answer in the affirmative.[83] What Gunther Schuller, the interviewer in this case, seems to have been referring to is exemplified very well by such passages as the opening of *Intégrales,* in which a succession of "sound elements" (in the sense of pitch content and registral placement) is repeated some fourteen times before its dissolution, but never with an exact repetition of dynamic or rhythmic indications. Such passages—which, as anyone even casually acquainted with Varèse's music knows, are numerous—are quite clearly the aural equivalent of multiple views of an object.

"GEOMETRICAL" STRUCTURE. Varèse became accustomed early on to critics' choice of geometrical metaphors to describe the sound of his music. That he seemed to approve of their efforts could easily be interpreted as simple acquiescence on his part in an attempt to escape from traditional types of description—types which, since they were all based on the conventions of the previous century, Varèse saw as a false set of standards whose employment could only lead to misunderstanding of his own musical aims. But there may have been more to it than that. Varèse appeared fond of Massimo Zanotti Bianco's short article for *The Arts* in 1925, which was entitled "Edgar Varèse and the Geometry of Sound," and he mentioned it on several occasions in his lectures.[84] Later, Varèse went his commentators one better and formulated the analogy to crystallization, drawing upon a mineralogist's definition of the phenomenon and translating it into his own terms:

> Conceiving musical form as a *resultant*—the result of a process—I was struck by what seemed to me an analogy between the formation of my compositions and the phenomenon of crystallization. Let me quote the crystallographic description given me by Nathaniel Arbiter, professor of mineralogy at Columbia University: "The crystal is characterized by both a definite external form and a definite internal structure. The internal structure is based on the unit of crystal which is the smallest grouping of the atoms that has the order and composition of the substance. The extension of the unit into space forms the whole crystal. But in spite of the relatively limited variety of internal structures, the external forms of crystals are limitless." Then Mr. Arbiter added in his own words: "Crystal form is a *resultant* (the very word I have always used in reference to musical form) rather than a primary attribute. Crystal form is the consequence of the interaction of attractive and repulsive forces and the ordered packing of the atom." This, I believe, suggests, better than any explanation I could give, the way my works are formed. There is an idea, the basis of an internal structure, expanded and split into different shapes or groups of sound constantly changing in shape, direction, and speed, attracted and repulsed by various forces. The form of the work is the consequence of this interaction. Possible musical forms are as limitless as the exterior forms of crystals.[85]

Was this Varèse's first encounter with such an analogy? Quite possibly not. Among his friends and acquaintances in the 1920s was Charles-Edouard Jeanneret, later known as Le Corbusier, who collaborated with Varèse during the 1950s on *Poème électronique*. Working with Amédée Ozenfant, Jeanneret wrote many essays on art—principally concerning what they called "purism"—including one entitled "Towards the Crystal" (1925), from which the following passage is taken:

> One can detect a tendency [in later cubist art] which might be described meta-phorically as a *tendency towards the crystal*. The crystal, in nature, is one of the phenomena that touch us most, because it clearly exemplifies to us this movement towards geometrical organization. Nature sometimes reveals to us how its forms are built up by the interplay of internal and external forces. The crystal grows, and stops growing, in accordance with the theoretical forms of geometry; man takes delight in these forms because he finds in them what seems to be a confirmation for his abstract geometrical concepts. Nature and the human mind find common ground in the crystal as they do in the cell, and as they do wherever order is so perceptible to the human senses that it confirms those laws which human reason loves to pro-pound in order to explain nature.
>
> In genuine cubism there is something organic, which proceeds outwards from within.[86]

If Varèse read this essay when it was new, then he might very well have absorbed and retained, even if unconsciously, some of the ideas contained in it. These ideas, resurfacing in his mind years later (stimulated, perhaps, by his renewed contact in 1956 with Le Corbusier after a hiatus of twenty five years), might have intrigued him enough to send him searching for a firmer basis for a musical analogy, rooted this time directly in scientific terminology.

Writing earlier than Ozenfant and Jeanneret, Apollinaire had defended the cubists' apparent fascination with geometry, countering their detractors with the observations that "geometrical figures are the essence of drawing" and "geometry, the science of space, its dimensions and relations, have always determined the norms and rules of painting." Yet, as he hastened to say, "The new painters do not propose, any more than did their predecessors, to be geometers."[87] And it should be pointed out that not all of the cubists were terribly eager for their work to be described as geometrical, for obvious reasons: "geometry" implied a level of abstraction or a coldness which they could not accept; and it implied a compositional procedure too calculated and mathematical, therefore (possibly) deficient in intuition. Kandinsky, as early as 1911, had asked: "Why restrict artistic expression to the *exclusive* use of the triangle and similar geometric forms and figures?"[88] Responses were not long in coming. Gleizes and Metzinger specifically repudiated the idea that "geometry" in their work was an end in itself: "For us, lines, surfaces, and volumes are only nuances of the notion of fullness"—that is, the expression of space without "the sensation of relief" that the old illusionist technique of perspective sought to provide.[89] Kahnweiler was equally adamant; the impression that some people had received of geometric forms in the paintings, he said, "is unjustified, since the visual conception desired by the painter by no means resides in the geometric forms, but rather in the representation of the reproduced objects."[90]

Varèse, of course, was not restricted to depicting three dimensions on a flat surface. Musical space could be inherently more than two-dimensional. Nevertheless, Varèse clearly felt an attraction for this concept in application to music, and it led him into some interesting observations which parallel those of writers on the visual arts. One notion that received a good deal of attention at the time was the possibility of access to a fourth dimension that would liberate painters (and sculptors) from traditional constraints. Here again, a juxtaposition of statements is revealing. Apollinaire:

Regarded from the plastic point of view, the fourth dimension appears to spring from the three known dimensions: it represents the immensity of space enternalizing itself in all directions at any given moment. It is space itself, the dimension of the infinite: the fourth dimension endows objects with plasticity.

Varèse:

We actually have three dimensions in music: horizontal, vertical, and dynamic swelling or decreasing. I shall add a fourth, sound projection—the feeling that sound is leaving us with no hope of being reflected back, a feeling akin to that aroused by beams of light sent forth by a powerful searchlight—for the ear as for the eye, that sense of projection, of a journey into space.[91]

Varèse at other times—including the same year, 1936, in which he gave the lecture just quoted from—referred to projection as a "third dimension."[92] It is evident from this that Varèse, like Apollinaire (in all likelihood), used dimensionality as a metaphor more than anything else, for there seems to be no consistent formulation of the concept. But certainly the vision of infinitude conjured up by Apollinaire must have appealed to Varèse.

Picasso

The cubist period left a lasting mark on Picasso's philosophy of art, insofar as any such philosophy can be defined.[93] Picasso was an artist to whom many listened.[94] Varèse must have heard him quoted frequently, and he even quoted him himself on at least one occasion. Some of the striking correspondences between statements made by Picasso and Varèse may be nothing more than coincidences—the product of similar aesthetic background and a common dislike for theoretical systems—but others do suggest a causal connection, formed by Varèse's reading or otherwise learning of Picasso's pronouncements. This is particularly likely to be true of the "De Zayas Statement" of 1923 and the "Zervos Statement" of 1935, both of which were published in places where Varèse would have seen them (in *The Arts* and *Cahiers d'Art* respectively). Some examples follow.

"To me there is no past or future in art. If a work of art cannot live always in the present it must not be considered at all."[95] Varèse echoed this sentiment in his 1959 Princeton lecture: "Listening to music by Perotin, Machaut, Monteverdi, Bach, or Beethoven, we are conscious of living substances; they are 'alive in the present.' "[96] For Varèse, this idea was obviously tied with "making it new," in the words of William Carlos Williams—precisely what the old masters must have done to produce living art.[97]

"There are miles of painting 'in the manner of'; but it is rare to find a young man working in his own way. . . . To repeat is to run counter to spiritual laws; essentially escapism."[98] Varèse agreed: "Music written in the manner of another century is the result of culture and, desirable and comfortable as culture may be, an artist should not lie down in it." In an earlier lecture, Varèse had already quoted from Romain Rolland's novel *Jean-Christophe*, about a young composer who had rejected "that bed all prepared for the laziness of those who, fleeing the fatigue of thinking for themselves, lie down in other men's thoughts."[99]

"I have never made trials or experiments."[100] Varèse never liked being called an "experimental" composer: "Of course, like all composers who have something new to say, I experiment, and have always experimented. But when I finally present a work it is not an experiment—it is a finished product. My experiments go into the wastepaper basket."[101] Picasso meant his statement in the same sense:

"Among the several sins that I have been accused of committing, none is more false than the one that I have, as the principal objective in my work, the spirit of research. When I paint, my objective is to show what I have found and not what I am looking for."[102]

Consistent with these feelings about his own work were Picasso's views on the historical position of cubism. He pointed out that cubism was an experimental or transitory art, as some had termed it, only in the sense that all art has these qualities. He said further: "Cubism is not either a seed or a foetus, but an art dealing primarily with forms, and when a form is realized it is there to live its own life." Twelve years later, speaking in the same vein, he said: "A picture lives a life like a living creature."[103] It is somewhat misleading to extract these statements from their contexts, for Picasso seems to have regarded the interaction between the work of art and its viewer as a far more subjective process than Varèse ever did. For instance, it is difficult to imagine Varèse applying to music Picasso's opinion that "when [a picture] is finished it still goes on changing, according to the state of mind of whoever is looking at it"—words which come just before the previous quotation.[104] Nevertheless, Varèse probably liked Picasso's evocations of animated art, for they correspond closely to his own depictions of "bodies of intelligent sounds moving freely in space" and "composing with living sounds."[105] They also fit very well with Hoenë Wronsky's definition of music as "the corporealization of the intelligence that is in sound," which Varèse never tired of quoting.

Concerning the process of executing a work and the fate of the ideas that initiate it, Picasso first expressed his opinion in general terms: "A picture is not thought out and settled beforehand. While it is being done it changes as one's thoughts change."[106] Later, this basic thought took a more definite form: "An idea . . . is a point of departure and no more. If you contemplate it, it becomes something else. . . . As far as I am concerned, at any rate, my original idea has no further interest, because in realizing it I am thinking about something else."[107]

For his part, Varèse found his own useful quotations:

> Braque was quoted in an interview as saying: "The picture is finished when nothing is left of the original idea." And Picasso, also in an interview last June, expressed very much the same thing: "One takes whatever one finds. . . . It (the painting) begins with an idea and then becomes something else entirely." This stirred a faint recollection and looking through my files I found in a 1924 number of *Eolus* what I had written in a similar vein to answer the question I was always being asked about the genesis of my works: "The impetus may come from an idea, an image, a phrase, anything that gives a shock, that turns on so to speak the emotional current. But this object which solicits the composer outside himself is only an ostensible motive and will disappear, finally eliminated by the work that is taking shape."[108]

Varèse could not have failed to notice that this depiction of compositional process is consonant with the process of crystallization already discussed. The two are really presented in the same terms, with the "constantly changing" sound shapes of the analogy to crystallization corresponding to the endless transformations of the original idea and its derivatives. On one occasion predating even the earliest Picasso source, however, Varèse propounded essentially the same concept: "Possibly in modern music we require some image or idea as a point of departure; nevertheless our tendency, I think, is to let the image or the idea become absorbed in the work itself and eliminated through the process of invention."[109] This suggests that he arrived at the idea independently, though the possibility should not be discounted that it had already gained a certain currency among artists in general.[110]

Following logically from the above is a strenuous opposition to the strictures of preconceived forms. Varèse's characterization of form as "the result of a process" led him into an analogy between a standard "historical" form and "a rigid box of definite shape," noting that if one's aim is to fill a box of this sort, one "must have something that is the same shape and size or that is elastic and soft enough to be made to fit in." However, a substance of harder consistency cannot be so forced; it will break the box—as, Varèse promised, his music would.[111] Picasso's analogy seems intended to make much the same point: "It's no longer reality that must enter my form. Otherwise, I'm like a pastry cook who makes molds, and I make all sorts of dough in order to put it into molds. 'That one's with ginger and that one's with pistachio.' And after that you no longer dare to set foot outside your mold."[112]

A marked distrust for prettiness or attractive details provides further grounds for agreement—not at all surprising, really, since the merely decorative had ceased to be of interest already to the cubists, and Varèse specifically rejected the anecdotal or picturesque with respect to timbre, at least. Comparison of quotations is instructive; what it suggests is more a similarity of approach than an identical procedure. Picasso: "When you begin a picture, you often make some pretty discoveries. You must be on guard against these. Destroy the thing, do it over several times. In each destroying of a beautiful discovery, the artist does not really suppress it, but rather transforms it, condenses it, makes it more substantial."[113] Varèse: "Even the most beautiful phrase goes into the discard if it is not structural, if it is only an imaginative vagabond."[114] This squares too with the dislike that Varèse and the cubists shared for "inspiration" and all its connotations.

"I like a certain awkwardness in a work of art."[115] Stravinsky has testified to the authenticity of this phrase; it certainly sounds quintessentially Varèsian, although we have no other corroboration for it. The juxtaposition of his words with an anecdote reported in Gertrude Stein's 1933 book on Picasso is probably more revealing of general similarities in aesthetic than of any direct connection in this instance. Here is Stein's paraphrase of Picasso, related in her inimitable style:

> When you make a thing, it is so complicated making it that it is bound to be ugly, but those that do it after you they don't have to worry about making it and they can make it pretty, and so everybody can like it when others make it.[116]

Awkwardness or ugliness, then, might serve as a kind of guarantor of originality.

Anti-cubism

The reaction of the cubists against impressionism is well documented, and Varèse went along with it: "I do not use sounds impressionistically as the impressionist painters used colors. In my music they are an intrinsic part of the structure."[117] However, Louise Varèse has verified her husband's friendship with the painter André Derain, who never became a cubist, and notes that one of Derain's favorite sayings, "Painting is made of light," was used analogically by Varèse to introduce his own dictum, "Music is made of sound."[118] This view of light is fundamentally contrary to cubist theory. Even for Cézanne, the ancestor whom the cubists all claimed, this was already a mistake. As Kahnweiler said, "Where his friends the Impressionists saw only light, he used light to shape the three-dimensional object."[119]

Among the artists discussed in this chapter, Delaunay, who first embraced cubism and then rejected it, would perhaps have been the most sympathetic to Derain's view. In the hands of the cubists, color had gained new importance compared to its role in previous art, but for some, particularly among the French, the cubists had not gone far enough. In a letter to Kandinsky, for example, Delaunay wrote: "The Cubist group of whom you speak experiments only in line, giving color a secondary place, and not a constructional one."[120] The very title of Delaunay's essay "Light" reveals a sensibility on the subject corresponding to Derain's. "Light in Nature," he said there, "creates the movement of colors"— from which all else flows.[121] He also had far more complimentary words for the impressionists than did his cubist compatriots.

On the balance, Varèse does seem to have leaned more toward than away from the attitude that color, though of more than decorative or ornamental significance, was less important than other factors (notably pitch and register) in shaping sound masses and setting them in motion. Nevertheless, he may have seen the views of Delaunay and Derain as a corrective influence, counteracting the cubists' tendency to think too much about form. Certainly he did not think of himself as a "cubist composer"; among the few direct references to cubism in the surviving record of Varèse's writings and interviews is the following particularly revealing quotation: "[The twelve-tone system] is important in the same way that Cubism is important in the history of the fine arts. Both came at a moment when the need for a strict discipline was felt in the two arts. . . . But we must not forget that neither Cubism nor Schoenberg's liberating system is supposed to limit art or replace one academic formula with another. . . . [They] are media and not finalities."[122]

No doubt at the time of Varèse's lecture (1948) this seemed a plausible analogy, although the historical perspective gained since then suggests that the twelve-tone system—perhaps in confirmation of the power of the reactionary forces which, in Varèse's opinion, were in control of musical thought—has proved far more durable than many would have predicted. Certainly Varèse's tone is dismissive neither of the dodecaphonists nor of the cubists. When, in a later interview, he said, "I respect the twelve-tone discipline, and those that feel they need such a discipline," one can easily imagine him saying the same, in the past tense, of the practitioners of cubism.[123] There is the underlying suggestion, however, despite the "liberating" qualities attributed to both systems, that the benefits they might bestow are not worth the dangers of adopting them, for strictness devolves into rigidity in all but the most masterful of hands. Varèse saw the problem as being not so much with the originators of such systems as with the imitators, but he acknowledged that there would always be imitators, therefore always a certain amount of mediocre art. The confusion of good with bad, which was to be avoided, was much more likely if everyone subscribed to the same methods. A real artist would constantly seek to invent new means of expression, as much to set himself apart from those with no ability to think for themselves as out of the sure knowledge that wholesale adoption of others' methods leads to stagnation. As Varèse put it, in his characteristically blunt fashion, "Anyone who does not make his own rules is an ass."[124]

FUTURISM

Varèse made no public claims of allegiance to the artistic tenets of futurism. In fact, he divorced his intentions from those of the futurists repeatedly and vehemently. The earliest evidence of this stance is found in a 1916 newspaper interview: "We . . . need new instruments very badly. In this respect the futurists (Marinetti and his *bruiteurs*) have made a serious mistake. New instruments must be able to lend varied combinations and must not simply remind us of the things heard time and time again."[125] Varèse referred here to the machines that Luigi Russolo and other futurist composers had assembled only a few years earlier for "concerts of noises"—machines that emitted readily recognizable and basically unaltered sounds from the world outside the concert hall. These were classified according to six "families of noises," of which the first comprised rumbles, roars, explosions, crashes, splashes, and booms, the second, whistles, hisses, and snorts, and so on. Despite Russolo's assertion that "the art of noise must not limit itself to imitative reproduction" but instead "will achieve its most emotive power in the acoustic enjoyment, in its own right, that the artist's inspiration will extract from combined noises," Varèse clearly remained unimpressed.[126] A year after the interview quoted above, he contributed to *391*, Francis Picabia's Dadaist periodical, an aphoristic statement about his compositional aims which reads in part: "Why, Italian futurists, have you slavishly reproduced only what is commonplace and boring in the bustle of our daily lives."[127]

   Yet the highly visible and sensational, though short-lived, nature of the futurist musical phenomenon ensured that it would be remembered with a vividness far out of proportion to its importance. And Varèse's daring use of large percussion forces in his works from 1921 on, and the tendency of hostile critics to call the results mere noise, made confusion between Varèse and the futurists all but inevitable—and not only in the so-called popular press. As late as 1955 Henry Cowell, who surely should have known better, wrote that Varèse was "the only composer connected with the futurist manifesto written at Milan in 1913 who has achieved a position of importance in modern music."[128] This statement prompted a fierce denial from Varèse of any such connection, in which he quoted the statement he had written for *391* thirty-eight years previously.[129]

Part of the problem was that many of Varèse's remarks, if interpreted superficially, could easily have been construed as expressions of the futurist musicians' aesthetic. For instance, he spoke of "the richness of industrial sounds" and of "the noises in our streets and our ports," which "have certainly changed and developed our auditory powers"; he saw in the ability to produce *"entirely new combinations of sound"* the possibility of "creating new emotions, awakening dulled sensibilities"; he "looked upon the industrial world as a rich source of beautiful sounds, an unexplored mine of music in the matrix"; the sounds he heard around him "from all directions" led him to imagine how "in just such complexity" they "could be transmuted into music."[130] But the crucial parts of these utterances—"in the matrix", "transmuted"—were overlooked. Even as early as 1930, pointing out the lack of "[musical] means of our own time," he mentioned some of the newer, "electrical" possibilities and cautioned that "these means must not be used simply for research into reproduction of sounds that already exist but rather ought to permit new creations according to new conceptions"—a thinly veiled criticism of Russolo and his school.[131]

Varèse probably issued his condemnations of futurist philosophy as a matter of public relations. He evidently felt it necessary to dissociate himself from those who hardly even deserved to be called composers. His thoughts about futurism in general, however, may have been rather different. We do know that he owned a copy of F. T. Marinetti's writings and approved (somewhat selectively) of what he read.[132] Might he also have read some of the more "technical" manifestos written by others, notably the futurist painters and sculptors? There is no way to be certain, but even if he did not, at least some of their ideas would have reached him through informal contact with artists. The futurists' pronouncements were widely distributed, and they were well known in Parisian circles, Apollinaire's included. There are numerous points of correspondence between the ideas of the cubists and the futurists, although ultimately the differences proved more significant. That the French and the Italians seemed in certain ways to be thinking along the same lines could only have encouraged Varèse, already inclined to eclecticism, to adapt ideas from both for his own purposes.

The two groups were able most readily to make common cause in the rebellion against outmoded concepts and irrelevant strictures. The futurists were as outspoken as the cubists against imitative, representative, and episodic tendencies carried over uncritically from old art and in use still as the result of "academic" thinking. If anything, the futurists were the more violent in their sentiments, even calling for the destruction of art from the past. (That they may not have advocated the literal realization of this call is beside the point; what *is* to the point is that they intended to sound dangerous.) Varèse could not have found himself in complete agreement—after all, he treasured much of the musical past—but certainly he admired their spirit, much as he admired the spirit of the Dadaists without embracing their iconoclastic tendencies or their concept of anti-art. Boccioni spoke of a new "plastic power" in futurist painting and sculpture that enabled the artist to create "new subjects which do not aim at narrative or episodic representation; instead it coordinates different plastic values of reality, a coordination which is purely architectural, free of all literary and sentimental influences."[133] Here we find a familiar disdain for the anecdotal, and for the values of another century. Among the exhortations of Marinetti that Varèse echoed was the famous "Let's murder the moonshine"—an expression of antisentimentality.[134]

Given the futurists' warlike tendencies, it should come as no surprise that they prized disequilibrium and conflict, even violence, in their work more than did the cubists. "There is with us not merely variety, but chaos and clashing of rhythms, totally opposed to one another, which we nevertheless assemble into a new harmony."[135] The idea of a clash out of which would emerge a "new harmony" was enunciated at around the same time, in not much different form, by such writers as Gleizes and Metzinger and Léger. Varèse seems much closer to the futurist version of this revolution in this autobiographical remark: "I became a sort of diabolic Parsifal, searching not for the Holy Grail but for the bomb that would make the musical world explode and thereby let in all sounds, sounds which up to now—and even today—have been called noises."[136] Phrases of Marinetti's such as "For the moment we are content with blowing up all the traditions, like rotten bridges" come to mind.[137]

Details of technique as described by futurist painters and sculptors recall the statements of Metzinger and others. Carlo Carrà, for example, enumerated some features of the new painting, among them: "Plastic complementarism (for both forms and colors), based on the law of equivalent contrast and on the clash of the most contrasting colors of the rainbow. This complementarism derives from a disequilibrium of form (therefore they are forced to keep moving)."[138] Elsewhere, he spoke of "constructions of arhythmical forms, the clash between concrete and abstract forms."[139] By "arhythmical" Carrà probably meant rhythm without perceptible regularity or patterns of repetition—precisely what Metzinger and Varèse termed "rhythm." The difference in viewpoint from the cubists is really a matter of tone: the futurists always conveyed such details in an atmosphere of power and vigor. But this is hardly a superficial matter, as the futurists' opposition to cubism (see below) shows.

Like the cubists, the futurists stressed the self-referential nature of their art and defended their right to adjust the details of a painting (or sculpture) according to the particular needs of the work. Boccioni, for instance, said, "A sculptural whole, like a painting, should not resemble anything but itself, since figures and objects in art should exist without regard to their logical aspect."[140] Another property held in common with the cubists was the employment of color and shading as integral structural features. Boccioni's offer of a choice between coloring in black or gray the edges of contours in sculpture so that they might "die away little by little and lose themselves in space," and doing without this technique of shading, instead letting live "the sinuosities, the discontinuities, the bursts of straight and curved lines, according to the direction which the movement of the body imposes on them"[141] is reminiscent of Gleizes and Metzinger's approach to the problem of the division of the canvas—for in their first alternative, just as in Boccioni's, one of the aims was to establish a central focus toward which the space encompassed by the artwork could refer. (Boccioni: "Thus I create an auxiliary chiaroscuro which forms a nucleus in the atmospheric environment."[142]) The coloring of edges also seems to represent the transference to sculpture of a technique similar to one described by Rivière, with similar intentions.

Spatial thinking was as key a concept to the futurists as to the cubists—their writings are full of references to structure in terms of volumes, masses, and planes—but with this important difference: the futurists put everything in terms of *motion*. The very foundations of their aesthetic required this, for the futurists saw their movement as the only valid response to the enormous changes that technology had wrought upon civilization. Speed was "a new absolute,"[143] an end in itself, inseparable from modern consciousness: "Living art draws its life from the surrounding environment . . . we must breathe in the tangible miracles of contemporary life—the iron network of speedy communication which envelops the earth . . . the spasmodic struggle to conquer the unknown."[144]

Varèse responded to the rapid pace of change in his world in similar fashion. Perhaps it was the futurists who brought him to this awareness, or perhaps he was caught up in it on his own.[145] Probably it was a little of both:

Speed and synthesis are characteristics of our epoch.[146]

New aspirations emanate from every epoch. The artist being always of his own time is influenced by it. . . . We do not think that the horse plow is still adequate for the needs of today. We are quite satisifed that Boulder Dam expresses us better than the Egyptian pyramids.[147]

The artist who is attuned to his era grasps, crystallizes, and projects its special character. . . . Whole symphonies of new sounds have come from the new industrial world, and all through our lives form a part of our daily consciousness. It would appear impossible that a man who occupies himself exclusively with sound could remain unchanged by this.[148]

Futurist painters and sculptors grappled with the problem of motion and how to *embody* it in their works, not simply depict it by illustrating one phase of a moving body. The motion itself had to be treated as if it were a tangible thing. Of all the futurist writers, Boccioni contributed by far the most extensive commentary on the subject. The crucial phrase, both for him and others, was "continuity in space." What they were looking for, said Boccioni, was "not the construction of an object, but the construction of an object's action. . . . A body set in movement, therefore, is not simply an immobile body subsequently set in motion, but a *truly mobile object*, which is a reality quite new and original."[149] The object, in fact, "has no form in itself"[150]—an idea which will already be familiar to the reader from earlier discussion. Boccioni saw a great danger in fragmentation, in which only a single stationary image represented an object in motion, or even several such images: "We are not trying to split each individual image—we are looking for a symbol, or better, a single form, to replace these old concepts of division with new concepts of continuity. Any dividing up of an object's motion is an arbitrary action, and equally arbitrary is the subdivision of matter."[151]

But this did not mean the mere delineation of trajectory. Rather than showing a body's "passage from one state of repose to another," Boccioni sought "the unique form that expresses its continuity in space."[152] Apparently there was some difference of opinion about this among the futurists, for the art form known as Photodynamism, a futurist invention, did indeed concern itself with showing motions from one point to another as if they had a solid form: "Remembering what took place between one stage and another, a work is presented that transcends the human condition, becoming a *transcendental photograph of movement*. For this end we have also envisaged a machine which will render actions visible"—that is, by means of "the motion and light which translate themselves into trajectories."[153] Particularly of interest to Varèse would have been the opportunities afforded by the medium as described by Bragaglia:

> To put it crudely, chronophotography could be compared with a clock on the face of which only the quarter-hours are marked, cinematography to one on which the minutes too are indicated, and Photodynamism to a third on which are marked not only the seconds, but also the *intermovemental* fractions existing in the passages between seconds. This becomes an almost infinitesimal calculation of movement.[154]

Photodynamism can be regarded as analogous to Varèse's employment of sirens in an attempt to use the spaces between the semitones of the tempered scale, not only in the first of his works to include sirens in the instrumentation (*Amériques,* completed in 1921) but also in experiments made long before, in Paris:

> When I was about twenty . . . my thinking even then began turning around the idea of liberating music from the tempered system, from the limitations of musical instruments, and from years of bad habits, erroneously called tradition. I studied Helmholtz, and was fascinated by his experiments with sirens described in his *Physiology of Sound.* I went to the *Marché aux Puces,* where you can find just about anything, in search of a siren, and picked up two small ones. With these, and using also children's whistles, I made my first experiments in what later I called *spatial music.*[155]

To return to the mainstream of futurism: Boccioni and others, seeking a way to make "continuity in space" possible in painting and sculpture, turned to several subsidiary concepts:

THE EXPRESSION OF MULTIPLE VIEWPOINTS. As for the cubists, the possibility of displaying several different viewpoints, as if the artist had seen an object from a number of different angles and had fused these views into one image, was tied to the concept of simultaneity. For Boccioni, if a spectator could see only one side of a sculpture at a time, its essential immobility would be reinforced. "My spiral, architectural construction, on the other hand," he said, "creates before the spectator a continuity of forms which permit him to follow ideally (through the *form-force* sprung from the real form) a new, abstract contour which expresses the body in its material movements." Thus would be suggested to the spectator "a continuity (simultaneity)."[156] To avoid the division of discrete images, Boccioni dispensed with "rigid profiles" in favor of profiles that each carried "in itself a clue to the other profiles, both those that precede and those that follow, forming altogether the sculptural whole."[157] It is likely that the futurist version of simultaneity, incorporating motion, is even more closely analogous to the hypothesized operations of simultaneity in Varèse's music than is the cubist formulation.

THE EXTENSION OF LINES AND BOUNDARIES OF BODIES INTO THE SURROUNDING SPACE. "Every object reveals by its lines how it would resolve itself were it to follow the tendencies of its forces."[158] Further, "lines and outlines must only exist as forces bursting forth from the dynamic action of the bodies."[159] By breaking down the distinction between the object and its environment, the futurists aimed to place the visual emphasis on motion. To paraphrase without (it is hoped) oversimplifying: since an object could move or be moved anywhere in space, there seemed no point in painting space as empty. To do so would isolate the object, freeze it into an arbitrary position—would in fact destroy motion:

> An infinity of lines and currents emanate from our objects, making them live in the environment which has been created by their vibrations. Areas between one object and another are not merely empty spaces but continuing materials of different intensities, which we reveal with visible lines which do not correspond to any photographic truth. This is why in our paintings we do not have objects and empty spaces but only a greater or lesser intensity and solidity of space.[160]

One result of this filling of space is that objects intersect with their environment. "Futurist sculpture," wrote the contemporary critic Arthur Jerome Eddy, "seeks to reproduce a figure or an object *attached to* and *a part of* its fleeting and flowing surroundings, its atmosphere, its *medium*."[161] Another result of extension of objects' lines and planes is that the objects intersect with one another. "Every object influences its neighbor . . . by a real competition of lines and by real conflicts of planes," wrote the futurists as a group in 1912.[162] Boccioni noted further that "objects never end; they intersect with innumerable combinations of attraction and innumerable shocks of aversion."[163] This kind of intersection was called *interpenetration* [or compenetration] *of planes*. It is likely that Varèse found the idea interesting. The dichotomy of attraction and aversion is strikingly reminiscent of a passage from a lecture delivered by Varèse in 1936. He spoke of moving sound masses in his music and continued, "When these sound masses collide, the phenomena of penetration or repulsion will seem to occur."[164] The same influence also shows up in his description of *Espace* ("Voices in the sky . . . filling all space, criss-crossing, overlapping, penetrating each other, splitting up, superimposing, repulsing each other, colliding, crashing"). In fact, the entire idea of extension of objects' lines and planes is markedly similar to Varèse's idea of projection. Boccioni's explanation of the concept of "dynamic continuity" or "dynamic form" to be used to avoid sharp differentiation of objects is of further significance in this regard: "*Dynamic form* is a species of fourth dimension, both in painting and sculpture, which cannot exist perfectly without the complete concurrence of those three dimensions which determine volume: height, width, depth."[165] Dynamic continuity was an added dimension just as sound projection for Varèse was a fourth dimension (see above, pp. 18–19).

On the other hand, to the extent that fusing objects with their environment was a *customary* procedure for the futurists, it would probably have seemed undesirable to Varèse from a musical standpoint, for he relied heavily upon differentiation: "In the matter of timbre, my attitude is precisely the reverse of the symphonic. The symphony orchestra strives for the utmost blending of colors. I strive to make the listener aware of the utmost differentiation of colors and densities."[166]

The mutual influence of expanding bodies implies the existence of competing centers of influence in the same futurist work. Boccioni hinted at this when he left the artist the option to omit the shading that directed all elements of the work toward a nucleus. Gino Severini was more explicit: "It is clear that in one and the same picture or work of art there may be more than one *centrifugal and centripetal* nucleus in simultaneous and dynamic competition."[167] The idea of competing centers potentially has a great deal to do with independently moving masses, and for this reason would have appealed to Varèse, who later spoke of "the movement of sound masses without relation to one another." Movement of forms had the power to change their original relationships, according to Carrà; Varèse could not have failed to notice the attempt to introduce a condition of constant change into art.[168]

Competing centers would also have served indirectly as an aid to the futurists in realizing another goal: elimination of stasis from their work by involving the spectator, thrusting both him and the artist into the center of things. The title of Carrà's short piece "Plastic Planes as Spherical Expansions in Space" evokes this scheme—a scheme imagined in detail by Boccioni: "The artist," he wrote, "finds himself at the center of spherical currents which surround him on every side." Further: "For us the picture is no longer an exterior scene, a stage for the depiction of fact. A picture is an irradiating architectural structure in which the artist, *rather than the object,* forms a central core. It is an emotive architectural environment which creates sensation and completely involves the observer."[169]

In Varèse's own words we find an echo: "It seems to me that [Milton Babbitt] wants to exercise maximum control over certain materials, as if he were *above* them. But I want to be *in* the material, part of the acoustical vibration, so to speak."[170]

THE "DOUBLE CONCEPT OF FORM." This was another useful way of thinking about objects whose presence in the artwork was to be de-emphasized or (ideally) even eliminated in favor of the action undergone by them. Thus Boccioni spoke of "*form in movement* (relative movement) and *movement of the form* (absolute movement)," which "can alone render in the duration of time that instant of plastic life as it was materialized, without cutting it apart by drawing from its vital atmosphere, without stopping it in the midst of its movement, in a word, without killing it."[171] This formulation is quite consistent throughout Boccioni's writings. He also called it "plastic dynamism," in an essay by that title in which he stated explicitly that the two kinds of motion took place simultaneously, one mixed with the other.[172] Since all motions take place in space, we can readily relate this double concept of form to Varèse's (and the cubists') two functions of space, in which space defines and is defined by the motions of objects. This focus on action and transformation makes form a "resultant" for the futurists just as much as for Varèse.

Criticism of Cubism

The futurists' opposition to the cubist aesthetic was based primarily on three problems that they had identified: that it was excessively static, not concerned enough with fluidity or motion, thereby perpetuating the mistakes of earlier art; that it was too cold, scientific, and intellectualized, leaving no room for intuition; and that it was limited by its preoccupation with geometrical forms.

On many occasions the futurists took particular pains to set themselves apart from the cubists: "They obstinately continue to paint objects motionless, frozen, and all the static aspects of nature. . . . We, on the contrary, . . . seek for a style of motion, a thing which has never been attempted before us."[173] The accusation of detachment and objectivity directed at cubist art was usually made by contrasting the futurists' direct involvement: "We do not superimpose concepts on to the object like the cubists. We futurists are right inside the object, and we live out its evolutionary concept."[174] Picasso, in particular, came under fire: "[His] concept of form is the result of dispassionate, scientific measurement, which kills the dynamic warmth, the violent action and the marginal variation which are precisely the qualities that allow the form to live outside the intellect, so that it can be projected into infinity."[175] Note the value placed here upon the intuitive approach to artistic solutions. It was symptomatic, according to the futurists, of the cubists' insistence upon distancing themselves from their material that their forms were artificial and unresponsive to human feelings. Boccioni explained: "In nature there can be no absolutely perpendicular lines and no absolutely horizontal lines. The only thing that is perpendicular or horizontal is a single point, situated at eye level; since the others—above, below, and alongside this point—all *lead off* around us in lines converging at infinity."[176]

Presumably Varèse would have sided with the futurists on some points and not on others. His remarks about cubism certainly suggest that he found the cubists' discipline too strict in certain respects. He would probably have agreed that motion—*real* motion—in painting and sculpture was worth attempting, although he might not have thought that the futurists had come any closer than others to achieving it. But Varèse could not have accepted the (apparently unconditional) ranking of intuition over intellect, which may have made him suspicious—as evidently it did other observers at the time—about the attainability of futurist aims in general.

KANDINSKY AND THE BLAUE REITER

It is even less likely that Varèse had any direct exposure to the theoretical writings of the blaue Reiter, based in Munich, than to those of the artists and critics of Paris and Milan. However, the Germans did have extensive contact with other, allied artistic movements outside Germany; Wassily Kandinsky, for example, maintained a regular correspondence with Apollinaire and Delaunay. The present-day distinctions between the cubists, the futurists, and the blaue Reiter group were apparently not made so sharply at the time these movements were being established.[177] The primary and overwhelming fact of newness and opposition to old ways must have encouraged artists of the time to think of themselves and their fellows as perpetrators of one big movement. This is reflected in the comment by Varèse placed as an epigraph to this chapter ("here and in Germany").

Varèse probably heard a certain amount through his friends at L'Abbaye de Créteil about what was going on in Munich. As with other ideas from the visual arts, remembering some things, forgetting or discarding others, he absorbed and transformed them into his own aesthetic. As the ideas of Kandinsky and his compatriots filtered through to the Parisians and in some instances blended with what was already there, so Varèse would have shared in this synthesis.

For the purposes of the present discussion, Kandinsky has been treated as the principal spokesman for the blaue Reiter. Kandinsky's writings occupy an important place in the artistic theory of the time; more than any of his contemporaries in Munich, he attempted to convey his aims and principles in written form. Four of his works serve here as sources of his ideas: "On the Question of Form" (sometimes translated as "On the Problem of Form") (1911); *Concerning the Spiritual in Art, and Painting in Particular* (1912); "Reminiscences" (1913); and *Point and Line to Plane* (1926). A few comments by other, related artists will be cited as well.

Among the most obvious parallels between themes in Kandinsky's writings and in the work of the French is the idea that the true artist must not be bound by rules. Kandinsky spoke of the "internal necessity" that served as the exclusive solution to the problem of art; it "was capable of overthrowing all known rules and limitations at any moment."[178] Elsewhere, he said that "one who knows the supposed rules of painting will never be sure of creating a work of art"—a statement closely resembling the aphorisms of Debussy and Busoni that Varèse was so fond of quoting— and further, that "there is no rule by which one can arrive at the application of effective form and the combination of particular methods precisely necessary in a specific case."[179] This directly parallels Varèse's remarks about the "exigencies of the particular work."

Rejection of rules meant being forced to think for oneself. Kandinsky advocated with his French counterparts a "reasoned and conscious" approach to painting, and stated that in his "compositions"—as he chose to call what he regarded as his most highly developed work—"reason, consciousness, purpose play an overwhelming part."[180] But not codification, which Kandinsky feared as keenly as the cubists did. Refusal to be bound by rules, too, went hand in hand with rejection of the representational and anecdotal. Kandinsky's formulation of "two branches of art," which were as valid for painting as for music—one the virtuoso type (representational), the other composition (absolute and nonobjective)—would certainly have appealed to Varèse, for Kandinsky identified composition as the product of the greatest advances in art.[181]

Perhaps the clearest of all correspondences between Kandinsky, the cubists, and Varèse lies in the idea of form as the outer expression of inner content or meaning. This idea is so extensively and forcefully presented in Kandinsky's writings that it is difficult not to believe that he was its originator, and that the cubists got it from him. In both "On the Question of Form" and *Concerning the Spiritual in Art*, form is defined in precisely these terms.[182] Varèse's pronouncement, "Form is a resultant—the result of a process," and his analogy to crystallization are direct parallels. His claims that "form and content are one,"[183] on the other hand, seem at first not to jibe exactly with Kandinsky's ideas about the relationship between the two, since in "On the Question of Form" we read that "the outer effect can be different from the inner."[184] It is more likely, however, that Varèse's insistence on the inseparability of form and content was meant to distinguish his compositional process from the process of filling predetermined forms with motivic, thematic, and harmonic material. Further, inner *is* different from outer in that, according to the crystallization analogy, the number of available internal structures is severely limited, while the number of possible external forms has no limit at all.

As to the question of nonobjectivity in new art and its possible relationship to musical structure, Kandinsky's views on objects in a painting correspond closely with those of the cubists: he described his developing "ability to *overlook* the object within the painting" as derived from the "effect of painting on the painted object, which can dissolve itself through being painted."[185] These words certainly have a resonance in Varèse's accounts of the fate of initial ideas in the course of executing a work. Here, however, is where this similarity between Kandinsky's and Varèse's ideas ends. For Kandinsky, the "object" clearly has nothing to do with the inner content or meaning; it may not even be so much as a point of departure.[186] Inner meaning cannot be directly viewed in the work of art; it is by definition subjective, a state of mind: "I still see *ahead* of me . . . the ever-increasing wealth of possibilities, the ever-growing depth of painting I cannot describe. And one must and *may* not describe such things; they must mature *innerly* in secret confinement and may not be expressed otherwise than by the painter's art."[187] This attitude may very well explain why Kandinsky found the approach of the cubists wanting: "Should [a grammar of painting] ever be achieved, it will be not so much according to physical laws (which have often been tried and which the cubists try today), as according to the laws of internal necessity."[188] But Varèse, trusting less to the vagaries of "inspiration" (a word which Kandinsky often used with far greater respect than Varèse ever did), at least provided for an object *to begin with* that could be obscured and finally dispersed: he was perhaps less abstractly inclined.[189]

Kandinsky's treatment of space in painting differs somewhat from its treatment by the French and the Italians. The inner/outer dichotomy, however, does have important relationships to the dual (internal and external) conception of space dealt with in the section of this chapter on cubism. In "Reminiscences," Kandinsky characterizes space as something to be moved within. For himself, the artist, he sought "to move in the picture, to live in the picture." For the viewer, he sought "the possibility of letting [him] 'stroll' in the picture, forcing him to forget himself and dissolve into the picture."[190] Elsewhere, especially in *Point and Line to Plane,* Kandinsky devoted considerable attention to the placement of forms within the frame of the painting—as, for example, when he speaks of the upper horizontal boundary as representing lightness and freedom, the lower boundary density and restraint, and states that this difference can be either dramatized or minimized by the placement of forms with respect to these boundaries.[191]

On the other hand, as Hayter has pointed out: "The interrelation between these [pictorial] elements and the space in which they are presented cannot be ignored. It should be obvious that such relation must modify the space itself, that a point in a closed volume sets up tensions throughout the volume, that the antithesis between space and object is illusory."[192] Kandinsky found that the elements in a painting either lie upon the *basic plane* of the painting in such a way as to emphasize it, or hover in space, thus avoiding the flatness of the plane, dematerializing it and creating a sense of depth.[193] That is, the elements used in the composition actually create the space of the composition. By unlocking "the vital forces which, in the form of tensions, are shut up within the elements," the composition is produced.[194] Even earlier in the same treatise, we read that Kandinsky's working method involved investigating elements in isolation, then in combination; thus it is really no surprise to find these elements acting as spatial determiners later on.[195] Also, for Kandinsky the element had two simultaneously existing natures: external (form) and internal (tension).[196] That is, the element, which in combination with other elements produced forms, was in *itself* a form of a sort. Analogously, space both determined and was determined by the form of a painting.

It is entirely possible that space became a primary concern for Kandinsky only after about 1920, when ideas of motion began to make their presence felt in his work for the first time. Certainly there is far more technical information about space and motion in *Point and Line to Plane* than in any of the pre-1920 writings. Kandinsky's comments about points set in motion are somewhat similar to the futurists' "double concept of form." He speaks, for instance, of the "double sound" that results "at the moment the point is moved from the center of the basic plane," consisting of the "absolute sound of the point" and the "sound of the given location in the basic plane."[197] Kandinsky's idea resembles even more closely Gleizes and

Metzinger's "center from which or toward which the gradations of color tend": "In sculpture and architecture, the point results from a cross-section of several planes —it is the termination of an angle in space and, on the other hand, the originating nucleus of these planes which can be guided back to it or can be developed out of it."[198]

These approaches to the problems of defining and operating within space would certainly have had some relevance for Varèse, particularly because for Kandinsky space was intimately connected with the realm of time, previously regarded as the exclusive property of music. If music could become spatial, could painting become temporal? Kandinsky thought so, particularly when the basic plane was allowed to disintegrate, for when this happened the elements formerly on it would recede, and "time is required to follow the form elements receding into depth."[199] For this reason, the old division between space and time as the domains of painting and music respectively had begun to collapse. "As far as I know," Kandinsky said, "this first became apparent to the painters."[200] And Varèse quite possibly was the first composer to implement the results of this crossover.

Kandinsky's approach to the various kinds of relationships of forms in space, in its regard for the power of context and of mutual influence of forms, reveals common ground with the cubists:

> The purely pictorial composition has in regard to form two aims:
>
>   1. The composition of the whole picture;
>   2. The creation of the various forms which, by standing in different relations to one another, serve the composition of the whole. . . . Singly they will have little meaning, being of importance only so far as they help the general effect.[201]

Varèse, with his attention to balance between sound masses and his use of "material elements at the same time in opposition to and in support of one another," shared this idea of interrelation.

Kandinsky's theories of form interaction provided for a considerable range of choices for the artist: "Since form is only an expression of content, and content is different with different artists, it is clear that there may be many different forms at the same time that are equally good."[202] But not arbitrary choice; Kandinsky was as firm as Varèse in his abnegation of such methods. (In the letter to Eddy: "You will have to admit that the element of 'chance' is very rarely met with in these pictures."[203]) The forms "must be fashioned in one way only; this, not because their internal meaning demands that particular means, but because they must serve as material for the whole."[204] How to reconcile the multiplicity of valid forms with the lack of available choice in shaping them? These criteria are not in real contradiction; there is more than one way to achieve a given result (that is, to express an internal content), Kandinsky was saying, but in order for this to be done the forms used had to be precisely tailored to the situation. Paradoxically, he also thought of every form as being "as sensitive as smoke," which "the slightest wind will fundamentally alter."[205] This paradox represents a problem for the composer too, who must create motion over time using structures that are nonetheless definable entities, such as chords or linear patterns, and that always threaten to call attention to themselves for themselves quite apart from their contextual role. These, in a sense (although it is obviously an analogy that cannot be carried too far), are akin to externalities for Kandinsky: if one becomes preoccupied with them, the outer takes over from the inner, resulting in lifeless compositions. The extreme mobility of forms "makes it perhaps easier to obtain similar harmonies from the use of different forms than from a repetition of the same one: apart from the fact that, of course, an exact repetition can never be produced."[206] Although more cautiously phrased here than by such cubist writers as Gleizes and Metzinger, the warning against repetition is no less striking. And in Varèse's "simultaneous interplay of unrelated elements that intervene at calculated, but not regular, time-lapses," the word *unrelated* clearly was meant in a special sense: not that the elements so treated would be juxtaposed arbitrarily, but that they would *seem* to be unrelated.[207] This had to do with inner versus outer meaning. As Kandinsky put it, the "construction may be composed of seemingly fortuitous shapes, without apparent connection. But the outer absence of such a connection is proof of its inner presence. Outward loosening points toward an internal merging."[208]

The blaue Reiter artists subscribed to the same basic principle of color and texture as agents of contrast as did the cubists and the futurists. They agreed that color, although greatly expanded in its range of possibilities in the new art, was still subordinate to form, for form could stand alone, but not color: it could not "dispense with boundaries of some kind."[209] Texture was subject to the same limitations: if it was allowed to become an end in itself, then the means would drown out the end: "the external has taken over the inner—mannerism."[210] On the whole, color was most useful as an agent of contrast, precisely as Varèse valued it for the delineation of sound masses. Texture, on the other hand, could be employed in two ways: in parallel to the forms of the composition, or in contrast.[211]

For color, the degree of contrast depended on the choice of forms, because "certain colors can be emphasized or dulled in value by certain forms." But further, and even more important, "an unsuitable combination of form and color is not necessarily discordant, but may with manipulation show fresh harmonic possibilities."[212] The deliberate use of contrast to produce "disharmony"—or what would in the past have been called disharmony—has clear connections to the striving for disequilibrium mentioned by cubist and futurist writers. Kandinsky emphasized that "the universal harmony of a composition can . . . consist of a number of complexes rising to the highest point of contrast. These contrasts can even be of an inharmonious character, and still their proper use will not have a negative effect on the total harmony but, rather, a positive one, and will raise the work of art to a thing of the greatest harmony."[213] Not only that, but "such really independent complexes can, of course, be subordinated to still greater ones, and these greater ones, in turn, form only a part of the total composition."[214] This idea of nested relationships relying upon contrast and developing over time is integral to Varèse's compositional methods. For Kandinsky, however, as for the cubists, contrast had an opposite number. Gleizes and Metzinger's two alternatives, allowing elements of a painting either to work together or to work independently, is analogous to Kandinsky's expression of the two great principles of abstract art: "the law of setting side-by-side or setting opposite (the two principles—the principle of the parallel and the principle of contrast.)"[215]

Comparison of Kandinsky's and Varèse's philosophies of art also directs attention to a side of Varèse that has not been sufficiently appreciated. One unfortunate result of the mistaken association of Varèse with the futurists was that he automatically acquired the same image of the hotheaded destroyer of the past that was the popular representation of the typical futurist. But Varèse's declaration that "the links in the chain of tradition are formed by men who have all been revolutionists!" should serve as a reminder that Varèse was really talking about forging continuity, not breaking it.[216] When he spoke of freedom for music, he did not mean irresponsible or unlimited freedom, freedom to do absolutely anything. He meant deliverance from outmoded practices statically and thoughtlessly perpetuated, from "bad habits" (*"erroneously* called tradition"), and from restrictions on the use of sound materials that modern technology had made accessible. This attitude squares with Kandinsky's: "Schoenberg realizes that the greatest freedom of all, the freedom of an unfettered art, can never be absolute. Every age achieves a certain measure of this freedom, but beyond the boundaries of its freedom the mightiest genius can never go."[217] Although Schoenberg did not call himself a revolutionary, clearly he met Varèse's requirements for this role: "No matter how original, how different a composer may seem, he has only grafted a little bit of himself on the old plant. But this he should be allowed to do without being accused of wanting to kill the plant. He only wants to produce a new flower. It does not matter if at first it seems to some people more like a cactus than a rose."[218] For his part, in "Reminiscences," Kandinsky discussed development in art, which for him did "not consist of new discoveries which strike out the old truths and label them errors" but rather took place in the form of "sudden illuminations" that showed "new perspectives in a blinding light, new truths which are basically nothing more than the organic development, the organic growing of earlier wisdom which is not voided by the later, but as wisdom and truth continues to live and produce. The trunk of the tree does not become superfluous because of a new branch; it makes the branch possible."[219] Change in art is slow but unceasing, and the true artist will participate in that change, although he will rarely know exactly where it is leading. Otherwise he would risk being trapped: " 'Truth' in general and in art specifically is not an X, not an always imperfectly known but immovable quantity, but [a] quantity [that] is constantly moving in slow motion . . . like a slowly moving snail that scarcely seems to leave the spot, and draws behind it a slimy trail to which shortsighted souls remain glued."[220] These "shortsighted souls" are, of course, next of kin to Varèse's artisans, who make no new tools but instead depend solely upon tools already invented.[221]

*   *   *

The correspondences revealed in this chapter are of two basic types: philosophical and technical. For the purposes of formulating a theory to account for the structure of musical compositions, the latter are of great potential importance; indeed, the strength of the technical correspondences has provided the real impetus to base a theory of structure for Varèse's music upon visual analogies. However, this is not to say that the philosophical correspondence—such as the idea of newness for its own sake, or of the self-referential work of art—are merely incidental. Without their presence to guide and suggest, any appearance of technical similarity would be fallacious. Only the philosophical correspondences can supply real assurance that technical similarities are more than coincidental— the sort of *apparent* correspondences that might occur between any two randomly chosen systems. Varèse would never have wasted his time with matters of technique for the sake of technique alone.

Besides the reasons originally given for treating cubism first, there is another, even more important: cubism has left far more traces in Varèse's writings and other recorded statements than has either futurism or the blaue Reiter movement. Those whom Varèse knew earliest evidently also influenced him to the greatest degree. Nevertheless, the foundations of Varèse's aesthetic do not really bear a cubist stamp. One reason is that the correspondences between the strands of artistic thought and what Varèse gleaned from them can be drawn in different ways, even though the correspondences offered by the different groups of artists are in some respects very similar. As examples, take the cubist idea of two available methods of dividing the canvas and Kandinsky's dual principles of parallel and contrast, or the dual nature of space (container and contained) expressed in one form or another by members of all three groups. In these cases, no single source is sufficient to explain what Varèse inherited; the resonances are all the richer and more interesting for the diverse voices that convey them.

The other reason is that the "cubist" strand itself should be identified as French as much as anything else. Much of what Ozenfant and Jeanneret, Picasso, De-launay, and the Orphic group had to say, by virtue of its historical setting or because of other factors, cannot accurately be classified as cubist, even granting that cubism was never a school and hence does not lend itself well to strict definition. In fact, these individuals have little in common other than having lived through the cubist period. Their common heritage has made it appropriate to consider their ideas and their effect on Varèse cubist-related; but their very presence on the scene ensures that even taking into account only the most direct influences—those which Varèse absorbed in his native country—it is impossible to impute them all to a single point of view.

The question of influence is a thorny one, even where there exists plentiful documentation—in the form of private notes or diaries, for example, or a carefully preserved private library. Lacking these in Varèse's case, one is forced to rely almost entirely upon hunches and circumstantial evidence. There are two points to be made about this. First, a good hunch can open doors whose existence one never even suspected before. Second, for our purposes today what matters more than the exact sources of Varèse's aesthetic—although such details are valuable information—is that the transmission of ideas both general and specific occurred at all. The strength of the correspondences revealed in this chapter encourages us to take Varèse's evident fascination with—and perhaps even in-depth study of—visual art and from it to make something both literal and intricate.

TWO

THE SPATIAL ENVIRONMENT: PROCESS, PITCH/REGISTER, AND SYMMETRY

The past twenty-five years or so have seen a wide-ranging, if somewhat sporadic, attempt on the part of theorists to come to grips with Varèse's compositional procedures.[1] Despite all the activity, however, little in the way of consensus has emerged. Numerous different approaches have been tried, but none has been developed beyond the scope of a single article. Has the intractability of Varèse's music discouraged continued study?

Varèse has long had a reputation for being difficult. His pronouncements about the "sterility" of analysis and his claims that his music is not based upon any "system" have forced theorists to reconsider the utility of traditional approaches, leading some to the conclusion that analytical methods which rely upon precise definitions of musical elements are inappropriate to the material. Apparently for this reason, the authors of several published studies have employed generalized, approximate analytical parameters.[2] Another, related problem is that, in the opinion of some, the various domains of musical sound appear to achieve relative levels of importance in Varèse's music far closer to equality than they do in the works of other, contemporaneous composers. Specifically, the usual hegemony of pitch is challenged by register, rhythm/duration, and timbre. An analytical method that responds to this perception by proposing to embrace all domains simultaneously cannot help but rely upon approximation.

Other writers apparently doubt either that Varèse was being completely forthright in renouncing his debt to other composers' methods or that he meant his self-imposed isolation quite so unequivocally. As might be expected, studies of this sort focus largely on pitch (that is, pitch *class*) and treat it in a relatively conventional manner.[3]

Unfortunately, much of this work, despite the occasional insight it affords, either is based upon fundamentally wrong assumptions or fails to follow through on what are ostensibly right ones. First, with respect to Varèse's originality—not of style, which is not at issue, but of working methods—it is not at all astonishing that Varèse's claims for himself provoked a certain amount of skepticism, at least initially. But now, especially since the various attempts to explain Varèse's work

39

through methods of organization known from other composers' work have all fallen short, the question should be asked: Why *not* take the composer at his word? Perhaps Varèse was pursuing artistic goals that others did not share. Such conjectures, of course, are not worth much without some form of supporting evidence. But in any case there is little wisdom in simply assuming, as has been done so often, that the history of compositional practice in the first half of the twentieth century is equivalent to the history of atonality and dodecaphony on the one hand and the vestigial tonality of neoclassicism on the other.[4]

Varèse's background is unique among the great composers of this century. This fact serves as a powerful support for and confirmation of our intuition: Varèse not only sounds different, he *is* different. And this difference is rooted, not in mere appearances, but in the essential facts of compositional procedure. Milton Babbitt's warning to those who would presume otherwise is well put: "The Varèsian opening statement . . . is of such a character as not to suggest that it is itself an instance of a familiar 'language' system, whose associated constraints would then be inferred, mistakenly and, for the coherent hearing of the rest of the work, disastrously."[5]

Second, approximate methods of musical analysis have always been suspect, and for good reason. If the only relevant outcome of exact notation—and performance—of a piece of music is an *approximate* phenomenon, then why would any composer take the trouble to specify his exact intentions in the first place? There is no reason to think that Varèse had less than exact results in mind, even though most attempts at analysis of his music have proved unequal to the task of exposing them.

To deal successfully with Varèse's music, the theorist must, first, accept the norms of Varèse's sound-universe as the *only* factors relevant to definition of structure in his work; and second, proceed inexorably from these to the formulation of a set of principles based upon a combination of rigor and flexibility. Here rigor means that the basic assumptions (whatever they are) set as hypothetical constraints upon the music ought not to change arbitrarily in the course of the analysis; but flexibility in the initial definition of principles is needed as well to admit a larger range of sound events than would be considered conducive to coherence in other, more extensively analyzed music.

In embarking on this study, I would not like to give the impression of claiming that I have done entirely without the help of others. Chou Wen-chung's *Musical Quarterly* article points in the right direction, arguing as it does from Varèse's own terminology; Wilkinson's article, despite certain flaws, is of substantial value; and Babbitt makes a number of useful points which have set the stage, as they were evidently intended to do, for more extended investigation.[6] What follows, however, is in all its essential aspects new.

THE COMPOSER SPEAKS

Varèse's remarkably original way of thinking about musical structure is accurately and consistently reflected in his writings and other recorded comments. Varèse resorted as a rule to rather enigmatic language when he talked about his music, but what he did say is far more revealing about the technical aspects of compositional procedure than has generally been recognized. The following passage provides a useful starting point:

> When new instruments will allow me to write music as I conceive it, the movement of sound masses, of shifting planes, will be clearly perceived, taking the place of linear counterpoint. When these sound masses collide the phenomena of penetration or repulsion will seem to occur. Certain transmutations taking place on certain planes will seem to be projected onto other planes, moving at different speeds and at different angles. . . . In the moving masses you would be conscious of their trans-mutations when they pass over different layers, when they penetrate certain opacities, or are dilated in certain rarefactions.[7]

Varèse's visual imagery has always been susceptible to interpretation as merely a rather involved metaphor. But this interpretation is unjustified. The visual analogy has a purpose, for the events described in such terms are in fact taking place literally *in* the music. "Spatial music" and "music in space" are phrases used by Varèse over and over again; the single unifying principle of his music is the manipulation of materials with reference to a *spatial* framework.

To what extent is physical space translated into musical space? More specifically, which attributes of physical space are employed in this translation? Varèse once said: "The new composers have not abandoned melody . . . there is a distinct melodic line running through their work. . . . But the line in our case is often vertical and not horizontal."[8] In this rather oddly phrased statement Varèse identified one of his primary concerns, which deserves considerable attention: the vertical dimension. There is, indeed, almost nothing in his music resembling melody or line in the traditional sense, as was noticed almost immediately by those who attended the Varèse premieres of the 1920s. Struck by the newness of what they heard, and searching for descriptive terminology appropriate to it, the critics found such evocative phrases as "blocks of sound," "cubical music," "skyscraper chords," and "the geometry of sound."[9]

The following basic assumption serves as a first step beyond intuitive judgments—however keen—toward solid theoretical gound: if the vertical dimension has primary status in Varèse's musical frame of reference, then the partitioning of vertically defined space takes on crucial significance. Varèse commented directly upon this feature of his composition: "Your main problem in the art of composing today," he was once quoted as saying, "is to see that the notes of your chords are properly spaced."[10] Elsewhere, he said that "taking the sonorous elements as a whole, there are several possibilities of subdivision with relation to the whole: into other masses, other volumes, other planes."[11] Using these possibilities of subdivision, Varèse sought the result that he described variously as "the sensation of non-blending" or "the movement of unrelated sound masses."[12]

However, identification of component portions of the whole does not in itself constitute much of an analysis. Exactly to what extent *are* these component masses unrelated? Surely not completely so, for complete separation would imply a technique of arbitrary juxtaposition and combination, precisely the sort of approach that Varèse criticized in the works of Cage and others ("so accidental that I can't see the *necessity* for a composer!").[13] Even in his early works Varèse occupied himself with "a way to project in music . . . how one element pushing on the other stabilizes the total structure, thus using the material elements at the same time in opposition to and in support of one another."[14] Perhaps the best way to describe what Varèse had in mind is with reference to more traditional musical techniques. As Varèse said, the movement of sound masses was meant to take over the function usually ascribed to counterpoint. Counterpoint was something about which Varèse had managed to learn a good deal during his student years in Paris, particularly from his classes at the Conservatoire with Charles Widor, whom— unlike any of his other teachers there or at the Schola Cantorum—he admired.[15] Varèse certainly must have developed a healthy appreciation for the fact that contrapuntal parts lead independent lives yet at the same time belong together, and that neither quality by itself is sufficient. Of course, the limits of tonal counterpoint proved far too rigid for Varèse to remain confined by them for very long, but some lessons one never forgets. In the music he later composed, the simultaneous occurrence of two or more sound masses suggests *in itself* that these masses have an aggregate function in addition to their independent functions.

In Varèse's program notes on *Déserts,* the idea of coexistent dependence and independence is quite clear: "The work progresses in opposing planes and volumes. Movement is created by the exactly calculated intensities and tensions which function in opposition to one another; the term 'intensity' referring to the desired acoustical result, the word 'tension' to the size of the interval employed."[16] As noted in chapter 1, the words "exactly calculated" are of considerable significance, but not in the sense of any pre-existent system of organization. Varèse remarked further about *Déserts* that "although the intervals between the pitches determine the ever-changing and contrasted volumes and planes, they are not based on any fixed set of intervals such as a scale, or series, or any existing principle of musical measurement. They are decided by the exigencies of this particular work."[17]

For this apparently self-generating method of composition, in which order is not imposed externally but grows in some fashion from within, Varèse found his best expression in the form of an analogy to the process of crystallization. The relevance of this analogy to Varèse's aesthetic backgound has already been discussed in some detail, but the possibility that its roots are in others' ideas should not be allowed to obscure the powerfully original significance it has for structure in his music. To recapitulate: Crystal form, in its standard mineralogical definition, "is characterized by both a definite form and a definite internal structure," the latter of which originates in "the smallest grouping of the atoms that has the order and composition of the substance." Extended into space, this internal structure produces the external form. Varèse showed special interest in the fact that "in spite of the relatively limited variety of internal structures, the external forms of crystals are limitless."[18]

The analogy to crystallization emphasizes growth through orderly expansion of a bare minimum of an idea, cell-like in nature. This may sound, in twentieth-century context, almost traditional. One might wonder, for instance, whether "crystallization" is simply synonymous with the generative-cell models of analysis propounded by George Perle and others.[19] But other statements by Varèse effectively refute this possibility: "There is an idea, the basis of an internal structure, expanded or split into different shapes or groups of sound constantly changing in shape, direction, and speed, attracted and repulsed by various forces. The form of the work is the consequence of this interaction."[20] The initial idea is not necessarily anything more than a point of departure. The basis of an internal structure, expanded into other configurations which in turn produce still others, may not appear more often than, or even stand in any direct, easily discernible relation to, other sound events that come into existence in the course of a work. Having appeared once, the initial event may never be heard again.

The formal implications of this technique are revolutionary indeed. Since for Varèse the form of a work is the consequence of the interaction and expansion of its materials, his statement "form and content are one" follows inevitably. That "form is a resultant—the result of a process"[21] leads to the striking conclusion that unity and continuity in the works of Varèse spring *at least* as much from the consistent nature of the manipulative processes applied to sound materials as from any overall similarity in the structure of the sound materials themselves.

To place process at a level of importance higher than result is to suggest that the music develops within a continuum of perpetual change. From some points of view such methods no doubt invite incoherent results, but clearly Varèse did not agree: "I think of musical space as open rather than bounded, which is why . . . I want simply to project a sound, a musical thought, to initiate it, and then to let it take its own course. I do not want an a priori control of all its aspects."[22] Logically, then, the exact repetition of any formation heard earlier in a work would be rather unlikely. In fact, instances of it are virtually nonexistent.[23] *Near*-exact repetition, however, is something else again. This kind of event, which involves reference to some previous material, resembles the more traditional process of thematic or motivic development and offers potential contradiction to the unidirectional nature of constant change. However, according to Varèse, "if the themes reappear, they always occupy a distinct function in a new medium"—an assertion which, as we will see, is entirely accurate.[24]

THE THEORY ITSELF

In a truly spatial context—an approximation of Varèse's working frame of reference—criteria of absolute size and distance, in the vertical sense, must form the basis of structure. Consistent application of such criteria has certain inescapable effects. First, inversional equivalence cannot exist, for in a framework based on absolute interval sizes a third, for example, obviously cannot serve the same function as a sixth. Second, octave equivalence must be ruled out as well, for in

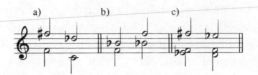

Example 2.1

spatial terms events in different registral locations occur in fundamentally different places. Thus the property of pitch class disappears. The designation "C♯," for example, can have no meaning unless its octave location is identified.[25] In example 2.1a the two intervals shown are spatially equivalent, but the two in 2.1b are not. In 2.1c the two groups of pitches shown are not spatially equivalent, even though both are instances of pitch-class set 3–2.[26] The term *pitch/registral* describes a condition in which pitch content and registral disposition are taken to define, as one, the nature of an entity. Under these conditions, the "equal-tempered" system serves simply as a neutral calibration of that portion of the frequency spectrum (seven octaves plus) available to conventional instruments. It provides a uniform measure of absolute interval size, of distance between upper and lower boundaries of sound masses.[27]

The properties of Varèse's music revealed by the analogy to crystallization indicate a means of describing activity within this sound space. The fact that a continuum of change represents unity means that the most important analytical considerations, in most situations, will be point-to-point connections. Because of the special nature of Varèse's procedures, immediate succession often reveals the strongest relationships between musical formations. Each new formation must result in some fashion from what has preceded it, in turn to be manipulated to produce the next formation. In defining the various kinds of manipulation and transformation, the theorist must distinguish them from one another, and from merely arbitrary operations, in useful and significant ways. He must ask: How is each succeeding development *precisely* meaningful? And how is the process involved consistent with other transformations at other points? For this purpose we will have recourse to several different kinds of operations, all of which exhibit the general property of *symmetry*.

On the simplest level, symmetry can describe individual formations.[28] In example 2.2a, E4 is symmetrically placed with respect to outer pitches C♯4 and G4 because it is precisely equidistant from both. In example 2.2b, middle pitches G4 and B4 are symmetrically placed with respect to C♯4 and F5 because the distance

Example 2.2

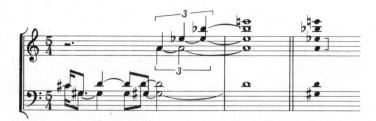

Example 2.3a: *Déserts*, mm. 21–22

Example 2.3b: *Intégrales*, m. 36, woodwinds

from C♯4 to G4, six semitones, is equal to the distance from B4 to F5. Either one or two pitches, then, may comprise the center of a symmetrical formation.

When a larger number of pitches enters the picture, more possibilities arise. In example 2.3a (*Déserts*, mm. 21–22), the order of intervals from top to bottom is the same as from bottom to top. The bracket marks the center of the formation. This kind of symmetry is called *mirror* type. In *parallel* symmetry, on the other hand, the sonority is divisible into two or more groups, each of which displays the same intervallic order from lowest to highest pitch. In example 2.3b (*Intégrales*, m. 36, woodwinds), the parallel symmetry of the two groups is shown by the brackets. These two types of symmetry may also operate simultaneously. In example 2.4 (*Intégrales*, m. 69), mirror symmetry accounts for the configuration extracted in (a), parallel symmetry for the extraction in (b).

This kind of all-inclusive symmetry does not characterize every collection of

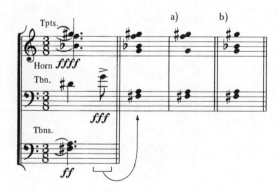

Example 2.4: *Intégrales*, m. 69

pitches in the music of Varèse. Frequently a given formation will exhibit no obvious properties of symmetry. This could be for any of three reasons: (1) the formation may not include everything happening in its particular location; (2) the formation may encompass two or more events that are independently functioning entities, not linked by any one expression of relation; (3) the formation may be transient, and accounted for by movement which occurs on a level distinct from that of immediate succession. What was said earlier about point-to-point connections still holds true; however, Varèse occasionally juxtaposes locally unrelated events in order to throw into relief certain transformations taking place over time spans of greater length.

Partial symmetry also has important functions. In example 2.5 (*Intégrales*, m. 78), the lower half of the structure does not replicate the spacing of the upper half. However, the middle segment, extending from C4 to F5, includes pitches E♭4 and D5, which divide it in the pattern [3][11][3]. The remaining segments of the chord, A1–C4 below and F5–G♯7 above, are equal in size. In this excerpt are other forces that operate together with intervallic symmetries; these come under the heading of timbral differentiation. Somewhat analogous to the role of color in the new art of the early twentieth century, Varèse's aspirations for timbre in his work included its removal from any "incidental, anecdotal, sensual, or picturesque" function and its use instead as "an agent of delineation, like the different colors on a map separating different areas, and an integral part of form."[29] Timbre, in other words, was for Varèse a partitioning device. In this role it is often, inevitably, tied to registral placement, but this is far from always being so. Registral overlap often poses analytical problems that only timbral differentiation can resolve. In example 2.5, timbre helps divide the sonority into groups (delineated by brackets). The instrumental groups comprising this chord are: low brass, A1–B2; middle and high brass, C4–D5; and woodwinds, F5–G♯7. Further, one result of the importance of timbre for Varèse is that the lowest and highest pitches of timbral groupings can serve, in the spatial sense, as demarcators. As with other means of distinguishing masses from one another, these boundaries of timbral areas take on a certain prominence in the texture. Thus, in the present example, the span

Example 2.5: *Intégrales*, m. 78

A1–C4 includes all low brass *and* the distance between them and the horn, at C4, which is the lower edge of the middle/high brass. The span F5–G♯7 is defined by the boundaries of the woodwind area. Another symmetry lies in the groups A1–B♭1–B2 and the analogously placed G♭6–G6–G♯7. These two segments produce a combination of mirror and parallel symmetry: mirror because the two groups are equidistant from the center of the entire chord, parallel because their internal structures present the same ordering of intervals, [1][13], from bottom to top.

Dynamics may act in conjunction with timbre to emphasize the symmetrical character of individual formations. The vertical structure in example 2.6 (*Déserts*, mm. 171–174), viewed as a whole, is not symmetrical. However, the lower part of the structure, E♭1–E2, is clearly set apart from the rest. This is brought about by means of dynamic and timbral contrast, for E♭1 and E2 are marked *pp*, while the other pitches are all emphasized in some way: either they are registrally and timbrally prominent (as is C♯6, for example), or they are accented, *fp*, at their entrances. The upper part of the structure in example 2.6 is symmetrical. Notice too that the symmetry is reinforced by timbral distribution: two pairs of instruments (trumpets and flutes) interlock, while a third pair, clarinets, brackets them. Meanwhile, the note G♯2 is emphasized over the others by repetition, instrumen-

Example 2.6: *Déserts*, mm. 171–174 (percussion of indefinite pitch omitted)

tation, and variation in loudness, and can thus be said to serve as a delimiting lower boundary, further isolating E♭1 and E2 from the symmetry above.

Types of Process

So far, we have seen structures which, considered by themselves, display various types of symmetry. Substantial though they may seem as musical "objects," however, these structures are not really objects at all, but manifestations of musical process. Larger contexts show how the principles of symmetry also control the workings of process. In example 2.7 (*Déserts*, mm. 29–30), the configuration given in the timpani at m. 29 is duplicated, [14] higher, in the brass at m. 30. This kind of transference of structure to a new pitch/registral level will be referred to as *projection*. (The timpani sonority is itself a projection of a segment of the chord in mm. 21–22, reproduced above in Example 2.3a.) The use of the term *projection* in this sense is meant to approximate the meaning that Varèse assigned to it. His definition of projection as "the feeling that sound is leaving us with no hope of being reflected back, a feeling akin to that aroused by beams of light sent forth by a powerful searchlight"[30] certainly suggests that the manipulation of musical elements in a spatial framework eventually produces radically different results from those of more familiar procedures. It also effectively conveys the sense that return does not occur.

Projection is brought about essentially through the movement of outer boundaries, and preservation of internal detail from one location to another is optional. In example 2.8 (*Intégrales*, mm. 177–181, 184–185), the sustained notes C5 (trumpet), C♯6 (oboe), and D7 (piccolo) form the configuration [13][13] in mm. 177–181. This is duplicated [10] lower in m. 185 by D4 and E♭5 in the clarinet and E6 in the piccolo. However, the B6 of mm. 177–181 has no correspondent in m. 185; hence the projection is only partial. Varèse employs partial projection far more often than complete duplication—the process of projection usually overlaps with other processes which bring about, simultaneously, other changes in the material.

Always, however, whatever is to be regarded as the product of projection must preserve some characteristic of its source. In the hypothetical situation illustrated by example 2.9, group (b) cannot be considered a projection of (a). Similar motion

Example 2.7: *Déserts*, mm. 29–30, brass and timpani

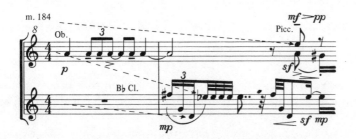

Example 2.8: *Intégrales,* mm. 177–181, 184–185 (lower instruments omitted)

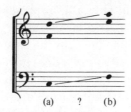

Example 2.9

is not sufficient. There is no interval of projection, because D5–A5 is not the same size as C3–F3. Spatial processes do not yield particularly useful analytical information if they are not interpreted in consistent and exact fashion.

Often used in conjunction with projection, *rotation* is closely related to parallel symmetry. The difference between mirror symmetry and rotation is that rotation implies a succession of events in which the first causes one or more others to occur. The transformation identified here as rotation is sometimes called *inversion,* used literally—in the sense meant, for example, when it describes the operation that produces the I-form of a twelve-note row from the P-form beginning on the same pitch. Use of the term *rotation* avoids potential confusion with inversion in the tonal sense.

In example 2.10 (*Déserts,* mm. 85–93), rotation is applied to a sonority of considerable temporal and spatial expanse. The boundary interval [54] of mm. 85–91 is duplicated in mm. 92–93; the internal structure, however, is reversed, as if the structure, while being projected, had been turned 180 degrees within the

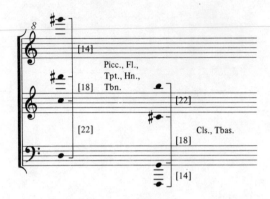

Example 2.10: *Déserts*, mm. 85–93

"plane" of the music. Note the change of instrumentation that occurs simultaneously with the reversal of the vertical order of intervals, effectively articulating this rotation.

Example 2.11 (*Intégrales*, mm. 151–154) illustrates the symmetrical process designated *expansion*. Measured from the outer edges of the first trichord (trumpets and horn), the distance B♭4–C3 is the same as the distance A5–G7. Pitches C3 and G7 are both outer boundaries; they represent, respectively, the lowest and highest points attained in this particular passage. (Embedded within this expansion is a rotation of smaller scope, shown by the crossed dotted lines.) That D3, not C3, is the lowest point in the final sonority does not interfere with the symmetry of expansion, which depends upon total space occupied over a period of several measures. The relationship is a typical one in Varèse's music, in that provisions for further progress are incorporated into the results of the operation. In this instance, while the dimension C3–G7 is the outcome of previous events, D3–G7 will control future developments.

Another example of expansion demonstrates further flexibility in the use of this transformation. The excerpt in example 2.12 (*Déserts*, mm, 46–53, with pickup) is bounded, temporally speaking, by brief silences and abrupt changes in instrumentation, both before and after. The first event in this clearly delineated

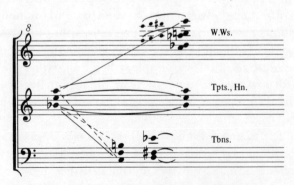

Example 2.11: *Intégrales*, mm. 151–154

Example 2.12: *Déserts*, mm. 46–53

Example 2.13: *Déserts*, mm. 81–82

section fills a space of [7], which is subsequently and rapidly enlarged. (Interrelations and interactions between component elements are not shown in the example.) The lower boundary of this passage, F♯1, is quickly attained, but the upper boundary, E♭6, does not appear until m. 51, at which point F♯1 is no longer sounding. Nevertheless, because mm. 46–53 comprise a unit by virtue of timbral and durational criteria, an overall symmetry is determined by the highest and lowest limits established for the whole passage. Symmetrical expansion occurs, since F♯1–G3 equals D4–E♭6.

Symmetric *contraction*, illustrated in example 2.13 (*Déserts*, mm. 81–82), is simply the reverse of expansion. Note that the initial event, F♯3–G5, is expressed as a temporal simultaneity, while E♭4–B♭4, the goal of the contraction, is not.

Extended Applications

In all but the briefest of excerpts, the individual types of process are usually combined. However, single varieties are powerful forces in some situations, as the next two examples demonstrate.[31]

Control of extended passages may be managed through multiple projections of single intervals. In example 2.14 (*Octandre*, II, mm. 39–66), some internal detail is omitted to clarify the larger picture.[32] The example begins at a point where the total amount of space in use is relatively small: [21], from B3 to A♭5. This is subsequently and rapidly expanded, although only partially through projection of [21]; the next prominent appearance of that interval is in the boundaries F♯3 (horn entrance, m. 43) and E♭5 (piccolo, m. 42; trumpet, 44; oboe, 45; highest

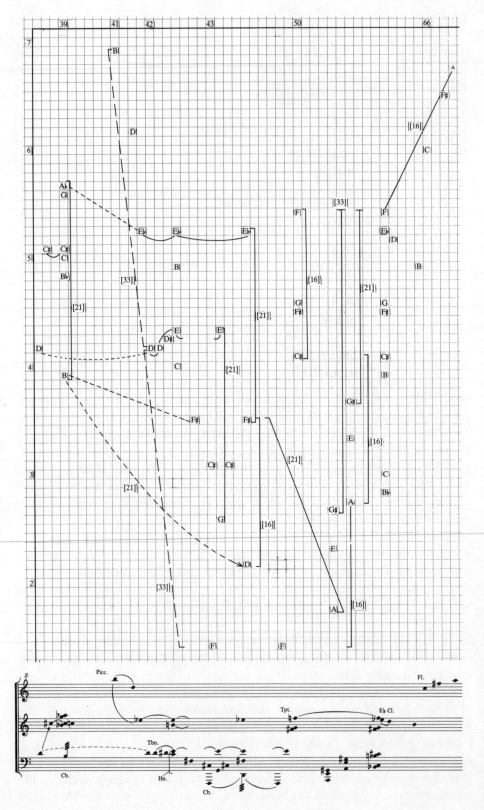

Example 2.14: *Octandre*, II, mm. 39–66

note in the texture until m. 50). It also occurs, somewhat obliquely, as the interval between the initial B3 (contrabass) and the contrabass D2 in mm. 46–47 (note, however, that both of these pitches are distinguished by being played "sur le chevalet"). The interval [16], D2–F♯3, first occurs in relative obscurity, merely as a kind of intersection between instances of [21]. In the passage beginning at m. 50, however, it emerges as the primary controlling factor in spatial structure: first, as the boundaries of the chord in the upper region, C♯4–F5, differentiated from the rest of the texture by its sustained quality. The lower region, slightly more complicated, consists of a succession of three chords. The first two of these form a pair by virtue of their rhythmic activity and their internal similarity: the second is the same as the first, [12] higher. The octave interval in this instance, since it is explicitly articulated, aids the association.[33] The distance from the former low boundary F1 to the lowest note of the second of these two new chords, A2, is [16]; and therefore, of course, so is the interval A2 to C♯4 (the lower boundary of the upper, sustained chord). Thus the entire space F1–F5, [48], has been trisected into [16]-spans. Meanwhile, [21] remains present, between the highest note of the lower, active chord pair (G♯3) and the highest note in the whole texture (F5). This spatial arrangement remains in place until m. 66; and even after this point [16] continues briefly in evidence, as the rapid notes in the flute rise to A6, [16] above the previous upper boundary.

One further detail to be noted in example 2.14 is the replication of [33] in mm. 39–42. The relevant events follow upon one another in rapid succession: from B6, the highest note in the passage, to the return of the D4 in the trombone (clearly meant, in this context, as a continuation after its temporary eclipse), to F1 in the contrabass, the lowest note in the passage. Thus D4–F1 stands as a projection of B6–D4. Because the lower boundary of the first span is the same as the higher boundary of the second, however, it could also be said that D4 is a midpoint in the defined space F1–B6. Relationships of this sort are quite common in Varèse's music, especially in situations where activity in a high region is suddenly superseded by activity in a much lower one (or vice versa). A fine example is found near the end of the second movement of *Offrandes* (ex. 2.15, "La croix du sud," mm. 40–43). In the first two measures of this excerpt the parts enter in pairs until the entire texture has accumulated (downbeat of m.41). The governing framework here is two equal spans: C2–B3, defined at the lower boundary by bassoon and at the upper by cello alternating with viola; and A4–A♭6 (upper woodwinds). The lower of these, however, changes timbrally as the strings, on (A♯-B)3, drop out (at that same downbeat of m. 41) and are replaced by the horn. This is a signal, or at least may be interpreted as such. The horn is the last part to sound in the entire texture so far discussed; its notes B♭3 and C♭4, together with the highest note (A♭6 in the piccolo), effectively predict the entrance of the new lower boundary, C♯1 in the harp (m. 42), for A♭6–C♭4 equals B♭3–C♯1. Thus A♯/B♭3, through its timbral change and its prolongation beyond the rest of the pitches in mm. 40–41, moves from an internal, secondary position into a primary role, equal in importance to original boundary pitch B3.

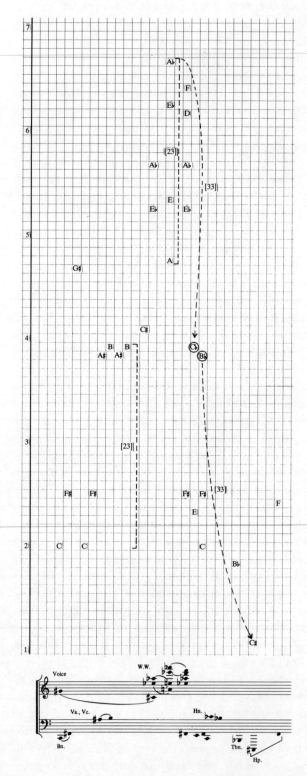

Example 2.15: *Offrandes,* II ("La croix du sud"), mm. 40–43

Combinations/Longer Examples

Far more common than instances of single processes are situations in which two or more operate simultaneously. In such situations, segmentational decisions may become rather complicated, and various agents of differentiation often must be invoked to explain structure. One relatively straightforward case is the passage shown in example 2.16 (*Déserts*, mm. 63–65), where Varèse achieves timbral separation by placing the first two trichords in the woodwinds and the second two in the brass. These two phases of activity together constitute the simultaneous employment of projection, rotation, and expansion. The two pairs of solid parallel lines show projection and expansion; the two pairs of crossed dotted lines show that rotation takes place as well.[34]

In a larger context, the configuration of combined processes becomes more complex: projection, rotation, expansion, and contraction all influence one another. Example 2.17 (*Ecuatorial*, mm. 211–220) is indeed rather complicated. Essentially what happens here is that a large space is reduced in stages to one much smaller. The large expanse B♭0–E7 is divided exactly in its middle by the highest note in the trombones (C♯4), a note which is given special emphasis by the glissando preceding it. The entrances of parts are staggered in typically Varèsian fashion, roughly in order from lowest to highest, and the highest pitches (D♯6 and E7 in the two ondes) enter as the others drop out. While these are held in mm. 212–213, other, lower notes appear, ending with the group D1–E1–F2 (m. 215), which is followed by a rest. The ondes' D♯6–E7 thus has an analogue in E1–F2; the presence of D1 makes the projection only partial, but this lowest pitch has other purposes. On the most local level, the entrance of D1 completes a secondary symmetry involving the duplication of the interval [19]: its first appearance occurs between E4 (lowest pitch in the trumpets, mm. 211–212) and A2 (lowest pitch in the organ, m. 213), then between D2 and A1.

Subsequent developments reveal that the placement of the lower boundary at D1 has further significance. The trombones, in sextuplets at m. 216, first outline G2–E4, then reach a semitone further to F4. Temporally adjacent events thus articulate the span D1–F4, which by virtue of *registral* proximity may be inter-

Example 2.16: *Déserts*, mm. 63–65

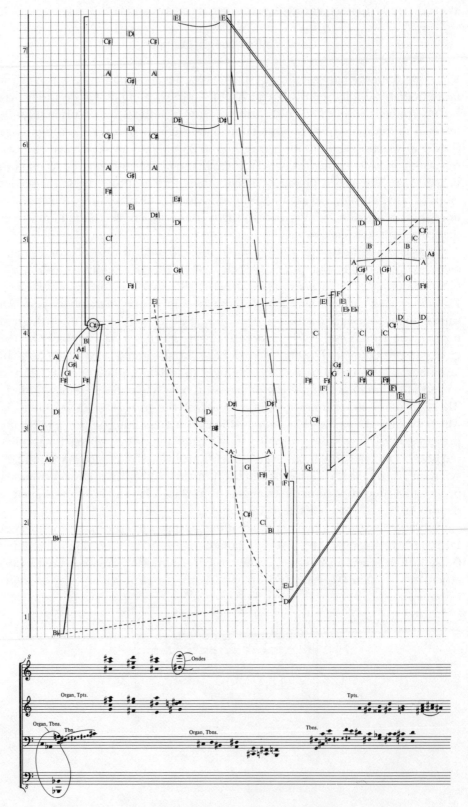

Example 2.17: *Ecuatorial*, mm. 211–220

preted as a projection of B♭0–C♯4 from m. 211. Next, trombones yield to trumpets (mm. 217–218), then rejoin them in mm. 219–220, where a span E3–D5 is delineated as a projection of G2–F4. Simultaneously, the large span D1–E7, formed earlier by temporal adjacency, contracts symmetrically to this same E3–D5. The confluence of processes suggests that the phenomenon referred to by Varèse as "penetration" of one sound mass by another has taken place.[35]

The next two examples, 2.18 and 2.19 (*Intégrales*, mm. 80–102 and mm. 126–135, respectively), are best considered together, for the second, because it is similar to the first in certain respects, raises the issue of repetition alluded to earlier. Side-by-side comparison of mm. 93–100 and mm. 131–134 reveals a resemblance that is certainly not coincidental. Some differences are evident—in rhythm, dynamics, accompanying percussion, and use of mutes—but pitch/registral relationships have been left intact.

Analysis of each excerpt in its immediate context helps explain the meaning of Varèse's remarks about the "distinct function in a new medium" of such reappearing material (see p. 43 above). In ex. 2.18, mm. 93–100 are preceded by a passage (mm. 80–93) dominated by a group A4–B6, which alternates several times with a lower pair of chords: G1–F♯2 followed by D2–E3. Embedded in this lower area are features of the upper, given in succession instead of simultaneously: the [11]-span G1–F♯2, an effect of the interlocked [11]s A4–G♯5 and B♭4–A5; and the [14]-span D2–E3, a projection of A5–B6. The two widely separated groups converge in a symmetrical contraction to the "melodic" component of mm. 93–100 in its eventual complete form. The pitches D4 and E4 are the first two presented in the melody, and F♯4 and C4 bracket the final interval (filled symmetrically by D4 and E4) in m. 100. The repeated trombone chord D♭2–A♭2–E♭3 comes about as a partial projection of D2–E3. Note that the space filled by the entire contents of mm. 93–100 (D♭2–F♯4) is congruent to the intervals of contraction G1–C4 and B6–F♯4. Finally, C4, the last pitch given in m. 100, is used together with B4 in m. 101 to effect a symmetrical expansion to the outer boundaries F♯1 and F7 in m. 102.

In the later excerpt (ex. 2.19), on the other hand, projection rather than contraction is the process primarily responsible for motion to the recurring material from the immediately preceding eleven-note sonority of m. 126, F♯3–C7. This chord can be partitioned in two ways: first, into overlapping woodwind and brass groups (B4–C7 and F♯3–E6, respectively); second, into three congruent segments at A♭4 and B♭5. These three segments are timbrally delineated, too: the lower F♯3–A♭4 encompasses trombones and horn and is set far apart from the high trumpets, and the upper B♭5–C7 is defined by the three highest woodwind instruments (piccolos and E♭ clarinet). In the first partitioning, the span B4–C7 corresponds to the distance (marked in the example by single brackets) delineated by D4 in mm. 127–133 and the trombone chord D♭2–A♭2–E♭3; and F♯3–E6 corresponds to the *interval* of projection, which can be read either as C7–D4 (marked with a double line) or as B4–D♭2. The second partitioning produces three segments, all congruent to the span of the trombone chord in mm. 131–134; in example 2.19, the lowest of these three is shown projected to m. 131.

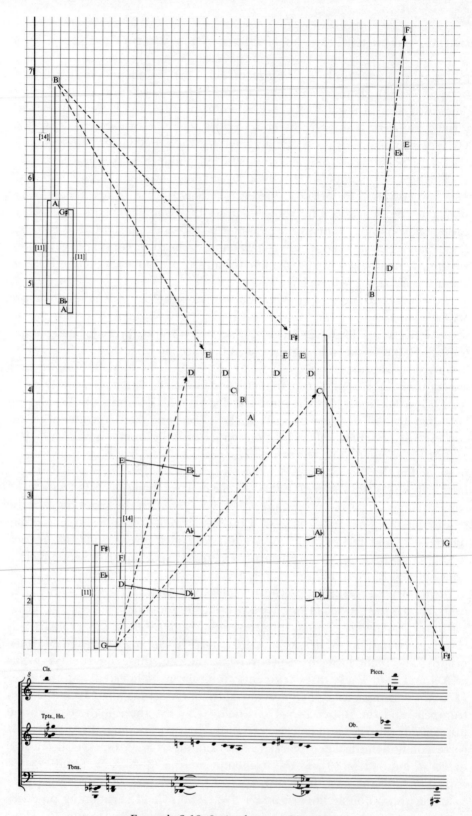

Example 2.18: *Intégrales*, mm. 80–102

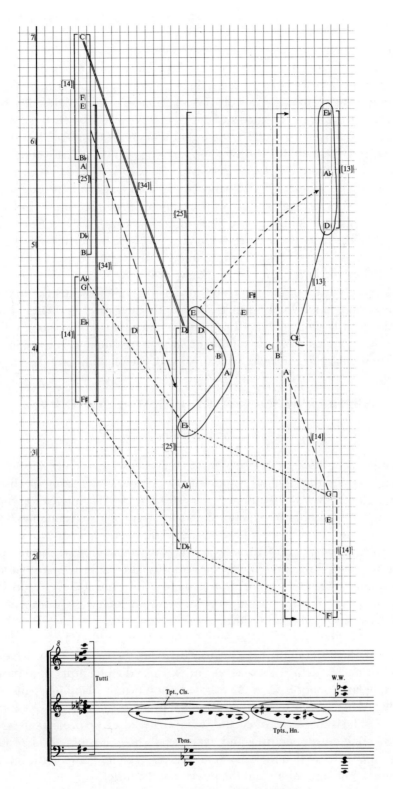

Example 2.19: *Intégrales,* mm. 126–135

The continuation of this passage emphasizes other features of its structure. The pitch E♭6 in m. 135, which remains the highest pitch for some time, is the same distance above D4 as D♭2 is below, hence participating in another instance of projection. Contributing as well to the attainment of this high point are the successively articulated [13]-spans C♯4–D5 and D5–E♭6. (D5–E♭6 is divided by A♭5 and stands in analogy to E♭3, the upper note of the trombone chord in mm. 131–134, and to A3 and E4, the initial upper and lower boundaries of the melody in those same measures.) Below, successive [14]-spans are given by the trombones (F1–G2) and the distance G2–A3 between the trombones and the lowest pitch of the melody. These are projections of the trombone span in mm. 131–134. Furthermore, while the double intervallic projections below A3 and C♯4 do balance one another, the real (that is, exact) symmetry here is expansion outward to F1 and E♭6 *not* from A3 and C♯4 but from A3 and B3, the last two pitches given in the melody before the introduction of the "new" C4.

The various facets of the "repeated" material have different structural meanings depending upon location in the work. In each case the material is fully integrated into its context. The effect is not so much that of return as of reference to an earlier point; and because of the disparity in treatment in the two locations, one tends to hear this reference as a function of the ongoing process.

FURTHER RAMIFICATIONS OF THE SPATIAL ENVIRONMENT

Approximation

As a matter of analytical strategy it is important to stick to exact relationships when defining structure through the symmetrical processes. Observations such as "this expansion is 'off' by only a semitone" are misleading; for if to miss exact symmetry by a semitone is within the realm of possibility, why not two semitones, or even more? Once any sort of inexactitude has been admitted, where does one draw the line? Nevertheless, situations do arise in which approximation is not only admissible but even necessary. Like their exact counterparts, approximate symmetries mean nothing in themselves; but approximations are if possible even more dependent upon the context, for they must occur in conjunction with intricate networks of exactly symmetrical relationships.

Example 2.20 (*Offrandes*, "Chanson de là-haut," mm. 32–35) is a case in point. Here the D2 tied over in the bassoon, together with the D4 and D6 which enter at the end of m. 32, define a space [48] in expanse divided at its midpoint. The succeeding large sonority at m. 35 is based upon two overlapping spans of [48], both divided in the same way as their common predecessor: A1–A3–A5 and G♯2–G♯4–G♯6. The whole series of events can be analyzed as two projections from the first [48]—one down, one up—and, taken as a whole, it could also be called an expansion were it not that there is a semitone discrepancy between the interval of expansion at the upper end and the interval at the lower.

One way of resolving the problem, of course, would be to dismiss the possibility

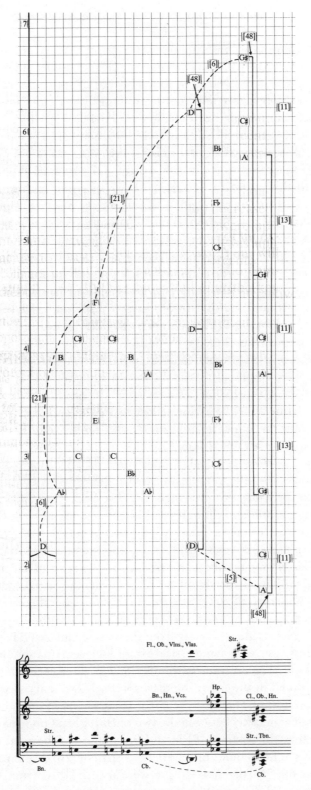

Example 2.20: *Offrandes,* I ("Chanson de là-haut"), mm. 32–35

that expansion plays any significant role at this point; but just because the discrepancy is so tantalizingly small, the analyst may wish to consider alternative explanations. In this case, there is no need to look very far, for there are several other symmetrical relationships embedded in this passage. First, the string parts in triplets and sixteenths in m. 32 fill the space A♭2–F4, [21], which is duplicated at the entrance of D4–D6 in the succession F4–D6, also [21]. Even more interesting is that the D2 already sounding at the beginning of m. 32 delineates another span together with the rapid notes in the strings: [27], divided [6][21]. We find a counterpart to this above in G♯6 above D6 (successive highest notes).[36] This symmetrical structure [6][21][21][6] accounts for the interval of projection from D2–D4–D6 up to G♯2–G♯4–G♯6. If the expansion were exact, then A1–A3–A5 would have to become G♯1–G♯3–G♯5, which would tend to mesh the two [48]s in m. 35 into one sonority rather than allowing their definition as separate regions. (Octave and compound-octave spans, which present special problems and demands in a spatially oriented analysis, are discussed later.) The overlapping, symmetrically partitioned [48]s in m. 35 also provide a composite vertical structure [11][13][11][13][11] which is itself symmetrical and which is duplicated in part by the repeated harp chords of m. 34: [11][13][11]: (C♭–B♭)3–(C♭–B♭)5. The upper part of this chord is [24] higher than the lower part, a partial projection of the [24][24] of m. 32. Notice also that the lowest interval of [11] in the A1–G♯6 expanse, A1–G♯2, is also given as a succession in the contrabass, from its A♭2 in m. 32 to the A1 in m. 35. The requisite network of symmetrical relationships is present, allowing the interpretation of D2–D6 progressing to A1–G♯6 as the *closest possible* to an exact expansion.

Use of the "as close as possible" alternative in analyzing symmetrical constructions also results in a good deal of useful flexibility where important spans overlap. A passage from near the end of the first section of *Déserts* (ex. 2.21, mm. 65–78) provides a brilliant, though complicated, example. In mm. 71–78 there are three successive, clearly defined spans: D♯2–F♯6, D♯1–G♯5, and C♯3–F7, of sizes [51], [53], and [52] respectively. One might conjecture that some sort of correspondence is intended here, despite its less than exact nature. In fact, the relationship does have some significance; however, the actual spatial manipulations have nothing directly to do with the three spans identified above, but rather with the preceding context and the overlap of material within the excerpt.

Example 2.21 continues directly from the passage analyzed in example 2.16, which consists of a perfectly symmetrical expansion occurring simultaneously with a double rotation. (The outcome of this motion is marked (a) in the graph; several of the events noted in the following discussion are also marked with lower-case letters in parentheses.) The next event, the [6] (C♯–G)4 in the horn, is placed as exactly as possible midway between the two pitch/registral units of m. 65; see (b). (The reason that this span is [6] in the first place will become clear shortly.) Succeeding this in fairly quick order are (c), a span of [26] divided at its midpoint and containing one [13] divided [4][9], as were all four [13]s in mm. 63–65 (see ex. 2.16); and (d), a second, lower [26]. We may regard these, then, as a series of partial

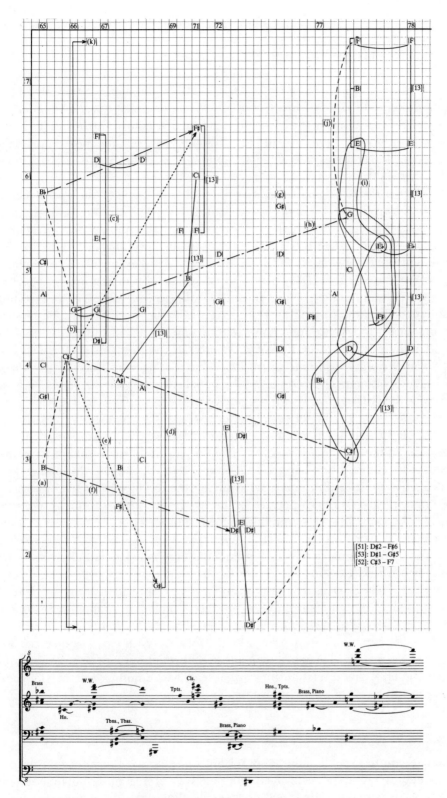

Example 2.21: *Déserts,* mm. 65–78

projections, as first the structure [4][9] is projected, then [13][13], then finally [26] *not* divided into [13]s. In the upper region, however, [13] continues to be projected in overlapping forms: A♯3–B4, B4–C6, F5–F♯6—followed by a transfer to the lower region: D♯2–E3. Before this last projection, occupied space is bounded by G♯1 and F♯6, a symmetrical expansion from the first note of the horn's [6]-span, C♯4; see (e). With the entrance of [13]: D♯2–E3, however, yet another, overlapping expansion becomes clear, from the outer edges of the expansion that ended in m. 65 [see (f): the diverging long-dash lines].

Measures 72–76 emphasize space divided into [6]-spans in the upper region and the last projected [13] in the lower; see (g). The proliferation of adjacent [6]s seems to represent a focus upon that feature of the immediately preceding measures—beginning with the (C♯–G)4 in the horn and also including the [6]s resulting from the overlap of [13]s in mm. 70–71. Further, the distance from the top of the lower region (D♯3; piano, m. 73) to the top of the upper region is exactly the distance of expansion from C♯4 down to G♯1 and up to the F♯6 just mentioned. The lowering of the lower spatial boundary to D♯1 in m. 75, besides serving the obvious function of lower reinforcement for D♯2 and E3 in mm. 71–74, also continues the projection of [13] (with E2) and prepares for the next big, culminating event, beginning in m. 77. The structure here first fills the space C♯3–G5, a symmetrical expansion of the initial (C♯–G)4; see (h). Its spacing, as shown by the circled groups of three pitches in the example, preserves the [4][9] subdivision. In m. 78, the series of interlocked [4][9]s is extended even further— see (i)—and the [6][7] partitioning produced earlier by overlapped [13]s also reappears in the very higest position. The framework of the resultant structure can now be read as four adjacent [13]s from C♯3 to F7, and also (by implication) as two adjacent [26]s. But that is far from all: the distance from *previous* to *new* low point, D♯1 to C♯3, is duplicated in the rise from *initial* to *final* high point in mm. 77–78, G5–F7; see (j). And finally, the distance D♯1–F7, if taken as a whole (that is, total space occupied in the entire passage), represents a symmetrical expansion from the same (C♯–G)4 in mm. 65–66 that expanded to produce the initial structure C♯3–G5 of m. 77; see (k).

It should now be clear that other near but not exact relationships may be read as by-products, though interesting by-products for all that. Among these are the vertical spans so close to identical in size listed above ([51], [53], and [52]) and the nearly exact expansion from D♯2–F♯6 to D♯1–F7. With exact symmetries accounting for spatial placement and delineation throughout a given passage, other more vaguely defined relationships are at least worth noting, for they may enhance the sense of continuity in progression.

Octaves

The decision to exclude judgments relying upon octave equivalence from our analyses presents no special problems for much of Varèse's music, but in situations where octave "doubling" or duplication is explicitly a part of the texture, treatment of the octave in all cases as simply a span of [12] which, except for its absolute size, is no different from any other interval becomes difficult to justify. Under the conditions of literally stated octaves, either in single sonorities or in parallel parts, it seems advisable to relax the outright prohibition of octave equivalence to allow that duplication may have other functions in addition to (and possibly even more significant than) the filling of particular volumes of space. One of these additional functions is simple reinforcement. According to one interviewer, Varèse stated that this was his practice in the orchestral works, at least.[37] This does not mean, however, that the analyst is freed from the necessity of dealing with octave-bounded spaces as parts of a spatially defined context. After all, the question of which part is the reinforcer, which the reinforced, must be answered. One part may have greater functional significance than another—or the space they encompass together may emerge instead as the most important feature. The introduction of octave spans offers an analytical alternative that might be called "flexible space": spatial volumes which may be variably expanded or collapsed by implementing the doublings for some purposes and ignoring them for others. The octave thus acquires unique properties, the most important of which, for the purposes of this chapter, are illustrated in the examples that follow.[38]

In example 2.22 (*Déserts*, mm. 238–242, with reference also to mm. 226–237), octave doubling appears on several levels of varying importance. Preceding the example proper is a sustained chord of several measures' duration, consisting of a lower region bounded by C2 and B3 and a registrally isolated high pitch, C#6. Immediately preceding the chord is D4, strongly emphasized through unison doubling; with the C#6 it encloses, spatially and temporally, the pitches Eb4, D5, and Eb5. Thus mm. 226–237 are defined, in their larger spatial disposition, by the congruent spans C2–B3 and D4–C#6. The inner pitches (B3 and D4), however, have the most to do with what happens next. Among the pitches in the complicated texture of m. 238 is B2. If B2 is taken as the representative of B3 in this instance (see dotted arrow from B3 to B2), then a symmetrical expansion can be read from B3 down to D1 (lowest note in the example)—and, in correspondence, D4 up to B5, the initial high point of the passage (top of the accumulative brass sonority of mm. 239–240). Here D4 also assumes some importance in itself, as the initial low point F2 articulates a span below D4 exactly as large as B5 above D4. As m. 240 yields to m. 241, the lower region now stands as a *contraction* from the initial boundaries of m. 238: that is, D1–B3 to E1– A3. At the upper end, Eb6 is reached, with longer-range significance for structure; for the total span E1–Eb6 is a projection of the space defined by the highest pitch of mm. 228–237, C#6 (and also the pitch of longest duration), and the lowest, D1, of the immediately succeeding section.

These manipulations, considered as a group, account for the larger dimensions of the sound masses at this point. Given their self-sufficiency, how is it possible to interpret the extension, in m. 242, to Eb7 as anything other than a doubling for the purposes of reinforcement? Of course (Eb–D–C#)7 *does* function as a reinforcement of (Eb–D–C#)6; its strengthening of this portion of the texture

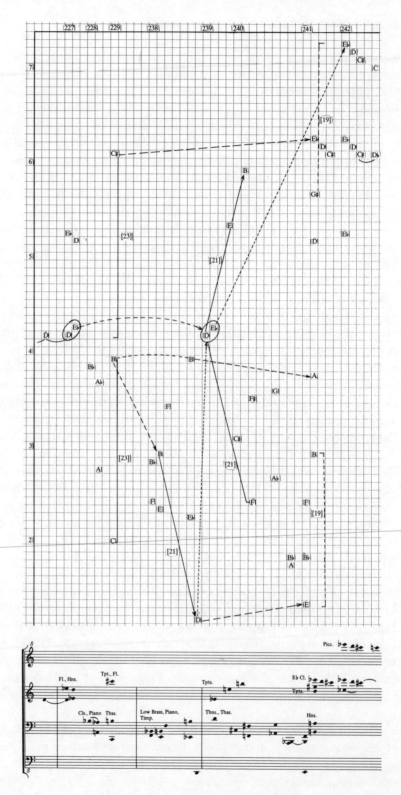

Example 2.22: *Déserts,* mm. 226–242

is part of the climactic effect of this measure. But the extension of occupied space to E♭7 serves as a culmination in other ways as well. First, it confirms the mediating role of the horn and trumpet entrances in m. 240, which occur immediately after the low point E1 is articulated: these introduce to the texture the configuration B2–A3–(D–G♯)5. The entrance of E♭7 completes a symmetry, in that E1–B2 is the same in size as G♯5–E♭7. Second, E♭7 completes a symmetry larger in both the temporal and the spatial sense: the two initial pitches of m. 239, (D–E♭)4, are now revealed as the mediating midpoint between the previous low point D1 and the new high point. D1 and E♭7 are, in addition, the outer boundaries of the entire passage, which lends this particular symmetry an even greater significance. The group (E♭–D–C♯)7, in turn, becomes the mediator for the next series of events, which ends this third of the four sections of *Déserts* (discussed in ex. 3.31).

Next is a passage previously examined at some length: *Octandre*, II, mm. 39–66 (ex. 2.14). The octaves articulated by the rhythmically active chord pair in mm. 50–51 were identified as an associative factor in that region. There can be little doubt that these octaves are meant to be heard as such, but this stops short of explaining why such an association is made in the first place. Providing an explanation here is particularly important, for in *Octandre* octaves of any sort—successive or simultaneous—are rare indeed, and they seem intended to attract special attention.

Once again, study of the context reveals a second function above and beyond reinforcement. The previous analysis of this excerpt has shown that both [33] and [21] have important functions. Of course, [33] is exactly [12] larger than [21], but before m. 50 no special relationship is expressed between them. In mm. 50–66, however, the spans [21] and [33] are united through the octave-related chord pair, for G♯3–F5 is [21] in extent, as already mentioned, while G♯2, the highest note of the first of the lower chords, forms a span of [33] with the same F5.

The last example in this section is taken from the orchestral work *Arcana*. In this composition, and in *Amériques* and *Ecuatorial* as well, thicker textures and demands of ensemble balance not common to the chamber pieces ordain rather more widespread use of octave doubling than is found elsewhere.[39] This excerpt affords an opportunity to observe the extended and multifarious applications of flexible spatial principles under such conditions.

Example 2.23 (*Arcana*, mm. 362–377; begin at rehearsal 35) begins with a chord in trumpets and trombones (actually the upbeat to m. 362) which if divided at the trombones' highest pitch yields two segments, [18]: E♯2–B3 and [20]: B3–G5. Prolonged through m. 363, this chord is succeeded immediately by material that, in its external dimensions at least, can be interpreted as the result of (partial) projections of the preceding upper segment. Of much greater significance for large-scale motion, however, are the entrances at m. 366, which involve two spatially distinct segments, an upper [18]: F4–B5 and a lower [20]: C♯2–A3. (Note that these segments are also temporally distinct.) Further, their composite range C♯2–B5 represents a symmetrical expansion, (a), from previous outer boundaries E♯2 and G5. An "exchange," (b), has thus taken place simultaneously with expansion, an operation which resembles that of ex. 2.16.[40]

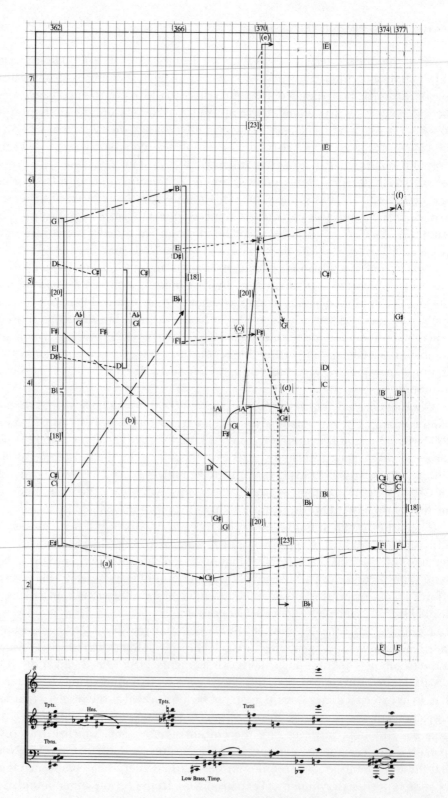

Example 2.23: *Arcana*, mm. 362–377

Next, [20] is projected with the entrance of F5 above A3, at (c). Pitches F#4–F5 in the trumpets may be regarded as a projection from F4–E5; they are projected in turn to form the edges of (G#–A)3–G4, at (d). Note that because A3 stands in relation to G#3–G4 as G4 to F#4–F5, this projection results in parallel symmetry. A3 has a residual overall significance as the upper boundary of the [20] in m. 366, and it now serves as the initiating low point, with F5 as the upper, of an immense symmetrical expansion to B♭1–E7, the boundaries of the climactic chord extending through m. 371, at (e).

Following this climax is a passage for percussion alone (mm. 372–373). Such hiatuses in pitched material sometimes have the effect of breaking local connections of the sort discussed in this chapter, and in this instance we find that the entrances in m. 374 and m. 377 present configurations that develop clearly out of material previous to the climax chord. The spaces filled by these new events are [30]: F1–B3 and [52]: F1–A5. They do not at first seem related to anything that has gone on in the passage so far, but if the lower doubling F1 is subtracted the situation becomes much clearer: F2–A5 is [40] in extent, which corresponds to the composite of the [20] C#2–A3 and its projection up to F5, already analyzed—a projection of C#2–F5, (f); and F2–B3 is [18], which is congruent to F4–B5 (m. 366). Thus the two span sizes with which the excerpt began have longer-range as well as local significance. As for F1, it has to do with deploying the large chord that enters at the very end of m. 377 (not included in this example).

Larger Temporal Spans

Whether there is anything like a global structure in any Varèse work, of the kind elicited by a pitch-class set or twelve-tone row analysis, is still an open question. In much of the Varèse oeuvre, however, there is no appreciable evidence that such a structure exists, nor is there much reason to suppose that it *should* exist, given the noncyclic, unidirectional nature of the processes so far discussed, the aesthetic philosophy which serves as their underpinning, and the analytical procedures, emphasizing point-to-point connection, that have grown out of them. Yet the idea that structure is "open rather than bounded," to use Varèse's phrase, does not exclude the possibility that motions across other than the smallest temporal spans may be subject to control by the same processes that provide point-to-point continuity. We have already seen some instances of this, although the spans of time involved are still rather short compared to the length of the pieces that contain them. The final example in this chapter, however, presents a series of clearly related motions which encompass 154 of the 224 measures of *Intégrales*— approximately one-half to two-thirds of its length, depending upon the performance—and which rely for most of their analytical support upon structures that in more locally oriented analysis emerge as particularly important, even culminating.[41]

Almost all local detail is excluded from example 2.24 in order to avoid distracting the reader from the larger motions. The first of these occurs from the large

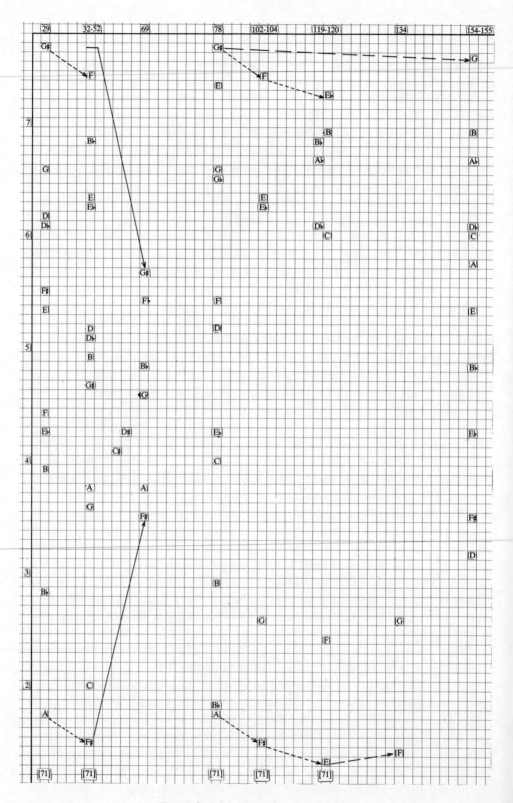

Example 2.24: *Intégrales,* mm. 1–154

sonority that forms in mm. 25–29, eventually filling the space [71]: A1–G#7, to the next large sonority, repeated continually throughout mm. 32–52, which fills a space exactly the same size as the first: F#1–F7. This projection, then, taken in aggregate, fills the space F#1–G#7; it also represents the total portion of the available sound spectrum occupied to this point in the work. The upheaval that follows m. 52 and brings to a close the first section of *Intégrales* comes to rest in m. 69 in a space bounded by F#3 and G#5—representing a symmetrical contraction from the previous boundaries.

By m. 78, another large expanse has been filled: A1–G#7, the same in size and spatial location as the first in the work. (The local means by which it is brought about, of course, are not at all the same as the events leading up to m. 29.) This [71] is followed quite a while later by another [71], F#1–F7 in mm. 101–104—remarkably, the same in size and location as the second such span in the work (in mm. 32–52). As in the first section, this chord pair defines the limits of occupied space from m. 71 on; these limits are superseded, finally, by a third large chord which is also [71] in extent: E1–Eb7 in mm. 119–120. These three [71]-spans can be taken to form a unit which expresses a connection to the final events of the second section of *Intégrales:* the low boundary reached in m. 134 and present until m. 143, F1, and the high boundary of the fermata chord of mm. 153–154, G7, stand as a symmetrical contraction (by [1] on either end) from the edges of the previously occupied space, E1 and G#7.

Several points now ought to be made. One is that none of this would be very interesting if the events selected to demonstrate large-scale motion were not in themselves supported by a network of symmetrically defined relationships ranging from the most minute details to aggregations of several measures or more. Another point is that absolute size, in the sense of sheer quantity of space encompassed, seems to be the criterion exerting the most control over these larger motions, at least in this case. Thus the relative brevity of prolongation of the structures F#1–F7 (mm. 101–104). E1–Eb7 (mm. 119–120), and the oblique relationship of the relevant structures in mm. 134–154 are for these purposes not factors which disqualify them from positions of potential importance. Their enormous vertical expanse alone elevates them to prominence. A third point is that while the mechanism of large-scale process in this example is scarcely obvious, still its relative simplicity is exceptional among the works of Varèse. No one at this point can state definitively that structures of this sort do not exist for the other works, but if they do exist they will probably be extremely hard to find. Since the possibility that a composer has intricately concealed a musical structure does not excuse an over-contrived analysis, future attempts to elicit the larger processes of Varèse's works may very well fail.

No doubt this is just what should be expected. Nothing in Varèse is obvious; this is precisely what has frustrated analytical inquiry into the music for so long. As noted in the introduction, to say that Varèse's approach is methodical is not at all the same as to say that it is systematic; for Varèse, systems belonged to textbooks and schools of thought. They were oppressive to him not only because they are boring but, perhaps even more important, because they are, artistically speaking, dangerous. What would be the point (he seemed to be asking) of writing a work whose organizational principles stood exposed for the world to see? Whatever originality such a work might exhibit would soon be lost sight of, buried under a mass of mediocre imitations. The most obvious, after all, is the soonest copied. This is a danger which, I believe, Varèse feared deeply, and his fear explains much of the reluctance to talk about his music in technical terms and his tendency to avoid the role of teacher.

There is another, more specific problem with structure that is too neatly laid out, especially with larger motions of the sort just discussed. If these become so unambiguous that they *immediately* engage the listener's attention, in a way that obviates any apparent need to consider the details of structure first and synthesize them into progressively larger frames of reference, then form becomes something external and imposed, rather than a real resultant. We know enough by now of Varèse's disdain for "traditional music boxes," as he called the "taught" forms, to be sure that he was not attracted by such solutions to the problem of form. Varèse did not make use of such short cuts, and none is available to us either.

THREE
THE SPATIAL ENVIRONMENT: INTERNAL STRUCTURE

TRICHORDS, DERIVATIVES, AND THEIR PROPERTIES

In chapter 2 analytical procedures were introduced which are based upon registral placement and disposition as factors of importance equal to pitch in the articulation of structure. Useful though these procedures have proved to be, they are not sufficient, mainly because projection, rotation, expansion, and contraction deal almost exclusively with the external dimensions of sound masses. Some other tool is needed for taking measure of internal details. What sort of tool might this be, and how would one go about inventing it?

Since the occupation and partitioning of space are primary concerns for Varèse, we might reasonably suppose that a study of intervallic content would offer the best access to the material. Not only does form equal content, according to Varèse, but—as he himself puts it—form results from the *density* of the content.[1] We might begin, then, by considering the relative importance of individual interval sizes, gauging this importance by frequency of occurrence. However, a wide variety of intervals can be found in any excerpt of even moderate length. Certain sizes may be more numerously represented than others, but even the least common usually appears frequently enough to make the presence or absence of particular intervals nearly meaningless as a structural criterion by itself.

This is not to say that dyads are of no use at all. In fact, the four spatial processes already discussed all depend upon dyadic relationships (upper and lower boundaries of sound masses) for their definition and implementation. To extend the application of these processes to internal structure, however, would pose enormous problems, for here the articulators of dyads could not be limited to highest and lowest pitches. The result of such analysis would be a tangle of "relationships" verging upon incoherence.

Groups of three pitches (trichords) are far more promising, for with trichords it is possible not only to define spatial configurations based on pairs of intervals but also to define relationships between trichords with a few simple operations. We are interested, of course, not in the pitch content but in the spatial qualities of these trichords—in other words, their *absolute intervallic content*. The system of twelve trichordal set classes, in which sets are defined and distinguished from one another by means of pitch-class and interval-class content, will not be useful here. Each trichord XYZ in a spatial environment, where X, Y, and Z are all different pitches,[2] consists of two registrally adjacent intervals XY and YZ, in which Y is the lower pitch of one interval and the higher pitch of the other. (For our purposes, it is not important whether X or Z is the highest pitch of the three.) We define adjacent intervallic content as primary, distinct from the boundary interval XZ (which represents external structure by defining the amount of space that a given configuration occupies). The appropriate label for a given configuration refers to adjacencies only, in the manner shown in example 3.1a. This configuration, rotated and preserved within the same space (G#–G), is shown in example 3.1b. The original configuration and its rotation are defined as equivalent and are referred to by the same series of bracketed numbers, the smaller interval preceding the larger as in the example: [3][8].

If [3][8] is now defined as a *basic form* in some composition, then, like any basic form consisting of two unequal adjacent intervals, it has three related forms, henceforth called *first-order derivatives*.[3] Example 3.2 illustrates the operations that generate these related forms: in 3.2a and b, the operation will be called *unfolding;* in 3.2c, *infolding*. In each operation, two notes remain stationary (one of which serves as a pivot and is circled in exx. 3.2a through 3.2c, while the third note moves about the pivot into a new location, giving up its original position. There are three pitches in the basic form, hence three pivots. A basic form together with its three derivatives will be called a *constellation*.

At first glance, it might seem that there would be six derivatives, rather than three, for each basic form, since each pitch may pivot about each of the other two. However, there can be only three distinct and different derivatives among the six, because for each of the derivative operations illustrated above there is one other which simply reproduces the same intervallic result. Example 3.3 diagrams one of the redundant operations for [3][8]. Note that the [3][11] thus derived is in rotational relationship to the one derived in example 3.2a.

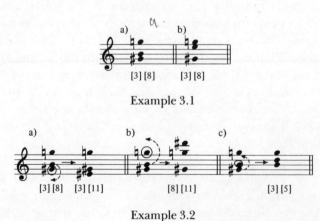

Example 3.1

Example 3.2

[3] [8]   [3] [11]

Example 3.3

Expressed in terms of X, Y, and Z, the intervallic adjacencies resulting from the derivative operations are as shown below. Note that the original boundary interval enters explicitly into the scheme only when it becomes an adjacency:

basic form: [XY], [YZ] (where [XY] is always < [YZ])

unfolding 1: [XY], [XZ]
unfolding 2: [YZ], [XZ]
infolding: [[YZ] − [XY]], [XY] if [[YZ] − [XY]] < [XY]
               or
               [XY], [[YZ] − [XY]] if [[YZ] − [XY]] > [XY]

The expression "[XY]," for example, means "the number of semitones in the interval XY."

A basic form made up of two equal adjacent intervals (such as [4][4]) has a more limited range of possibilities, for infolding reduces it to a dyad, and it has only one distinct unfolded form. A configuration consisting of two or more intervals of equal size in adjacent disposition is more accurately interpreted as the result of single-interval projection. Since repeated extension does not efface its original spatial identity, a single interval may build upon itself to form a chainlike pattern. There is no inherent limit to the extent of such a pattern. Example 3.4 (*Déserts*, m. 166) shows a spectacular chain of [5]s embedded in a larger texture.

A few other properties of spatial trichords can be mentioned at this point. One is that the derivative operations are reversible: having obtained an unfolded derivative of some basic form, one may retrieve the basic form simply by folding back in. The same may be done with an infolded form (by folding back out). However, in the latter case there is a choice of two routes to follow: one unfolding will return the original basic form; the other will return a trichord not in the original constellation.[4]

The reason for this is that the first property (that from each trichord can be derived two unfoldings and one infolding) has a corollary—namely, that each trichord itself is the infolding of two different forms but the unfolding of only one. For instance: [1][6] is the infolding of both [1][7] and [6][7], but the unfolding of [1][5] only, as shown in example 3.5. Intersections between constellations have considerable implications for analysis and will be taken up in subsequent examples.

The relationships outlined here for trichords could conceivably be defined for larger collections of pitches. However, even for tetrachords the number of deriva-

Example 3.4: *Déserts,* m. 166

tives would increase to the point of being unwieldy. To mention but a few of the complications involved: each pitch would have more than one available pivot (three, in the case of a nonsymmetrical form); two pitches could be moved about a single pivot, either in the same direction or in two different directions; and new questions of equivalence would arise—for example, whereas [3][8] and [8][3] are rotationally equivalent, the same is not true of [2][3][6] and [3][2][6], even though their adjacent intervallic content is identical.[5]

Note, however, that the decision to define spatial operations in terms of trichordal groups has nothing to do with the literal size of pitch groups in Varèse's music. After all, trichords are no more common than groups of several other cardinalities. It should already be evident that the operations to which spatially defined trichords can be subjected are capable of producing pitch groups of any

Example 3.5

size. The choice of the trichord as unit is based upon the unique characteristics of groups of three in a spatial context, not upon any empirically observed preference on Varèse's part for sound masses, or even subdivisions of masses, made up of three notes.

Spatially defined trichords may be used to measure intervallic consistency in whole works or sections of works. Generally speaking, the fewer constellations invoked to describe the spatial lattice, the more consistent—and coherent—the analysis will be. Since the total number of possible forms, even up to an arbitrary limit on the external size of any single form, is very large, the description of structure in terms of a small number of constellations should constitute significant information about the music. But spatial trichordal analysis may reveal a shift in emphasis in the course of a work from one group of forms to another or the introduction of new forms in conjunction with types already present. For this reason, the composite repertoire of trichords for an entire composition is usually somewhat larger than the collection of trichords in use at any single point. Individual forms often serve localized, specific purposes, or even control entire sections, then vanish from the texture, recurring only sporadically or not at all. This is perfectly in keeping with Varèse's compositional aims. He spoke of his music as "a journey into space," with the attendant implication that the journey is one-way, beginning in one place and ending in quite another.[6]

It might seem, since the trichordal forms are fixed—in the sense that they seem to be the results of musical transformations rather than descriptions of the transformations themselves—that to employ them in analysis is to be too preoccupied with secondary matters. To prevent this from happening, the analyst must remember that the trichords are not static objects, congealed lumps of sound, but rather manifestations of process. One might think of them as *images* of musical progression. Coherence in the overall picture of a composition drawn by an analysis is directly dependent upon the clarity with which the origins and destinations of these images are determined. In example 3.6 (*Nocturnal*, mm. 53–60), a trichordal form standing alone is succeeded temporally by two instances of one of

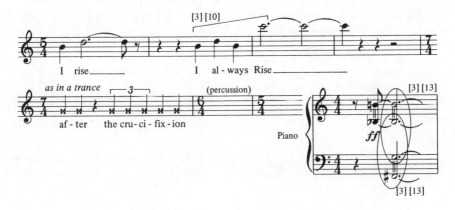

Example 3.6: *Nocturnal*, mm. 53–60 (percussion omitted)

its derivatives. More important than the fact of finding [3][13] twice in the boundaries of the piano clusters is that the first, solitary form has *produced* the others: that the original material has expanded, and that its intervallic characteristics have been spread over a larger space.

The application of trichords and their derivatives to analysis of Varèse's music demonstrates, even in isolated situations, their power to describe process. The bass staff of example 3.33 shows one such detail (*Intégrales,* mm. 82–83, trombones). This progression of two chords stands alone in its registral location and is preceded and followed in that register by silence. Form [3][8] is succeeded immediately by [3][11]; the two are in derivative relationship. Another example introduces the possibility of reading connections between temporally nonadjacent passages. In situations where the composer has clearly intended a reference to earlier material, such connections may have considerable analytical value. The two excerpts from *Intégrales* (mm. 105–106, mm. 144–145) shown in example 3.7 are timbrally, rhythmically, and registrally similar, yet the adjacent intervals are not the same. However, the second trichord, [5][6], can be obtained from the first, [5][11], by infolding. (Note, by the way, that there is no pitch-class set correspondence between the two passages; in those terms the sets would be 3–4 and 3–5 respectively.)

In both example 3.33 and example 3.7, the schematized formation of derivatives outlined in example 3.2 is not duplicated exactly. That is, the simple unfolding or infolding of one trichord does not necessarily produce the other *in its actual spatial orientation.* Once created, the new configuration usually must be projected, or rotated, or both, into place. Thus, the mechanics of obtaining derivatives are not synonymous with musical process; they participate in that process but are almost always combined with other spatial operations to yield the final musical result.

Notice also that we have said nothing up to now about identification of the basic form; we have only identified a derivative relationship between two trichords. Looking at the examples above, we might be tempted to assign this identity to the first trichord of each pair, but often there are reasons to do otherwise. In fact, the exact identity of the basic form (as opposed to its derivatives) is often in flux. In isolated situations, where a complete constellation is not presented, it is not always

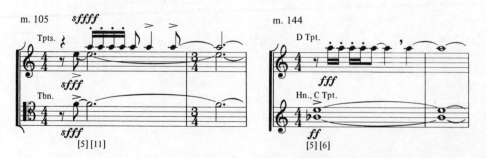

Example 3.7: *Intégrales,* mm. 105–106, mm. 144–145

possible to label the basic form, only to state that a derivative relationship exists between the two forms present. Once the context is enlarged, however, an analytical decision about the identity of the basic form can usually be made.

In example 3.8 (*Octandre*, II, mm. 17–20) the first event is a well-articulated, registrally isolated pair of chords reiterated many times in various different rhythmic patterns before its dissolution (in m. 36). The form [1][7] progresses to [1][8] (ex. 3.8a). Since either could just as easily be the basic form, we would need go no further to describe the relationship between the chords *as separate entities*. However, taking into account the intervals formed by the juxtaposition of the two chords (ex. 3.8b), we find trichords A♭2–(D–E♭)3 and (G–A♭)2–D3, both [1][6]. Therefore, [1][7] would be the better choice as basic form in this particular situation, for [1][6] is the infolding of [1][7] but bears no direct relationship to [1][8].

Additional evidence that [1][7] is a basic form in this passage can be adduced by expanding the field of operations to include the chords as units in juxtaposition with other units which enter and are repeated. The outer boundaries of the first, higher chord, (D–B♭)3, with respect to the lower boundary of the group (E♯–F♯–A)4 in m. 20, produce the configuration [7][8]: (D–B♭)3–E♯4 (ex. 3.8c). Like [1][6], [7][8] is a derivative of [1][7] but not of [1][8].

Identifying the basic form in one place, however, is no guarantee of having found it everywhere. Another example, taken from *Offrandes* (ex. 3.9, "La croix du sud," mm. 6–12), shows that the form designated as basic may change in the course of a passage. The entrance of the voice in m. 8 creates relationships with previous, surrounding material, notably the sustained D3 and A3, and the C6 which forms the lower boundary of the high strings/winds region. These relationships can be expressed as [7][10]: (D–A)3–G4 and [3][7]: (D–F)5–C6. The configuration [3][7] is also found twice in the voice: G4–(D–F)5 and (G–B♭)4–F5. As in the example from *Octandre* above, we have a choice: either [3][7] or [7][10] would

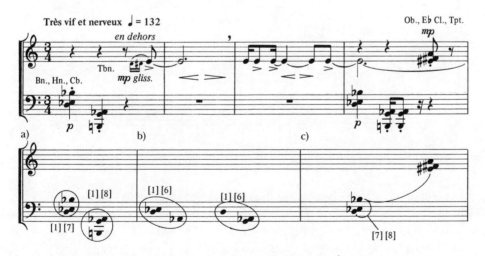

Example 3.8: *Octandre*, II, mm. 17–20 (piccolo and E♭ clarinet omitted)

Example 3.9: *Offrandes,* II ("La croix du sud"), mm. 6–12

serve equally well as the basic form. Here we might choose [3][7] because it occurs first and because it appears three times. As the first phrase of the text concludes (m. 12), [3][7] appears again in the voice—as (F♯–D♯)5–G♯4, a projection of the voice's first [3][7]—but then becomes associated with [3][10], [10][13], and [3][13]. The last of these is especially important, incorporating as it does the last three notes in the voice. Neither [10][13] nor [3][13] can be derived directly from [3][7], but both are unfoldings of [3][10]. Since [3][7] can now be read as an infolding of [3][10], and since [7][10] is absent from this particular location, [3][10] is the best choice for basic form.

  Other factors may work against a shift of basic form identity, even where one might easily be read. In example 3.10 (*Density 21.5*, mm. 31–33, mm. 44–46), the situation in b, if considered by itself, seems straightforward enough: two interlocked instances of [3][13] are followed immediately—in fact, are overlapped—by [3][10]. Temporal precedence and number of occurrences would seem to make the choice of [3][13] as basic form almost automatic. However, the similarity between b and a is striking: both consist of a steep ascent to a relatively high register and are followed by the insistent repetition of a small number of pitches in a wide variety of rhythmic patterns. Undoubtedly this connection is meant to be heard. In 3.10a, [3][10] is the basic form; thus, the best expression of the continuity implied from mm. 31–33 to mm. 44–46 would be to call [3][10] the basic form in both passages, with [3][7] and [3][13] its infolded and unfolded derivatives respectively.

  Sometimes the basic form is not literally present in the texture. In the opening of the second movement of *Octandre* (ex. 3.11: mm. 10–21), part of which is analyzed in ex. 3.8, the first structure formed is [2][11]: (E–G♭)5–F6.[7] In m. 20 the

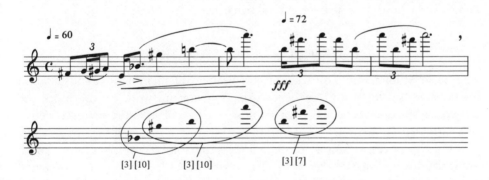

Example 3.10a: *Density 21.5,* mm. 31–33

Example 3.10b: *Density 21.5,* mm. 44–46

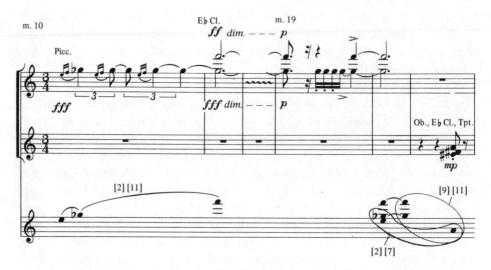

Example 3.11: *Octandre*, II, mm. 10–21 (lower instruments omitted)

group (E♯–F♯–A)4 enters, spatially adjacent to the [2][11] above. Its upper boundary can be juxtaposed against the upper material in two ways: one, with the piccolo part above, yielding [2][7]: A4–(E–G♭)5; the other, with the sustained piccolo-E♭ clarinet dyad, yielding [9][11]: A4–G♭5–F6. None of these configurations can generate the other two directly, but all three are derivatives of [2][9].

INTERACTION OF CONSTELLATIONS

The constellation is only a measure of potential; not all members of a constellation are necessarily used in any one section or even in any one work. Furthermore, the term *basic form* does not usually apply to the contents of an entire texture, even at one particular moment in a composition. Only rarely, and only for relatively short periods of time, does a single constellation assume total control. Far more typical are situations in which a basic form and its derivatives are confined to one spatial region of a texture, sometimes a very small region indeed. Progress must be described by the action and interaction of two, three, or even more constellations simultaneously.

The opening of *Intégrales* (ex. 3.12) is a case in point. The initial trichord, [2][6], presented throughout as a brief figure, is joined by two new entities, both also trichords: (1) a chord in the high woodwinds; (2) a chord in the trombones. Chord 1 is [6][8], an unfolded form of [2][6]. Chord 2 is [4][9], which is not related to [2][6]; however, as [4][9] it embodies a range of spatial characteristics which eventually have a great deal to do with this opening passage. Notice first that its external interval is [13], which is exactly the distance between its highest note, C♯4, and the lowest note of the motive, D5. A linking form may be read, expressing the spatial relation between the two trichords: E3–C♯4–D5, or [9][13], which is an unfolded derivative of [4][9].

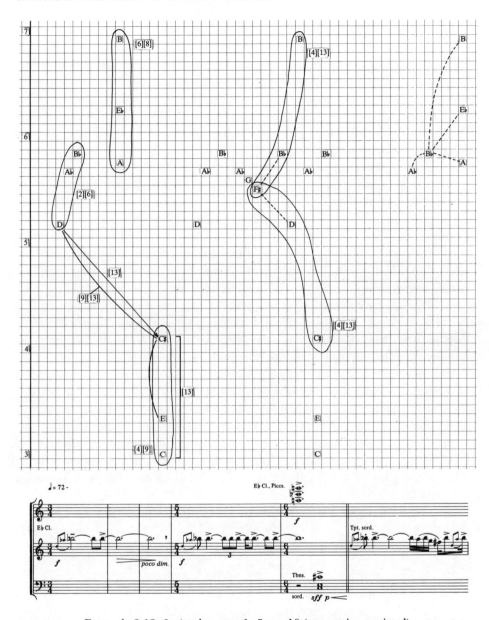

Example 3.12: *Intégrales,* mm. 1–5; m. 10 (percussion omitted)

As the passage continues, with the three entities maintained in static continuity[8] until m. 25, an elaboration of the figure (m. 10) yields new information. The complete form of the figure, of which the original [2][6] now turns out to be the skeleton, is symmetrical in itself, in that the interval of [8] is split into [4][4] by the F#5. Just as this happens, chords 1 and 2 reenter, with the following results: first, the upper [4], together with the upper boundary of chord 1, forms [4][13], another derivative of [4][9]; second, the lower [4], taken with the upper boundary of chord 2, also forms [4][13].

The opening of *Intégrales* has other spatial potential, some of which is eventually exploited. To what degree such exploitation takes place in any piece is a matter of compositional choice. The existence of potential spatial relations does not preordain their activation any more than the statement of the prime form of a twelve-tone row would demand the eventual employment of all its possible transformations. Among those potential forms that surface later in *Intégrales* are [2][13]: (Ab–Bb)5–B6, which is formed by the upper two notes of the figure and the uppermost note of chord 1, and [1][5]: (A–Bb)5–Eb6, inherent in the position of the lower two notes of chord 1 with respect to the highest note of the figure.

New forms arising from the combination of forms already present in the texture are, in fact, often detectable as the implications of earlier material even before they are explicitly stated. A passage from *Déserts* (ex. 3.13, mm. 21–36) provides an apt illustration. In mm. 21–29 the texture is firmly under the control of [6][7] and its derivatives. In m. 30 a sudden upheaval takes place, still completely controlled by [6][7], but the new juxtapositions of material have implications for later developments which are realized in mm. 35–36 (flute and piccolo), where [13]-spans are presented at a distance of [3]. The interlocked [3][13]s D5–(Eb–F#)6–G7 might be regarded simply as a projection of the structure Bb3–B4–D5–Eb6 in m. 30 if the latter were explicitly delineated. In m. 30, however, the configuration [13][3][13] is still only potential, not actual.

The mere fact of its creation does not mandate extensive use of a form in a composition; instead, the trichord may simply be reabsorbed into the texture. Thus there is a difference between spatial manipulations of momentary effect and manipulations whose effects are more far-reaching. Since trichordal forms are only measures of process, without intrinsic value, it follows logically that "recurrence" of a form at some point after its eclipse may not be—in fact, almost certainly is not—"the same" form at all. That the label is identical is likely to be only a

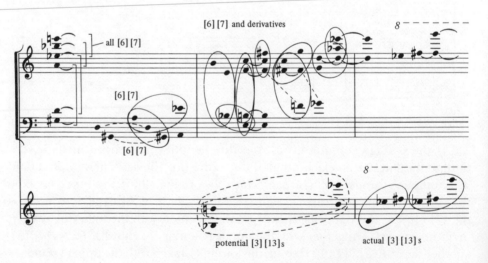

Example 3.13: *Déserts*, mm. 21–36

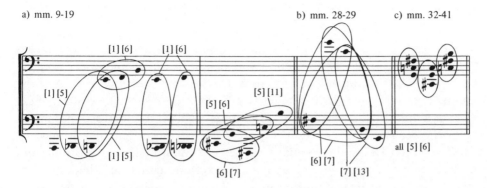

Example 3.14: *Nocturnal*, mm. 1–41, low registers

coincidence. If the work is truly to "flow as a river flows," in Varèse's words, then return or restatement in the conventional sense is an improbable phenomenon.[9] Like Heraclitus, who could not step into the same river twice, we will never hear the same Varèse twice.

The opposite process, separation of intertwined forms, may also occur, although unambiguous instances of it are much rarer than instances of combination. The three excerpts from *Nocturnal* in example 3.14 display all of the pitched material in the lower registers of this work up to m. 41. The first passage, example 3.14a, shows [5][6] and [6][7] in combination, in approximately equal strength. In examples 3.14b and c, we see that mm. 28–29 and mm. 32–41 are the exclusive provinces of [6][7] and [5][6] respectively. Note that in mm. 32–41 a single instance of [5][6] is succeeded by two others—one lower and one higher—together forming a configuration characterized by parallel symmetry.

CRITERIA FOR SEGMENTATION

Enough examples have been presented up to this point for the reader to have gathered that a given texture may be divided in different ways. To avoid leaving the impression that finding spatial relationships is an arbitrary or ad hoc process, I will enumerate the criteria for segmentation and describe some of their applications in analysis.

First and foremost among the associative forces in a spatial context is literal, registrally expressed symmetry. This aspect of structure is always available as grounds for segmentation, but it need not be invoked exclusively, or even invoked at all. Rather, other criteria may either act with registral adjacency or override it momentarily. Principal among these criteria are *timbre, rhythm/duration, linear succession,* and *dynamics,* applied separately or in combination.

Let us return to example 3.8 for a moment. The initial part of the analysis dealt only with literal adjacencies: first, within each chord separately, then between the two chords considered in vertical alignment. In order to read [7][8]: (D–B♭)3–E♯4, however, two elements were disregarded: (1) the internal structure of the chord bounded by (D–B♭)3, and (2) the trombone figure (D–D♯–E)4. Both of these would interfere fatally with the [7][8] segmentation if registral adjacency were the only possible means of associating pitches. But linear succession makes the association of the [1][7]–[1][8] chord pair with the [1][3] above it readily perceivable; by this means, we can "hear around" the trombone part. And the rhythmic presentation of the pitches (D–E♭–B♭)3 ensures that we always hear them as a unit. Juxtaposed against other units of this sort—such as [1][3] in this case—the *boundaries* of the unit acquire an importance that they would not otherwise have. Under these conditions, perception of the chords as distinct and separate entities depends as well upon timbral differentiation and rhythmic elaboration, for both are especially important to hearing passages in which the rate of pitch change is zero or near zero. In such frozen situations, so characteristic of Varèse, the prominence of timbral and rhythmic factors tends to make the listener aware of the individual quality of each entity. One may reasonably expect to hear intervals *between* entities and to hear the interval defining the amount of space that each entity occupies. In example 3.8, therefore [7][8] is a viable segmentation. None of this mitigates the importance of literal adjacencies as forces in generating derivatives or the distinction made between external (XZ) and adjacent (XY and YZ) intervals for that purpose. Once generated, however, any entity may lead a life of its own. These are, after all, "bodies of intelligent sounds moving freely in space."[10]

Dynamics as a segmentational criterion usually function in combination with other factors, but occasionally they acquire primary significance. Consider example 3.15, taken from the first movement of *Octandre* (mm. 8–10). Two interlocked [3][8]s and their derivative [3][11] appear first, followed, in a long ascent from E4 to G6, by two interlocked [8][11]s, unfolded derivatives of [3][8]. The intervening B♭4, at *mp*, can be separated from the surrounding notes, all at *f*, *ff*, or *ffff*. Rhythm also supports this segmentation, for E4, C5, B5, and G6 all carry accents (> or ‿), while B♭4 has none.

Two earlier examples can be studied for segmentations based on rhythmic and durational accents. In example 3.10b, m. 44, the E5 is omitted from the linear succession and [3][13]: A4–B♭5–C♯6 is read. The relevant criterion here is dura-

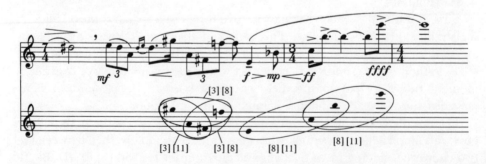

Example 3.15: *Octandre*, I, mm. 8–10, oboe

tion, for E5 is shorter than any of the pitches surrounding it. In example 3.9, mm. 8–9, voice, E5 is bypassed in linear succession to obtain two forms of [3][7]. This is justifiable on the grounds of rhythm: given the textual setting of these pitches, E5, set on the end of "femmes," will receive less stress than the pitches on "Les," the beginning of "femmes," "aux," and "gestes."

A distinction has been drawn between *real* segmentations, of the kind identified in examples 3.14 and 3.15, and *potential* segmentations, which only foreshadow real segmentations, pointed out in examples 3.12 and 3.13. The difference, however, is not always obvious. Why, for instance, in example 3.12, is [1][5] not a real segmentation? The answer is that it would be, if either (a) one segmentational criterion delineated this trichord unambiguously or (b) a constellation to which [1][5] belonged exerted palpable control over structure in this passage. Neither condition is met. Constellations [2][6] and [4][9] comprise a coherent and all-inclusive structure, while [1][5] is merely an isolated by-product.

Continuation of analysis from the point where example 3.12 leaves off (ex. 3.16, *Intégrales*, mm. 25–29) provides a good opportunity to observe the activation of potential segmentations. The first new form, [5][6], is completed by the entrance of E5 in the D trumpet part. This pitch links by virtue of registral adjacency with the two lower notes of chord 1 (see ex. 3.12), A5 and E♭6. Form [5][6] is an unfolding of [1][5], but the immediately subsequent articulation of [5][11]: F4–(E–A)5 shows that [5][6] is the basic form here, with both the real segmentation [5][11] and the potential [1][5] its derivatives. In fact, a real [1][5] does enter the texture and take its place as another registral adjacency, (D♭–D–G)6.

Meanwhile, the trumpet dyad F4–E5 has been surrounded symmetrically by F♯5 (clarinet) and E♭4 (horn). Again by registral adjacency, two instances of [2][11] are formed; these are realizations of the potential [2][13]: (A♭–B♭)5–B6 of mm. 1–25, in the form of infolded derivatives. Next, the pitch F♯5 establishes a connection, by linear succession, to G6, generating [2][13]: (E–F♯)5–G6. Below, through a combination of linear succession and registral adjacency, another [2][13] is formed: A1–B♭2–C3. Finally, a single instance of [5][13], a realization of the potential [5][8]: B♭5–(E♭–B)6 of mm. 1–25, occurs as the highest three notes of the accumulated chord: (D–G)6–G♯7. Example 3.16 also shows that the formerly exclusive components of structure, [4][9] and [2][6], continue to participate in structure here. Still other potential forms arise from the new juxtapositions of material, to be realized in their turn at a later point.[11]

Conjunction of forms may also lead to activation of their own derivatives. Often a fairly routine event, this may have special significance depending upon the spatial operations involved. In example 3.17 (*Octandre*, I, m. 11) a symmetrical configuration of linked [1][10]s embodies two potential [10][11]s, as shown. Shortly thereafter, [10][11] occurs as a real segmentation, and its external span may be read as a projection of the composite span of the two [1][10]s.

That trichordal forms are embodiments of relationships, not things in themselves, permits their use to represent connections between proximate material even where no literal simultaneity or direct linear succession exists. Example 3.18,

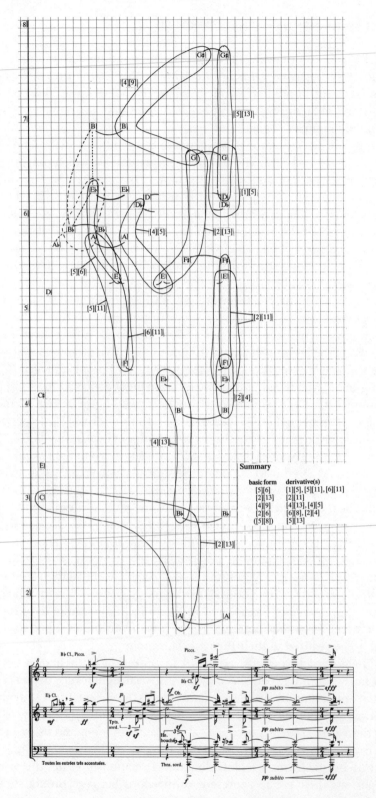

Example 3.16: *Intégrales*, mm. 25–29

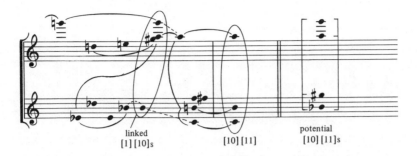

linked
[1] [10]s

[10] [11]

potential
[10] [11]s

Example 3.17: *Octandre*, I, m. 11

taken from the same context as example 3.9 (*Offrandes*, "La croix du sud," mm. 4–8), shows [3][11] and [3][8] expressing an analogy between material near the harp and bassoon parts, which are obviously very similar. (In example 3.9 this sort of connection produces the segmentation [7][10].)

Linear succession is a more complicated phenomenon in a spatial context than it might at first seem. For this reason, a bit more should be said about it. Every linear succession in a spatial context is ultimately reduced to vertical form. The ambiguity, if there is one, arises when the contour of the linear succession is not simple, uninterrupted ascending or descending motion. Example 3.19 illustrates with two successions of pitches.

Undoubtedly, however, such ambiguity is intentional. The result is that several (at least potentially) equally viable segmentations may be extracted. Consider mm. 18–20 of *Hyperprism*, included in example 3.25. Reduced to strictly vertical terms, these six notes fall into a symmetrical pattern: [6][2][3][2][6]. In strictly linear terms, the pattern is asymmetrical, but if it is divided in the middle (that is, the linear middle, between the G and the B♭), two mirror-related forms of [5][8] are produced. Now divide the group asymmetrically, separating the last five notes from the first one (which is valid for dynamic, timbral, and rhythmic reasons). The first three of these five form [3][8]: B4–(G–B♭)5. An analogous, mirror-related [3][8] is also present, but not as a linear succession; instead, it is a registral adjacency, (G–B♭)5–F♯6.

INTERACTION WITH SPATIAL PROCESSES

The system of trichords and derivatives and the processes of projection, rotation, expansion, and contraction defined earlier arise from common assumptions about the nature of musical space as Varèse regarded it: a neutral spectrum calibrated in semitones, in which volume of space and its partitionings, almost entirely unfettered by the obsolete notions of octave and inversional equivalence, are the primary structural determinants. To explain how, more specifically, the trichordal system and the spatial processes are related is not a simple task, for neither do they act independently, nor is one simply a function of the other. The following

Example 3.18: *Offrandes,* II ("La croix du sud"), mm. 4–8

Example 3.19a: *Octandre*, III, mm. 43–44, piccolo

Example 3.19b: *Offrandes*, I ("Chanson de là-haut"), m. 14, clarinet

examples illustrate the various ways in which they reinforce and complement each other in musical situations.

Trichordal forms may join to produce what can be called "rough symmetries": intervallic configurations which are not precisely mirror- or parallel-symmetrical, but in which the trichordal components are arranged symmetrically among themselves. Example 3.20 (*Hyperprism*, mm. 45–46 [and until m. 58]) illustrates. In this graph some details have been extracted for the sake of legibility and placed to the right of the heavy line. In these measures, which begin a pitch-static section extending through m. 58, two forms of [2][11] appear at the outer extremes in mirror-symmetrical orientation. Exactly midway between them are [2][9], the infolded derivative of [2][11], and another form of [2][11]. Just within the outer boundaries of the entire chord are two [4][11]s, also in mirror arrangement. In the middle, overlapping with [2][9], are [3][8] and its derivative [3][11]. As in the *Octandre* passage above (ex. 3.8), the repetition of entities over several measures provides a large number of associative juxtapositions from which structure may be deduced.

Example 3.21 (*Offrandes*, "Chanson de là-haut," mm. 30–31) presents an interesting analytical problem. The content of these measures can be separated into registrally overlapping groups defined on the basis of rhythm (and, as an auxiliary consideration, timbre). The higher two of these groups are exactly the same size, [27], but the lowest is different: [32]. This lowest "group," however, is actually two separate entities, which form a symmetry of their own: [7][9][7][9], reading from bottom to top. The only element that does not participate in this arrangement is the trombone's A♯3, which, taken with the lowest note G1, forms a span of [27].[12] The pitch A♯3 has other functions as well: the segmentation B2–A♯3–D♯4 is [5][11], formed by the conjunction of the two [27]s identified above. Further, (F♯–A♯)3–D♯4, [4][5], corresponds to registral adjacency G♯5–(C–F)6. A rough (and partial) symmetry of trichords is combined with regional and partially concealed symmetries of larger spans.

Both the preceding examples suggest that specific trichordal forms may act to

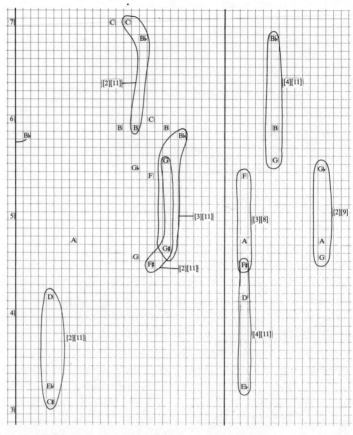

Example 3.20: *Hyperprism*, mm. 45–46 (and until m. 58)

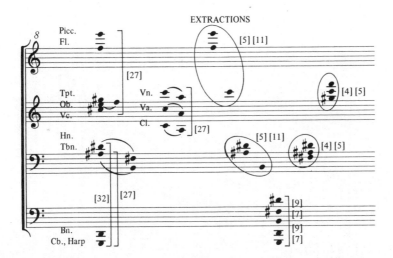

Example 3.21: *Offrandes,* I ("Chanson de là-haut"), mm. 30–31

define processes in action by themselves serving as boundaries. Conversely, an otherwise bewildering array of trichords may be explained by external spatial design. In example 3.22 (*Octandre,* III, mm. 18–23), we follow developments in the upper region only. From an interlocked complex of [3][8] and [3][11], [3][8]: G4–(D♯–F♯)5 is extracted. After an interruption in the form of a partial projection (G4–D♯5 to G♯4–E5), a change of instrumentation occurs simultaneously with the reappearance of [3][8], rotated and projected up [4] with respect to its first occurrence. Next, B4–(D–B♭)5 expands symmetrically to B♭4–(E♭–B)5, or [5][8]. At this point, the registral gap between upper and lower material is narrowed considerably with new material in the bassoon and horn parts. The pitch E4 in the horn, in fact, becomes the midpoint of mm. 20–22 (C♯2–G6). Linked to the B♭4–B5 structure above, E4 moves up [2] to F♯4–C5–D♭6, immediately joined by G6 to form a mirror-symmetrical configuration [6][13][6], read as interlocked [6][13]s. The F♯4 is sustained and becomes detached from the upper parts, which, moving on their own, contract symmetrically to [2][11]: E♭5–(D–E)6, then are rotated and projected up [7] (m. 23) to B♭5–(C–B)6, also [2][11]. The order of spatial operations, then is projection/rotation, expansion, projection, contraction, projection/rotation—a symmetrical arrangement itself, in that its retrograde is identical (remembering that contraction reversed becomes expansion and vice versa). The kaleidoscopic succession of forms thus takes place within a framework which controls many details of pitch movement.

Example 3.22 suggests that as literal, thoroughgoing symmetry in a musical texture becomes more pervasive, the importance of the trichordal forms decreases. By and large this is true. Another example, taken from the end of Varèse's last (and incomplete) work *Nocturnal* (ex. 3.23: mm. 88–93) amplifies the point.[13] In these, among the last measures that Varèse ever completed for performance, the trichordal structure pales in significance compared to the mirror symmetry of

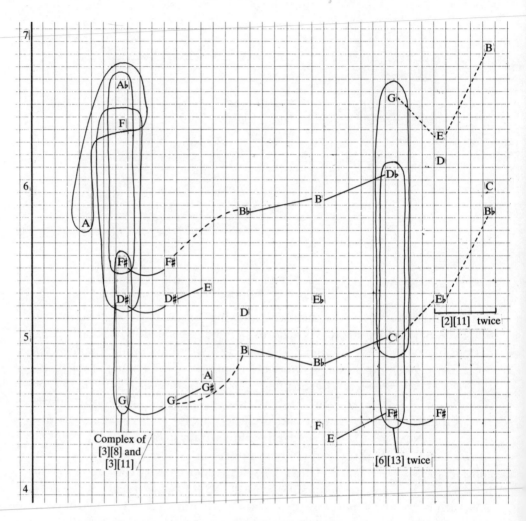

Example 3.22: *Octandre*, III, mm. 18–23 (lower instruments omitted)

Example 3.23: *Nocturnal*, mm. 88–93

the passage, which controls not only the spacing of each chord by itself, but also the movement of the outer boundaries from one chord to the next.[14]

The last example in this section illustrates the control exerted upon the placement of trichordal forms both through larger considerations of delineating space and through elements held in common between the trichordal types. The large chord that begins example 3.24 (*Arcana,* mm. 180–198; begin three measures before rehearsal 18) has a number of significant structural features, but for the present purpose we will consider only a few of them. First, it has a well-defined midsegment, articulated by the horns (with English horn and Heckelphone) in the final, two-beat triplet of m. 181. Above and below this area (G♯3–B♭4) are two outer segments, identical in size but defined in slightly different ways: C♯1–G♯3, from the lowest note in these measures to the lower boundary of the horns' triplet, and C♯5–G♯7, encompassed by the lowest and highest notes in the simultaneous two-beat triplet in the woodwinds.[15]

The second significant feature of the large chord is the internal structure of the midsegment: its trichordal components are [3][8] / [3][11] and [6][8], as shown in the example. These have a great deal to do with what happens next—and so does the space in which they are confined, for the next pitched events occur both through projection of the interval [14] (that is, B♭4–G♯3 to G♭2, m. 187) and through a new juxtaposition of the trichords: A2–(E♭–F)3, or [2][6], is the infolded derivative of [6][8], and (G♭–A)2–F3 is [3][8]. This juxtaposition also gives birth to [2][11]: G♭2–(E♭–F)3, which in conjunction with its "parents" soon assumes equal importance. At m. 191 the rapid woodwind figures enter, with [2][11]: F♯5–(G–F)4 defined by the first E♭ clarinet part alone and both [2][6] and [3][8] by the subsequent combination of the two E♭ clarinet parts. The new lower boundary F4, which remains in force for several measures, is [23] above G♭2. As the material in the clarinets is expanded through newly articulated versions of the three constellations, the upper boundary E6 is eventually reached (piccolo, m. 196), thus constituting a projection of [23]: G♭2–F4 to F4–E6. As this happens, a shift occurs in the relative importance of the three constellations in the texture, with [2][6] taking over from [6][8] as a basic form (and joined by *its* infolded derivative [2][4]) but reduced to a connective role. In this function, however, it is joined by the others, which contribute to the move down to B♭2 via successive new low points: first (F–E♭)4–(B–A)3, interlocked instances of [2][4] and [2][6]; then B♭2, which completes the large-scale [8][11], F4–A3–B♭2, and the more immediate [2][11], (B–A)3–B♭2.

Inevitably, the point is reached where other forms develop out of the complexity of events within this rapidly expanding space: notably, [3][10] and [6][7], with still others in potential to be realized later. [3][8] remains a primary component up to and including the big change in texture at m. 198, but the other two are eclipsed. The culmination of this passage with respect to upward expansion, A7 in m. 198, provides a final link to the motion away from the chord in mm. 180–181, for the distance [17] from E6 to A7 is the same as from C♯1 (lowest note in mm. 180–181)

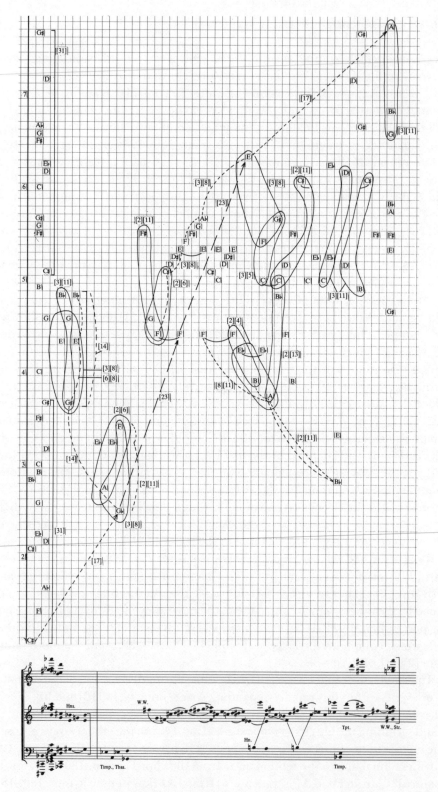

Example 3.24: *Arcana*, mm. 180–198

to Gb2 (lowest note in mm. 187–190). Thus a mirror-symmetrical series of ascending motions can be charted: [17][23][23][17].

EXTENSIONS OF THE TRICHORDAL METHOD

Intersections and Second-Order Derivatives

An intersection between two constellations occurs when two basic forms hold a first-order derivative in common. For example: [3][7] and [4][7] intersect in [3][4], the infolded derivative of both. In example 3.25 (*Hyperprism*, mm. 18–23), as noted, the beginning of the flute solo can be segmented in two ways, yielding two instances each of [3][8] and [5][8], interlocked. As the solo continues, two new forms (among others) come into existence: Bb5–(Db–F♯)6, by registral adjacency, and (F–Ab)5–Db6, by a combination of registral and linear adjacency. Both are [3][5], the infolded derivative of both [3][8] and [5][8].

More distant relationships may be expressed through *second-order derivatives*. For instance, we can say that [2][3] is a second-order derivative of [5][8] because [2][3] is a first-order derivative of [3][5] and [3][5] is a first-order derivative of [5][8]. Such relationships do not at first seem to mean much, for taking the derivative of a derivative obscures the original intervallic content almost entirely. However, the connection can be explained by *families* of constellations linked by a common form. The intersection in example 3.25 implies the existence of a family; this is set forth below.

Basic Forms:	[3][8]	[5][8]	[2][3]
Derivatives:	[3][5]	[3][5]	[3][5]
	[3][11]	[5][13]	[2][5]
	[8][11]	[8][13]	[1][2]

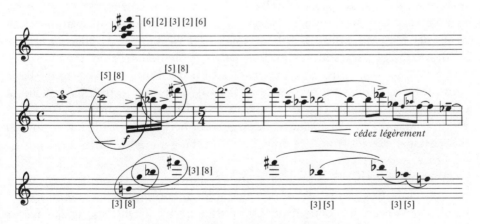

Example 3.25: *Hyperprism*, mm. 18–23, flute

Another, based on the common form [2][11], would yield the following:

Basic Forms:	[2][9]	[2][13]	[11][13]
Derivatives:	[2][11]	[2][11]	[2][11]
	[2][7]	[2][15]	[11][24]
	[9][11]	[13][15]	[13][24]

As in the case of single constellations, the derivative process identifies potential only. In the second family above, for example, the forms [11][24] and [13][24] are not likely to have much analytical importance, for [24] is the rarely used double octave.

Recall example 3.9, in which the basic form identity changes in the course of several measures. Where such metamorphosis takes place even more rapidly, a family of constellations may be better suited to describing what is actually happening. On an even more local level, a derivative of a derivative may be implemented momentarily. Example 3.26 (*Intégrales*, mm. 32–52 and 44–45) shows such a situation. (Only the groups in mm. 32–52 relevant to analysis of mm. 44–45 are labeled.) The initially puzzling intrusion into the otherwise purely pitch-static alternation extending throughout mm. 32–52 can be explained by invoking [9][11]—a derivative, not of [2][11], but of *its* derivative [2][9]. This analysis explains mm. 44–45 as a momentary extension of mm. 32–52's "normative" structure, in that [2][6] and [2][11] each appear for this moment in more than one form.

Micro-structure

Earlier it was suggested that an arbitrary upper limit might be imposed, varying slightly from piece to piece, upon the external size of trichordal forms. This is usually a de facto limit, because registral adjacencies exceeding [13] or [14] are relatively rare. Larger gaps may be incorporated into trichordal structure by momentary implementation of second-order derivatives—as in example 3.33 (*Intégrales*, mm. 80–83). Earlier the trombone chords were analyzed as successive [3][8] and [3][11]; also shown is an alternative segmentation based upon horizontal considerations but preserving the two vertical [3]s. If [3][7] is taken as the basic form, then it implies the existence of [7][10], a derivative that has no literal existence at this point. However, one of *its* unfolded derivatives is [10][17], a registral adjacency which includes the large space between high and low regions in this passage. (Recall from example 3.11 that the generating form need not be explicitly present.)

As a rule, too, there is a lower limit on size of forms. This is also arbitrary, but it is consistent with Varèse's use of space and spatial concepts, in that manipulations involving intervals smaller than a certain size are not all that interesting. No matter whether they are infolded or unfolded, groups of small intervals do not fill a great

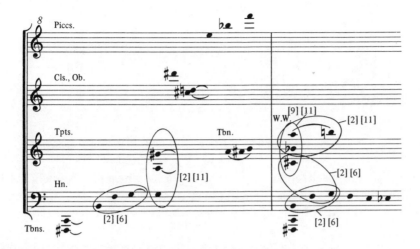

Example 3.26: *Intégrales*, mm. 32–52; mm. 44–45

deal of space, and one cannot move very quickly through space with them. The smallest form used so far in this chapter in an analytical situation is [1][5], as the infolded derivative of [5][6]. Groups of smaller external (XZ) compass than [6] are relegated to the realm of *micro-structure*. Micro-structure usually exists as a static by-product of trichordal form structure, although occasionally it takes a more active role—that is, occasionally the intervallic characteristics of the material are appropriately described in terms of a micro-structure. All possible unequal divisions of spaces smaller than [6] can be found in a single family of forms, a double constellation:

Basic Forms:	[1][3]	[2][3]
Derivatives:	[1][2]	[1][2]
	[1][4]	[2][5]
	[3][4]	[3][5]

Note the intersections with some of the larger (or macro-) forms already used in this chapter. The chains [1][1] and [2][2], as in the case of larger intervals, are regarded as accumulated single-interval projections.

In a nonspatial context, such close groupings of pitches might have a great deal of significance, but in this environment they have little structural weight. They are associated here in a largely undifferentiated fashion not only because it is possible to do so, but also because the exigencies of spatial manipulation demand it.

The most interesting uses of micro-structure involve repeated replication (projection) of a cell-like component. A fairly lengthy example occurs at the opening of *Octandre* (I, mm. 1–6). In example 3.27 the descending oboe line consists of a series of overlapping [1][2]s, some rotated with respect to the original. The last of these, (F–F♯–G♯)4, is projected to a spatial location detached from the

Example 3.27: *Octandre*, I, mm. 1–6

chain of other groups through the interval [4], the last linear succession in the oboe (m. 5), and occurs as C♯4–(B–A♯)3 in the clarinet. This final [1][2] thus depends from the lowest note (C♯4) reached by the oboe. The original pattern, disrupted, ends.

Occasionally, micro-structures express relationships between nonsimultaneous events similar to the analogical functions assumed by real trichords (for instance, forms [3][8] and [3][11] in ex. 3.18). In example 3.34c (*Intégrales*, m. 106, repeated many times thereafter until m. 117), a two-chord sequence proceeds by contraction. The outer interval is not the same above and below, but the two groups connecting the extremes are both [1][3] (see dotted boundaries in 3.34d).

Trichordal Complexes

Situations arise from time to time where a wide variety of forms must be read at once. Usually this is due to an especially neutral manner of presentation, in which no one form or group of forms stands out. In such situations structure is best described not in terms of the behavior of individual form types but rather in terms of their behavior with respect to other types. What develops is a collection of trichordal complexes in each of which two or more basic forms and their derivatives remain spatially associated for some time.

Interaction of forms in these cases is usually rather complicated, and example 3.28 (*Intégrales*, mm. 71–78) is no exception. At the outset things seem fairly simple: interrelated [1][13]s, one [4][9], and one [1][9]. As registral space opens into the lower region, we find [1][13] occurring several more times, twice in association with [2][13]. The entrance of the trombones presents a new, somewhat troublesome problem, for their two registrally overlapping dyads may be segmented in four equally valid ways (see extractions). Further complications ensue: the last trombone dyad forms [5][11], obliquely, with the lower boundary of the trumpets/horn trichord G3–(G♯–A)4, then [6][11] with the C trumpet in m. 77.

There are now seven different constellations present in the lattice, which would have rather dismal implications for analytical coherence were it not that the associations developed in the sparse texture of the opening measures of this passage are maintained, in large part, during the movement to the climactic chord of mm. 77–78. In the upper region, [1][13] and [4][9] continue in complete control; in the lowest region, [1][13] and [2][13] remain associated. In all, [1][13]

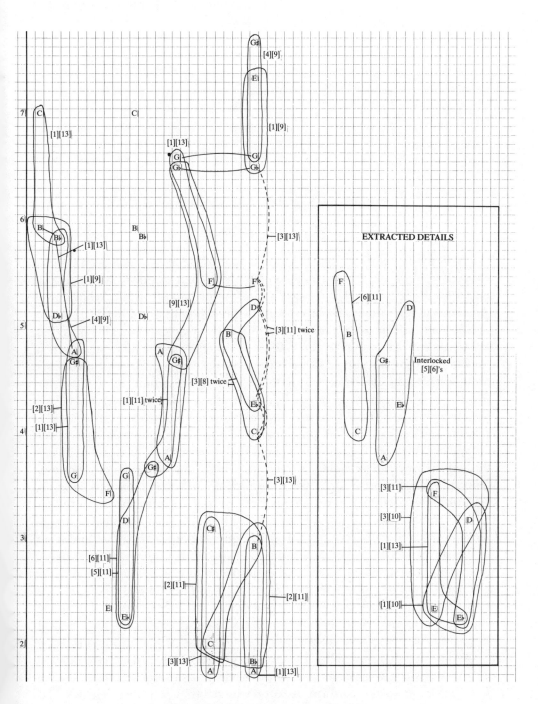

Example 3.28: *Intégrales*, mm. 71–78

has disappeared from the middle region but remains at the outer extremes. Meanwhile, [3][11], [6][11], and [1][10] all progress to the middle region, while [1][10] drops out at the final chord. As for [3][10] (represented in the final measures of this passage by [3][13]), its associations are twofold: with [1][13] and [2][13] below and with [3][11] in the middle. The composite configuration of [3][11] and [3][13], completely mirror-symmetrical, extends across all but the outermost edges of the chord in mm. 77–78. Notice that, just as in the original association (D–F)3, the [3] remains the common interval ((C–E♭)4 and (D–F)5).

SOME PROBLEMS OF THE TRICHORDAL METHOD

Octave Equivalence

The derivative operations for trichords in a spatial context have been defined irrespective of octave and inversional equivalence, but this does not imply that such equivalence is entirely irrelevant to analysis of Varèse's music. What Varèse apparently accomplished, however, was the limitation of its influence to certain specific kinds of situations, and in such situations he adapted it to his purposes. Some applications of octave equivalence to Varèse's music were discussed in chapter 2. The implications of limited octave equivalence for relationships defined through trichordal constellations are the subject of this section.

First, some definitions are needed. In tonal, atonal (pitch-class set), and twelve-tone theory, octave and inversional equivalence are understood, in the main, as different aspects of the same phenomenon. The present discussion, however, distinguishes between the two. Inversional equivalence refers specifically to intervals and their octave (or double-octave, etc.) complements, while octave equivalence refers to intervals and their octave (or double-octave, etc.) compounds. Substituting actual values, one could say that inversional equivalence would exist if [3] were an equivalent expression for [9] (or [9] for [15]), and that octave equivalence would exist if [3] were an equivalent expression for [15], or [27], and so on.

We can dismiss the first of these outright. A spatial environment would collapse upon the introduction of inversional equivalence; under such conditions pitch relationships would be much more efficiently (and accurately) described with pitch-class sets. Octave equivalence, however, is different, *if* it is consistently employed with reference only to interval sizes and not to the positions of individual pitches. That is, octave equivalence does not mean that a pitch in one octave means the same thing as it would in any other octave, but that an interval enlarged or shrunk by an octave (or compound octave) has, *for some purposes only*, a meaning equivalent to its unaltered form. A further limitation upon the scope of octave equivalence in Varèse's music is that octave doubling must be literally present.

Octave doubling occurs in several different ways. There are four discernible categories, in two pairs: the single, isolated instance of doubling, as opposed to the phenomenon of parallel parts; the undivided octave, as opposed to the divided octave. These categories combine in four different ways.

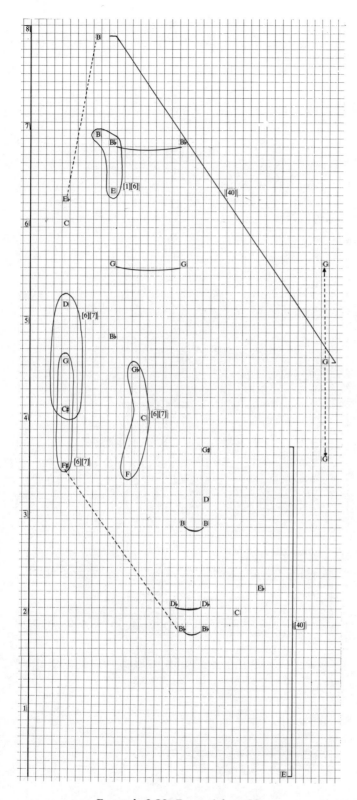

Example 3.29: *Ecuatorial*, m. 23

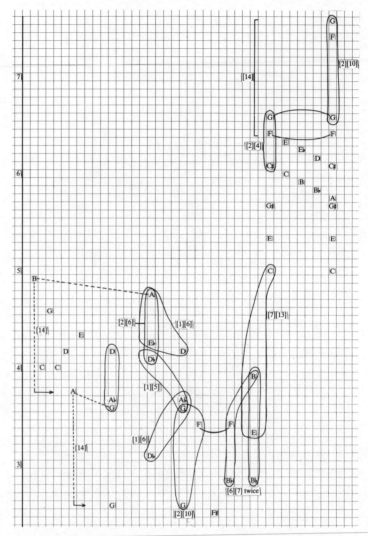

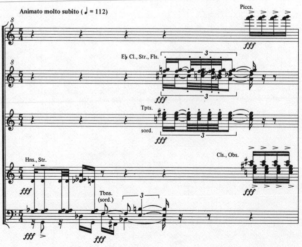

Example 3.30: *Amériques*, m. 8 (with reference also to mm. 1–7, alto flute)

THE SINGLE UNDIVIDED DOUBLING. Usually this is not problematic. Example 3.29 (*Ecuatorial*, m. 23) presents a typical instance. There is no need to assign B6 and B7 to a single trichordal form—in fact, B7 may stand outside the trichordal structure entirely, represented by its "octave equivalent" B6, which belongs to the form [1][6]. Why is B7 there at all, then? It functions as the upper boundary of a large symmetry of spans, each [40] in extent, as shown by the brackets in the example.

UNDIVIDED DOUBLINGS IN PARALLEL PARTS. This situation is potentially problematic but simpler to handle analytically than divided doublings (see below) because the texture is relatively sparse in most cases. A short passage appears in example 3.30 (*Amériques*, m. 8). The pitch G2 is excluded from the general trichordal structure but participates in larger, external spatial delineations, notably the projection of the [14] that defines the opening alto flute melody. Conceivably, however, G2 could belong to a localized form, [2][10]; as shown, this results in a projection of structure from the lowest to the highest reaches of space occupied by m. 8. As for the lower D♭ (in octave 3), it is fully incorporated into the trichordal structure. Octave doubling, then, need not be explained exclusively as such.[16]

A beautiful example of undivided parallel octaves appears at the end of the third instrumental section of *Déserts* (ex. 3.31, mm. 240–246).[17] The pitch series (E♭–D–C♯)6 occurs first, undoubled, in m. 241, then in m. 242 doubled at the octave above. At m. 243 the lower C♯6 is sustained, and C7 and C8 appear (piccolo and piano). Thus the octave doubling mediates between octaves 6 and 8 as space in use is steadily expanded to the highest point (C8). This makes the simultaneity C♯6–C7 analogous to the linear succession C♯7–C8. All of this activity is well knit

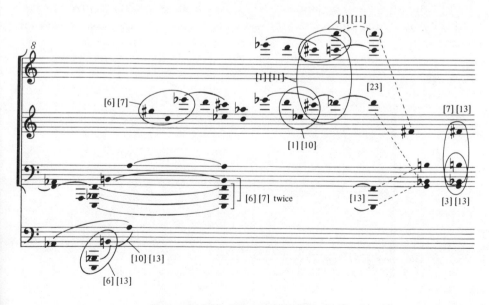

Example 3.31: *Déserts*, mm. 240–246

together by the trichordal forms, especially the constellation [1][10], as shown. Meanwhile, in the lower region, from a complex consisting of [6][7] and [10][13] a single interval E1–F2 is extracted, preparatory to forming the prolonged sonority of mm. 246–263. The [13] from below and the [23] (D♭6–C8) from above are projected to m. 246 to merge in a classic instance of penetration.[18] Trichordal consistency is maintained. Notice that the [1][10] complex, having served its temporary purpose, vanishes from the picture. Octave equivalence also assists in this penetration, as C7 stands for C8 in mm. 244–245.

THE SINGLE DIVIDED DOUBLING. In order for the single divided doubling to function as a real doubling, it must be reinforced by other factors, such as simultaneous attack. In example 3.32 (*Hyperprism*, m. 42) the C♯4 in the horn cannot effectively function as a doubling of C♯6 in the flute even though the two pitches end up sounding simultaneously. The internal structure of the chord is readily explained with trichordal forms, as shown. (See example 3.26 for another instance of non-doubling: B2 and B5.)

By the criterion of rhythmic simultaneity, the doubling shown in the upper region of example 3.33 is real (*Intégrales*, mm. 80–83). Which of the As is more essential to structure? It would seem at first that this question must have an unambiguous answer. If in some sense these two As mean "the same thing," then one of them must simply be there to provide reinforcement: to "double." In trying to eliminate one or the other, though, we quickly discover that both perform vital structural functions. Take away A5, and not only is B6 left out of the trichordal structure, but the association of constellations [1][10] and [1][13], important to the connection with m. 78 (see ex. 3.28), is lost as well. Take away A4, and the [10][17] linking upper and lower regions disappears. Of course, the relative locations of the altered structures could be adjusted to restore those lost relationships, but this would interfere with other relationships later in the work. A reasonable conclusion to draw at this point is that A4 and A5 are integrated into structure much as any

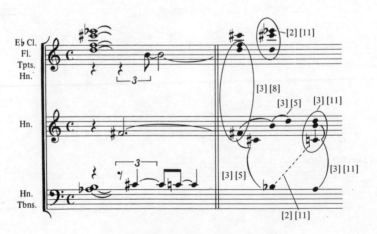

Example 3.32: *Hyperprism*, m. 42

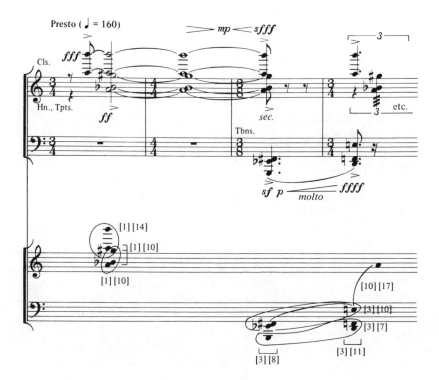

Example 3.33: *Intégrales,* mm. 80–83 (percussion omitted)

two pitches *not* at the interval of [12] might be. In general, single divided doublings do work in this fashion, and might even be better termed "octave duplication" than "doubling."

In example 3.30 above, the flutes and piccolos present two simultaneous doublings—(F–G)6 and (F–G)7—that in the technical sense are divided, in that each divides the other. We should recognize, however, that this is really a "double doubling"—and undivided, because no other pitches occur in the space F6–G7. Example 3.30 shows that the upper F and G contribute both to the local [2][10] connection and to the delineation of a [14]-span.

MULTIPLE DIVIDED DOUBLINGS. These are by far the hardest of the four types to deal with. One might begin with the provisional assumption that the doublings are present at least partly for spatial reasons, not merely for reinforcement; but if a spatial approach does not yield a coherent analysis, then other possibilities must be considered. The orchestral works *Amériques* and *Arcana* are particularly problematic in this respect.

Some situations involving multiple divided doublings are fairly straightforward, such as example 3.34 (*Intégrales,* mm. 101, 105, and 106, and until m. 117). Segmentation of the two rapidly alternating chords in m. 106 (Example 3.34c) strictly according to registral adjacency produces the analysis shown in example 3.34d. The constellation [3][10] springs from the oboe figure in m. 101, [3][13]:

Example 3.34: *Intégrales,* m. 101; m. 105; m. 106 (and until m. 117)

B4–D5–E♭6, and the constellation [5][6] from the trumpets/trombone trichord directly preceding (exx. 3.34a and b respectively). The constellation [1][10] is held in common between the two chords, and the micro-structures [1][3] connect the outer boundaries. Interesting results, however, are produced if the upper doublings are removed: as example 3.34e shows, [3][10] and [5][6] respectively now control the entire structure. Which analysis is correct? Both are, for they reveal simultaneously existing versions of the same material. The two analyses suggest that the doublings are present largely for reasons of continuity, for without them the connective material noted above disappears.

Octaves in parallel parts are sometimes clearly integrated into the trichordal structure, as in example 3.35 (*Ecuatorial,* m. 19). Constellations [2][11] and [6][7] unite in a well-connected lattice. In other situations things are not so simple. The following excerpt from *Offrandes* (ex. 3.36, "La croix du sud," m. 21) is given twice to show (1) the correspondence between horizontal and vertical dimensions, and (2) the other trichordal forms that comprise structure. Of all the constellations present,[19] only [1][7] is not represented in the immediately preceding music—and even [1][7] provides a link to m. 21 through the vocal upbeat (B4–G5, in m. 20).

Example 3.35: *Ecuatorial*, m. 19

a)

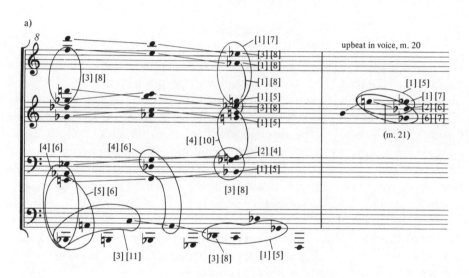

b)

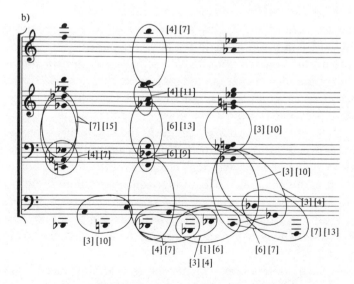

Example 3.36: *Offrandes*, II ("La croix du sud"), m. 21

The note-against-note texture continues through m. 24. Measure 22 is a partial repetition of m. 21; in m. 23 the instrumental parts have the same pitches as in m. 21, but the voice part is different. This produces a few shifts in internal structure, including interlocked [1][3] micro-structures in the voice which duplicate pitches found an octave higher in m. 23 (and, of course, in m. 21 as well). Measure 24 is very like m. 23, except that Varèse brings some parts down an octave and leaves others as they are; the result is what might be termed "octave compression." Most of the new spatial arrangements produced by this compression belong to constellations found in the previous measures of the passage. All in all, the spatial information is conveyed in extremely dense fashion; in fact, the rate of information over time approaches the level of "rapid motion."[20]

Rapid Motion

Compared to other music of the first half of the twentieth century, the works of Varèse are characterized by a rate of pitch change (with respect to time) which is on the whole rather slow. Even to the uninitiated listener, in fact, this is one of the most striking features of Varèse's style. It is the product of prolongation, often through repetition, of single configurations or series of configurations. In its extreme form, Varèse's technique of static continuity produces a peculiar kind of "frozen" music, as in the opening of *Intégrales* (mm. 1–25 and, later, mm. 32–52). But even apart from such cases of stasis, the typical sound event in Varèse lasts much longer than one in, say, Schoenberg. It is also a different kind of event. Affecting the shape of Varèse's structures are other striking phenomena, such as enormous dynamic contrasts, frequent interjection of silence, and a vast palette of timbral differentiation. These act together with long durations to divide a work into temporal successions of readily discernible entities.[21]

The implications of Varèse's techniques for analysis are considerable, for one effect of their application is the extremely clear delineation of processes in action. Initiation and termination of individual operations are often quite unambiguous. But although these are normative conditions for Varèse, not every measure of his music exhibits them. Consider the passage quoted in example 3.37 (*Intégrales*, mm. 53–70). From m. 62 to m. 69 conditions reign which distinguish this passage radically from what has preceded it, even to the point of seeming incongruous— for, if mm. 1–25 or 32–52 of *Intégrales* are frozen music, then these measures are in a liquefied or perhaps even gaseous state. In analytical terms the problem is that the sudden acceleration to a very high event-density makes the implementation of the aims stressed earlier in this chapter—to focus more on process than result—a formidable task. Because so much is happening all at once, the processes become fiendishly difficult to unravel, and the analyst is left grasping at straws: the trichordal forms themselves, which, even if their existence is merely fleeting, are at least identifiable.

The best recourse in such cases is the expedient compromise. Trichordal forms are useful as a means of describing spatial layout even in these moments of

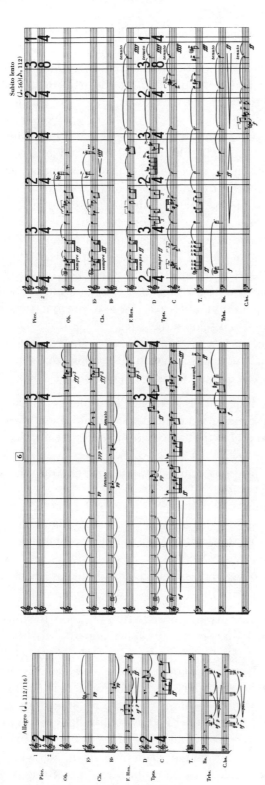

Example 3.37: *Intégrales*, mm. 53–70 (percussion omitted)

(apparently) near-complete formal dissolution, but they must be employed rather in the manner of a repertoire, a composite vocabulary of forms previously used in the piece, and applied simultaneously, in many overlapping forms. Analysis in most such cases becomes something like an assay in the metallurgical sense, and as such does have a certain validity, even though it is to some extent at odds with the methods used elsewhere.

Closer examination of the complicated passage quoted above reveals that its texture is formed in a basically additive way, much as Varèse's accumulated single sonorities are (for example, mm. 25–29 of this same work, discussed in ex. 3.16). The difference here is that the components of the texture, once they enter, remain rhythmically active. In m. 65, for example, four different rhythmic patterns sound simultaneously, in addition to a sustained pitch in yet another part. Not only is each component fragmented by its rhythmic treatment, so that its pitches are heard both singly and in groups, but the whole texture is rhythmically fragmented as well. Analytical difficulties are further intensified by the restricted registral space employed. Sheer vertical distance in a larger, less densely filled space would separate some components to such a degree as to prevent trichordal relationships from forming; here this is seldom the case.[22]

Segmentation of such a texture must take into account every rhythmically defined component in juxtaposition with every other component. If this is to yield plausible results, a few ground rules are in order. The following five are useful:

1. Any registral adjacency is a potentially viable segmentation.
2. Any linear succession is a potentially viable segmentation. This can involve successive attacks in the same part or successive attacks in different parts.
3. Notes attacked simultaneously, or two notes attacked simultaneously followed by a third in linear succession, or vice versa, comprise potentially viable segmentations.
4. Two notes attacked simultaneously, or in linear succession, or serving as the external boundaries of a unit, may form a segmentation with a note already sounding if that third note is registrally adjacent to at least one of the other two pitches.
5. Pitches that form a repeating unit may be interpreted as either sustained or attacked.

Note that these rules are in part tailored to this situation; the third quickly becomes ambiguous if applied to any context in which more than three notes enter simultaneously.

Because the analysis of rapid motion, as defined above, is of a largely quantitative nature, we will ignore "sports," or trichordal forms that appear only once or twice. Some segmentations yield micro-structure, to be dealt with separately.

So much information is generated by comprehensive analysis of this passage that it is impossible to represent all of it legibly in a single graph. We will therefore examine only a few trichordal types at a time, beginning with the four in m. 53, some of which provide direct connections from preceding material.[23] Example

3.38 shows that the constellation [5][6], represented by [5][11] and [6][11], is the most important in this respect and continues to be crucial to structure almost until the end of the rapid motion passage. Next is [5][8], here as [5][13], which exists only in potential form in the preceding section (mm. 32–52: A4–D5–E♭6), but which in m. 53 is a prominent linear succession and appears often in the subsequent passage. Constellation [6][7] is quite important in mm. 32–52, but after its appearance as a registral adjacency (A4–(D♯–A♯)5) in m. 53 occurs only a few more times. Constellation [4][7], represented in potential form in mm. 32–52 as (F–A)3–G♯4, has a prominent role at the outset of the rapid motion passage, but after m. 62 it vanishes completely.

Example 3.39 displays the occurrences of constellations [2][11] and [3][10]. The first of these is prominent in mm. 32–52, but the other exists there only in potential: G3–(G♯–B)4. Shortly after its first real appearance (mm. 62–63: (G♯–B)4–A5) is a major articulation of [3][10]: the juxtaposition of the three sustained pitches G♯4, D♯5, and A5 with the alternating dyads in the woodwinds and horn produces several forms. Both [2][11] and [3][10] continue to appear frequently until the end of the passage, where [2][11]—and almost everything else—suddenly disappears, leaving [3][10] as the sole component of the final chord.

A few other constellations, mostly of minor importance, appear in the passage: [2][6], [3][8], [4][9], and [1][10]. The most significant of these is [2][6], carried over from mm. 32–52 and resurfacing most explicitly in mm. 68–69 as [2][4]: (C♯–D♯–G)4 in the tenor trombone.

On the level of micro-structure there is nothing strikingly regular—as is usual for micro-structure—but a series of [2][3]s can be traced through the densest part of the passage (mm. 64–67), beginning (from below) with (E–F♯–A)3 and extending up to F♯5. The [2][3] cells do not occur all at once, or in any particular order; the rule applying to segmentation for these components is that the pitches comprising each component should occur at least relatively close together temporally, even if the result would not be a viable segmentation under the rules established above for real trichords. Above (D♯–F♯)5 two more pitches form links in a chain of [3]s; this is an outgrowth of the bisection of the [6] (D♯–A)5 by the entrance of F♯5 in m. 63. An analogous formation appears in a lower location: B3–(D–F–G♯)4.

To some extent, the trichordal forms do sort out the intervallic content of these measures. One notices from the graphs, for example, that most of the more frequent forms tend to occur in clusters, corresponding to the moment-to-moment changes occurring in different regions. Aside from this general observation, what else can be said about structure? As one might expect, analysis of the larger design is difficult given the speed with which everything moves. One view of spatial manipulations is presented below.

The entrances of the D trumpet and the bass trombone in m. 62, which occur at the very outset of rapid motion, outline an interval of [16] (ex. 3.40). The two parts then rise to G♯4–A5, a [13]-span, where they are joined by a new group in the woodwinds and horn filling F4–F♯5, also [13]. These together comprise another span of [16] (ex. 3.41). Also present is the C trumpet, really in continuation from

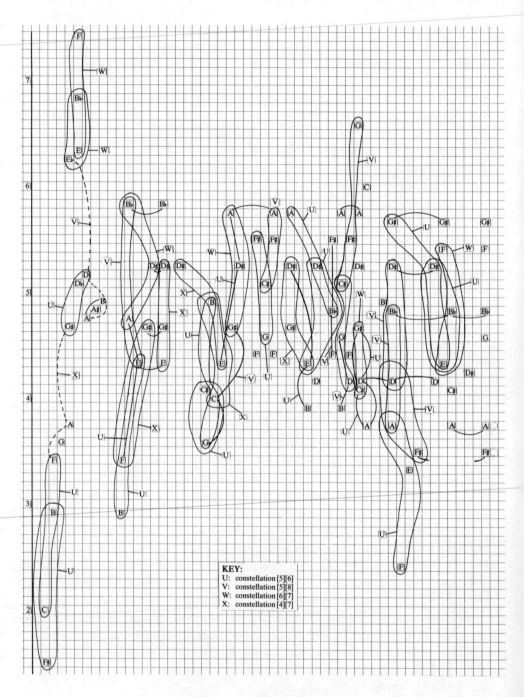

Example 3.38: *Intégrales*, mm. 53–69

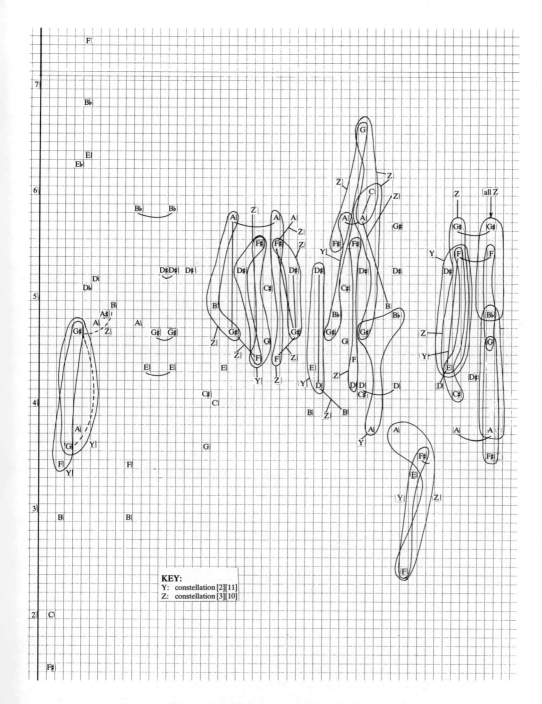

Example 3.39: *Intégrales*, mm. 53–69

Example 3.40: *Intégrales*, m. 62, D trumpet and bass trombone

Example 3.41: *Intégrales*, m. 63 (C trumpet and tenor trombone omitted)

m. 62. In m. 63 its briefly sustained D♯5 forms the trichord [6][7] with G♯4–A5. Recall that the bass trombone part rose from G3 to G♯4, a span of [13], adjacent to and the same size as the interval filled by [6][7]. Thus we now have, as total space in use in mm. 62–63, a span of [26] bisected by G♯4, and two overlapping [16]s (ex. 3.42).

In m. 64, the tenor trombone enters (B3–D4) just as the C trumpet begins reiterating the interval E4–D♯5. These two parts together form yet another [16], which then coexists with F4–A5. Example 3.43 compares the overlap of these two

Example 3.42: *Intégrales*, mm. 62–63

spans of [16]

Example 3.43: *Intégrales*, mm. 62–64

Example 3.44: *Intégrales*, mm. 65–66

simultaneous [16]s with the successive [16]s G3–B4 and F4–A5, revealing an interesting relationship: the first two (of mm. 62–63) overlap by [6], and the second of this pair is [10] higher than the first; the second two (mm. 63–64) overlap by [10], and the second is [6] lower than the first.

Now (m. 66) the woodwind/horn group ends with a sudden ascent to G6, doubling its previously occupied space from [13] to [26]. Thus F4–F#5–G6 is analogous to G3–G#4–A5 of mm. 62–63 (ex. 3.44). The ascent to G6 also implies an interval of [16] above D#5, thus doubling the [16] B3–D#5 as well (also shown in ex. 3.44).

Near the end of the passage (m. 67; see ex. 3.45) the contrabass trombone outlines a [13], F2–F#3. Above, the next part to move is the C trumpet in m. 68, from E4 to F5, also [13]. Immediately adjacent above each of these is a [3], yielding two [16]s. The last chord (m. 69) embodies this relationship: a span of [26], it is divided into two [13]s and contains a [16], F#3–Bb4. The F#3–G4–G#5 structure parallels the other, earlier bisected-[26] structures; this last one is really a chain of three [13]s, for the contrabass trombone rises [13] and then is sustained to become the lowest note of the final chord.[24]

There is more. Example 3.46 shows that the chord in m. 69 is a culmination in other ways. The movement from the outer limits of mm. 62–69 to the final chord is not quite a symmetrical contraction, for G6–G#5 is [11], while F2–F#3 is [13]. But the low [13] *contains* an [11], linear succession F2–E3. Is there a complemen-

Example 3.45: *Intégrales*, mm. 67–68; mm. 69–71

tary [13] associated with G6–G♯5? Yes: F♯5–G6, which is the upper [13] of the bi-sected-[26] structure identified earlier in example 3.44.

A comparison of the summary of relationships in example 3.46 with example 3.39 shows that the constellation [3][10], so obviously important in the final chord in m. 69, is also intimately bound up with the other larger structures that lead to that final chord. Thus a relationship has been established between the trichordal forms and the larger spatial manipulations in the passage.

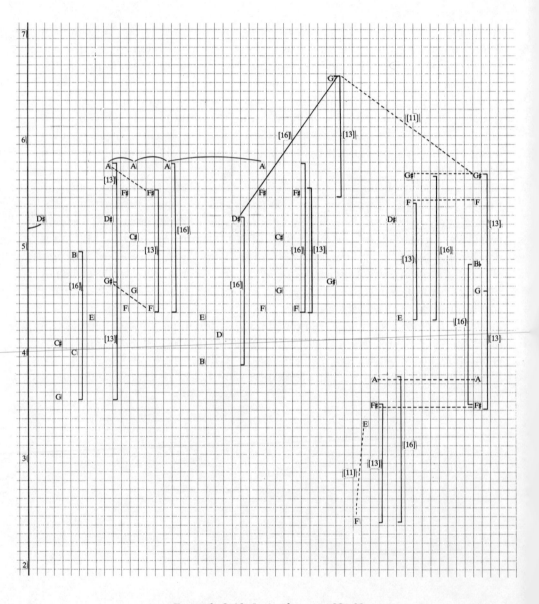

Example 3.46: *Intégrales*, mm. 62–69

LONGER ANALYSES

In this section, the openings of two works by Varèse are presented to show how trichordal forms can be applied effectively to the analysis of longer passages than have served as illustrations up to this point. (For analyses of even larger scale, see chapter 5.)

Octandre, I, mm. 1–12 (Composite Graph: Example 3.55)

The micro-structure of the first six measures of *Octandre* has already been analyzed in example 3.27. Not enumerated there were the real trichordal forms presented simultaneously (see ex. 3.47). The first two, [2][11] and [1][10] overlapped, become quite important in the structure of the first movement. As the oboe line descends, the overlapped configuration is projected down [4], with [1][9], a derivative of [1][10], connecting the original to its projection. With the F♯4, a new trichord enters the picture: [1][5], as a linear succession. Its local cause is the bisection of (C♯–B)4. Also formed at this point is [5][6]: (C♯–F♯)4–C5. As the oboe line reaches F4, two potential segmentations arise. These are [1][6]: (F–B)4–C5, and [6][7]: F4–(C–G♭)5, connected by the derivative relationship.

The completion of the connected micro-structure [1][2][1][2] . . . at A4 immediately precedes the entrance of the clarinet [8] below, and its line reaches A♯3 at a point [11] below A4. This [11] is neither the external interval of [1][10] nor an adjacency in [2][11], but rather the external interval of [3][8], formed by division at the clarinet's first note C♯4 (see ex. 3.48). The [3][8] is the realization of another

Example 3.47: *Octandre*, I, mm. 1–4

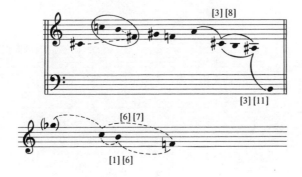

Example 3.48: *Octandre*, I, mm. 4–6

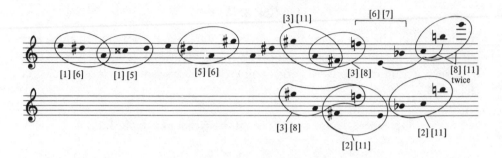

Example 3.49: *Octandre,* I, mm. 6–9

potential form: note that each of the overlapped [2][11] / [1][10] pairs in the oboe contains a [3][8] in its highest, lowest, and last notes. Below the A♯3 enters B2 in the contrabass, a projection of the [11]-span which also forms a [3][11] with the clarinet A♯3–C♯4.[25]

Above A4 the oboe proceeds to articulate real forms of [1][5] and [1][6] (mm. 6–7; see ex. 3.49). This, together with the previous association of a real [1][5] and a potential [1][6], is a clear instance of intersection of constellations, for [1][6] is both the unfolding of [1][5] and, later and more clearly, the infolding of [6][7]. Another unfolding of [1][5], [5][6], succeeds the two smaller forms.

The next pitch evolution occurs in m. 8, where the pace of events undergoes a sudden acceleration. First come the intertwined [3][8]s and [3][11] analyzed above in example 3.15; then, overlapping with these and the succeeding [8][11]s, two linear successions of [2][11] (see ex. 3.49). The high G6, besides completing the last [8][11], also completes a larger symmetry about A4, shown in the pitch/registral graph of mm. 1–12 in example 3.55. The adjacent [11]-spans below A4 are now balanced by adjacent [11]s above A4: G♯5–G6.[26]

The next measures, in which all but two of the remaining instruments enter, are even more complicated. The rapidly rising flute figure (m. 10, ex. 3.50a) preserves some pitches from the last of the oboe solo in mm. 8–9, projects two

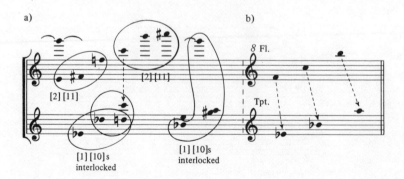

Example 3.50: *Octandre,* I, m. 10

others up [12], and adds a new one, C♯7, to form two instances of [2][11]. The lower of these duplicates an instance in the oboe, and the other is rotated with respect to it. As the flute line rises, trumpet and clarinet enter, trumpet with E♭4–D♭5, clarinet with D5. These together comprise [1][10]—and the upper two of these pitches, together with C6 in the flute (which occurs nearly simultaneously with the clarinet entrance), form another [1][10] in mirror relation to the first. There are now two mirror-related pairs in m. 10, and a third is quickly formed, again from adjacent [1][10]s (see ex. 3.17 above): B♭4–(G♯–A)5–G6. This can easily be read as a projection from the first adjacent pair. Also interesting at this point is the linear succession in the trumpet, [7][11]: (E♭–B♭)4–A5, which stands as a projection of F5–(C–B)6 from the flute (see ex. 3.50b). The gap between [2][11]s in the flute part is thus finally incorporated into the overall scheme.

One other instance of [2][11] is present in m. 10: E♭4–(D–E)5 (ex. 3.51). Its juxtaposition with the lower of the other [2][11]s in that measure embodies two potential [3][8]s and one [3][11]. The progression of potential to real has now come full circle: first (mm. 1–4) [3][8] existed in potential form, partly produced by [2][11]; next, after [3][8] emerged as real (m. 6), it overlapped with [2][11] in more or less equal strength (mm. 8–9); now it returns to potential status.

With the entrance of horn and bassoon in m. 11, (C–B)4 appears, completing a symmetry with (C–B)5 (oboe, m. 9) and (C–B)6 (flute, m. 10). The [11]-span has now been projected both up and down [12].[27] The chord formed in m. 11 and prolonged through m. 12 (ex. 3.52) includes these pitches and several others in a

Example 3.51: *Octandre*, I, m. 10

Example 3.52: *Octandre*, I, mm. 11–12

Example 3.53: *Octandre*, I, m. 10

instances of [10] [11] bracketed

Example 3.54: *Octandre*, I, mm. 10–12

configuration worth studying in detail. At the bottom, [7][11] is found again, but now in somewhat oblique form: (C–B)4–F♯5. This is probably a sign that it is being reabsorbed, and in fact, the intervening F5 means that this segmentation should be regarded as potential. The precedent for the actual adjacency [6][11], other than its status as a derivative of [5][6], lies in the juxtaposition of the entire clarinet part in m. 10 with the sustained oboe pitch G6 (to which it is registrally adjacent; see ex. 3.53). The three highest notes in the chord form [3][8], showing the reemergence of this form into actuality. The transference from its previous, lower appearance balances the opposite motion of [6][11] from high to low.

The overall structure of the chord bounded by C4 and C♯6 is symmetrical, with [11]s at either end. The remaining two pitches, (F–F♯)5, may be separated from the others on the basis of rhythmic segmentation. The structure (C–B)4–A5–G♯6 can also be interpreted as overlapped [10][11]s in mirror relation. This is a significant development, as example 3.54 shows: just as the union of [1][10]s in mirror relation, twice, produced potential forms of [10][11], derivative of [1][10], so now two [10][11]s are united (still only as potential forms) in mirror relation: [11][10][11].[28]

Ecuatorial, mm. 1–18 (Composite Graph: Example 3.62)

MEASURES 1–5. The opening of this work is similar to the opening of *Octandre* in its initial motions across small intervallic spaces. As in *Octandre,* the micro-structures are articulated simultaneously with larger spatial forms. The initial gesture of two descending [1]s, however, also includes an octave "doubling," C♯6. This and the fact that C♯ 5/6 is much shorter in duration that either B♮4 or B4 suggests that the first pitch might be separated from the second and third for certain purposes (ex. 3.56a). On the other hand, B4 in trumpet and piano is

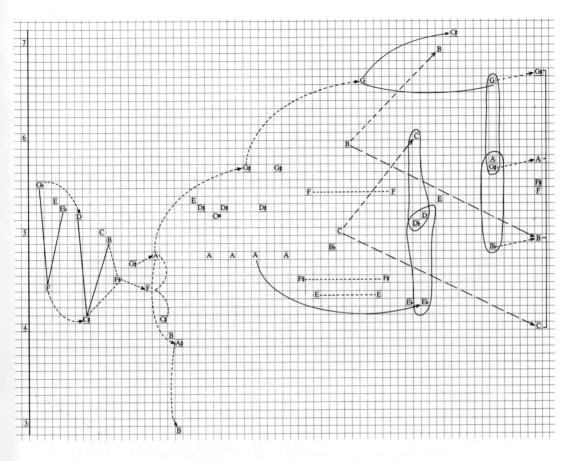

Example 3.55: *Octandre,* I, mm. 1–12

distinguished from the other two, which appear in the piano only, by timbral means (ex. 3.56b). This dichotomy plays a crucial role in the articulation of space in these first measures of the passage.

The group C♯5–(B♯–B)4 is extended in chainlike fashion down to (A♯–A)4 in mm. 3–4. The intervening E5 produces the first real trichords in the work: [1][5] and [1][6] (ex. 3.57). Three more forms are then quickly articulated, as shown. One might expect [6][9]: E♯4–(D–G♯)5 to be a viable segmentation as well, but this

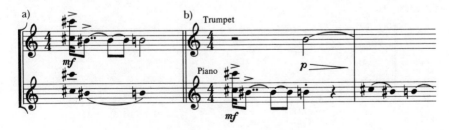

Example 3.56: *Ecuatorial,* m. 1

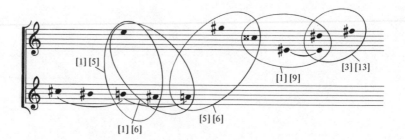

Example 3.57: *Ecuatorial*, mm. 1–5

is an isolated form which has no force in the rest of the passage. The other trichords form a connected structure.

Looking at the segmentation as a whole, we might note that it has a certain unsatisfactory quality. Three constellations are bunched together with no clear relationship expressed between them other than that they coexist during these five measures. But perhaps this amorphous character is intended, and the material presented as a partially inchoate mass to be shaped and directed in subsequent developments.

At any rate, there are other features of structure that should be pointed out. First, on the level of micro-structure, the [1]-chain from C♯5 to A4 is doubled in extent to reach E♮4 (refer to ex. 3.62). This movement is analogous to the doubling of C♯5–(B♮–B)4 to reach A4. Second, above, the filling of space by [1]s is extended by the registral association of pitches (C×–D♯–E)5. Third, the dual segmentation of C♯5–(B♮–B)4 takes effect in terms of *entire* space filled in mm. 1–5 (excluding C♯6, about which more will be said later), [15]: E♮4–G♯5, and the *final* span [13]: E♮4–F♯5 (mm. 5–6). The [15] is a symmetrical expansion from pitches C♯5 and B♮4 (dotted arrows in ex. 3.62), the [13] an expansion from B♮4 and B4 (solid arrows).

MEASURES 6–11. The group (D♯–E–C×)3, a projection of micro-structure, also projects both the final and the total spans of mm. 1–5 below the previous lowest point, E♮4. The connecting trichordal forms are [1][13] and [2][13], presented here in equal strength; both will be used later (ex. 3.58). Through [2][13] it is possible to read a connecting form engaging the final boundaries of mm. 1–5: [13][15], an unfolded derivative of [2][13].

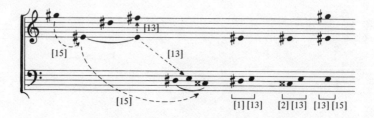

Example 3.58: *Ecuatorial*, mm. 4–6

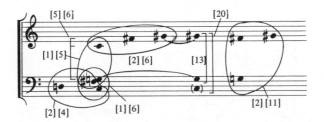

Example 3.59: *Ecuatorial,* m. 8

The last pitch of three in the projected micro-structure connects through the trombone parts to (C–F♯)3, forming [2][4] (ex. 3.59). Simultaneously [2][6]: C4–(F♯–G♯)4 is presented in the trumpet. Note that [2][4] exists in potential in mm. 1–5, by a combination of registral and temporal association: (D–E–G♯)5. Also in the complex of m. 8 are several instances of [1][5] / [5][6], an instance of [1][6], and one of [2][11], all representatives of constellations presented earlier. In the [13]: F×3–G♯4 sustained beyond the other pitches we recognize an analogy to E♯4–F♯5, the sustained pitches of mm. 5–6. This [13] is *contained* in a larger span, the entire range of m. 8: C3–G♯4, [20]. An analogous situation exists in mm. 1–5 if C♯6 is taken into account, for E♯4–C♯6 is also [20] (see ex. 3.62).

MEASURES 12–18. The basic motion of these measures is a vast expansion of occupied space both below and above. The trichordal content so far exposed in the piece is partially separated at this point, with a structure formed entirely from constellations [5][6] and [6][7] below and a thinner texture of [1][12] and [6][7] above. These registral regions are articulated successively, and can be treated separately for the moment.

Below (mm. 12–13; see ex. 3.60), an interlocked [1][5] / [1][6] complex continues to express the close derivative relationship between the two, but the advent of two forms of [5][11] implies a competing constellation, [5][6]. This dichotomy is

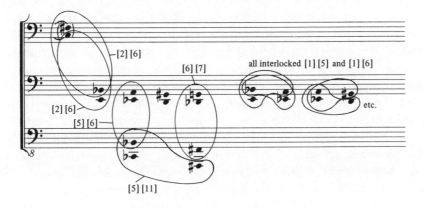

Example 3.60: *Ecuatorial,* mm. 8–12

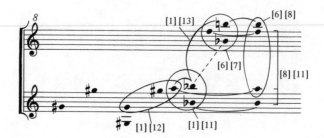

Example 3.61: *Ecuatorial*, mm. 14–18

not resolved, but later in the work, beyond the portion of it analyzed here, it becomes more convenient to interpret [1][5] and [1][6] as the infolded derivatives of [5][6] and [6][7] respectively.

Above (mm. 14–18; see ex. 3.61), the G♯4 spins off octave equivalents in octaves 3 and 5 before interlocked members of constellation [1][12] reach up to B6. The [6][7] formed at the top stands in analogy to F♯1–(C♯–G)2 below; notice that in both of these the lowest pitch is accompanied (and, above, replaced) by a pitch one octave lower. The resulting spans of [25] have important meaning for the overall spatial design, as diagrammed in example 3.62. The sustained configuration B♭4–A5–(F–B)6 consists of an interlocked [6][8] and an [8][11], which is new and will affect later developments in the work.

All of this motion takes place within a framework that exhibits various kinds of symmetry. The relationships are expressed in the graph that appears as example 3.62.

The foregoing analyses indicate that *Ecuatorial* and *Octandre* are different sorts of pieces—and, in fact, the character of each work as revealed in its opening measures remains consistent throughout. One might feel tempted to conclude that *Octandre* is better organized, but this is not so; it is simply more economical in its means. Part of the somewhat lavish effect of *Ecuatorial* is Varèse's extensive employment of octave doublings, virtually absent from *Octandre*. As mentioned in chapter 2, such doublings contribute to the fluidity of spatial structure, but the effect on trichordal structure is to introduce an enormous variety of constellations in rapid succession. In the opening passage the separation of some forms from others does seem to act as an articulation of the rather undifferentiated complex in the first measure; but another constellation enters the picture in m. 15, and yet others follow soon after. Furthermore, the interlocked [1][5]s and [1][6]s in m. 12, incorporating and magnifying as they do the features of those forms interlocked in mm. 3–4, seem somewhat undifferentiated themselves. It is almost as if Varèse, working with a larger canvas here than in *Octandre*, found it necessary to blur some of the smaller details in order not to distract from the bigger picture (the larger spatial manipulations). Thus the point of the "parallel tritones" in m. 12 is that they create a *region* of [1][5] and [1][6], not that they articulate individually presented instances of these forms.

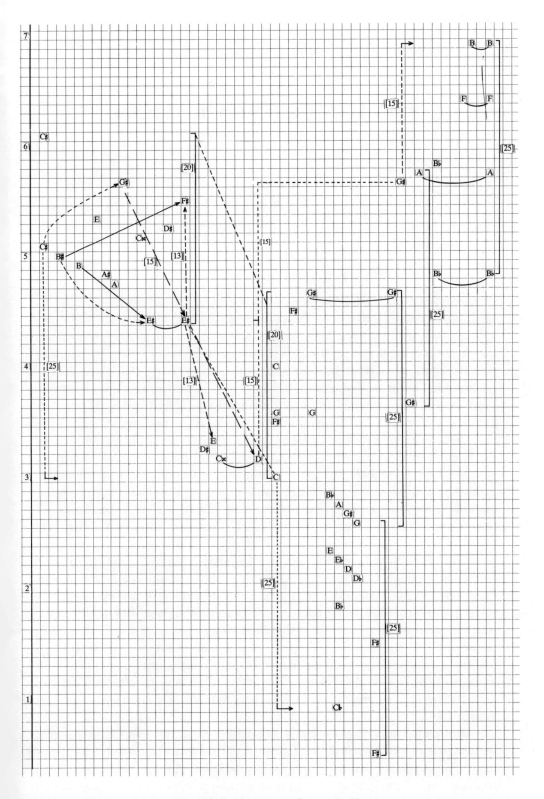

Example 3.62: *Ecuatorial*, mm. 1–18

FOUR
RHYTHM AND DURATION

Up to this point the reader has been compelled to accept on faith the validity of a sweeping hypothesis: that of all the domains of musical sound, pitch and register—or, as they are called here, pitch/register—are primary in the music of Varèse. Answering the questions that such a hypothesis raises, however, cannot be put off forever. What basis exists for it, other than the assertion that it is true? Why pitch/register and not rhythm, duration, timbre, or loudness (dynamics)? Or why should *any* domain or combination of domains be considered primary? Questions like these have been asked before, and the range of responses—including none at all—has been extremely varied. Perhaps this accounts more than anything else for the diversity of analytical strategies that have been applied to Varèse's music.

The lack of consensus implies something else as well: that such pre-analytical matters have not always received adequate attention. Too much has been taken on faith, too many assumptions left unexamined. There is always the chance, of course, small though it may be, of obtaining interesting, even useful analytical results simply by asserting a hierarchy of domains without dealing with the objections that might be raised to such a hierarchy. After all, who can hope to defend an opinion to everyone's satisfaction? But this approach also has its drawbacks, the main one being that the results obtained are, by definition, entirely subjective and thus can be peremptorily dismissed by anyone who doesn't agree with the initial assumptions. Perhaps it is time to try to curb the seemingly endless round of "Well, I hear it this way" and "Well, I hear it that way," which resolves nothing. Not, of course, that it is possible to do away with subjectivity entirely; but its scope can be limited. By arriving at a hypothesis by a more careful route one can focus the essential arguments and begin at least to replace the current confusion of approaches.

Some scholars and critics have said, explicitly or implicitly, that Varèse assigned the domains of rhythm, duration, timbre, and loudness a status equal to that of pitch. The possibility that this is true cannot be ignored, for if the claim could be substantiated, then the inevitable conclusion would follow that any analysis of a Varèse work which proceeded from the assignment of primary importance to a single domain would be invalid. But there is no way to prove the truth of this claim except to demonstrate it in analysis. How would such an analysis be conducted? To consider pitch, register, rhythm, duration, and so forth all on an equal footing, there would have to be some sort of continuum that included all these domains: a scale of values held in common.

As an example, consider the hypothetical assertion that dynamic levels in some given instance are as important as the pitches subjected to these fluctuations in loudness. "As important," though, in what terms? To make sense of this statement one would have to find a way of expressing the information conveyed by the pitches and that conveyed by the dynamics as components of a single analytical image. Even to express pitch in terms of dynamics and vice versa would not be sufficient, for that would produce two images, not one. But where is the common scale of values? Unfortunately, the only available candidate seems to be the finished, composed musical context itself, which deposits us back at our starting point. In other words, to demand equality of domains under analysis is to declare analysis irrelevant or futile.

Thus we are forced to consider alternatives. One, in fact, is suggested immediately above: that each domain in turn be used to express the others, or—again—the information conveyed by them. This procedure would result in several parallel analyses, all presented in different sets of terms. Presumably, the next step would be to reconcile them somehow. Since we already know that no *real* unification is possible (owing to the lack of a common scale of values), this reconciliation would involve assessing the relative power of the various analyses. Two outcomes of this assessment are possible: either that different analyses would work better at different points, with none dominating the others; or that one analysis would emerge as more powerful than the others. If the first, then in order to avoid a fragmentary and disjointed presentation the analyst would probably have to present all of his analyses in full, either successively, or in parallel, or via some combination of the two approaches. In the event of the second outcome, on the other hand, the most powerful of the domains could simply be designated primary and could carry the main thrust of the analysis, with supplementary information interjected from the analyses according to the other, secondary domains. From the approach adopted in the previous two chapters, it is obvious that this has proved itself the relevant outcome for Varèse's music. What remain to be explained are the reasons why pitch and register together have been accorded primary status.

Determining the relative importance of the various domains in Varèse is not easy. We may make some headway, however, by asking the right questions. To ask "Aren't they all equally important?" or even "Which is the most important?" is to phrase the question in an unhelpful way; it leads to arguments that can have no convincing resolution. Instead, let us ask: "Which comes first?" Which domain, or combination of domains, forms the initial idea that is then sharpened, clarified, made more definite by the others? Making the initial idea more definite, it must be added, is not tantamount to explaining the compositional process as part of the work itself. Quite the opposite: one would imagine the composer's intention to be that when the finished piece is heard the process of composition should *not* be obvious. Picasso's statement, "I want to get to the stage where nobody can tell how a picture of mine is done," can readily be translated into musical-compositional terms.[1] A piece, after all, should not be expected to display its own analysis, as if it were transparent and its skeleton visible. Part of a work's appeal, it might even be argued, is a certain mysterious quality. But the possibility that our appreciation of this quality constitutes part of our aesthetic experience does not rule out our attempting, as another part of the experience, to penetrate whatever mysteries the work of art presents.

This brings us back to the question we were asking. To decide which domain comes first and serves as the framework to which all the others are applied certainly does not exclude those others from consideration. Evaluated by itself, the initial framework is likely to have a neutral cast, one which admits of many possibilities of interpretation and development but cannot be directed toward any one of them without the additional qualities imposed by the other domains.

Next, criteria for selection of a primary domain are needed. These are potentially of two kinds: general, arising from the exigencies of the compositional medium, and specific, having to do with Varèse's individual techniques. The most important criterion of the first type is what might be called relative exactitude of sound shape. On the basis of exactitude, two domains can be relegated immediately to secondary status where compositions for conventional (non-electronic) forces are concerned. Timbre, for one, is not nearly so susceptible to regulated gradation or precise definition as is pitch. Any competent composer is aware of this. Karlheinz Stockhausen wrote that he turned to electronic music as a means of obtaining timbral control that was not available through conventional instruments. He found, for example, that a unified timbral continuum could not be set up between the clarinet and the piano.[2] Varèse undoubtedly dreamt of a time in the future when electronics would make possible great improvements in control. Yet he never claimed any function for timbre in his works except as "an agent of delineation." He did remark on its potential as a contributor to other structures comprising the overtones of written pitches, but invariably such remarks were couched in the conditional tense. Any more powerful role for timbre would require the invention of new kinds of instruments.[3]

Granting, for the sake of argument, that Varèse may have attempted some rudimentary control over structures resulting from combinations of partials, we would want to know next what factors were involved in producing the desired result. One important variable for such a purpose, certainly, would be loudness. The lack of precise indications for dynamic levels effectively prevents a composer from exerting the same control over overtone complexes as over written (or "fundamental") pitches. This is so simply because loudness plays a crucial role in determining which partials are heard in what degree of strength relative to others. And while a vast range of dynamics is available with conventional instruments, no exact calibration of this range is possible. Electronic music has long since removed this obstacle, for there precise decibel levels are easy enough to specify. But *f, mp,* and the like are only crude approximations compared to the precise frequency relationships in the domain of pitch.

Rhythm and duration, however, cannot be dealt with in such summary fashion, for they share exactitude of notation with pitch and register. Now, therefore, we must pass to the second criterion: the specific nature of Varèse's own procedures. To a certain extent, the distinction implied by the terms *rhythm* and *duration* is misleading, for Varèse included durational considerations under the rubric of rhythm in such statements as "In my own works . . . rhythm derives from the simultaneous interplay of unrelated elements that intervene at calculated, but not regular, time-lapses."[4] Here a mode of organization is alluded to, or at least hinted at, that might well rival pitch in degree of complexity and precision. Furthermore, on a level of shorter time-spans, such as a beat or a measure, a wide variety of rhythmic detail is generally evident in Varèse's music. Varèse's rhythmic patterns are complicated in a way that is quite different from his contemporaries'. It is a quality especially audible in the writing for percussion, and does in fact seem to have a great deal to do with the importance of percussion in most of his works, but it is certainly not confined to this instrumental group. Varèse introduced, for all practical purposes singlehandedly, a far wider range of rhythmic stratification than had been dreamt of by Western composers up to that time: from passages of rhythmic unison (complete coordination) to situations in which every part can be distinguished from every other purely on the basis of rhythm (complete independence). Is it possible, then, that among his reasons for doing so was the intention of placing rhythm/duration in the role of primary, controlling domain—either by itself or in parallel with pitch/register? Perhaps this induces a version of the first outcome mentioned above, in which each of the two domains would require treatment in turn as primary.

To assert this now, however, would be leaping to conclusions. Let us return to the statement of Varèse quoted earlier concerning "simultaneous interplay of unrelated elements." Consider, together with this explanation of the origins of rhythm in his music, the statement that "rhythm . . . is the generator of form." First, we saw in chapter 2 that the phrase "unrelated elements" must be understood in a special way. It does not imply that the elements have nothing to do with one another, but rather that their independence might be compared to the independence of contrapuntal lines in other music. Rhythm is one means by which elements may be associated in the same musical context, but it is not the only one.

Second, the statement that rhythm is the generator of form might be taken to suggest that the pitches, together with the other forces (timbral, dynamic) shaping them, are merely the conveyors of rhythms which are themselves, in aggregate, the primary determinants of form. But equally plausible is that rhythm is the generator of form only in the sense that it is responsible for setting sound masses in motion. In fact, this is more plausible, for the idea that rhythm *derives* from the interplay of elements suggests strongly that these elements have some sort of prior existence. This, of course, is only suggested by Varèse's words, not explicitly set forth. As was made clear in chapter 1, nearly everything Varèse said admits of multiple interpretations; his aesthetic ruled out attempts to be absolutely rational and unambiguous. Analytical choices must be based on what seems the best available evidence. Under this interpretation, rhythm maintains a considerable importance. As the generator of form, it is by definition part of the content, for as Varèse also said, "Form and content are one." But from an analytical point of view, rhythm cannot be identified as the origin, the Ur-material from which this music is constructed.

Returning to general criteria, we find other reasons why a conclusion of this sort might be expected. Limits are eventually imposed by the exigencies of history even upon revolutionaries. For centuries before 1900, Western music had been consistently and overwhelmingly pitch oriented. Some of the heirs to this tradition saw a need to make fundamental changes. But even so, is it really likely that one composer at the beginning of the so-called "post-tonal" era—a name which in itself refers primarily to changes in pitch usage—all on his own could have forced pitch to accommodate rhythm as its equal? Even granting how different Varèse's music is from that of his contemporaries, even granting that he did assign greater structural roles to timbre, dynamics, and rhythm than they had filled before, still this is not to say that these domains were raised to a status equal to that of pitch. Not even a great revolutionary can change everything at once. One of the compromises that Varèse had to make was to acknowledge the sovereignty of pitch—although, as we have seen, he was able to mitigate this sovereignty by introducing register as an essential factor in the definition of structure.[5]

Part of Varèse's lifelong struggle was with others' minds: those of fellow musicians who preferred the old ways or, at most, ways diverging only minimally from what was already familiar; those of the heads of foundations and of commercial enterprises who would not build or support efforts to build new sound technologies. The other part of his struggle, which no one talks about much, surely must have been internal—for even if Varèse was unfettered by the limits of others, certainly he had limits of his own to deal with. Varèse was often called as "visionary," a "precursor," a figure "ahead of his time." How he hated those epithets! "The artist is never ahead of his time," he would retort, "but is simply the only one who is not way behind." Perhaps this means that anything he could have conceived or dreamt of was by definition "of his own time," but it does not imply that the things conceived or dreamt of could be realized, or that conceiving of something would be the same as realizing it, much less using it. Varèse's much-admired aphorism, "Sometimes one sees so far that expression refuses to follow as though it were afraid," certainly shows that he understood the limits under which he worked.[6] If we accept the idea that artistic practice is in a continuous state of evolution, then we must admit that all artists are transitional figures, as Picasso said. For this reason "the liberation of sound" is bound to mean something different now from what it meant a generation ago, and from what it may mean a generation hence.

While rhythm/duration, with respect to pitch/register, is clearly a secondary, contributing domain, not all secondary domains are of equal stature. The roles of timbre and loudness as partitioning devices have been illustrated in enough contexts by now for the reader to have a clear idea of how they operate in general, but there is a great deal more to say about rhythm, even though its partitioning role has been touched upon as well. As Varèse's remarks about it imply, it does have special significance. Our analytical appreciation of the music, therefore, can be considerably enriched by a closer study of the diverse functions of rhythm, which vary according to the type of context. Of particular interest in this connection is the writing for unpitched percussion, and its use both in conjunction with pitched material and in solo passages (and pieces) will be considered. The vast resources of rhythmic stratification that Varèse introduced will be assessed, particularly with reference to the writing for percussion, but in other situations as well. Also to be examined is the idea of formal delineation as a function of the reuse of material. And the phenomenon of pitch stasis, including "frozen music," in which other domains become especially active and prominent, will be studied as a special way of controlling durational structure.[7]

At approximately the same time that Schoenberg began producing works in the twelve-tone idiom, with rhythmic and metrical characteristics that were, at least on the local level, much simpler and more regular than in his earlier music, and at a time when Stravinsky had embraced an ostensibly conservative, neoclassical style that brought with it a more rigidly controlled approach to rhythm and meter, Varèse's first mature works exhibited exactly the opposite tendency. Starting with *Amériques* and continuing throughout his career, Varèse's penchant for rhythmic complexity seems to have been aimed at nearly complete and constant disruption of pulse, of any semblance of regularity in beat pattern. This tendency has roots in his aesthetic background; as noted, Varèse despised what he viewed as the monotony of repetition, including metrical reinforcement. In fact, he apparently sought as nearly complete a divorcement as possible of rhythm from meter. Recall his statements that "rhythm is too often confused with metrics" and that "cadence or the regular succession of beats and accents has little to do with the rhythm of a composition." Here Varèse spoke of music in general, not just his own, but the attitude revealed still reflects a determination to avoid any such confusion in his music. Clearly he felt that radical solutions were required. It is difficult to find passages in Varèse where the beat, or even some simple subdivision or compound of it, is literally stressed for more than a couple of measures.

These qualities are strongly suggestive. Although they do not mandate anything, certainly they would not lead us to expect neat, exact durational schemes: the sort, for example, in which some number of beats or measures in one section is balanced by exactly the same number in another section, or in which a simple proportion expresses a relationship between two sections. By disrupting the pulse, Varèse succeeded in controlling the passage of time in ways that are not entirely unprecedented, but which still are remarkably powerful in their ability to overcome and neutralize what might be called "objective time" or "clock time." When within successive measures, or even within the same measure, the beat is divided in so many different ways, into equal and unequal parts of varying dimensions, one would certainly not be inclined to try measuring durational structure through additive, cellular processes of the sort, for example, that Boulez has adopted for the study of Stravinsky's music.[8] Time is still a factor—how could it not be?—but it does not always tick by in identical, discrete quanta. Neat schemes of any sort are incompatible with Varèse's aims. They smack too much of externally imposed, predetermined form. Varèse wanted to "paint a seemingly unpredictable picture" which nevertheless was "calculated" in all its essentials. Only by calculation, paradoxically, could he ensure that unpredictability would not be compromised by inadvertent repetition.

From the foregoing we can reach a general conclusion: absolute (that is, exactly measured) duration is irrelevant in most analytical situations. This is another reason that the graphs of chapters 2 and 3 assign no uniform calibration to the horizontal axis—aside, that is, from the pragmatic value of allowing as many pitch/ registral events as possible to be represented on a single graph. Nevertheless, beatcounting is not always inappropriate. It is useful in situations where duration has independent stature, where pitch events have temporarily ceased to progress, resulting in a static oscillation between two or more configurations or irregularly spaced repetitions of a single configuration. In these situations, duration assumes the function of directing progression, and it becomes necessary to measure it in some way. By doing so, we learn a great deal about the shapes that these pitchstatic passages take and the developments that eventually bring them to an end.

Related to the deliberate avoidance of metrical reinforcement is the use of complicated cross-rhythms, one of Varèse's principal means of separating and distinguishing sound masses. The point of presenting complicated and conflicting rhythmic patterns is often not so much the resultant rhythm of their simultaneous presentation as it is the stratification possible in such situations.[9] Emphasis upon this stratification is often provided by other forces, usually timbral and/or registral. The large number of percussion instruments typically included in a Varèse work and the large number of ways in which they may be played—always specified carefully—afford the composer a huge range of timbral possibilities. The various ways in which this range is put to use will be detailed below. It should also be noted, however, that complex cross-rhythmic passages do not always signal an intention to differentiate internally. In extreme cases, no matter how accurately the passage in question is performed, the result is a sound entity that in the aggregate is unique but of which the component parts are indistinguishable. This is obviously more likely to be true where the texture is dense and the duration relatively brief.

PITCH STASIS

There are varying degrees of pitch stasis, the most extreme of which is called here "frozen music." Varèse's use of pitch stasis is extensive. Although every instance is unique in terms of such specific attributes as pitch content, durational scheme, and rhythmic patterns, there is a general procedure which all have in common: a collection of pitches (or indefinite pitches where the stasis is conveyed by percussion) in a particular registral disposition and, in the case of the oscillating type of stasis, in fixed groupings is repeated several times and undergoes in the process a rhythmic elaboration. Usually in no two repetitions is the rhythm exactly the same. As this process is carried out, elaboration and variation in other domains (timbre and dynamics) may also occur; this is frequently true of the frozen situations mentioned above. The pitch collection may be in a single part, or a single chord played by several instruments, or a series of events in different parts or groups of parts. When the repetition ends, the musical progression continues by motion that provides a strong contrast to pitch stasis, although often this following material is related in some direct and clear-cut way to the immediately preceding events, as can be seen from some of the examples below. Usually the motion is markedly faster, in terms of pitch change over time, although not always sufficiently so to qualify as a passage of the rapid-motion type discussed in chapter 3. The pitch repetition acts as an accumulator of tension, which is released when the repetition is finally superseded. This may explain why one pitch-static section hardly ever follows another directly.

A few examples of relatively brief pitch stasis illustrate the process on a small scale. At the opening of *Octandre,* first movement (ex. 4.1, mm. 1–5), the solo oboe states the basic pitch series G♭5–F4–E5–D♯5 three times in succession. The second occurrence is only slightly altered from the first and is related to the more considerable rhythmic transformation of the third in that in the second occurrence (m. 2) the last two notes are repeated, whereas in the third (m. 3) the first two are repeated. The progression of increasing degrees of rhythmic metamorphosis is typical of pitch-static environments. But the essential rhythmic "shape" is maintained—is in fact exaggerated, with the long E5 becoming even longer compared to the other pitches in the third occurrence. The resumption of pitch change in m. 4, as pointed out in the discussion of example 3.47, is carried out by means of projection: D5–C♯4–C5–B4 together are [4] lower than the initial four pitches. Here, however, no repetition takes place; in fact, the rhythm is completely uninflected (each successive pair of pitches occurs at a distance of an eighth), a development which has the effect of canceling the rhythmic relationship established in the first three measures.

Example 4.1: *Octandre,* I, mm. 1–5

A more extended example of pitch stasis occurs at the beginning of *Offrandes*, first movement (ex. 4.2). The D5 is subjected to some timbral fluctuation as it is passed back and forth a few times from its initial location in the muted trumpet to the oboe. Then, shortly before the accompanying material in the strings and horn drops out (m. 7), it is expanded to the five-member collection in m. 6. The continuation of the trumpet part unaccompanied has the interesting effect of narrowing and intensifying the musical focus from its initially diffuse quality, a development emphasized by the abrupt shift to a tempo three times the speed of the opening, so that the quick figure originally in thirty-seconds at quarter = 44 is now even faster (sixteenths at quarter = 132). After the third occurrence of the complete five-note form, a process of abbreviation begins to intrude (mm. 10–11), with a concomitant shift in rhythmic contour (F♯4 is extended, C5 in m. 11 slightly de-emphasized), although D5 remains dominant. The emphasis on G5 at the fermata in m. 13, together with the reversal of the original order of G5 and E♭5, seems to be the transformation that finally brings this pitch-static passage to an end, as the trumpet moves almost triumphantly to B5, precipitating a shower of new events which gradually subsides over the next few measures.

Offrandes, unlike most of the later works, contains very few pitch-static passages—and no other as dramatic or extended as this first one. In part this is because it is a vocal piece (both *Ecuatorial* and *Nocturnal* are like *Offrandes* in this respect) but it is also because of its early date of composition. In *Amériques,* pitch stasis has a similarly special function; it occupies rather little of the work, and even in those passages that have static elements the procedure is not always the same as it is in the later instrumental pieces. For example, in the long "Grandioso" section near the end (mm. 459–510, beginning at rehearsal 44), certain elements—the dirge-like figure in the trombones and the reiterated chords, for example—are established right at the beginning and maintained throughout, but other ele-

Example 4.2: *Offrandes*, I ("Chanson de là-haut"), mm. 6–14, trumpet

ments, not reiterated, are also brought in in a steady stream. As in *Offrandes,* the most striking instance of pitch stasis is found in the opening measures (ex. 4.3, mm. 1–7). In the seven occurrences of the alto-flute figure the only rhythmic changes from one to the next are the durations of the longer two notes, initial B4 and final E4. These change according to independent schemes until the last three repetitions of the figure, in which B4 is a dotted eighth in duration and E4 a triplet eighth plus eighth (including the value of the following rest) each time, although even here a slight fluctuation occurs as an accelerando (m. 5) is followed by return to original tempo (m. 7). When the repetitions are broken off, the change is abrupt: a jagged rhythm and new pitch material as the full orchestra enters in m. 8.

The move toward greater rhythmic regularity seen in this example is another possibility in the treatment of pitch-static material. Superficially considered, it would seem more or less diametrically opposed to the type of treatment exemplified in the passage from *Offrandes* above. Its effect, however—the conclusion of stasis—is the same. From this we can conclude, provisionally, that the appearance of a discernible pattern, yielding a directional change of some sort, is crucial to the conclusion of stasis.

In the case of the *Amériques* example, the tension is generated by repetitions that are almost exactly alike. The only other instruments sounding are the harps, in featureless ostinato, and the bassoon, which at first (m. 3 to downbeat of m. 5) interjects a chromatic figure at irregular intervals but eventually lapses into a sustained pitch. However, it is not only the close conformity of the last three versions that should be noted. The shortening of the durations of B4 and E4 to three-quarters and five-sixths of a beat respectively means that the duration of the entire figure is much shorter than any of the previous versions. Overall, then, an

Example 4.3: *Amériques,* mm. 1–7, alto flute

accelerando takes place, a pattern which may be identified as the inducement to end the pitch-static passage.

Something quite similar to this occurs at the opening of the second movement of *Octandre* (ex. 4.4, mm. 1–11, piccolo solo). The grace-note figure leading to G♭5, which is prolonged by staccato repetition and/or sustention, sets up a series of nine durations which moves from fairly long (seven beats) to short (one beat), then back again to almost as long as the first (six beats). Finally, the series ends with the lengths ⅔, ⅔, 1⅔: in other words, a two-beat triplet (with the last note extended). This regularity and abbreviation act together to bring an end to this particular pitch stasis; the eighteen beats of G♭5 sounding together with F6 effectively separate the opening measures from the next pitch-static section, which brings several elements into play (mm. 17–35). Note that the sustained G♭5–F6 pair (mm. 11–16) is not *in itself* an instance of pitch stasis, in the sense that the term is meant here, for there is only one long duration, no series.

In this and other similar passages the process of rhythmic elaboration seems intended to act upon the pitches until the accumulated tension results in rupture of the confining stasis. At least, that is one possible interpretation. However, there are other ways of looking at it. If rhythm is indeed acting upon pitch in these instances, then one must conclude that it is a force which is essentially independent of pitch, since it apparently "behaves" in various ways at different points, subjecting some pitch groups to a temporary stasis while leaving others unaffected. If instead we were to regard the pitch groups as "bodies of intelligent sounds moving freely in space," in Varèse's evocative words, then we might view the process of rhythmic permutation and elaboration which occurs in some cases not as a behavior forced upon these sounds but as one which they adopt of their own free will. However, there *is* something about the varied repetition that suggests a struggle to break free of confinement. Perhaps it would not be going too far to suggest that, in some figurative sense, they are captured.

This phenomenon has been studied by others, with different results. Robert Morgan, in "Notes on Varèse's Rhythm," begins with a general observation about Varèse's pitch structures that "the pitches . . . don't want to go anywhere" of their own accord, and concludes that the rhythmic procedures are designed to induce movement where none would otherwise occur.[10] Morgan chooses as an illustration the opening twenty-five measures of *Intégrales,* a good example of frozen

Example 4.4: *Octandre,* II, mm. 1–11

music; what is unclear about Morgan's formulation is why, if all of Varèse's pitches are reluctant to move onward, only a few groups exhibit the behavior of the *Intégrales* example.[11] One might conclude to better purpose that despite an absence of counterpoint—which, on an intuitive level, seems to be what Morgan is responding to—the pitches *do* want to go somewhere, that they do so by means of the processes discussed in chapters 2 and 3, and that when they are *prevented* from going a struggle ensues, ultimately resulting in escape.

The next logical question is: what motivates the choice of one pitch collection over another as a candidate for stasis? It is not possible to provide a definitive answer, but the question does lead to some useful observations. In keeping with the idea that the relevant structures in Varèse are processes and not objects, one must beware of the temptation to regard the pitch collections held in stasis as special in themselves—as if they were being featured, elevated to prominence beyond other collections dwelt upon for shorter periods of time. Absolute time or clock time, as mentioned, is not a reliable indicator of real duration in Varèse anyway; it is not the length of time that a collection is held in stasis which produces the sensation of accumulating tension, but rather the irregularly spaced repetitions and the various other manipulations that accompany them. It might happen, for example, that pitch stasis would be used to separate preceding and following events which had greater importance to the continuum of process than the events in stasis. Or the tension generated by a pitch-static section could be used to place emphasis not upon the section itself but upon what it led to. This alternative applies very clearly to the *Offrandes* passage just discussed: the rapid succession of events that follows upon the trumpet's attainment of B5 completes a double projection from the opening measures.

Besides this, however, pitch stasis may have other functions. We saw in chapter 1 that this phenomenon is analogous to certain techniques of early twentieth-century painting and sculpture, particularly the expression of multiple views of a single object according to cubist and futurist theory. For visual artists this was a way of showing the true nature of the scene or object depicted: that is, not so much a thing in itself as something integrated with its surroundings. For Varèse, pitch-static techniques were in all likelihood a way of expressing not only the variety of internal relationships of the material subjected to such treatment but also the multitudinous connections to its context. At points where processes of various sorts are intermingled, are realized or initiated at the same time, pitch stasis serves as a way of revealing numerous completions and departures. Most important, because pitch/registral progress has been halted, all of these relationships are revealed, in a sense, *at the same time*—despite the objective lapse of time during the pitch-static passage. Varèse's intentions in adapting the idea of multiple viewpoints to music thus seems to have been exactly the opposite of the artists' aspirations. Jean Metzinger, for instance, identified the technique as a way to achieve temporality in painting: "Formerly a picture took possession of space, now it reigns also in time."[12] Even this reversal, however, makes sense if we take into account the possibility that the painters, in their quest to incorporate time—

previously the province of music—into their work, and Varèse, in his quest to bring a sense of space—conventionally regarded as the realm of the visual—into his work, might have traveled the same road, but in different directions.

Example 4.4 approaches the condition of frozen music. There is no clear-cut line of division between this extreme form of pitch stasis and the types illustrated in our previous examples, but at least it is possible to identify the two principal factors which determine the overall degree of intensity of a pitch-static passage (as distinguished from the way in which tension accumulates in the course of a passage). One, naturally, is length—measured by number of repetitions, not by number of beats or units of clock time. The other is the relative purity of the stasis—that is, whether and to what extent the pitch/registral groups, once set, are interrupted or intruded upon by new pitch events. Roughly speaking, the greater the length of the passage and the fewer the interruptions by foreign material, the more likely the passage is to sound frozen, hence more intense than other, related passages. In practice, pitch stasis is hardly ever 100 percent pure (examples of varying degrees of purity are presented below). If relative purity of stasis is conducive to the creation of intensity, then one might expect also that the fewer in number the discrete elements involved in the stasis, the more intense it would be. To a certain extent this is true, although in practice a larger number of elements is usually associated with a longer period of stasis; thus the effect is one of mutual cancellation more often than not.

We begin our examination of frozen music with two relatively simple passages from the second and third movements of *Octandre*. These are analytically more straightforward than other similar passages because no percussion parts are involved and because the timbral and dynamic domains as well as the pitch/registral are static, allowing concentration upon rhythm and duration.

In the second movement, mm. 50–66 (diagrammed in ex. 4.5) consist of two different sonorities which alternate in succeeding measures. Excluding the prominent F5 (trumpet) in the first and (E♭–D)5 (E♭ clarinet) in the second, the two

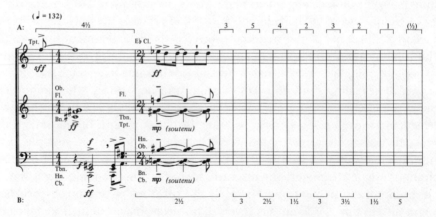

Example 4.5: *Octandre*, II, mm. 50–66

sonorities are also distinguished by their dynamic levels (*ff* and *mp* respectively). In addition, in all but two of its occurrences the first sonority is rhythmically active internally, with effects upon the pitch/registral structure discussed in chapter 2 (see ex. 2.14). From the diagram in example 4.5, we see that the series of durations does indeed follow an irregular pattern. Regarded by itself, the first sonority progresses essentially from a relatively long to a relatively short duration, while the second may be said, slightly less convincingly (that is, if the two 1.5-beat durations are ignored), to progress from short to long, with a very big increase at its last occurrence. This combination of extreme abbreviation with extreme prolongation results in the end of stasis. In overview, it is reasonable to say that while on the local level the movement of succession from one sonority to another is unpredictable, still a general move in one direction is discernible throughout the entire passage.

Measures 24–39 in the third movement (ex. 4.6) are somewhat more complicated. Here there is only one chord, but the figural component has an independent rhythmic structure. Once again, the ensemble rhythm seems to sputter unpredictably—at least until the last seven measures of the passage—but overall

Example 4.6: *Octandre*, III, mm. 24–39

there is movement in the direction of regularity. There are three stages in the ensemble stasis (we will examine the trumpet part shortly). First, mm. 24–26 are framed by the chord in crescendo; the second stage (mm. 27–32) is all *fff* and consists of the same rhythm played twice (see brackets in the example), followed by an appended series of progressively longer durations: 1.5, 2, and 3 beats. The third stage (mm. 33–39) is a series of seven half-note durations, each in crescendo *p* to *sff* except for the last: *p* to *f* and back to *mp*. As for the trumpet part, it progresses independently through four complete statements of (G–F–E)5 over the duration of the first two stages of the chord stasis; the first and third of these are quite short, the second and fourth quite long by virtue of extreme prolongation of both G5 and E5. In the third stage the trumpet begins in synchrony (m. 33) with the ensemble chord but moves out of phase immediately, managing only four complete statements and an incomplete fifth to the ensemble's seven attacks. Here truncation (of the trumpet figure) is associated with the end of stasis, as was also the case in the passage from *Amériques* (ex. 4.3).

It will not have escaped the reader's attention that the two passages discussed in examples 4.5 and 4.6 are related in an obvious way: the figure (F–E♭–D)5 in the second movement is used in the third, two semitones higher. By itself this connection would, perhaps, be only mundane; what makes it compositionally interesting is that the figure is associated in both locations with static treatment. Otherwise the two passages are thoroughly different, neither the harmonic nor the rhythmic structure of the one bearing any resemblance to that of the other. There is a built-in fundamental rhythmic contrast because (F–E♭–D)5 is partitioned consistently, in conjunction with the harmonic alternation, while (G–F–E)5 is not.

Sometimes the end of stasis is associated with an absolute regularity, unmitigated by factors such as the truncation noted above. In such cases the regularity is the signal, but it also constitutes part of the surprise, or the unpredictability, of the situation—for here not only pitch/registral relationships but also durational relationships are frozen, along, most likely, with timbre and dynamics. Example 4.7 (*Intégrales*, mm. 32–36; mm. 44–45) is a case in point. This stasis takes the form of an alternation between the groups marked (a) and (b) in the example; (a) first appears alone (mm. 32–33), then a second time (mm. 34–35) and thereafter with the cumulative sonority (b) (m. 36). The pattern of durations is shown by the table of numbers to the right of the musical notation. Group (a) remains, through m. 46, longer than or equal in duration to (b); alternation no. 5 is an exact repetition of no. 2, and no. 6 is closely related to no. 4, although this is the one point in the passage where foreign material intrudes, shown as (c). The intensification of the durational relationship between (a) and (b) represented by no. 6 next leads to a reversal (mm. 47–52), with (b) now longer than (a). These last three alternations are precise duplicates of one another. As for the intrusion, its foreign nature seems balanced by the regularity of what follows, but eventually this regularity itself becomes a disruption, for nothing we have heard in the piece up to this point leads us to expect it. The tension built up by the repetition is finally dissipated in one of the most violently rapid passages found anywhere in Varèse (mm. 53–69).[13]

Table of Durations (in quarters at ♩ = 60)

	(a)	(b)
1.	9	–
2.	6	5
3.	4	4
4.	5	2
5.	6	5
6.	5½ (c)	2
7.	4	5
8.	4	5
9.	4	5

Example 4.7: *Intégrales*, mm. 32–36; mm. 44–45 (percussion omitted)

Extreme regularity is applied in a more concealed way in the passage illustrated in example 4.8 (*Arcana*, mm. 418–426). Here the principal component is a steady stream of quintuplets in several parts, in an irregular pattern which becomes even more jagged after m. 421, when rests begin to break in. (Only the highest voice of the quintuplet texture, for the sake of simplicity of presentation, is shown in the example.) Additional irregularity is supplied by eruptions in the lower instruments and percussion and in the percussion alone. There would not at first appear to be any evidence of periodicity, either in the sequence of pitches or in the intrusions of rests; the end of the passage, if anything, seems even more irregular than what precedes it. Note, however, that one striking feature of the quintuplet material is the peak represented in the contour of the highest line (and of the other

Example 4.8: *Arcana,* mm. 418–426

parts in general) by each occurrence of A♯6. Note further that the A♯6s are not at all evenly spaced throughout the passage; instead, they occur in clusters. In the initial measures of the passage, a segmentation conforming with the occurrences of these clusters produces an irregular series of durations; but at the end, if a segmentation is drawn at the first of a cluster (or single occurrence, where these are isolated) of A♯6 and at the points where the other notes resume—either immediately, or after a rest—then a regular pattern emerges, as shown by the numbers above the example (expressed in fifths of a beat).

Patterns of a more approximate sort which are equally effective in bringing stases to an end involve an accelerando or ritardando; in such situations, although the exact durations of the repeated pitch units remain unpredictable, the effect of the speeding up or slowing down is to reduce the number of possibilities and focus the ear's attention upon one aspect of rhythmic development. This will be perceived as a qualitative change from the circumstances immediately preceding—just as is the imposition of exact repetition—and foretells the resumption of pitch/registral change.

A passage from *Déserts* (ex. 4.9, mm. 124–132) conveys the effect of abrupt acceleration after two leisurely accumulations of the components of the repeated group. It should be noted that this pitch stasis leads to another pitch/registral structure, rotated with respect to its predecessor but much shorter and not prolonged through stasis.[14]

As for retardation in stasis, a clear-cut example occurs in mm. 80–92 of *Intégrales* (ex. 4.10). There are three components in this section: a single repeated sonority in the upper parts, (A), which will be the main focus of our investigation; a brief interjection by the trombones, (B), repeated once; and an independent development in the percussion (not shown). The high sonority is first prolonged in a series of durations, numbered 1 through 7 at the top of the example. Each of these is divided into two phases: rhythmic activity in small values is followed by a longer sustention. This alternation changes near the end (m. 90). The successive *total* lengths of these segments reveal no discernible pattern; the ratios, however, between rhythmically active and sustained portions of each segment have more significance. (As elsewhere, included in the duration of a segment are any following rests before the beginning of the next segment.) The first four of these ratios vary widely, but the last three, roughly 1:3, 1:4, and 1:3, are much closer and represent a kind of increasing regularity (see chart at the right of the example). After the last of these active/sustained segments, a series of increasingly longer values begins, at the second note of the two-beat triplet in m. 90. In terms of quarter-note beats, these are: $\frac{2}{3}$, $\frac{7}{6}$, 1 $\frac{1}{2}$, and 2 $\frac{1}{2}$ (note that the point of division which produces the last two is the accented cutoff in the trumpets and horn in m. 92). The convergence of ratio sizes in mm. 88–90, followed by the effective ritardando in mm. 90–92, impose a regularity which signals the end of stasis.[15]

In all but two of the excerpts examined so far the change inducing the disintegration of stasis appears only near the end. Sometimes, however, dynamic elements seem to be in competition with static elements right from the beginning, so that a progression may be read through the entire passage. Eventually, the force behind this progression accumulates to the point where the elements responsible for the stasis are overcome, usually abruptly. This technique bears a certain resemblance to that of partial and developing stases discussed in conjunction with later examples, although there the "impurity" in question is produced by continual introduction of new pitch material.

A notable example of steady progression is found in *Ionisation* (ex. 4.11, mm. 38–42), where a combination of rhythmic and timbral differentiation sets up two alternating textures: one of unison triplets, the other of quicker, irregularly spaced bursts of notes (not shown in the example). The first phase of this stasis consists of the progressive shortening of the triplet figure, from 3 beats to 1 $\frac{2}{3}$ to 1, while the length of the entire repeated unit remains the same. Next, an ambiguity

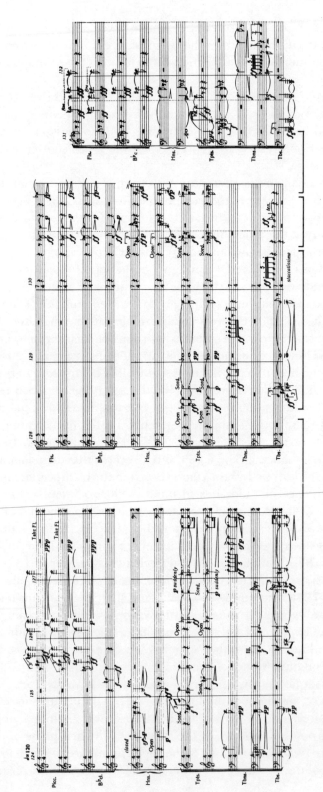

Example 4.9: *Déserts*, mm. 124–132

Example 4.10: *Intégrales*, mm. 80–92

is introduced in the form of a duple group (m. 41, first beat) which combines instruments from both textures; however, the characteristic triplet of the first texture is reasserted immediately afterwards and then proceeds to be further abbreviated. The group of two sixteenths and an eighth at the end of m. 41 is notated literally as occupying a whole beat, but its three attacks are closer together than those comprising the triplet. The last occurrence of this component is only a single attack. The net effect of this passage, then, is the telescoping of one component while the other continues more or less unaffected. (But the triplet texture has not been permanently eliminated, for it enters again in m. 44. See ex. 4.14.)

A study of example 4.12 (*Intégrales*, mm. 135–143) reveals two types of steady progression which converge to bring about the abrupt end of pitch stasis. The static elements are two trichords that always enter in the same order and in their alternations segment the passage into a series of durations, each consisting of the pair of trichords plus the rest separating one occurrence of the pair from the next. No real pattern, other than a general tendency toward shorter total duration, results from this segmentation; however, the durations of the trichords them-selves, disregarding the rests for the moment, do become progressively shorter until m. 141. The one-beat duration reached at this point is maintained for the last

Example 4.11: *Ionisation*, mm. 38–42, triplet texture

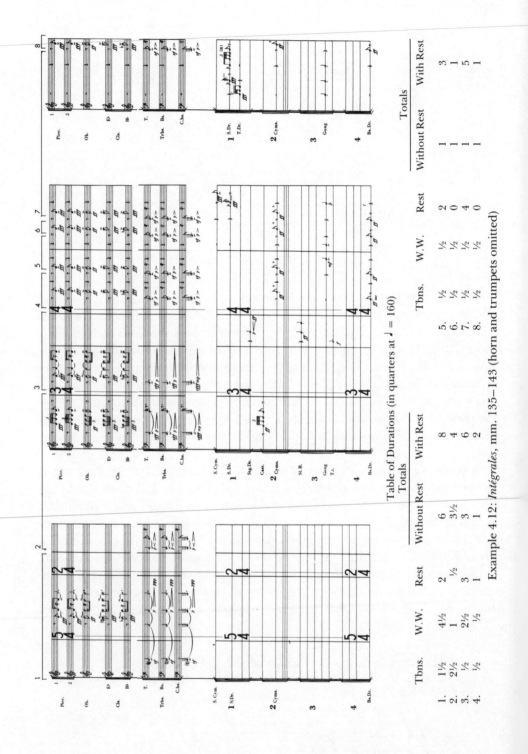

Table of Durations (in quarters at ♩ = 160)

Example 4.12: *Intégrales*, mm. 135–143 (horn and trumpets omitted)

five appearances of the trichord pair, in precisely the same rhythm as well (two eighths). Meanwhile, among the rests another pattern emerges: the first (two beats), m. 136, is entirely empty; the next longer rest (three beats) is empty of pitches but marks the first independent use of percussion in the passage; the last rest (four beats), across mm. 142–143, likewise has no pitches but is filled by the entrance of elaborate material for snare and tenor drums.

In both of the preceding examples the immediate cause of the end of stasis (the extreme abbreviation of the triplet texture and the last burst of pitched material, respectively) may be assessed as the product of a progression extending throughout the static passage. Where no apparent connection of this sort exists, two causes may be identified—one immediate, the other general—for bringing stasis to a conclusion. The next two examples provide some idea of the diversity possible under the application of this technique.

Example 4.13 (*Octandre,* II, mm. 17–36) continues from where example 4.4

*new element; stasis effectively dissolves at this point.

Example 4.13: *Octandre,* II, mm. 17–36

above ends. As mentioned, the sustained dyad of mm. 11–16 is not part of a static section, although in its rhythmically active form it does play a part in the present example. The four components are labeled (a), (b), (c), and (d); the collection is not complete until m. 20. Of the four, (d) has the most consistent function, for it is clearly used as a demarcator. One might almost call it cadential. The rhythmic reduction focuses on attack points in the interest of assessing this demarcating role accurately. Sustentions are indicated only where they result from the immediately previous attack: that is, if (b) were to enter and sustain, for example, while (a) then entered with staccato chords, after which (b) continued to sound, then the duration of (b) after the (a) chords had ceased would be indicated by a rest; on the other hand, if (c) were to enter and sustain without any of the other components becoming involved, then its duration would be shown in noteheads.[16]

There are two reasons why (d) has a more specific function than any of the other components in this passage: first, because it is used less often; and second, because its occurrence is always (except for the very end, where the stasis dissolves) followed by a rest. The first of the five locations of (d), in m. 20, is followed by one beat of rest (m. 21). The second, much more rhythmically elaborate occurrence (mm. 25–26) precedes two beats of rest (m. 27). The third (m. 31), which occurs in the same rhythmic pattern with (a) as it did at the beginning of the second occurrence (two-beat triplet in m. 25), is cut off sharply. Further rhythmic development of (d) has been put off for a moment. In the meantime (m. 32), three beats of rest intervene, after which (d) dominates, serving in mm. 33–35 as demarcator for the entire static section, as it already has for the subsections.

A progression, then, is clear: from one to three beats of rest. Besides this quantitative progression there is a qualitative one: m. 21 is the first rest (that is, in this case, an *attack* rest) of any kind in the stasis; in the attack rest in m. 27 we hear the sustention of E4 in its new timbral guise (horn taking over from trombone), which is a new kind of event in the passage; m. 32 is an actual rest, completely empty of sound. This shock of silence, together with the ensuing elaboration of (d) comprising its last two occurrences, may be considered the immediate cause of dissolution of stasis, but the overall function of (d) is just as important in controlling events.

The same kinds of control are exerted in *Ionisation*, mm. 44–50 (ex. 4.14), although the specific means chosen are quite different. This passage bears some relation to the previous stasis in the work, discussed in example 4.11: the triplet texture is carried over, although now separated into two distinct functions, and the brilliant, irregular rhythms of the *tarole, tambour militaire*, and *caisse claire* have been to some extent "regularized" into quintuplet patterns. The contrast between the two textures, which are always presented in alternation, is thus very clear cut, being both timbrally and rhythmically based. To this extent it is static, or frozen. Relative pitch is also static; in conjunction with the constant rhythmic unisons the only distinction made is between high and low (hereafter referred to as H and L, respectively). The variable elements are length of phrase and order of H and L, to which we now turn our attention.

Example 4.14: *Ionisation*, mm. 44–50

The initiating event, HLL as a triplet, becomes a point of reference throughout these seven measures; it may be understood as a beginning each time it occurs. To a certain extent it is balanced by another triplet-based event in a different group of instruments, in the pattern HL on the last two parts of the triplet, which serves a terminating function. Between initiation and termination comes the quintuplet texture. Phrase 1 (m. 44) has one quintuplet. In phrase 2 (m. 45), again there is one quintuplet, but with a rest on the third of the five (slight irregularity introduced); further, the termination leads, not directly to a new initiation, but to a two-beat extension of the quintuplet texture, with additional rhythmic elaboration. Phrase 3 (m. 46) is of the same duration as phrase 1, but the quintuplet texture is interrupted by a rest and does not continue to the downbeat of beat 3. Phrase 4 (m. 47) has a new element in the thirty-second note of beat 3; again the terminator does not lead to the initiating triplet, and this time the extension (mm. 47–49) is not only much longer but also more irregular, and is essentially in two parts

(2 + 6.5 beats). The first part of this extension, with its accented LH succession, duplicates the sound of events which ended the quintuplet texture in phrase 1 and the extension of phrase 2, but leads instead to a development of the HL succession. This takes place in three distinct phases, marked by brackets in the example, and leads neatly into the terminator group. Phrase 5, the last, regains the three-beat length of phrases 1 and 3 but ends in an approximation of the triplet-based terminator, produced by placing a rest on the fourth of five in the quintuplet.

The last events of phrase 5, given by the quintuplet texture, also present L and H simultaneously—a unique event in this static passage. This, the assumption of terminator role by a different group, and the effective neutralization of the sense of the quintuplet pattern in the last beat comprise the local, immediate inducement to end of stasis. Less immediate but no less telling is the relative brevity of the last phrase. An overview of the entire passage also reveals a pattern of development which eventually dissolves the stasis: beat-by-beat alternation of textures (phrases 1 and 2) interrupted by extension of one texture; resumption of "normal" alternation (phrase 3 and beginning of 4), followed by even more florid extensions and utter disruption of whatever sense of pulse has survived to this point; reassertion of normalcy at end of extension and beginning of phrase 5, immediately nullified by destruction of both quintuplet and triplet. Indeed, this final destruction is practically inevitable given the accumulated irregularities of the material preceding it.

Partial Stasis

We have already seen several instances in which pitch stasis occurs simultaneously with independent, nonstatic material in the percussion. This approach to assertion of self-sufficiency in the percussion as an instrumental group will be addressed in detail later in this chapter. Less common in Varèse are passages in which some but not all *pitch* elements are held in stasis; they demonstrate, however, that stasis under such conditions is subject to essentially the same constraints and is controlled by the same sort of rhythmic/durational principles that we have seen in more purely static situations.

In mm. 135–147 of *Ecuatorial* (ex. 4.15, including upbeat to 135), a partial stasis is in effect. While the voice and the two Ondes Martenot parts pursue their own courses of development, a series of brief events interspersed with rests of varying length unfolds in some of the other instruments. The elements involved are labeled (a) through (d) in the example, and accumulate over a period of time representing approximately four-fifths of the total length of the passage. Formally speaking, mm. 134–147 divide into three sections, the second of which is an abbreviated and otherwise slightly altered version of the first. Note that (a) in the first section is followed once by voice and ondes, twice more by silence; the section then ends with the succession (b)(a)(c), again followed by silence. The second section recognizably parallels the first: (a) followed by voice, entrance of ondes delayed this time. The intrusion between static elements, like the beginning of the

Example 4.15: *Ecuatorial*, mm. 135–147

first section, is considerably longer than any of the other intrusions; this is also only the second vocal entrance. Both (a)-initiated segments in the second section are slightly shorter than their counterparts in the first (durations in the example are indicated in thirds of a beat). The process of abbreviation now continues: there is no third (a)-initiated segment in the second section, and the (b)(a)(c) succession of the first now becomes (b) followed by (a) and (c) together. The total duration of these three components is the same (six thirds, or two beats) as in the first section, but the subsequent rest is abbreviated.

The third section is devoted to the introduction of the last remaining static element, (d), and the subsequent imposition of relative durational regularity which ends the passage. As the brackets show, if the last two measures are partitioned so that pitch elements are grouped with any rests that separate them from the next pitches, then three segments of lengths, 5, 5, and 6 result. It is as if the completion of the collection of static elements permitted the stasis-ending regularity to occur—not an exact regularity, but one that is nevertheless perceived as much *more* regular than anything that has preceded it. Here as well we find a culmination of the general tendency expressed throughout the passage away from long silences between the static elements. This is not a straight-line decrease, as can be seen by tracing the progression from its beginning, but the overall direction is clear.

Developing Stasis

This would seem at first glance to be a contradiction in terms. But the classification is useful, for it includes situations in which elements introduced initially give rise to others, some of which may eventually disappear and/or be replaced, while at least part of the initial content remains in place throughout. A classic example of developing stasis is the opening of *Déserts* (ex. 4.16, mm. 1–20). The dyad F4–G5, which begins the piece, fills the role of constant element.[17]

There are three principal stages in pitch/registral development. In the first, a duplicate span of [14] enters (m. 6), followed quickly by the splitting of both [14]s into adjacent [7]s (m. 7). The second stage is concluded by the projection of E3–F4 to Bb1–B2 and the simultaneous disappearance of (D–A)2–E3. The third stage introduces C#4 and proceeds in a fairly intricate rhythmic pattern to the upheaval at m. 21. These stages suggest divisions at m. 10, beat 3, and m. 16, beat 1, points which follow relatively long, unbroken sustentions and thus act as natural pauses. The durations of the three resultant segments are, respectively, 38, 23, and 19.5 beats (level (a) in ex. 4.16). The impression of steadily decreasing length is strengthened even further if the first C#4 is also taken as a point of division (19.5 becomes 11.5, 8).

From this point of view, then, the developing stasis displays structure much like that of a purer type of stasis. Like the excerpts in examples 4.13 and 4.14, the opening of *Déserts* seems to incorporate procedures of both long and short range which eventually bring an end to stasis: the former including progressively shorter

Example 4.16: *Déserts,* mm. 1–20 (percussion of indefinite pitch omitted)

segment length and generally increasing rhythmic activity, the latter represented by the especially complex cross-rhythms of mm. 19–20.[18] However, other ways of partitioning this passage can readily be imagined. For example, we could interpret the *attacks* of newly introduced elements as the beginnings of new segments, rather than taking, as we have done at level (a), the entire duration of the initial appearance of a new element as an act of closure. Under this change of divisional criterion the durations would be, in order, 23, 30, 14, and 13.5; see level (b).[19] The relative durations now reflect the number of new elements brought in at the beginning of each: four added pitches in the second segment, two in the third, one in the fourth. This scheme can also be regarded as based on the degree to which pitch/registral structure is affected (that is, the more activity, the longer the segment): intervals are both projected and split in the second segment, whereas only projection occurs in the third. The fact that only a single pitch is introduced in the fourth segment is compensated for by the more complicated relationship it bears to previous events; 13.5 is not much shorter than 14.

Is it possible to reconcile these two apparently conflicting segmentations? Probably not, for the ambiguity seems integral to the passage. Not only are elements presented simultaneously at length, rather than in the oscillatory patterns of previous examples; but, further, pitch/registral development takes place, and placement of points of division becomes a subtler matter of interpretation than it is under more purely static conditions. This ambiguity may provide some idea of the magnitude of the difficulties that the analyst would encounter in attempting to apply these segmentational procedures to nonstatic situations. In other words, where pitch/registral development takes place at all, it is the primary focus of attention, leaving durational considerations in the background.

Stasis as Termination

Earlier the point was made that the sheer number of repetitions in a pitch-static situation leads, seemingly inevitably, to an accumulation of tension that requires dispersal in some fashion, usually through subsequent rapid pitch development. Thus the placement of a pitch-static passage at the end of a section, or (especially) at the end of a work, would seem calculated to deny any sense of closure. Varèse, in fact, did not often use the stasis as termination, but two instances of this phenomenon, both in *Déserts,* are prominent enough to demand attention: mm. 244–263, which end the third instrumental section and immediately precede the final interpolation of organized sound, and mm. 312–325, the last measures of the piece. The pitch/registral groups of the second passage are those of the first transposed down [3], and they are used similarly (not identically).

Even from a cursory examination of these passages it is clear that they differ significantly from most other examples of stasis in their low dynamic and rhythmic profiles, frequent silences, and sparse scoring. None of these qualities alone would be sufficient to overcome the natural tension-accumulating tendency of pitch repetition, but together they are suggestive. Less obvious are the characteristics inherent in the durational structures of both, which makes these passages, in different ways, both self-sufficient and (implicitly) open-ended.

We will examine the earlier passage first. The rhythmic plan in example 4.17 shows that two kinds of events are held in stasis: the single note F#4 and the chord (G–Bb)2–B3. These form two kinds of durational units: the note alone (labeled N), and the note followed by the chord (N + C). In the basic gesture, which becomes established during roughly the first half of the passage, the note enters first, followed by the chord, followed by the note again. This succession N, C, N may be extended in any or all of its components; thus the first two larger units of the passage, bracketed in example 4.17, both begin N, N + C. The initial N of the second unit (m. 249), owing to its equidistant spacing between adjacent events, may also sound as an extension of the terminal N of the first unit.

In the second half of the passage, the basic gesture becomes more regularized in some of its aspects, more erratic in others. The terminal N of the second unit (m. 253) serves as a link, since it can easily sound as the initial N of a succession N, N + C, N. Next, however, N + C, N (with the terminal N always overlapping with the immediately previous C) becomes the expression of the basic gesture in mm. 254–260. This can be heard as the core of the first unit of the passage (see m. 246), but also as a condensation of the general form N, N + C, N of mm. 244–253, in

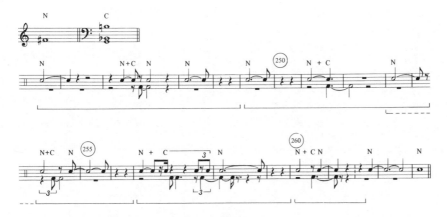

Example 4.17: *Déserts*, mm. 244–263

which the elements were set apart by rests. The effect of the regular alternation in mm. 254–260 is almost lulling, even though the actual durations (considered as exact numbers of beats) are quite irregular, and despite the brief rhythmic disruption in m. 257, where N + C is extended. One might think at first that the constant shifts in instrumentation of these components would tend to prevent equilibrium from being reached; from m. 249 on F♯4 is never heard twice in a row in the same instrument, and the chord is never heard twice in the entire passage in the same disposition of parts. If anything, the opposite seems to be true, which is perhaps not so surprising when one considers that in many other stases the reiteration of elements in exactly the same instrumentation is a contributing factor to the generation of tension. The last two segments (mm. 261–263) are all N, and no rest intervenes between them, the first time that this has happened in a successive N pair. The disappearance of chords and rests has the effect of smoothing out the texture and leaves the stasis demanding no resolution, although it could accommodate various continuations. In this connection, it should be mentioned that the composition of these measures posed an unusual problem: the music here was designed to suit two different performance options.[20] The increasingly neutral quality of the stasis has a special utility under the circumstances.

Like other referential material in Varèse, mm. 312–325 have much the quality of an echo. A number of changes have been made with respect to the earlier music to indicate that this passage occupies a new position, including the transposition down [3], different assignments of instrumental parts to the voices of the chord (as in the earlier music, constant shifts and avoidance of repetition are the rule), and the coloring of N and C with suspended cymbal and gong respectively. The durational plan is quite different, as is shown in example 4.18, but bears some resemblance to that of the earlier passage. The succession N, C, N can still be considered the norm, but here, at a point quite remote from the source, the echo has become somewhat distorted: N, N, N + C, N is now the first unit (mm. 312–318); N + C, N the second, with a subsequent N (m. 321) serving potentially either

Example 4.18: *Déserts,* mm. 312–325

as an extension of the terminal N of the second unit or as the initial N of a third; the third unit has no terminal N and for this reason deserves special attention.

In one respect, the scheme of mm. 312–325 seems at first to reverse the gradual imposition of regularity often displayed in static passages. If the lengths of individual components are considered separately, without reference to the normative groupings discussed above, then a pattern emerges, as shown by the first system of brackets below the staff in the example: three segments (N, N, N + C) of 6.5 beats each, then two of 3.5 each, concluding with three successively longer spans. This segmentation, however, can be regrouped as a series of overlapping durations (see second system of brackets) to combine symmetry with successively longer durations: 13, 13, 13.5, 15, 15. This pattern, unlike anything in mm. 244–263, competes with the vestiges of the N, C, N based segmentation, effectively expressing its altered nature by comparison to the earlier passage.

The event at the very end (mm. 323–325) is of a type not found anywhere else in either passage: in this N + C segment, N endures beyond the sounding of C, as if in imitation of N + C, N, but is completely different in effect: the omission of a new attack on E♭4 results in an elongation which merges almost imperceptibly with the final, beaten silence. There is a fairly strong suggestion at this point of a continuation beyond what is actually heard: the sound, projected into the infinite reaches of space, has passed beyond the point of audibility but has not ceased to live—as befits the "intelligent sounds moving freely in space" so crucial to Varèse's special attitude toward musical materials. Like its predecessor in *Déserts,* then, but for different reasons, this stasis both terminates and deliberately foregoes termination. One is tempted to speculate that the idea of using stasis in this way came to Varèse late in life, since the phenomenon is apparently unique to *Déserts,* his last completed work for conventional instruments. It would be interesting indeed if evidence should turn up in the later sketches (or even in *Etude pour Espace*) of analogous procedures.[21]

THE ROLE OF PERCUSSION OF INDEFINITE PITCH

Of all the distinctive features of Varèse's music, the one most widely recognized as unique is the writing for indefinitely pitched percussion instruments. Varèse has been lauded for his achievements in this realm; certainly no other Western composer has yet surpassed them. His special love for these instruments—for their seemingly endlessly varied possibilities of timbral combination, and for the discoveries waiting to be made with every exotic newcomer to the percussion section, be it wooden drums, anvil, or metal sheet—suggests that the percussive component in his scores deserves special attention. Since by definition the music for this group does not involve exact pitches, assessing its role (or, more precisely, its roles) demands an approach to analysis different from any adopted to this point.

As already mentioned, exactness of sound definition assumes priority in an analytical situation. The scoring for percussion in Varèse is always precise in its specifications of instruments and its prescriptions for playing them, including any special techniques that may be called for: unusual types of striking implements, such as knitting needles or twigs; unusual types of preparation, such as the leather cushion used for muffling the lath in m. 276 of *Déserts;* even different sizes of instruments that are not usually available in more than one size, such as the slap stick. Clearly Varèse took unusual pains to define *as closely as possible* the sounds to be obtained from the percussion. From the point of view of pitch and timbre, however, the results are bound to be less than exact, for the instruments them-selves—even the most common ones—are far less standardized than are their pitched counterparts. The variety of materials used in construction, not to men-tion the slight variations in drum sizes and cymbal diameters, means that to work in this medium is to accept less specifically predictable results than when writing for winds and strings.[22] A composer can only count on relative pitch, and then often only within one group of instruments. For instance, calling for a set of three Chinese blocks, a tenor drum, and a bass drum would most likely guarantee a collection of five sounds ranging from high to low (the lowest Chinese block sounds higher than the tenor drum), but how would this collection mesh, say, with another group consisting of high and low cymbals and medium and low gongs? It would almost certainly not be possible to set up a reliable scale involving all members of both groups; more likely, either the groups would be used separately in analogy to the pitched instruments, or the timbral differences between the percussion groups would be exploited to reinforce an intended differentiation between pitch groups, or both.

The pitched spectrum, by contrast, is based upon extremely precise frequency specifications and provides a uniform and consistent calibration of sound space. This kind of continuum, to which everything pitched can be related, is a powerful tool. However much Varèse might have wished to work outside the continuum—and there is plenty of evidence that he did, even to the extent of writing an entire piece that excludes definite pitches—he had nothing of comparable power to serve as a permanent substitute, and he knew it. In writing for pitches, while awaiting technical breakthroughs that would free music from the tempered scale, Varèse was forced into compromises he would not otherwise have made, but this is really beside the point. What matters is that the pieces we have now are written principally for pitches and must be interpreted through the nature of the pitch continuum as it existed then and as it exists now.

Varèse did not like the descriptor "unpitched" as applied to percussion; referring on one occasion to *Ionisation*, he called it his "work for unpitched instruments, although that is stupid for everything is pitched if but relatively."[23] In the words "if but relatively" lies the significance of Varèse's percussion writing with respect to pitch. From his statement that in the percussion section "there exist definite soprano, alto, tenor, and bass groups, susceptible of combination in four-part harmonies" it can readily be inferred that these terms refer to relative ranges and to harmonies of relative highness and lowness.[24]

It was Varèse's particular genius, however, to turn to his advantage what others might have perceived as inadequacies. The very fact that these percussion instruments have no definite pitch *does* free them, to the extent that their functions may occupy a spectrum ranging from close analogy to pitched events to none at all. By the same token, a greater or lesser degree of rhythmic resemblance between simultaneously or successively presented pitched and unpitched components may be used to depict relationships ranging from rhythmic unison to complete independence.[25]

In situations where the percussion scoring has been made quite closely analogous to scoring for pitches, pitched events tend to be perceived as a separate sphere of activity, essentially different from material that does not share this crucial characteristic. Even in the presence of unpitched events, then, pitched material has the requisite coherence to maintain a continuity of its own. For this reason, to the extent that they bear any relationship at all to pitched material, unpitched events take place in a kind of shadow world, where, singly or in groups, they reinforce, reflect, prefigure, or otherwise complement events in the pitched sphere.

Of these relationships, the most straightforward is reinforcement; in its simplest, purely rhythmic form it requires no illustration. Combined with timbral reinforcement, it becomes compositionally more specific and more interesting to talk about. In *Intégrales*, mm. 187–189 (beginning four measures before rehearsal 19), an uncomplicated instance of rhythmic combined with timbral reinforcement results in a palpable stratification. The entrance of two new reinforcing instruments in m. 189 after three occurrences of tam-tam and bass drum emphasizes the entrance of new pitched elements into the texture; further, because these elements are higher and of different timbral quality, the new reinforcing percussion sonority (gong and crash cymbal) takes on these characteristics as well with respect to the first percussion pair. In example 4.19 (*Hyperprism*, mm. 30–33) a succession of two chords is reinforced rhythmically in the percussion.[26] A clear timbral distinction is also made between the two: four percussion instruments play in

Example 4.19: *Hyperprism,* mm. 30–33

mm. 30–31, while four others, forming quite a different timbral mix, play in mm. 32–33. Furthermore, as indicated at (a) in the example, the second chord represents a symmetrical contraction from the first, and the more compact range of the second percussion sonority reinforces this as well: from the lowest sound in mm. 30–31 (bass drum) to the highest (cymbals) is a larger vertical distance than from the tam-tam to the single crash cymbal in mm. 32–33. In both of these examples the sound of the percussion instruments produces auras of approximate pitch around definite focuses, but clearly these auras do not interfere with the operation of the pitches themselves as exactly determined elements in spatial manipulation.

From rhythmic unisons we proceed to situations where pitched events are succeeded by unpitched ones which resemble them in some fashion. The range of possibilities, from specific to general resemblance, is large. In example 4.20 (*Déserts*, m. 47), the motivating force is literal reflection in the indefinite world of events originating as definite pitches. Four brass are balanced against four metallic percussion instruments. The initial event in the brass, F♯3, is followed by three more pitches: two lower than F♯3 and one higher, entering in ascending order. Then, in the percussion, one metallic instrument enters, followed by three more in succession: one lower and two higher.[27] For both the pitched and the unpitched group the last three instruments enter in order from lowest to highest, yet the resultant vertical order in the percussion, respective to the *initial* sound in the group, is a mirror image of the pitch order.

Slightly less specific but no less significant is the role of the percussion in the opening of the same piece (ex. 4.21, *Déserts*, mm. 1–11). The initial events in the developing stasis of the pitch material, discussed in example 4.16 above, are paralleled by the entrances of two suspended cymbals (m. 3) and three gongs (mm. 10–11). There are other parallels as well. Recall that in the opening measures first undivided, then divided dyads are presented; corresponding to these in the percussion are the two suspended cymbals (high, low) and the three gongs (high, medium, low) respectively. Notice as well that among the pitches there is a high group followed by a lower, a succession also duplicated by the relative pitch of the two percussion groups. Finally, the suspended cymbals assume two other specific functions: a timbral link at m. 5 between the flute/clarinet pair and the trumpets that momentarily succeed them on the same pitches; and rhythmic unisons at m. 10 emphasizing G5–C5. The use of rhythmic unison demonstrates that a pairing of pitched and unpitched sounds need not remain fixed. Here the change is particularly appropriate to the context of development within stasis.

Unpitched events appear less often as initiators of such relationships with pitched events, but even so this role for percussion can be an important composi-

Percussion:

1 = suspended cymbal
2 = high gong
3 = medium gong
4 = low gong

Example 4.20: *Déserts*, m. 47

tional device. In mm. 91–93 of *Intégrales* (rehearsal 9) the regular pulses in the gong and crash cymbal, which begin at the same point as the last attack of the pitch stasis, contrast strongly with the irregular rhythms of the measures preceding and serve as a bridge to m. 93, where the same quarter-note pulse—now on the beat— is taken up in trombones and percussion and continues intermittently through m. 100. More gradual but equally compelling as a transition in what happens in *Déserts*, mm. 87–92 (ex. 4.22), where a rather diffuse percussion texture built from isolated figures in thirteen different instruments leads to rhythmic unanimity in mm. 91–93 in just three instruments.[28] This change corresponds to the shift in the pitched instruments from the statically prolonged sonority of mm. 85–91 to the projected and rotated duplicate which begins to enter at the upbeat of m. 92 (see ex. 2.10), but it is the fact of contrast, not any specific rhythmic or timbral link between pitched and unpitched, that serves as the means of analogy. The change is timed differently in the two spheres: already in m. 88 we hear the figure in the snare drum that eventually becomes the basis of the new percussion texture of mm. 91–93, and this entire texture is already present in m. 91 before even the first pitch of the rotated sonority has entered. In addition, the single bass drum stroke at the downbeat of m. 92 prefigures the very low note (F1) which enters on the third beat of that measure as the bottom of the sonority.

Of these cause-effect successions in percussion and other instruments, perhaps the most interesting are those in which a reciprocal relationship exists. In mm. 23– 29 of *Déserts*, for instance (ex. 4.23), the low clarinet note is followed by high gong, then two pulses and another sustained note in two other percussion instruments. The pulses could be interpreted as responses to the figure D3–G#2 in the timpani (m. 23). By means of the triplet-based figure connections are made from the new rhythmic elaboration (m. 26) in the field drum to the clarinets (mm. 26–27) back to the field drum in m. 28. One receives the impression of a rhythmic evolution at each successive entrance, for the approach to and departure from the triplet figure is changed each time (although in ways that convey a clear resemblance). The even eighths in the wood drums and suspended cymbal at mm. 28–29 are another offshoot of the jogging triplet rhythm—and also, of course, an extension of the ascending motion in mm. 27–28. The triplet rhythm finally is picked up at m. 29 in the timpani and developed furiously—with the sixteenths now serving to concen- trate the gesture—precipitating the pitched upheaval in m. 30 (not shown in the example). The duplication of pitches D3 and G#2 from m. 23 to m. 29 means that the timpani part frames these measures, although it is clear that the progression to m. 30 could not have been carried through by the timpani alone. The sparse texture of these measures, intervening as it does between the denser scoring of mm. 21–22 and m. 30, provides an element of contrast and time for the elements of the chord in mm. 21–22 to be absorbed before further development is under- taken. For another, the development up to and including the precipitating rhythm of m. 29, and the resultant accumulation of intensity, are probably necessary for the upheaval at m. 30 to be convincing. Both the pitch and the rhythmic level lend the impression of departure from and return to the timpani: in the use of pitches,

Example 4.21: *Déserts*, mm. 1–11

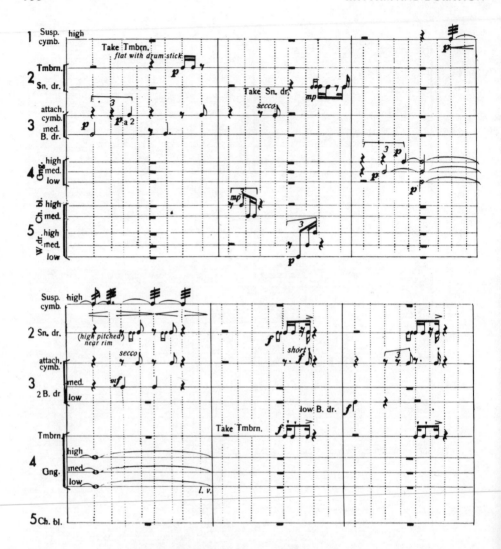

Example 4.22: *Déserts*, mm. 87–92, percussion

with no change (D3 and G♯2 move to the clarinets in m. 27); in the rhythm, as noted, with a significant difference.

On a grosser level, the entrances of the percussion section as a group often simply alternate with activity in the rest of the ensemble. A common gestural sequence in Varèse, for instance, begins with complex pitch activity and is followed by sustention in some or all parts; at this point or shortly thereafter the percussion, as if catalyzed by the pitches, often enters solo. Straightforward examples occur in *Ecuatorial*, mm. 14–18, with percussion entering in m. 16, followed by gradual diminuendo in all parts; in *Arcana*, following m. 242 (four measures before rehearsal 23) in *Intégrales*, mm. 101–103, where the percussion responds on the local level to the high woodwinds of m. 101, and on a larger scale breaks free from

Example 4.23: *Déserts*, mm. 23–29, clarinets and percussion

its exclusively reinforcing role in mm. 93–100. This escape from the role of
rhythmic doubling is also evident in *Amériques*, mm. 47–57 (rehearsal 5), where the
initial rhythmic activity is shared (through reinforcement) by the percussion,
which then departs on its own in m. 55. Earlier in *Amériques*, the first entrance of
the percussion comes in m. 9, after an abrupt surge in the pitched material in the
previous measure. Here there is no pitch sustention but, instead, a repetition of
the alto flute-harps pairing of the opening measures. In *Arcana*, mm. 28–31, the
percussion section is set apart in a unison rhythm which, although irregular, is
clear and distinct, in marked contrast with the orchestral rhythms before and after
it. The reverse is true in *Ecuatorial*, mm. 41–43 (beginning six measures before
rehearsal 4), where the rhythms in all five percussion parts in m. 42 are different
from one another (and are based on four different subdivisions of the beat),
resulting in a thicket of sound that stands in opposition to the unison rhythms of
the brass in mm. 41 and 43. Here the percussion seems intended to be heard as an
undifferentiated whole, rather than in stratification. This is also true of passages in
which the percussion serves the function of ostinato.

In summary, Varèse's unpitched percussion often fills a role that complements
the pitch material. Other evidence of this tendency can be found where activity in
the pitches—in terms both of speed of pitch change and of rhythmic intricacy—
increases to the level of the rapid motion discussed in chapter 3. At such points the
percussion usually disappears entirely, as it does in the rapid motion from *Intégrales* (mm. 53–69) analyzed in that chapter. Later in *Intégrales*, at the onset of the
complexities of mm. 117–126, the percussion again falls silent. And in the de-

veloping stasis of the opening of *Déserts* analyzed above, by m. 12, when rhythmic activity in the pitched parts has considerably increased, nothing further is heard from the unpitched component, and it stays out while pitch development continues and accelerates over the next several measures, entering again only when the accumulative chord of mm. 21–22 has begun to die away.

Activity of Percussion During Pitch Stasis

Pitch stasis would seem to present perfect conditions for prominent, independent development in the percussion. However, the percussion responds in a wide variety of ways to pitch stasis, all of them involving some degree of dependence. Unpitched development, where it does occur, is carried out at least in part in coordination with the articulation of durational units by the static pitch material. The next few examples are all taken from *Intégrales* and deal with the varying functions of percussion in several pitch-static passages.

The much-analyzed opening, mm. 1–25 (see ex. 4.24), is a classic instance of pitch stasis. From moment to moment the percussion presents a constantly shifting picture of instrumental combinations and rhythms; no two are alike. But the variety is not evidence of complete independence. In this passage the percussion's conformity to pitch-determined structures is actually more significant than its divergence. Rhythmic unisons are combined with timbral amplifications at mm. 8, 14, 16, and 22; more important, the changes in instrumental combination in the percussion are in general coordinated with the boundaries of the durational

F = figure (first occurrences: skeletal form, E♭ clarinet, m. 1; complete form, C trumpet, m. 10)

C = chords (first occurrences: B♭ clarinet and piccolos, m. 5; trombones, m. 5)

(See ex. 3.12)

List of percussion instruments and abbreviations

Suspended Cymbal	(S. Cym.)	Tambourine	(Tamb.)
Snare Drum	(S. Dr.)	Gong	(Gg.)
Tenor Drum	(T. Dr.)	Tam-Tam	(T.-T.)
Castanets	(Ctts.)	Triangle	(Tgl.)
Cymbals	(Cyms.)	Crash Cymbal	(Cr. Cym.)
Chinese Blocks	(Ch. Bl.)	Twigs	(Tw.)
Sleigh Bells	(Sl. B.)	Bass Drum	(B. Dr.)
Chains	(Ch.)		

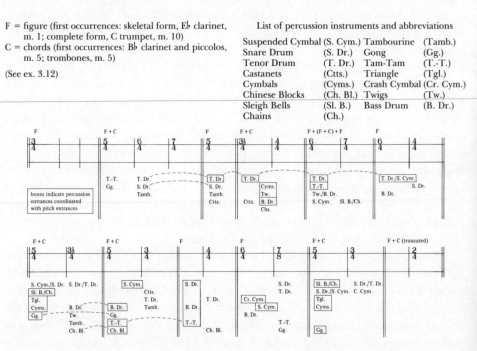

Example 4.24: *Intégrales*, mm. 1–25

units—although occasional overlap and frequent use of one or two common instruments in adjacent pairs of units slightly blur the correspondence. (In the example, dotted ties show where particular percussion instruments continue recognizably across unit boundaries.) Minor shifts within units generally correspond to entrances of the two trichords (woodwinds and trombones), even if not precisely coordinated rhythmically, or mark the point at which all elements of the unit have entered and sustain together. This passage is a kind of exposition for the percussion, in that the resources for the piece are set forth here. To some extent, like the pitches, it is static, in the sense that the available components are juxtaposed and combined through continuous rhythmic changes. Of the fifteen percussion instruments employed in this passage eleven have been heard at least once by m. 10, and of the remaining four only the Chinese blocks are used prominently (m. 15). On the other hand, the complete lack of repetition among the combinations chosen suggests that the percussion is meant to some extent to portray an ongoing progression, in the same way that the durational units do in their constantly varying lengths.

The next pitch stasis, mm. 32–52, is considerably different. Here there is no question that the pitched and unpitched elements are closely coordinated. A durational analysis of the passage (ex. 4.25) shows that the stasis consists of the alternation between two distinct blocks of material in the wind instruments: low sounds alone, (L), and a wide-spectrum configuration, (L + H). Always associated with (L + H) are suspended cymbal, crash cymbal, gong, tam-tam, and bass drum.[29] Associated with (L) are bass drum, tam-tam, and any or all of the following: Chinese blocks, sleigh bells, tenor drum, and snare drum.[30] There is only one exception to this pattern: the crash cymbals rubbed together at m. 37 as part of the group associated with (L). And at m. 44, where the one intrusion of foreign pitched material occurs in what otherwise would have been an (L) segment, the percussion compensates by omitting all but the "basic" bass drum and tam-tam. Other aspects besides these combinations are fixed: bass drum and tam-tam always enter in unison with the trombones in (L); gong, crash cymbal, and suspended cymbal always enter in unison with the trumpets in (L + H). Overall, these factors lend the passage a rigid and tightly controlled character, as opposed to the more flexible, almost open quality of mm. 1–25.

Measures 79–93, also discussed in a previous example (4.10), could most justifiably of all passages in *Intégrales* be described as a case of independent percussion. As in mm. 1–25, the percussion parts consist of a kaleidoscopic series of variations in instrumental combination, but unlike the earlier passage, the timing of these changes does not correspond very closely to the boundaries of the pitch-static units as delineated in example 4.10. There is, however, an approximate correspondence between the shifts in the percussion and the alternation between rhythmically active (A) and sustained (S) material in the pitched parts, as shown in example 4.26. Interestingly enough, the percussion turns out to be grouped quite clearly by bar lines. Also notice that the two trombone interjections are clearly emphasized, via rhythmic reinforcement, by the percussion.

Example 4.25: *Intégrales*, mm. 32–36, percussion and winds (rhythm only)

The last example of this group treats mm. 105–117. Not included among our earlier examples of pitch stasis, this passage could best be classified, based solely upon the behavior of the pitched material, as one in which specific, disruptive events toward the end eventually interfere sufficiently with the stasis to end it (see ex. 4.27). The pitched elements are in two groups, labeled A and B in the example. Throughout, each A forms a pair with the subsequently entering B; A always enters first and is sustained through the duration of B. At the sixth occurrence of this pattern, the B from the fifth occurrence is sustained through the following A, which has not happened up to this point. Then the sixth B breaks off in its two-chord alternation after the second chord instead of the first, which is also a new

Example 4.26: *Intégrales,* mm. 79–93, percussion and winds (rhythm only)

Example 4.26 *continued*

Example 4.26 *continued*

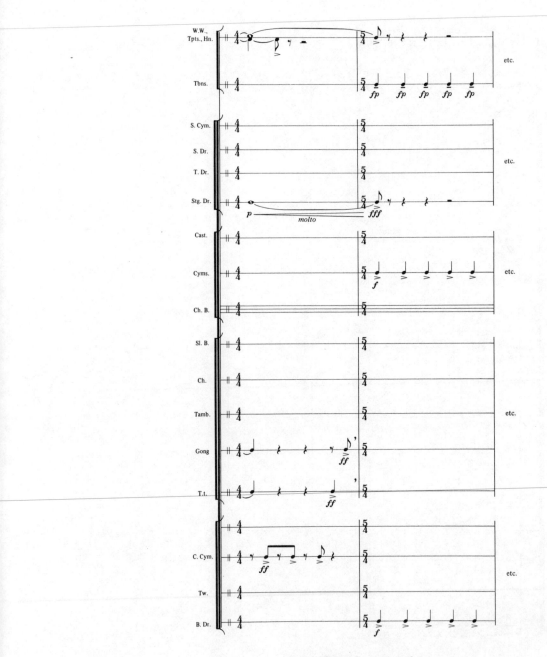

Example 4.26 *continued*

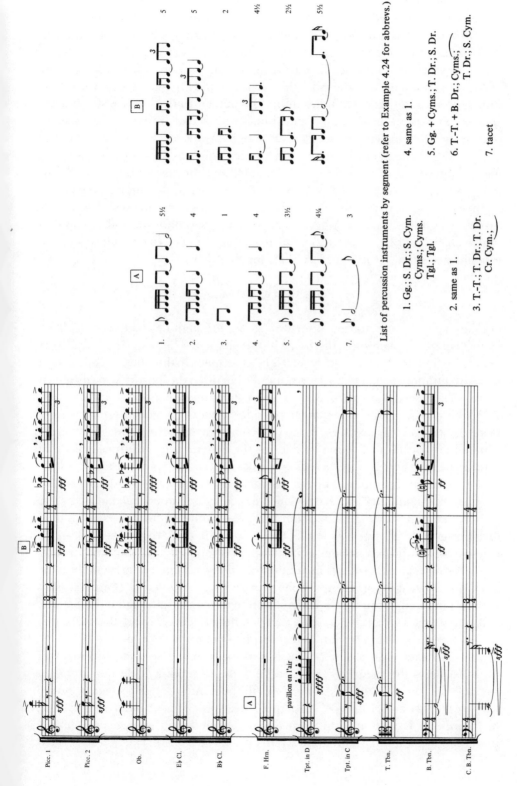

Example 4.27: *Intégrales*, mm. 105–117

event (truncation). Truncation of a more drastic kind follows immediately, as the seventh A is succeeded by new material instead of a response by B in m. 117.

By contrast, the percussion provides a thread of progression in which the rate of change steadily increases. (Refer to the numbered lists of instruments in ex. 4.27. The entrances of the percussion are in rhythmic unison with the components of A: one or two parts together with the trombone and C trumpet, then the others with various of the repeated notes in the D trumpet. In the lists the successively entering percussion instruments [individuals or groups] are separated by semicolons.) In no. 3 the change is slight, although significant. No. 4 returns to the norm of nos. 1 and 2; no. 5 represents a bigger change, as the cymbal sound joins the reinforcement of trombone and trumpet, and the suspended cymbal's entrance is delayed to reinforce B rather than A. The pace of alteration is accelerated further in no. 6, with the entrance of bass drum and the roll in crescendo on the suspended cymbal. And the biggest change of all is saved for the end: no percussion at all.[31] The percussion thus plays an overall dynamic role that bears a close resemblance to its role in mm. 135–143 (see ex. 4.12).

Percussion as Ostinato

Ostinato is, in Varèse's terms, a form of stasis, although of a kind not precisely equivalent to the pitch stasis discussed in this chapter. The frozen characteristics tend to be both timbral and rhythmic. The ensemble rhythm, both locally and in terms of durational scheme, varies constantly, but often the individual parts repeat more or less exactly (at irregular intervals) a rhythmic cell of some kind.

In this role unpitched material can provide continuity while changes are taking place elsewhere in the texture. This too is a complementary function, but of a very generalized sort. Under these conditions the timbral and rhythmic links that connect pitched and unpitched regions do not for the most part exist, a condition as close to literal realization as possible of the idea of unrelated sound masses. The percussion is in another space, one which has, at least temporarily, nothing to do with the semitone-calibrated spectrum. In *Ecuatorial* the percussion section is used extensively in this manner; examples can be found in mm. 99–101 and 106–114, where the percussion continues uninterrupted through the big pitch articulation at m. 111. *Amériques* also makes use of this technique to some extent, notably in the pitch-static passage beginning at rehearsal 39 (mm. 419–441). The percussion here is composed to convey a feeling of noninvolvement; although it doubles the triple- and quadruple-forte crashes, these do not effectively break the continuity of the entire percussion section in pianissimo—not for a while, anyway.

An elaborate example of percussion ostinato in the second movement of *Offrandes* bears the notation, "La batterie dans un sentiment de monotonie et somnolence." In example 4.28 (mm. 4–7), the beginning of this passage is shown. This is a true ostinato, with a period of three measures; it has an independent logic, not coordinated with that of the pitched parts, which meanwhile present a steadily unfolding structure (partially analyzed in exx. 3.9 and 3.18). The notes in dotted

Example 4.28: *Offrandes*, II ("La croix du sud"), mm. 4–7, percussion

circles ("accentuées légèrement dominant") participate in the ostinato but also occur on their own—in mm. 1–3, for instance. The ostinato is truncated near the end of its third period (m. 12) but resurfaces in mm. 25–27 and 45–47, and bits and pieces of it are also scattered elsewhere in the movement. Used in this way, the static, repeated material conveys the sense of an undercurrent to the music, not really involved with it and essentially unchanging. Its mysterious quality is entirely appropriate to the text, a poem by José Juan Tablada entitled "La croix du sud" ("The Southern Cross").[32]

Combination of Complementation and Independent Development

The percussion in the third and final large section of *Intégrales* shares with that of the second movement of *Offrandes* the characteristic of independence and displays it in a similar manner, by periodically submerging and resurfacing. The differences between the two are, first, that in the third section of *Intégrales* the reappearances of the percussion have a distinctly complementary function vis-à-vis the pitched material, and second that the percussion is evolving rather than static. As to the first, the percussion begins the section unaccompanied, and its appearances thereafter (until m. 217, after which it disappears until its reinforcement of the final chord of the work) are mostly either solo or set against minimal activity in the pitched parts. Thus pitched and unpitched exist throughout the section in a kind of balance, although only rarely are specific connections made between their components. The second is executed subtly: the rhythms and instrumentation chosen for each successive appearance are similar enough to their predecessors in the piece to be associative but at the same time altered enough to qualify as a portrayal of evolution.[33]

The process begins at m. 158, three measures before rehearsal 16 (mm. 155–157, also solo percussion, continue the diminuendo of the climactic chord of the previous section). Here the two most important associative elements are introduced: the Chinese blocks, in linear presentation, and snare drum/tenor drum, in a quick burst. The blocks' material has the character of a solo line, and becomes analogous throughout the passage to the various pitched solo lines: oboe at m. 161, D trumpet at m. 174, trombone at m. 186, and so on, although there is almost never any more specific connection made between them.

In mm. 174–176 the percussion returns, with the two associative elements present again, in amplification: snare and tenor drums have acquired the suspended cymbal, and their group is enlarged temporally as well, while the blocks' line is longer and more florid. A third element introduced here, consisting of sleigh bells and chains, has a definite timbral resemblance to the high woodwind chord at m. 175.

The measure of solo percussion at m. 183, together with the material at m. 186, exaggerate the previous successive presentation of snare/tenor drums and blocks in that there are now two intervening measures in which no percussion is heard. Here the snare/tenor/cymbal group is developed further, adding the timbre produced by striking the shell of the tenor drum. The high, "dry" qualities of this group are amplified by the introduction at this point of castanets, tambourine, and twigs.[34] At m. 186 the sextuplet in the blocks is a specific link to the trombone's rapid notes.

The reinforcing roles taken in mm. 187–189 have already been mentioned. At m. 190, a snare/tenor/cymbal burst occurs, which, though coordinated with the pitch climax, is rhythmically a solo figure. The grand outburst at mm. 195–197 is also coordinated with pitch development. The techniques are analogous: almost every instrument comes into play in both realms (in the percussion, this means almost every instrument heard so far in the section in an independent role; only twigs are omitted), and each, once it has entered, plays one pitch or a short figure in constantly varying rhythm. Thus pitched and unpitched exhibit a parallel stasis. The appended block figure (m. 198, the last appearance of this instrument) connects clearly to the sixteenths in the clarinet leading into m. 199.

In its last two appearances the percussion texture continues to change by small degrees. At m. 213 it begins as if prematurely, with castanets and suspended cymbal taking reinforcing roles in m. 212. The use of the triangle with suspended cymbal at this point serves to isolate and emphasize one facet of the element to which the cymbal still belongs. In some respects m. 217 is a direct parallel to m. 213, as the rhythmic figures are closely similar in the castanets, tenor, and snare, and the reintroduced tambourine and sleigh bells represent a slight shift in timbre. The overall sound is higher and provides a convincing connection from the high woodwinds in mm. 215–216 and their reappearance in m. 218.

Percussion Alone

Not every solo percussion passage in Varèse can be considered truly independent. In the solo excerpts from *Intégrales* just analyzed, for instance, the continual resurfacing of a specific texture works against hearing any excerpt as self-sufficient. *Ionisation,* naturally enough, stands as the premier example of percussive self-sufficiency—but it is also possible for brief solo passages, set off by pitched material, to assume this quality. *Déserts* provides a number of instructive examples, two of which are analyzed below.

Measures 264–269 (ex. 4.29) are a special sort of solo percussion passage: drums only. Five distinct pitch levels are called for, numbered in example 4.30 from (1), highest, to (5), lowest. The excerpt begins with a rhythmically complementary relationship between (2) and (3). Together these initially form the middle of the total range, framed in the next measure by highest and lowest. Next, with respect to (2) and (3), (5) and (4) form an analogous pair in inversion, although temporally much compressed compared to its predecessor. These pairings leave (1) isolated, and in a sense it maintains its isolation throughout, for its roll, shaped by crescendo and diminuendo, is the only element with a consistently different dynamic shape. But the temporal proximity of (5) and (4) may be taken as an indication that (1) and (2) might develop a paired relationship by virtue of their own proximity, which begins at the end of m. 265 and becomes simultaneity, thus even more intensely proximate. Thus, even though (2) and (3) maintain their successive complementary relationship through m. 267, (1) and (2) establish a pairing which exists in tandem with (2) and (3) during this period. Further, the roll in (2), which (3) does not have, increases the resemblance between (1) and (2), and its extension in (2) at m. 267 to the duration of a whole beat consummates the relationship.

Meanwhile, (3) has been developing a distinct character of its own: in mm. 266–268 its figure is precisely the same at each entrance. Thus, through these measures (and, in retrospect, beginning with the last half of m. 265) the succession (5)(4), (1)(2), (3) becomes increasingly clear. Finally, in mm. 268–269, (3) is left completely alone. The overall process could be described as the establishment of (relative) pitch symmetry to the midpoint represented by (3). The *idea* of symmetry can already be detected in the pairs that begin the passage, subsequently supplanted by relationship of outer pairs to a central focus, a kind of contraction. It is

Example 4.29: *Déserts*, mm. 264–269

not difficult to make a connection from this to the accumulating sonority which follows in the pitched instruments in m. 270 and radiates outward from the (approximately) central pitch that sounds first.

Earlier in *Déserts*, mm. 200–203 also exploit the possibilities of relative pitch, here in combination with a greater timbral range. The opening (see ex. 4.30) places two timbrally similar instruments in complementary opposition: rhythmically alternating and (with respect to relative pitch) in inversion. The clear timbres of the wood drums and Chinese blocks are succeeded, in m. 201, by the "fuzzy" timbres of guiro, maracas, and snare drum. The clear sounds, as perhaps is suggested by the use of the highest block at the end of m. 200, migrate in m. 201 to the high-pitched claves. Among the fuzzy sounds, only the maracas preserve any

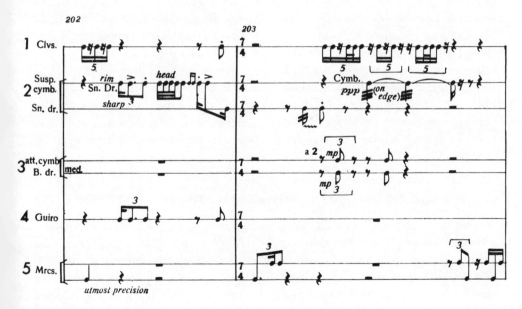

Example 4.30: *Déserts*, mm. 200–203

distinction in pitch level within the same instrument.[35] In m. 202 the snare responds to the claves with a variation of the rhythm of its last three pitches and the clearer timbre produced by playing on the rim. At the same time this first figure (second beat) is heard in unison with the guiro, thus ensuring that the connection with the fuzzy group is preserved. This connection is strengthened by the return to the snare head in the third beat. At the end of the measure claves and guiro are united rhythmically, an event which suggests convergence of the two timbral groups. A clear pitch distinction is made in the snare drum/side drum figure on the fourth beat, answered (in approximate inversion) in m. 203, in the maracas.[36] Measure 203 is marked by a widening of the total range (to include bass drum), the uniting of the fuzzy and clear timbres of high instruments (respectively, claves and suspended cymbal, the latter played near the edge), and a final figure for the maracas.

Taken in context, the passage could be said to resemble, in its beginning with sounds that are *almost* definite pitches, the music that immediately precedes it: m. 199, a remarkable 11/4 measure, at the same constant soft dynamic level indicated for mm. 200–203, and characterized by a maximal clarity of pitch definition, in that eleven different pitches are presented—each only once, and only one at a time—of which no two form an octave or octave compound.[37] As for what follows, the expansion noted in m. 203 also occurs in the pitches in m. 204. Analogously to the high emphasis in m. 203, the high notes in 204 are emphasized by the opening from near the bottom which soars to the top, and by the high pitches sustained into m. 205.

In short, the vast variety of possible combinations among the percussion instruments need not be an obstacle to analysis. The intricate details of Varèse's percussion scoring do present a potential pitfall, in that one runs the risk of becoming preoccupied with the intricacy for its own sake and feeling compelled to classify all of its aspects. Ultimately, however, like all other features of Varèse's music, the percussion must function as part of process, and thus the role of the constantly changing percussion textures may satisfactorily be explained as a way of portraying the unidirectional and irreversible nature of that process. That is, the primary significance of the fact that a particular percussion texture at a particular point in a work is not a repetition of a previous texture and will not itself be repeated later on may very well be simply that it *is* unique.

THE ROLE OF RHYTHM IN "MOTIVIC" OR "THEMATIC" REFERENCE

Arnold Whittall has found a singularly apt phrase for process in Varèse: "organic athematicism."[38] Even references to previous points in a piece do not violate the principles indentified in this phrase, for however much the material in question may resemble other material heard before, it is always integrated into its actual context. Thus the facile analogies that have been made between Varèse's recalls of earlier moments and the "cross-cutting," deliberately discontinuous splicing techniques of avant-garde film makers do not stand up to scrutiny. Varèse may have intended the sensation of flashback in some cases, but not a sensation of temporal rupture. The feeling of going onward and outward, on "a journey into space," is always present. The references are not turnings inward or backward; rather, they are indicators of how far the piece has come in its progress from the original music. Supporting this interpretation is the fact that no reference is ever an exact repetition: these musical fragments, echoing and resounding across the expanse of the composition, undergo permanent changes. Of course, it is perfectly possible Varèse's techniques have inspired younger composers to attempt compositional procedures analogous to cinematographic cross-cutting, the sort of thing which has been termed "anti-teleological" in some quarters. This response to Varèse's work would not necessarily be artistically invalid. The same can be said of the admiration reportedly expressed by such stalwarts of the avant-garde as Earle Brown and Morton Feldman for the "it-ness" of Varèse's sonorities, for their supposed self-sufficiency as objects—"coming from nowhere, going nowhere."[39] Such reactions and interpretations only demonstrate that evolution eventually produces offspring only remotely resembling the ancestors.

Apart from this, is Varèse's music thematic in a more traditional sense? After the earlier resolution of the process-object dichotomy in favor of process, any suggestion that Varèse's music is thematic should be viewed with skepticism. The recurrence of recognizable versions of earlier material should not be construed as evidence of thematic structure. This material is indeed *transformed,* but not exactly *developed.* For one thing, its presence is not pervasive enough. Even in *Arcana,* where the well-known three-note figure (see m. 1: A–B♭2–C3) may have a unifying, continuity-producing effect, the problem with the connections established through the figure is not that they are false, but that they are too obvious—in the end, they don't tell us very much about the real sources of continuity.

The same can be said of the figure in *Amériques* that appears initially in the alto flute (m. 1). Of all the instances of reuse in Varèse, this perhaps resembles most, although even so only vestigially, the process of thematic development: the figure reappears in recognizable form in different rhythms, in new instrumentation, and even with its pitch structure altered. Nevertheless, there is never any attempt to create a feeling of *return* with the figure. Rather, there is a palpable sense of irreversibility about the process, for once the alto flute has given up the figure it can never recur there. Notice, too, that the original form is first quoted nearly verbatim, then in versions that resemble the original to progressively lesser degrees—first with harps and bassoon (mm. 9–10), then with harps only (mm. 19–21), then again with harps, but joined by new material before even a full statement is completed (mm. 26–27), then, finally, alone (mm. 43–46), ending with the initial B explicitly taken over by another instrument. From this point on not only does the figure never appear again in the alto flute, but the alto flute itself disappears from the orchestration for the rest of the work. Compare Varèse's characterization (quoted earlier) of the initial idea in a composition as "only an ostensible motive which will gradually disappear as though absorbed, and finally eliminated, by the work that is taking shape."[40]

For all that, however, reference in Varèse is not uninteresting as a phenomenon. Beyond the obvious fact of resemblance, references to previous material often provide clues, principally through their various rhythmic associations, to continuity. This is demonstrated in a particularly vivid way by *Arcana,* which makes more extensive use of reference than any of Varèse's other pieces. There are at least a dozen readily recognizable figural fragments and rhythmic patterns involved in the network of reused material, but not all of them are referenced throughout as distinct, isolated entities. Some instead develop links to one another through certain of their characteristics. From this it follows that not every reference to previous material is equally specific; some, because of their multiple significance, are necessarily more diffuse. Further, some passages that occur as references, but which have distinct qualities of their own as well, may in turn become referents themselves.

Among the referenced materials of *Arcana* are four items of varying degrees of

Example 4.31: *Arcana,* occurrences of repeated-note figure

importance which through reuse become linked, some more directly than others. The first of these is also the most prominent, if prominence can be measured by number of references. It first appears in m. 32, horns (see ex. 4.31a) and will be called the repeated-note figure. In this and its next two appearances, all in the same passage (mm. 36 and 39, exx. 4.31b and c), the rhythmic form remains precisely the same up to the sixth note. After this initial group of occurrences, however, the figure undergoes a rhythmic transformation: the five thirty-seconds beginning on an upbeat become a one-beat quintuplet beginning on the beat (m. 59, ex. 4.31d), which in turn becomes the recognizable rhythmic association for most subsequent references. Note also the broadening of textural reference in mm. 128–130 and 160–161, where the figure is portrayed by all or most of the orchestra at once; this will have significance later on. Clearly related to the repeated-note figure at its inception is the second item, the "tune" in high wood-winds, xylophone, and glockenspiel beginning at m. 79 (ex. 4.32a). The link here is quite specific, consisting of a single-pitch quintuplet, followed by a rest, then a longer note still on the same pitch. Subsequent references to this focus upon other features unique to the tune, as examples 4.32b (mm. 215–217) and 4.32c (mm.

a) mm. 79-91, oboes; doubled at 8ve, E♭ Cl., Fls., Xylo;
         doubled at 15th, Piccs., Glock.

b) mm. 215-17, oboes; same doublings as at m. 79 (B♭ Cl. added at 8ve)

c) mm. 283-84, oboes; same doublings   m. 285, rhythm only:
         as at m. 215 (Glock. tacet)   high W.W. and Tpts.

Example 4.32: *Arcana,* occurrences of "tune"

Example 4.33: *Arcana,* occurrences of sixteenth stream

283–284) show. All three are also associated through a similar accompanying percussion texture (not shown). The last of these passages, mm. 283–284, leads directly into quintuplets (m. 285), which serves both to recall the associations made in m. 79 and to incorporate the expanded textural range of the repeated-note figure.

The third item from *Arcana* is the stream of sixteenth notes in high strings/high woodwinds in mm. 46–48 (ex. 4.33a). It is referenced very shortly thereafter (mm. 53–55, ex. 4.33b) in juxtaposition with material in the lower instruments, then much later but still in recognizable form in mm. 234–237 and 393–394, in both cases with lower material in triplets against the sixteenths. This rhythmic metamorphosis also has future significance. In fact, it is foreshadowed, if not exactly paralleled, by what happens to the fourth item in its initial form in mm. 92–96 (ex. 4.34a). Here, triplets begin and are subsequently opposed by groups of four. The reference at mm. 301–327 (ex. 4.34b) preserves this rhythmic feature along with the pitch/registral relationship of mm. 92–96, as does the last reference of this group, mm. 403–409 (ex. 4.34c).

We have identified the following:

Item	Label
1	repeated-note figure
2	W.W./Xylo./Glock. "tune"
3	sixteenth stream
4	triplet vs. quadruplet

Example 4.34: *Arcana,* occurrences of three versus four

These materials, and the changes imposed upon them through referencing, have a great deal to do with what happens in the passage immediately following the second reference to item 4 (mm. 410–426). The relationship triplet vs. quadruplet flows directly into triplet vs. quintuplet and thus represents an extension of the relationship embodied in item 4: three divisions of the beat → four → five. However, as can be seen from example 4.35 (mm. 410–411) the registral and textural location of the opposed rhythmic patterns is not that of mm. 403–409: the triplets have been shifted to the lower instruments, and the quintuplets have taken a higher position than their quadruplet predecessors'. The resemblance to the disposition of the triplet vs. quadruplet in the later references to the sixteenth stream (item 3) is strikingly clear, as is the overall contour of the quintuplet line, with a single predominant pitch from which the line makes periodic and momentary departures. As this occurs, however, many of the quintuplet groups, at least

Example 4.35: *Arcana*, mm. 410–411

up to m. 414, remain on one pitch, inevitably suggesting the form of the repeated-note figure, item 1. Item 2 does not figure directly in this passage; its effects, as noted, were felt earlier.

In overview, the repeated-note figure and the W.W./Xylo./Glock. tune formed a relationship of reciprocal influence; a similar association joined the sixteenth stream and the triplet vs. quadruplet idea; finally, features of items 1, 3, and 4 are combined. Of these, 1 is represented in the most general terms, and one might ask whether the successive quintuplets here really constitute a reference to the specific quintuplet form introduced as the repeated-note figure. As if in affirmative answer come mm. 427–431, which are not just a reference to the general figure, but refer to one particular form of it, mm. 104–108. The incipits of the two are juxtaposed in example 4.36. Besides drawing the connection between the two uses of the quintuplet, mm. 427–431 also reinterpret mm. 104–108 (previously only a reference) as a referent in their own right. These passages are the only two uses of the figure at a soft dynamic (the brass muted and marked lontanissimo—in both cases contrasting with what immediately precedes—and both are associated with almost exactly the same ensemble of unpitched percussion instruments (used here in complementary fashion).

This analysis leaves out a great deal of what could be said about referenced material in *Arcana,* for there are other points of contact between these and other identifiable entities. However, it should suffice to illustrate the special function of rhythm in providing continuity. Not all of Varèse's pieces work this way. Although

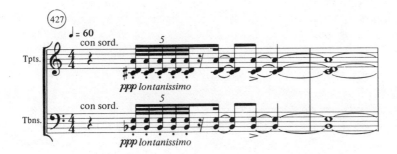

Example 4.36: *Arcana,* brass (repeated-note figure)

referenced material is common to all, what is referenced is not necessarily combined or subjected to any other sort of metamorphosis that could be regarded as compositionally significant. *Ionisation* is another work in which extensive use is made of rhythmic reference, in alliance with timbral reference; a few especially interesting instances of rhythmic reference through metamorphosis should be mentioned.[41] Two elements from the opening measures are displayed in example 4.37: in (a), the tenor drum and bass drums in m. 1 and m. 4—Slonimsky's "characteristic figure"[42]—and in (b), the bongo figure beginning in m. 9. The first recognizable reference to (a) comes early on, in mm. 13–14. Already the rhythm is slightly altered, smoothed out (ex. 4.38a). The LHHLH pattern of ex. 4.37b turns up in the snare drum/tenor drum pair from m. 23 on, also with a slight alteration (ex. 4.38b). Of major significance in the transformation of both (a) and (b) is the forte-fortissimo section, mm. 38–50, which divides into the two static passages discussed in detail earlier. (Refer to exx. 4.11 and 4.14.) In mm. 38–41 the HLL pattern of (a) has become thoroughly regularized into a triplet continuing the process begun in m. 13. All instruments in the texture involved in the triplets that make any distinction at all in pitch conform to this pattern. In mm. 44–50 the triplet texture continues, here portrayed by the same three drums that gave (a) its original form. Opposed to and in alternation with it are the quintuplets, which refer more or less exactly to (b): the LHHLH pattern is preserved, and the placement of accents in the first quintuplet divide the group analogously to the division imposed by the two sixteenth notes in the bongos at m. 9.

In the Varèsian context, dealing with the notion of referenced material is made particularly difficult by the conditions imposed upon analysis: we are constantly tempted to think of the materials and their references as *things* which stand primarily for themselves rather than as representations of something else—the process of the work. None of us can completely escape the principles of "thematic

Example 4.37: *Ionisation*, mm. 1–4, tenor and bass drums; mm. 9–11, bongos

analysis" inculcated in elementary theory classes, in which we all looked for themes, motives, and their recurrences as if they were objects because it was easier than finding what it was that they were making happen—or rather, of what they were really just the outward manifestations. In an abstract art, which music surely is, ultimately *nothing* has the status of object; nonetheless, there may be a sense in which for some music—perhaps for much music—themes and motives are concretions, if only because people insisted and still insist upon thinking of them that way. Further, it would be naive to suggest that the tendency to think of musical entities in this manner, probably more characteristic of the era which was waning during Varèse's youth than of any other era in the history of Western music, was brought to an abrupt end in, say, 1910, or that Varèse himself managed to cast aside completely the effects of being exposed to such tendencies in his formative years. Even if some of the painters to whom he listened sought to focus upon process rather than object, not everyone was of the same opinion, and in any case old habits die hard. We would ignore at our peril the possibility that what we have been calling Varèse's "references" are in some sense "recurrences": not just ghosts, but full-bodied recreations. Hence the preceding discussion of "items" whose existence is established not just by a single occurrence to which all subsequent similar passages are subsidiary, but by several or even many occurrences. As long as we don't confuse this process with thematic development we will not have compromised our original principles.

   The whole subject of rhythm/duration has long been problematic in analytic discussions of Varèse's music. Some difficulties remain to be disposed of, but in this chapter techniques have been found for dealing with this domain which disperse some of the mystery—not to say mystique—surrounding it. This will, it is hoped, make further fruitful consideration of rhythm/duration's true role in

Example 4.38: *Ionisation*, mm. 13–14, tenor and bass drums; mm. 23–24, snare and tenor drums

Varèse possible. To this end the special conditions that bring rhythm and duration to structural prominence, both in general terms and in specific situations, have been addressed. Still to be considered is the overall function in context of pitch-static passages and passages largely or wholly controlled by percussion of indefinite pitch. Do they represent breaks in the pitch/registral continuum, or arbitrarily obsessive treatments of particular phases in its process? Part of the problem here is that it is hard to generalize, for there are many purposes to which these devices may be put. The full-length analyses in the following chapter provide some indication of the range of possibilities.

FIVE

ANALYSES

Depending upon individual inclinations, the reader may regard the contents of this chapter either as a continuation of the previous text or as a kind of reference material. That is, while there is something to be gained from reading each of the two analyses presented here straight through, from beginning to end, it is also possible to examine the treatment of isolated short sections without following the analysis closely from the beginning. The choice of works for this chapter is largely the outcome of pragmatic considerations. Both *Hyperprism* and *Density 21.5* are fairly short and are composed for sufficiently different media to demonstrate the wide applicability of the analytical procedures developed in the three preceding chapters.

HYPERPRISM

Measures 1–11

Pitched material begins in m. 2; from here through m. 11 C♯4, carried mainly by the trombone but also doubled by and passed occasionally to the horn, dominates the texture (see ex. 5.1). Glissandi ending on C♯4 occur from above and below. These define an area initially bounded by B3 and F4—not quite symmetrical about C♯4—but the symmetry is completed in m. 11 when the horn, having superseded the trombone permanently as the conveyor of C♯4, appears with the figure in example 5.2. This imitates the other quick-note figures that have converged to C♯4, but it is not a glissando. Together with the timbral alteration of C♯4, this can be taken as a signal of imminent change.

The pattern of durations established by the alternation of C♯4 between trombone and horn also works in favor of an end to pitch stasis. Example 5.3 sets forth this scheme in beats, beginning with the trombone's first entrance. Because the trombone alone presents the glissandi it has a prominence as a solo instrument which is not entirely faithfully represented by the number of beats that it occupies.

Example 5.1: *Hyperprism*, mm. 2–4, horn 1 and trombone

Example 5.2: *Hyperprism*, m. 11, horn

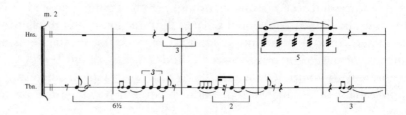

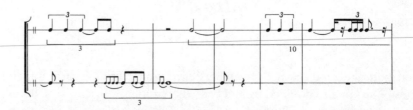

Example 5.3: *Hyperprism*, mm. 2–11, horns and trombone, rhythmic scheme

A glance at the score, however, shows plainly that the horns do become more and more active rhythmically with each successive entrance (see ex. 5.4 below), and that their parts in m. 7 seem to provoke the especially intricate outburst in the trombone in mm. 7–8. The durational series here, interestingly enough, has an underlying regularity: trombone 3, horns 3, trombone 3. The last segment, however, disrupts the regularity by continuing to an extreme level the tendency of the horns' part to increase in importance, a development which is reflected in the beat count for the horns: 3, 5, 3, 10 at successive entrances.

The percussion meanwhile plays both an independent and a supporting role.

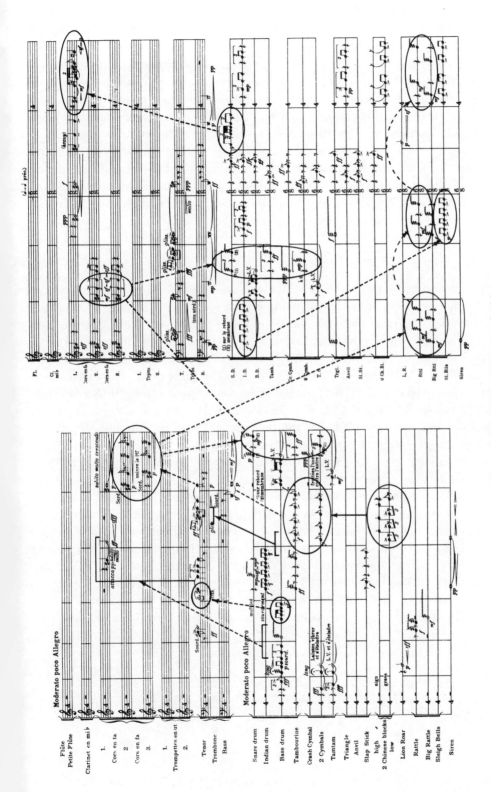

Example 5.4: *Hyperprism*, mm. 1–11

No parallel stasis here: percussion begins the piece, and both the combinations of instruments in use from moment to moment and the rhythms that they play are in constant flux through m. 11. There is only a rough and rather tenuous correspondence between the points of the trombone/horn alternation and the changes of percussion instrumentation. Example 5.4, however, reveals the rhythmic connections between the pitched and unpitched realms—connections which, although not precise imitations, nevertheless produce a network of mutual, approximate influence involving such characteristics as alternation, rolls, flutter-tonguing, and crescendo. Near the end of the passage, coinciding with the end of the trombone part in m. 9, there is a move toward coalescence, with a larger number of instruments in ensemble than has been heard up to this point. This has a climactic effect on the local level that contributes to sectional articulation.

Measures 12–18

From the upbeat to m. 5 onward, D2 has also been present, albeit intermittently, as the real lower boundary. This pitch influences events at m. 12: the top pitch in the texture becomes C6, which is the same distance, [23], above C♯4 as D2 is below. As for C♯5, which appears simultaneously with C6 in m. 12, together with F4 it is a projection of the interval A3–F4, the boundary of the sound mass previously maintained about C♯4. The pitch F4, then, is the pivot in this instance of self-projection (see detail, ex. 5.5). At the same time, a relationship is clearly established between C♯5 and C♯4. The literally stated interval of the octave, which suggests that the new pitch has the potential to represent the old, develops a longer-range significance as the piece progresses.

The upbeat to m. 15 contains new pitch material: the horns enter with [4][4]: (D–F♯–B♭)4, a configuration which corresponds exactly to the arrangement of C♯4 and the outer boundaries of the material that surrounds it in mm. 2–11, A3–(C♯–F)4. Again projection has occurred (ex. 5.6). The particular level to which this formation is projected places D4, the bottom edge, as far below C♯5 as C6 is above C♯5: both are [11]-spans and figure in this new development as well. Adjacencies are also significant: outer boundaries D4 and B♭4 form an instance of [3][8] with C♯5, while C♯5 and C6 form [3][11] with B♭4 (detail, ex. 5.7). The [11]-span also influences the next two events in the pitch domain. First (again see ex. 5.6), it produces F1 and E2, by projection, in the trombones of the downbeat of m. 15.

Example 5.5: *Hyperprism,* mm. 2–12

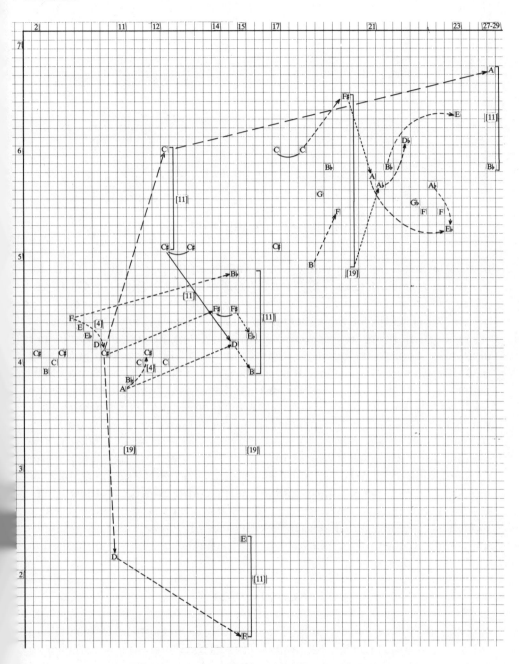

Example 5.6: *Hyperprism*, mm. 1–29

Second, B3 and E♭4 in the trumpets, while clearly on one level a projection of the
[4]-span components of (D–F♯–B♭)4, also contribute to a timbral area together
with the horns, bounded by [11]: B3–B♭4. Registral proximity, and the fact that
the five pitches in this group cease to sound at the same point, reinforce their
articulation as a unit. The entrance of B3–E♭4 also reinforces the control of the

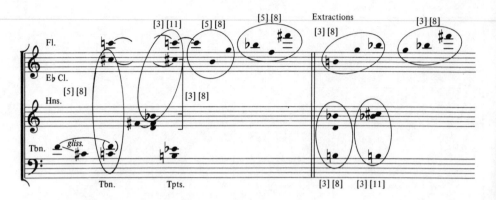

Example 5.7: *Hyperprism,* mm. 12–19 (with reference to mm. 1–11)

internal structure of this passage by constellation [3][8], for two additional instances are formed. These are [3][8]: B3–(D–B♭)4, and [3][11]: B3–B♭4–C♯5 (ex.
5.7).

The adjacent [4]s, the subsequent projection of a single [4], and their combined
crescendo in m. 16 are succeeded immediately by a clearly recognizable reference
in the percussion to the opening: cymbals, tam-tam, and bass drum in a triplet
pattern, the same series that served as upbeat to m. 1. The referential nature of this
pattern is a clue to its earlier significance. Its distinct, relatively pitched structure
(high, middle, low) can be interpreted as an imitation of the three pitches that form
the adjacent [4]s. Further, since these [4]s themselves refer to the framework A3–
(C♯–F)4 of the opening passage, the introductory percussion outburst is also
plausibly related to pitch-defined space. More generally, the descending series in
the percussion of m. 16 reflects the delineation of space in the pitch entrances of
mm. 12–15: high (woodwinds), middle (horns and trumpets), and low (trombones). The percussion parts in mm. 17–18 also refer to the opening passage,
though less specifically than does the triplet of m. 16. They are cast in a responding, complementary role, as pitch activity ceases (for the moment) after the motion
of the preceding measures.

Measures 19–23

Juxtaposed with the middle-range material, the placement of F1–E2 maintains a
continuity with the first eleven measures. There, D2–A3 was the lower segment in
the symmetrical arrangement, and this distance, [19], reappears between E2 and
B3 in m. 15. It has further implications for structure in m. 19, as the next new
space, B4–F♯6, also [19], outlined by the figure in the flute (see ex. 5.6). Together
with C6, the figure has an independently symmetrical construction, revealed by
the verticalization of its components: the resultant interval pattern is
[6][2][3][2][6]. This feature also affects the linear dimension, as the circled
segments in the example indicate. This pattern (both segments: [5][8]) has not

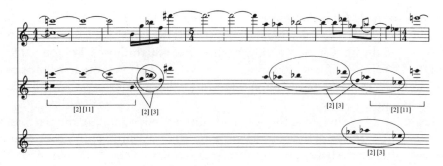

Example 5.8: *Hyperprism*, mm. 17–23, flute and E♭ clarinet

previously been identified in this piece, yet it does occur earlier in oblique (thus potential) form (see ex. 5.7). Note that [5][8]: (C–F)4–C#5 accounts for C4 in m. 12, a pitch up to now omitted from the analysis. Other important aspects of the flute figure are the linear adjacency [3][8]: B4–(G–B♭)5 and the registral adjacency [3][8]: (G–B♭)5–F#6.[1]

The flute solo continues in m. 21 with a chromatic group (A–A♭–B♭)5 that might be thought of as arising indirectly from the glissandi of the opening. More important is that the placement of these three notes engineers a shift of symmetrical focus from the span B4–F#6 (of which A5 and A♭5 represent a symmetrical contraction) to further activity initiated by (A–B♭)5. Durational criteria place these two pitches in prominence; they begin and end a series set apart by longer notes from what precedes and follows (ex. 5.8). The dyad (A–B♭)5 is the point of departure for symmetrical expansions that extend to D♭6–G♭5, the next two pitches in linear succession, and to E♭5–E6, the last two pitches of the flute solo (ex. 5.6).

Example 5.8 also shows other details of linear succession on a local level. Note that [2][3]: (A♭–B♭)5–D♭6 pairs with [2][3]: (A♭–F–E♭)5, bisecting the [10]-span E♭5–D♭6. The second of the resulting [5]s, because of the presence of G♭5, has its own internal symmetry, [2][1][2], and can be read as interlocked [2][3]s. The symmetry revealed by verticalization of the flute figure in mm. 18–19, mentioned earlier, also proves to be the source of these [2][3]s, as the segmentation in example 5.8 shows. The last three notes of the flute solo form [2][11] and complement another instance of that trichord which is stretched across mm. 17–19. This other [2][11] includes the first two notes of the solo and C#5, which formerly sounded below C6. These configurations occur as congruent delimiters at either end of the solo line.

Measures 23–29

The sonority B♭5–A6 in mm. 27–29 serves the long-range function of balancing the total use of space from the beginning of *Hyperprism* to this point (ex. 5.6). The counterpart to F1–E2, B♭5–A6, is as far above the original center C#4 as the other

[11] is below it. As for its local functions, the segmentation [5][13]: E♭5–(E–A)6 is relevant (derivative of [5][8]), as is [7][11]: (E♭–B♭)5–A6, which has an interesting precedent in the upbeat to m. 15. Of the three notes in the horns, F♯4 sounds first; with the C♯5 and C6 already sounding, it results in [7][11]. As noted, the process at work in m. 15 relies primarily upon other formations; thus the earlier [7][11] is a potential segmentation.

From m. 23 to shortly before the end of this section (m. 29), the percussion exhibits a high degree of independence, initiated by its entrance in a complementary role after the relatively rapid pitch presentation of the flute solo. As in the third section of *Intégrales,* the percussion also gives some impression of resurfacing with material clearly related to previous events. Contributing to this impression are the alternating rolls in cymbals and tambourine, together comprising a two-beat triplet (m. 23; see m. 5); alternating rolls in the rattles (m. 24; see mm. 6 and 17); the snare drum figure in m. 25, which refers to m. 21; and an elongated version (m. 25) of the crashing triplet figure that opens *Hyperprism* and returns in m. 16. This now takes place in entrances a beat apart, and because the single crash cymbal has been added there are four components, arranged in descending order of pitch.[2] This has the effect of recapitulating the registral space—as m. 16 did—but with a pronounced emphasis upon the higher end. From here to m. 29 the lower drums fade out while the other instruments, mainly high-pitched, dominate the percussion texture. In the crescendo at m. 29 this reinforces the completion of overall spatial symmetry at the high end, with the entrance of B♭5–A6. (Even in the tam-tam, which has a low component in its sound, the high harmonics are expecially audible when the instrument is played loudly.)

The pitches of mm. 21–29 have already been discussed in some detail, but further analysis yields other information, which becomes important in the connection with the passage beginning at m. 30 (refer to ex. 5.9). The flute solo may be segmented with special attention to the two descending gestures: one from F♯6, the other from D♭6. If the space filled by each of these is paired with the consequent descending semitone, the trichordal forms that result, [1][9] and [1][7] respectively, can be regarded as derivatives of a [1][8] that is not literally present. Also present, in potential only, are derivative-related [3][7] and [3][10]. Finally, the last two pitched events of the passage are single intervals: [13] and [11]. Their explicit isolation in this context suggests that they are to some extent independent entities.

Example 5.9: *Hyperprism,* mm. 21–27, flute and E♭ clarinet

Measures 30–42

The relationship between pitches and percussion in mm. 30–37 has been treated already (see discussion accompanying ex. 4.23). In the pitch realm by itself, the symmetrical contraction to the second chord (m. 32) and the expansion back out to the repetition of the first chord (m. 34) have been identified. What remains to be discussed is the internal structure. Owing to the registral overlap of the two timbral groups—horns and trombones—several segmentations are possible in both chords (see ex. 5.10). In the first, literal registral adjacencies present [1][9] and [3][10], lower and upper, the latter of which is the realization of the potential [3][10] of mm. 22–23. Alternatively, if the boundaries of the trombone interval are juxtaposed with F3, one of the horn pitches that they enclose, another form of [3][10] results.[3] Taken together with the uppermost pitch in the horns, G♭4, the trombones also form [10][13], an unfolded derivative of [3][10]. The second chord is made up of interlocked [1][10] and [1][8]—both derivatives of [1][9]—and forms of [5][8] and [4][11], the first expressed by horns alone, the second by trombones plus the highest horn pitch. Form [4][11] is not related directly to [7][11], but the two hold a central form, [4][7], in common, suggesting that this last may be the basic form of the constellation in this part of the piece.

Along with the contractive and expansive motions of [4] between the two chords, the graph in example 5.11 also shows that internal motions of [4] "double" and strengthen the external ones. The sixteenth-note figure in m. 33, horn 1, bears an interesting relationship to these, in that its boundary pitches E♭4 and G3 bisect two of the [4]s. The figure also provides a specific link to an earlier point, the trichord [5][6]: G3–(D♭–G♭)4, with respect to the last three pitches in the previous section, B♭5–(E–A)6. This trichordal resemblance would be of very minor interest were it not that G3 can be paired with E4 (by linear criteria) and that the two pitches are octave-related to G2 and E3. Looking ahead now to mm. 37–38, we find that the interval G3–G♭4 rises to a prominence that is only hinted at in mm. 33–34. In a way, G2–G♭4 (boundaries of the first chord and thus all of mm. 30–37) are *represented by* (though not equated to) G3–G♭4. In retrospect, this explains the

Example 5.10: *Hyperprism,* mm. 30–33, brass

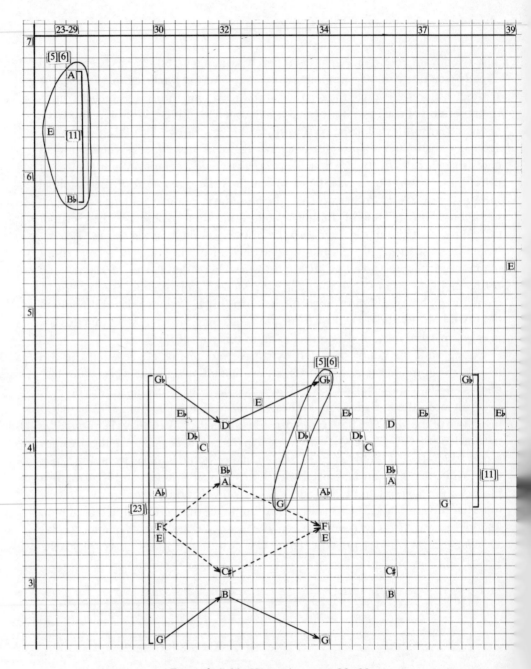

Example 5.11: *Hyperprism*, mm. 23–39

succession B♭5–A6 (m. 29) to G2–G♭4, which is otherwise puzzling, since the two
intervals are not the same size. This idea of a pitch being temporarily or locally
represented by one an octave above or below is not new to *Hyperprism* at this point,
as C♯5 did the same for C♯4 in m. 12 with respect to C6, and in the process
produced the same size pair of intervals, [11] and [23]. We can trace the following

sequence (referring to exx. 5.6 and 5.11): the distance [23]: D2–C♯4 (mm. 5–11) is matched in expansion by C♯4–C6; the C♯5 enters to stand in place of C♯4; the resultant [11] is projected to B̀3–B♭4 and F1–E2, F1–E2 achieving larger significance in the completion of the symmetry with B♭5–A6. Thus B♭5–A6 still stands, at several removes, for the original [23]—an interval which is restored in m. 30 as G2–G♭4, then collapsed once again to G3–G♭4 (mm. 37–38).

The interval G3–G♭4, subdivided by E♭4, marks the resurgence of [3][8], which together with the trichordal types developed in the preceding measures leads into the rapid motion of mm. 40–42. Example 5.12 shows the pervasive influence of [3][8], [3][10], and [1][9], the last now a basic form embracing [1][10] and [1][8] (m. 32: see ex. 5.10). At approximately midway through the rapid motion the constellation [4][7] reenters the lattice. It seems to be eclipsed at the final position of m. 42 but is actually carried to the lower region of the pitch stasis that begins in m. 45. At the moment of m. 42, [3][8] dominates, supplemented by [1][9] (as [1][10]) and [3][10]. Somewhat more weakly represented—really only in potential—is [2][11]: (C–D)5–C♯6 and D5–(C♯–E♭)6 (circled by dotted lines), which is, however, an important precedent for the trombone-horn group that begins m. 45.

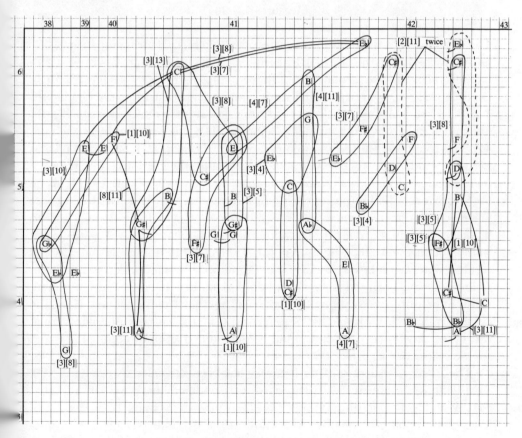

Example 5.12: *Hyperprism*, mm. 38–43

The overall spatial delineation of mm. 30–42 is fairly straightforward (see ex. 5.13). After the boundary interval G3–G♭4 in mm. 37–39, the higher pitch that first supersedes G♭4 as upper boundary is E5, [10] higher. If this interval of [10] is regarded as a center, then the [11] below it (the original G3–G♭4) effectively "predicts" another [11] above E5. The pitch E♭6 turns out to be the upper boundary of the entire rapid-motion passage (through m. 42). Now, if G3 stands for G2 in this manipulation as well as in the others discussed, then this symmetry encompasses mm. 30–37 as well. Furthermore, the linear succession G3–E♭4 represents [20]: G2–E♭4. In turn the linear succession E♭4–E5 (m. 39) also serves as a center, with the interval of [20] below it matched above by E5–C7, the upper boundary of the pitch-static passage beginning in m. 45. More locally, the lower boundary A3 can also be accounted for by this same complex of relationships. The pitch E5, besides being a member of an interval and of several trichords, also stands literally alone in mm. 39–40 for several beats. Taking E5 as a center, we find that from it radiate two members of the constellation [3][8]—upward, [3][8]: E5–(C–E♭)6; downward, [8][11]: E5–G♯4–A3. In this, as in many of Varèse's expanding motions, the lower boundary is more quickly attained than the upper.

Measures 43–58

The mechanism by which the boundaries of the pitch-static formation in mm. 45–58 are reached is, on the face of it, a nearly exact expansion, from A3–E♭6 to C♯3–C7. Several factors are responsible for the semitone discrepancy (refer to ex. 5.13). On the local level, two related but distinct symmetries produce the outer limits C♯3 and C7. First, a chain of [11]s results from C4 (last pitch attacked in m. 42), B4 (only pitch held over from mm. 42–43 into m. 44), and B♭5 (next new pitch, m. 44). This chain predicts the lower boundary C♯3, [11] below C4. Second, if B4 and B♭5 are considered by themselves, juxtaposed against the previous lowest note A3, then the adjacencies [14][11] can be said to add a symmetrically placed [14] above the [11] to reach C7. The position of C7 has already been explained as the outcome of a manipulation of larger scale. Thus, if the expansion to the pitch stasis were to be perfectly symmetrical, E♭6–C7 would have to be matched by A3–C3, which would not only make the extension of the [11]-chain impossible but would as well result in outer boundaries C3–C7. Octaves and octave compounds to this point in *Hyperprism* have been scrupulously avoided except in situations where, as noted, substitution or representation of one pitch by another seems intended. Here, the possibility that C3–C7 would not be perceived as a "real" space is especially strong, for these octave-related pitches would be maintained as outer boundaries—and for a considerable length of time.

The internal structure of mm. 45–58 has been discussed as example 3.29. To the rough symmetry of trichordal forms outlined there we can add that the forms [2][11], [1][10], and [3][8] have clear precedents in m. 42 (see ex. 5.12). These, on the basis of what we now know of the previous passage, are supplemented by various derivatives of [4][7] (ex. 5.14). Form [4][11]: E♭3–(D–F♯)4 is a

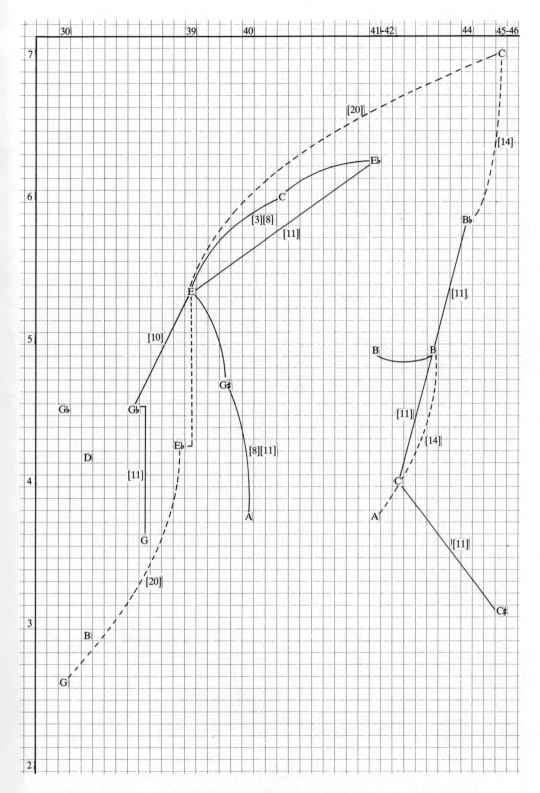

Example 5.13: *Hyperprism,* mm. 30–46

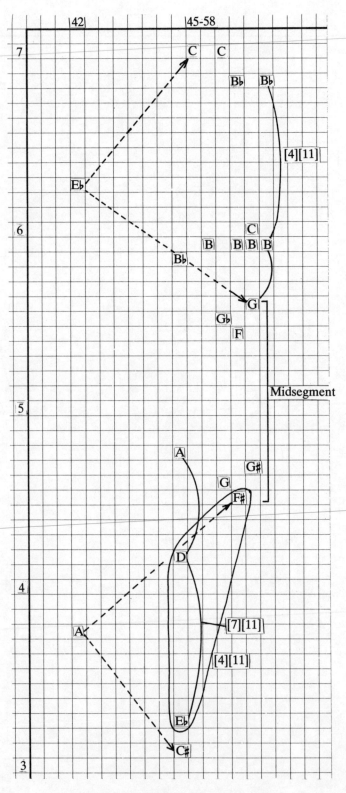

Example 5.14: *Hyperprism*, mm. 42–58

straightforward registral adjacency, but the other instances deserve special explanation. The four components of this stasis can be grouped according to several
criteria, one of which is rhythm. All have different rhythmic characters, but the
trombones and horns have in common the steadiness of repeated notes and
relatively regular metric form, while trumpets and woodwinds belong together on
the basis of their irregular and slightly more complicated pitch presentation. Thus
the trichord [7][11]: E♭3–(D–A)4, which groups the upper interval of the trombone-horn trichord with the sixteenths in the horn, is a viable segmentation. As for
[4][11]: (G–B)5–B♭6, it is the result of juxtaposition of the last interval in the
trumpets, m. 58, and the last, sustained interval in the woodwinds.

The association of trumpets and woodwinds also accounts partially for a larger
aspect of spatial design: together these two groups delineate F♯4–C7, which
amounts to a projection from the boundaries of m. 42, A3–E♭6 (see ascending
dotted arrows in ex. 5.14). Grouping trombones and trumpets on the basis of
another segmentational criterion, timbral resemblance, produces a correspondent
to this span in C♯3–G5 (descending dotted arrows). A third basis for segmentation
is relative registral position: high (woodwinds), middle (trumpets and horn), and
low (trombones and horns). The middle group is bounded by F♯4 and G5, which
define a segment situated exactly midway between outer boundaries C♯3 and C7.

The durational structure of mm. 45–58 is diagrammed in example 5.15, with
instrumental cues only (not complete contents of the score) provided on the staff
lines. The return of the percussion in m. 48 in a complementary role suggests that
this passage can be segmented according to the successive entrances of pitches and
percussion. In example 5.15a the segmentation is carried out strictly according to
this criterion. The two big pitched segments exist in approximate balance at either
end of the passage; if the first of these is grouped with the duration of the first solo
percussion segment, which actually takes place together with sustained pitches,
then the balance is improved, yielding 19 and 17 beats respectively.[4] Thus the
percussion in m. 56 sounds like a compressed version of mm. 48–49; the analogy is
strengthened by pitch sustentions in both locations. Another kind of balance holds
between mm. 45–47 and 56–58: respectively, before and after the first and last
percussion "intrusions" the pitched material lasts 11.5 and 10.5 beats.

Throughout the passage the pitched instruments and the percussion maintain
a roughly inverse relationship, if relative importance is measured in length of
respective segments. The pitches begin in control and then are nearly eclipsed by
the sudden strength of the percussion (mm. 50–54), then rise steadily to prominence again as the percussion falls away.

All of this is evidence of a thoroughgoing process in the passage, unlike the
changes introduced near the end of stasis illustrated in chapter 4. The balance
described above becomes even more precise and symmetrical once the subdivision
of the larger segments in example 5.15b is taken into account. Among the pitches,
the first subdivision is drawn at the entrance of the trumpets, last of the four
components to appear. In the last pitched segment the division occurs instead at
the trombones' entrance (m. 58), because here they are the last of the four to enter.

Example 5.15: *Hyperprism*, mm. 45–58

Among the percussion bursts a *relatively* long rest before reentry is taken as an appropriate point of division. The only exception made is at m. 56, where the last burst is grouped with the pitched material, as this last event in the percussion does not initiate a new segment; the pitches continue. It is really a termination.

Measures 59–68

The new section beginning at m. 59 comes about both through projection of large spans and the extension of extant trichordal forms (refer to ex. 5.16). The low F1 heard first is a projection below C♯3 (previous low point) of the span C♯3–A4 formed by the association, noted earlier, of components from the pitch stasis. Shortly thereafter, the E2 added in the second horn part brings about [2][9]: E2–(C♯–E♭)3.[5] At this point the basic form identity shifts to [2][9], with derivatives

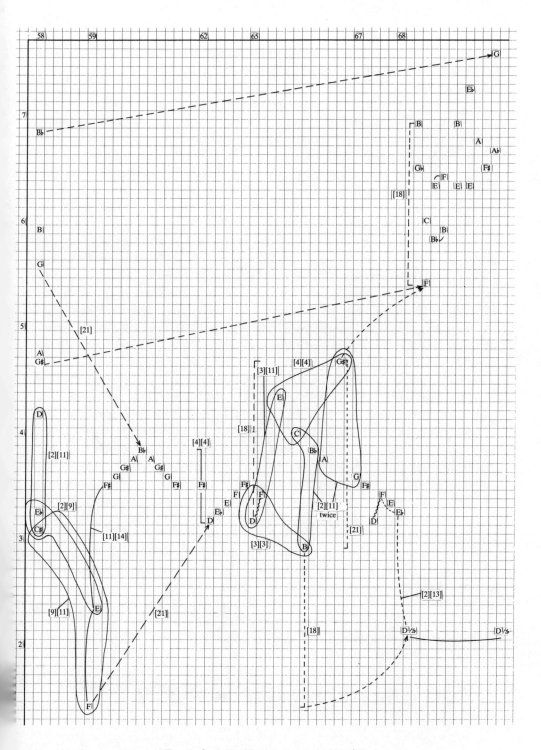

Example 5.16: *Hyperprism*, mm. 58–75

[2][11] and [9][11]; the latter occurs immediately as F1–E2–C♯3. Next, the entrance of F♯3 in the first horn brings in the large unfolded derivative of [3][11], [11][14]: F1–E2–F♯3 (recall that [3][11] is a component of the passage in mm. 45–58, as shown in ex. 3.27).

In m. 62 the trombone is reasserted as a solo instrument and takes over F♯3 from the horn. The glissando (in the horn) in m. 61 up to B♭3 and back is balanced in m. 63 by a glissando up from D3. The surrounding of a central pitch by [4]s clearly evokes the opening of the work, together with the instrumentation—the percussion is once again quite active. In a reversal of the role of the adjacent [4]s at the opening, however, those of mm. 61–63 serve as a contraction, as shown in example 5.16, from previous boundaries (final upper position of brass, m. 58, and new lower boundary, also brass, m. 59).

For those who cling to the belief that Varèse was secretly a twelve-tone composer, the solo trombone passage that follows (mm. 63–68) is a favorite example for analysis. The significance, however, of the nearly complete "descending chromatic scale" in mm. 66–68 pales by comparison to the elegant spatial layout. Example 5.17 shows how the pitches of relatively longer duration divide the passage into groups labeled (a) through (e). Within this framework a segmentation of trichordal forms is developed (again see ex. 5.16) quite consistent with the controlling forms of the preceding music. The order of pitches between C4 and G3 inclusive, groups (c) and (d), form an obvious symmetry. The [3][11] just before, (D–F)3–E4 in group (b), is related somewhat more subtly. First, the uppermost pitches of the two groups (c) and (d), C4 and G♯4, form with the uppermost pitch of (b) a pair of adjacent [4]s, as if in projection of the relationship (D–F♯–B♭)3 of mm. 61–63. Second, a principal event in group (a) is the alternation of F♯3 with F3, as if to suggest the possibility of substitution. The interval (D–F)3, then, could stand for (D–F♯)3, and with the lowest pitch of (c), B2, in fact does so as a member of a pair of adjacent [3]s, in imitation of the [4]s. Thus B2–(D–F)3 and (C–E–G♯)4 constitute a symmetry by implication.

The boundaries of groups (a) through (d) also act in conjunction with F1 (m. 59) to control overall spatial delineation. From low point F1 to new low point D3 is the same size span as from B2 (next low point) up to G♯4, high for the entire passage. Further, the repetition of the glissando D3 to F3 in m. 67, as part of (e), suggests a correspondence between D3–G♯4 and F1–B2. These two spans of [18] have a further effect upon the music beginning at m. 68.

The last of the solo groups, (e), demands special comment. The first part of it,

Example 5.17: *Hyperprism*, mm. 64–68, trombones

(F#–F–E–Eb)3, is a repetition of (a) with part of the glissando elongated and reversed. It also stands as an extension, all in semitones, of the micro-structures resulting from the juxtaposition of (c) and (d). The segmentation given in reduction below example 5.17 shows this relationshp.

The last note in the solo (m. 68, actually played by the entering bass trombone) is also the most difficult to deal with, since it has been deliberately placed outside the semitonal continuum. Perhaps inspired by the performance direction ("laughing") for the trombone at m. 67, some have interpreted this as Varèse's way of playing a joke on analysts and at the same time avoiding the "closure" that would result from completion of the twelve-pitch-class set. The pitch-class-oriented analyst, on the other hand, would like very much for this note to be a Db; in an attempt to get around the problem, one writer has even interpreted it as both D *and* Db.[6] From one point of view the ambiguity is actually useful, in that the note standing halfway between D and Db in the second octave, paired with Eb3, can resemble both the [14]-span of (b) and the [13]-spans of (c) and (d). On spatial grounds, however, there are better reasons for calling the pitch "D-like" than "Db-like." Locally, with (Eb–F#)3 and/or (Eb–F)3, D2 would yield trichords [3][13] and [2][13] respectively. There is little reason for the reintroduction of [3][13] at this point, but [2][13], as a derivative of [2][11], is well connected. A longer-range link arises from the juxtaposition of D2 with the lower boundary of the succeeding material (woodwinds, mm. 68–75), which is F5. The span D2–F5 is equal in size to that used in the entire passage mm. 59–68: Fl–G#4 (curved dotted arrows in ex. 5.16).

The percussion of mm. 59–67 is highly active, remaining so even as the trombone moves rapidly through pitch changes in mm. 65–67. Thus its function here is largely independent, but in one respect at least there is a coordination between pitched and unpitched: as the trombone becomes a solo instrument at m. 63, both the instrumentation and the character of what is played change in the percussion. The long held notes in horns and trombone in mm. 59–62 are reflected in the sustained rolls and the "laissez vibrer" indications for metallic instruments and siren. These disappear at m. 63, replaced now completely by short, angular figures in keeping with the irregular, almost jazzy character of the trombone part.

Measures 68–76

This section has three boundaries: initial, final, and total, all important (ex. 5.16). The initial limits F5–B6, [18], correspond to those of the two [18]-spans discussed previously. The total space occupied in these measures, F5–G7, is related by registral (not temporal) proximity to the composite of the final position of trumpets and woodwinds in the stasis ending at m. 58: G#4–Bb6. There is an obvious timbral link here as well in the combination of Eb clarinet and piccolo, neither of which has been heard since m. 58.

The final boundary, Ab6–G7, is best explained as a component of internal

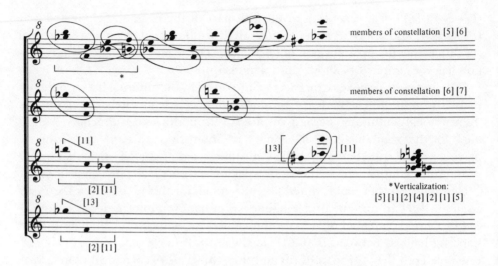

Example 5.18: *Hyperprism*, mm. 68–75, piccolo and E♭ clarinet

structure. This, as a result of a new juxtaposition of intervals [11] and [13] (first two notes in piccolo and E♭ clarinet respectively), is dominated by constellation [5][6] (ex. 5.18). Supporting roles are filled by [2][11] and [6][7]—each of the instrumental parts in m. 68 by itself is an instance of [2][11]. Their composite, including the trills, is mirror symmetrical, as shown in the verticalized extract in example 5.18. The interval [11]: A♭6–G7, then, is a projection of both intervals in the forms of [2][11], a phenomenon that is emphasized by the proximate position of F♯6, yielding yet another instance of the same trichord and bringing [13] into the final manipulation as well.

The percussion for mm. 68–71 is confined to Chinese blocks and, intermittently, slap stick. The choice of blocks, with their clear, almost definitely pitched sounds, emphasizes the timbral shift and the clear, crystalline sound of the woodwinds at this point. The blocks also prefigure the quick, plunging rhythms of the

Example 5.19: *Hyperprism*, mm. 68–69 (trombones omitted)

woodwind figures (ex. 5.19). Percussion takes on a complementary role at m. 72, entering in numbers and gradually gaining momentum as pitch change ends in the woodwinds. The intensification by means of quick notes and crescendo is a product of mutual influence between the two realms. Finally, the crash cymbal, entering unnoticed in m. 75 at *pp* as everything else reaches maximum loudness, continues past the abrupt cutoff in the other instruments, as if in echo (m. 76).

Measures 77–89

The solo percussion "interlude" of mm. 77–83 is marked "Vif très souple, mystérieux"; the last of these adjectives seems especially appropriate. This passage too is a kind of echo, but its components are so minimal that it really can have no specific referent. The only even remotely possible candidates are a few moments of the pitch-static passage (mm. 45–58) and the rhythmic unisons of mm. 30–37 (with horns and trombones). Measures 30–37, a briefly prolonged static alternation between two chords, relates—to this extent—to the present passage, which takes the form of an ostinato disrupted after several periods (ex. 5.20). The resemblance is strengthened by the clear timbral reference of the three unison horns in mm. 84–85, immediately succeeding the interlude, to mm. 37–38.

The three horns begin the final passage of *Hyperprism,* but their timbral reference is not matched by any striking pitch- or interval-based similarity (ex. 5.21). Instead, the material takes on the characteristics of mm. 68–75, becoming a mixture of [2][11] and [6][7]. Here [2][11] is no longer the basic form; control once again has passed to [2][9], represented as B♭3–(C–A)4, with its two derivatives [2][7] and [2][11].

From this point to the end of the piece larger intervals and larger spatial manipulations take over for the most part, so that trichordal forms have only limited relevance. Initial low point B2 is succeeded by B1, completing a relationship spanning the entire range of this passage and incorporating the end of the previous one: A4–G7, a span of [34] defined by previous and new high

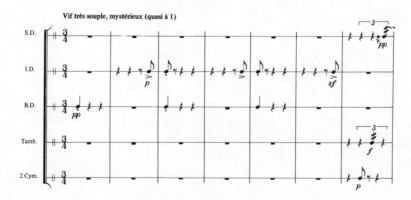

Example 5.20: *Hyperprism,* mm. 77–83

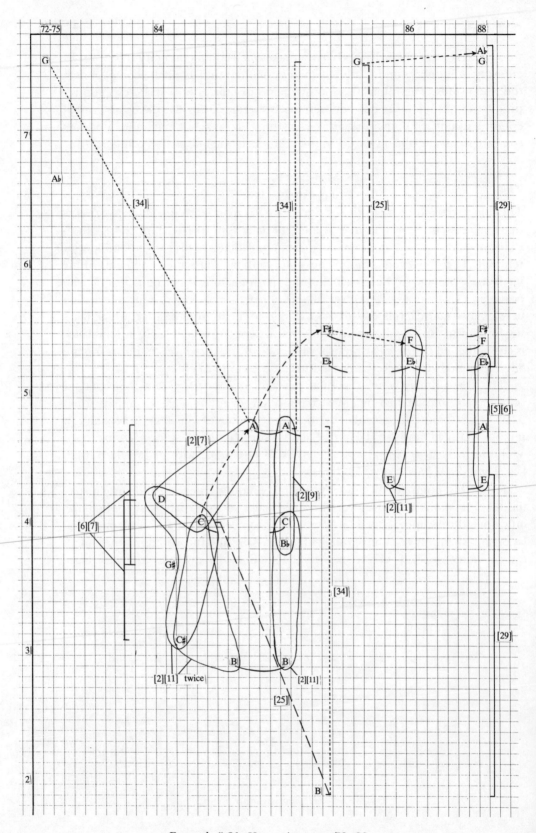

Example 5.21: *Hyperprism*, mm. 72–89

boundaries, is projected to B1–A4. Next, the linear succession C4–B2 represents the less literally stated C4–B1, [25], defining a space that is projected above F♯5 to G7 (first trumpet and piccolo). As for F♯5 itself, the linear succession C4–A4 in the horns (m. 85) is extended in a [9]-chain (dotted curved arrows) to produce the higher pitch. As other pitches enter, B1 forms an interval of [29] with E4 that is projected to the space defined by E♭5 (E♭ clarinet) and A♭7, top pitch (piccolo trill). The entrances of E4 and F5 also result in a projection of [2][11] to E4–(E♭–F)5. The trichord [5][6]: (E–A)4–E♭5, at the same time, preserves features of internal structure developed in conjunction with [2][11], with which it remains associated here.

The last pitches to enter the texture in the accumulative chord of mm. 85–89 are significant in three respects. First, F5 (trumpet 2), the penultimate entering note, stands with A♭7 in the piccolo (last entering note) as an expansion of the span F♯5–G7. Second, F5–A♭7 also contributes to overall spatial balance in the final passage, since it corresponds in size to the space opened by the initial gesture, D4–B2 (expanded down an octave by representative B1). Third, the added emphasis upon the high end of the spectrum supplied by F5 and A♭7 is given greater force by the simultaneous dropping, at m. 88, of the lowest three pitches (B1, B♭3, C4) and their replacement by three metallic percussion. The tam-tam retains a shadow of the lower pitches, but its high harmonics together with triangle and crash cymbal are clearly aimed in the opposite direction.

Hyperprism is not what one would call a big work—in performance it lasts about four minutes—but its brevity does not interfere with Varèse's characteristic travel to an end very different from his starting point. What the work does, it does compactly and efficiently. It can be regarded as the first fruit of the maturation of Varèse's technique, an event which, as noted in the introduction, gave the composer the ability to accomplish his aims in a remarkably wide range of media.

The terse, even laconic quality of *Hyperprism* is as evident at a larger-scale level as it is on the level of local connections. One prominent piece of evidence for this is the condensation through reference of mm. 30–37 into the "mysterious" drum-beats and the triple unison horns of mm. 77–85, but the reference and the condensation go further still. Preceding m. 77, the piccolo-E♭ clarinet passage (mm. 68–72) precipitates a massive outburst in the percussion (mm. 72–76). These measures for woodwinds actually serve a dual referential function: first, as shown above (ex. 5.16), they restore the registral region abandoned after m. 58 by means of timbral resemblance, trichordal connections, and projection of larger spatial dimensions. Second, the pitches' coming to rest on an [11]-span in m. 72 and sustention in crescendo with percussion entering in a complementary role clearly recall mm.23–29, which work in similar fashion (except that in the earlier passage the [11] enters in m. 27, some time after the percussion has been set in motion). Together with mm. 77–85, mm. 68–76 refer to (approximately) mm. 23–37, and in fact reach as far back as m. 18, the beginning of the flute solo (see chart in ex. 5.22). The woodwind material of mm. 68–72 thus incorporates

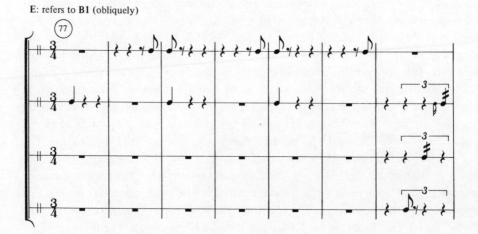

Example 5.22: *Hyperprism*, referential relationships

F: refers to **B1** (rhythm) and **B2** (texture)

Example 5.22 *continued*

features of two previous passages (mm. 18–29 and 46–58), collapsed into one reference near the end. Because the number of possible referents in the work is relatively small, such general kinds of references function as unifying forces. But their general nature also ensures that they do not confuse or otherwise interfere with the more specific continuity produced by spatial-manipulative processes.

DENSITY 21.5

This is one of Varèse's most extensively analyzed works; several studies of the entire piece have been published. *Density 21.5* is the only Varèse work that is compact enough (61 measures for a solo instrument) to be feasible as a subject of full-length analysis within the limits usually placed upon length of analytic prose.[7] The present analysis is essentially independent of its predecessors. All of them have interesting and valuable features but are also problematic in various ways, ranging from a tendency to leap to conclusions and arrive at an inclusive frame-work which is essentially imposed upon the piece and for which there is insuffi-cient support (Wilkinson), to an obsession with irrelevancies (the "statistical" approach of Gümbel), to an inability usefully to synthesize the results of meticu-lously detailed examination (Nattiez).[8]

That *Density 21.5* is for a solo instrument has been identified by at least one writer as a primary fact about the piece, as if it had some fundamental effect upon the conditions under which analysis could be carried out.[9] But there are really only two important differences between *Density 21.5* and the rest of Varèse's oeuvre, and they are self-evident. First, available registral space is relatively small; second, since no literal simultaneity of pitches is possible, linear detail must take on a more extensive role than it would otherwise—and, inevitably, become more crucial to segmentation. The processes remain the same. As in the works for multiple parts, intervals presented in linear fashion are interpreted variously as vertical adjacen-cies. In roughly the first third of the work trichordal forms play only a secondary role; instead, micro-structures serve initially as the important groupings. This is unusual for Varèse, but the compositional decision that it represents is clearly not *mandated* by choice of medium.[10]

Measures 1–5

The opening figure articulates a chromatic trichord, [1][1]: (F–E–F♯)4. This figure, in its various transpositions, will be referred to as group (x) and is identified by the solid boundaries in example 5.23. The G4 in m. 2 brings a second group, [1][2]: (E–F♯–G)4, an unfolding of (x), into potential existence. This will be referred to as group (y) and is marked by dotted boundaries. By registral association group (y) *is* a kind of succession, even in its first appearance in m. 2. The implicit relationship between the pitches (E–F♯–G)4 is made explicit in mm. 3–4 in the form of a direct linear succession and again in mm. 4–5, in reverse order. Symmetrical properties also suggest assignment of structural importance to group (y), for the articulation of space bounded by C♯4 and G4, divided evenly by E4, also becomes clear in the course of the opening measures—especially in m. 5, where the last gesture is devoted solely to expressing this framework. Group (y) outlines the interval (E–G)4 and thus serves to fill an interstice of the symmetry.

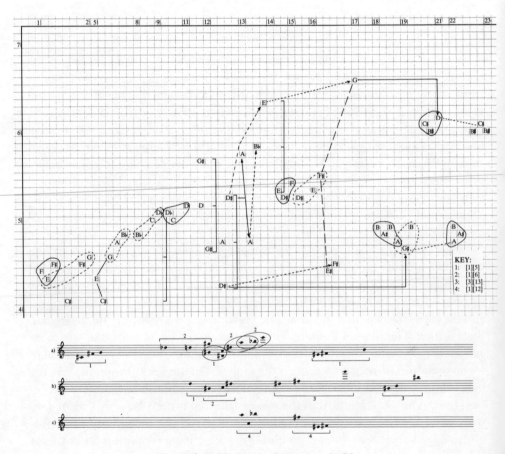

Example 5.23: *Density 21.5*, mm. 1–23

Measures 6–10

Expansion of occupied space proceeds by extensions of group (y): (G–A–B♭)4, then B♭4–(C–D♭)5. Up to the point where D♭5 is reached, in m. 9, total space employed so far in the work is [12] in extent, double the initial [6] covered by (C♯–G)4. The new space G4–D♭5 opened in mm. 6–9 is bisected [3][3] in analogy to (C♯–E–G)4 below. And the initial high point, G4, now stands in the same relationship to the outer boundaries C♯4 and D♭5 as did E4 to C♯4 and G4 at the beginning—that is, it bisects the space in use.

Measures 11–14

Expansion of space by one more semitone, to D5 in m. 11, at once completes a second group (x), resulting in a chain of three linked (y)s with an (x) on each end, and sets off a new series of developments. With D5 a sudden, radical change occurs: rapid expansion of occupied space through articulation of larger intervals, in the form of projections of previously articulated structures. The structural framework (C♯–G)4–D♭5 serves as the template for these new formations. Notice that G♯4–(D–G♯)5 and (D♯–A)4–D♯5, both bracketed in the graph, are projections of that original configuration. Further, A5 appears in m. 13, which enlarges the previous [6][6] formation by one more [6]. This results in a pair of interlocked [6][6]s sharing the common segment A4–D♯5. The repetition of A4 in m. 13 emphasizes the [12]-span A4–A5 as a significant segment, and its extension to B♭5 is analogous to the extension of C♯4–D♭5 to D5, thus also a projection of the structure [1][12].

The E6 in mm. 13–14, a major structural articulation, has two distinct functions. First, in retrospect it is clear that D5 is a point of rest before the burst of activity leading up to m. 14, by virtue of its temporal value in comparison to the notes that precede it. Pitches D♯5 and E6 are similarly situated with respect to their contexts, duplicating the relationship between C♯4 and D5 (projection of [13]). Second, B♭5–E6 is the counterpart to (D♯–A)4, in that these two segments form a mirror symmetry about A4 and B♭5. Note that A4–B♭5 is given as a direct succession in m. 13.

Measures 15–17

The appearance of the [6]-span B♭5–E6 poses the possibility that another [6][6] structure will be formed—realized with E5 in m. 15, the first note of that measure. It is also the first note of a new instance of (x), given in the distinctive rhythmic pattern of the opening. Again, too, (x) is succeeded by (y), but in rotation this time: (D♯–E–F♯)5 in m. 16. Implicit also in mm. 15–16 is the segmentation (D♯–F–F♯)5, by virtue of the emphasis placed upon the dyad (D♯–F)5 in m. 15. This corresponds to (y) in its original orientation. In all, some similarity is maintained with the opening of the piece, but the altered arrangement of details foretells differences in continuation. These differences arise almost immediately, as a new high point (G6) is reached in m. 17. Gestural similarity with mm. 13–14 is evident. Attainment of G6 is accomplished through a symmetrical operation centered about F♯5: [13] on either side. The symmetry is shown in the diagram by the lines of dashes radiating from F♯5. As for the formation [1][12]: (E♯–F♯)4–F♯5 embedded in the symmetry, it has clear precedents (see ex. 5.23).

Articulation of the interval F♯4–G6 as a direct succession reflects the gestural parallel with mm. 12–14 noted above: the distance D♯4–E6, [25], was formerly expressed as a symmetrical configuration involving several pitches but now appears as a single linear succession. The quick attainment of G6 thus reflects a condensation not only on the level of gesture but also with respect to details of spatial manipulation.

Measures 18–23

In terms of temporal order of presentation, what happens in mm. 15–16 now occurs, in mm. 18–19, in reverse. Group (y) follows (x) within the space of [3], but this [3] is given as a descent rather than as an ascent: (B–G♯)4. The (x) that follows, C♯6–B♯5–D6, is a rhythmically elaborated version of the initial form and is significant spatially, the outer edges of the new space, G♯4 and D6, standing in symmetrical contraction from the composite of D♯4–E6 (mm. 12–14) and F♯4–G6 (mm. 16–17). The union of these two large spaces is justified by the procedural links between them discussed above.

In mm. 22–23 the size of the lower group first presented within the space (B–G♯)4 undergoes shrinkage in two stages: first to (A–B)4, then to (A–A♯)4. The connection to the earlier presentation is established by the repetition of the figure (B–A♯–B)4. In m. 22 (A–B)4, rather than being given as a straightforward succession, now occurs with A♯4 filling it in. In its new context, (A–B)4 can also be interpreted as an effect, or projection, of the span B♯5–D6. In turn, when (A–B)4 shrinks to (A–A♯)4, there is a response in the upper register, in m. 23: B♯5–C♯6.[11] The net effect of this attenuation above and below is to reduce occupied space by means of another symmetrical contraction ([1] on each end). From the outer boundaries D♯4 and G6, then, the size of space in use has been reduced by [12]: [6] above and below. The fact that these two interval sizes, originally employed as vehicles in the expansion of space, are now used for contractive purposes serves to complement the opening music and to provide a strong sectional articulation.

Measures 24–28

In terms both of general registral location and of the placement of pitches within it, these measures bear a distinct resemblance to the opening (refer to ex. 5.24). The special percussive device, pioneered by Varèse in this piece ("notes marked + to be played softly, hitting the keys at the same time"[12]), is used only in these measures, and it has the effect at once of marking them as a reference and

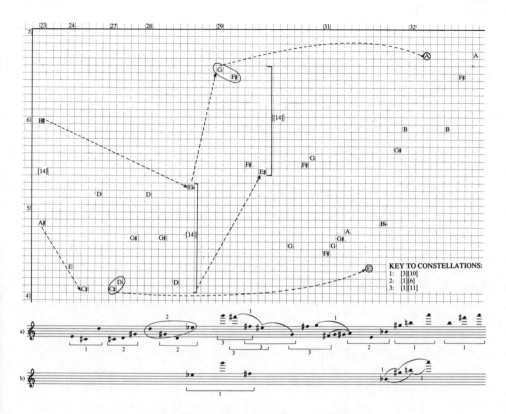

Example 5.24: *Density 21.5*, mm. 23–36

distinguishing them from their referent. The presentation in fragments and the performance direction "sharply articulated" are further aids to drawing this distinction. Varèse lends the material new significance by selecting only a few elements for treatment here. Measures 24–25, for instance, are devoted to an extremely abridged presentation of the space C♯4–D5, which originally required ten measures to delineate fully. The trichordal form [3][10], embracing the entire pitch content of this abridgment, is new information produced by a juxtaposition of intervals that previously had separate and distinct functions. One may confidently expect this conflation to have consequences for spatial development. In m. 26 the complete span C♯4–D5 is summarized in a single interval. Measures 27–28, in completing the passage, extend the network of subtle references. The [1][6]: (C♯–D–G♯)4 is certainly a familiar configuration. See (a) and (b) below the graph in ex. 5.23. The derivative-related [1][5] and [1][6] are formed by many intervallic adjacencies in the spatial layout. With one isolated exception, however, in those first 23 measures ([1][5] in mm. 1–2), no instance of either trichord is stated as a literal, linear succession, which suggests that they are best relegated to potential status before mm. 24–28. The same is true of [3][10] (line (b) in ex. 5.23), which besides (C♯–E)4–D5 in mm. 1–11 exists twice in potential as derivative-related [3][13].

Example 5.25: *Density 21.5*, detail

The real form of [1][6] in m. 27 also brings a new element into play: the pitch D4. In m. 28, it becomes clear that the structure (D–G♯)4–D5 is a reference to the bisected [12]-spans of m. 12—specifically to G♯4–(D–G♯)5, with which it has an interval (and the triplet rhythm) in common. Next appears [6][7]: (D–G♯)4–E♭5, derivative of [1][6], lending constellation [1][6] further substance. At the same time, the percussive notes G♯4, D5, and E♭5 form another [1][6]. The analogy is suggested by the fact that all three members of the [1][6] in m. 27 are percussively stressed.

The interval [13]: D4–E♭5, finally, also suggests an analogy—namely, to C♯4–D5. Armed with this information, one can extract the segmentation shown in example 5.25 (detail), which is based on a framework of [1][12]s. Recall that the configuration [1][12] is already implicit in the span C♯4–D♭5 expanded by [1] in m. 10, and that it becomes a linear succession in m. 13 and acquires further significance in m. 16 (see (c) in ex. 5.23). The union of the [1][12] components in mm. 24–28 yields the entire span of the passage, [14], which, as shown in example 5.24, can now be construed as a projection from the previous inner boundaries delineated by A♯4 and B♯5 (m. 23). Further, the configuration [1][12][1] of mm. 24–28 can also be regarded as a double infolding, in that A4 and C♯6 (outside the [14]-span in m. 23) now have counterparts in D4 and D5, inside the [14].

Measures 29–32

The idea of abridged presentation in mm. 24–28 is taken, in mm. 29–30, a step further: the succession (G–F♯)6–(F♯–E♯)5 is a projection of the same [1][12][1] structure just discussed (again see ex. 5.25). Having become a descending gesture, it is also a rotation. Note also that G6 represents a regaining of the highest pitch heard so far in the work. In six measures (24–29) the entire registral space of the first seventeen has been recapitulated.

Next, with the triplet [1][11]: G4–(F♯–G)5, [1][12] is also drawn into trichordal structure. This process begins with the form [1][10]: G4–(E♯–F♯)5, which holds [1][11] in common with [1][12] as basic form. The entrance of F♯4 articulates [1][12] once again, as F♯4–(F♯–G)5. The quick chromatic run from F♯4 to A4 that opens m. 31, juxtaposed with (F♯–G)5, accomplishes two things. First, the initial F♯4 completes (very briefly) a structure [1][11][1] with the pitches above it—an infolding with respect to [1][12][1]. Second, the boundaries (F♯–A)4 combine with their immediate predecessor G5 to form [3][10], its constituents in reverse order with respect to [3][10]: (C♯–E)4–D5 in m. 25. The new [3][10] is now projected to produce the two linked forms shown in example 5.24. The linear succession [1][6]: (E–A–B♭)4, which connects these events, is preserved approximately in the same registral position that [1][6] occupies with respect to [3][10] in mm. 25–27, and an analogy is effectively made, for [1][5] is a derivative of [1][6].

The influence of constellation [3][10] is actually more pervasive in this passage than has been shown. The linked [3][10]s occupying the space B♭4–A6 also express, implicitly, two mirror-related forms of their derivative [10][13] (ex. 5.24b). Looking back, we find the arrangement F♯6–E♯5–G4, also [10][13], in m. 30 (ex. 5.24a). This is not an uninterrupted linear succession, but it effectively becomes one if F♯6 is taken as a momentary representative of F♯5. Thus [1][10] and [10][13] are connected briefly in a way unrelated to the processes of trichordal derivation. Further, [3][13] connects m. 28 and m. 29. Here we might say that F♯5 stands for F♯6 in linear succession, but the interval G6–F♯5 is a viable segmentation anyway by durational criteria, for the two pitches serve as initiator and terminator of the quick figure.

The boundaries of the ascent extending through mm. 31–32, E4–A6, represent a projection from previous boundaries D4–G6 (mm. 28–29). This is an interesting but perhaps not entirely satisfactory analysis, since the registral space of the entire piece up to this point, C♯4–G6, is so clearly delineated in mm. 24–29. However, if these outer pitches are each grouped with the pitch immediately adjacent to form dyads (C♯–D)4 and (F♯–G)6 (circled in ex. 5.24), then it becomes clear that the boundaries are still projected to E4–A6, at the same time completing two instances of the familiar micro-structural grouping [1][2], or (y).

The roots of this correspondence actually extend some distance back into the piece. Looking at example 5.23 again, we see that even after m. 11, where literal expansion of space in use by micro-structural projection ceased, a thread of micro-structural continuity proceeded, at first implicitly, then explicitly again as far as F♯5 in m. 16. At this point, however, this continuity was definitively supplanted by the material in mm. 17–23, where two spatially separated micro-structural complexes took over the function of outer boundaries. The significance of this event for mm. 24–32 should now be evident: micro-structures [1][2], now articulated over larger temporal spans, continue to control the outer edges of space in use.

Measures 32–36 (Example 5.26)

The pitches B5–(F♯–A)6, prolonged in stasis throughout these measures, are reached through infolding of [3][10] to [3][7], as set forth in example 3.10. As such stases go, this one is brief, but it is not simple. Defining the repeated unit is the main analytical problem here. The three pitches are not simply given over and over again in the same order; if the recurrence of B5 is taken as the relevant point of articulation, then some units remain incomplete, and another (mm. 34–35)

Example 5.26: *Density 21.5*, mm. 32–36

itself contains much repetition (ex. 5.26a). A better but still not completely satisfactory approach (ex. 5.26b) would be to treat the third and fourth beats of m. 32 and all of m. 33 as a unit. This has the advantage that the same order of pitches occurs in m. 34 (up to the penultimate note in that measure), but the remaining elaboration has no place in the scheme. Best of all is 5.26c, in which the complete repeated gesture is interpreted as the first two beats of the stasis. The next four notes (m. 33) constitute an appended elaboration. A second full version of the gesture occurs in m. 34, with another appendix which begins in the manner of the first but then changes (longer F♯6, marked here with an asterisk) and dwells upon the upper two pitches. At the end of m. 35, sustaining into m. 36, the appendix turns out to be a third full occurrence of the gesture with an elaborated midsection. Technically speaking, then, this stasis decelerates, although the number of elements is not really large enough to produce a convincing sense of ritardando: 2, 4, 2, 7.75; or 6, 9.75. On a different level, the alternating A6 and F♯6 of mm. 34–35 do contribute a sense of deceleration (example 5.26d), as there are four pairings of these pitches with a ritardando in each set of two, and the last set is slower than the first.

Measures 36–40

The descent at the end of m. 35 points to the further descent made in this passage and at the beginning of the next (mm. 41–43). The interval A6–C6, [9], is projected immediately in the descent from C6 to E♭5 (ex. 5.27). This parallel is enhanced by the counterpart of B5, a semitone below the first [9]-span—D5, a semitone below the second.

The chromatic group prolonged in mm. 38–40 presents only obliquely the order corresponding to the opening figure of the work. The contents of this group are interpreted by subsequent events to express their relationship to the opening. For the moment, this short stasis is devoted to presenting the three pitches in all six

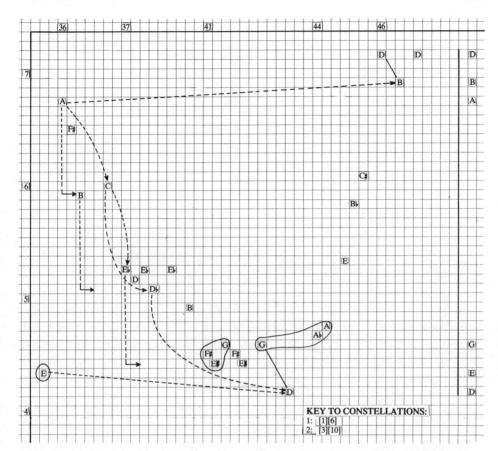

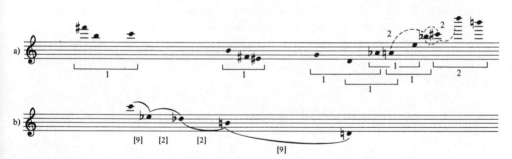

Example 5.27: *Density 21.5,* mm. 36–50

possible orders, as shown by the detail (ex. 5.28). The pitches (E♭–D♭)5 in m. 40 restore, with the immediately preceding D5, the order with which the series began, which effectively frames the entire presentation of the chromatic group, for it is the only one of the six orders that appears more than once. Furthermore, these pitches set forth the boundary interval [2] as an unambiguous descending motion, undivided by a third pitch or by a rest. The immediate result is the projection of [2] downwards, to B4.

Example 5.28: *Density 21.5*, mm. 37–40

Measures 41–45

The figure in m. 41, in its placement at this pitch level, completes several spatial relationships. First, it stands in analogy to the previous chromatic group, offering an explicit reference to the opening that was only implicit in mm. 38–40. However, the relationship is more than gestural. The space filled by (F#–E#–G)4, [2], is [4] away from the last pitch, B4, of m. 40; thus it is both the agent of and a participant in the unfolding, [2][4], of the [2][2] just formed. As shown in the extracted detail (ex. 5.29), the placement of both of these chromatic groups with respect to B4 is explained by unfolding. Spatially speaking, it is as if Db5 and D5 were pivoted about Eb5, opening up the [4]-span B4–Eb5, which becomes the [4]-span (G–B)4 as the entire chromatic group is simultaneously pivoted about B4.

The two chromatic groups define a span of [10], E#4–Eb5, which represents another in the series of descending [10]s initiated by A6–B5 and continued by B5–Db5. In the last beat of m. 43, the boundaries (E#–G)4 of the chromatic group are stated in direct succession—in mirror analogy to (Eb–Db)5 above—and are combined with D4. This bears a rotational resemblance to m. 31 (see comparison in ex. 5.30a); the analogy is continued and affirmed even more strongly by the succeeding Ab4 (m. 44). Together with the chromatic group itself, this new development duplicates the spatial layout of mm. 1–2 (comparison in example 5.30b); thus mm. 43–44 have a double resonance.

In the larger context, shown in example 5.27, the pitch D4 is revealed as the lower boundary for a considerable length of time. As such, it has a two-pronged significance. First, it completes a chain of [11]s C6–Db5–D4 overlapping with the [9]-chain A6–C6–Eb5 mentioned earlier. Thus Eb5 divides C6–Db5 as [2][9]. Recall that [2]: (Eb–Db)5 is projected to Db5–B4, so that Db5–D4 is also divided

Example 5.29: *Density 21.5*, mm. 38–43

a)

b)

Example 5.30: *Density 21.5*

[2][9], in rotated relationship to its parent configuration (ex. 5.27b). Second, the succession (G–D)4, marking the point at which the prolongation of the chromatic group is abandoned, represents one end of an expansion completed in m. 46 by D7.

Meanwhile, the ascending series of pitches in mm. 44–45 takes place in analogy to the ascent in mm. 31–32. Although the order of adjacent intervals is not identical to that of the earlier passage, the trichordal forms are related as members of the common constellation [3][10]. (The interpretation of [3][13]: Bb5–C#6–D7 as the unfolding, [3][10]: (C#–B)6–D7 as the basic form was explained in ex. 3.10.) In the later passage the influence of constellation [1][6] extends to a higher point, as line (a) below the graph in example 5.27 shows. In the process a micro-structure [1][1]: (G–Ab–A)4, plausibly interpeted as a mirror of the chromatic group (E#–F#–G)4, is generated.

Measures 46–50

With D7, an expansion by [5] on each end from G4–A6 is completed. Like the attainment of outer boundaries E4–A6, the expansion to D4–D7 is also controlled by micro-structures. The agent in the earlier motion, to E4–A6, was [1][2]; now an unfolding, [2][3], is brought to bear. The two structures in question are ver-ticalized for convenient reference in the extraction to the right of example 5.27: (D–E–G)4 and (A–B)6–D7.

The pitch stasis in mm. 46–50, diagrammed in example 5.31, represents an increase in intensity from that of mm. 32–36 on the basis of three criteria: greater length, fewer pitches (more repetition), and higher register. The common tri-chordal form and the clear intention that B6–D7 be heard as an intensification of (F#–A)6 in mm. 34–35 (itself an intensification in that earlier context) ensures that the listener will make the connection. Here a regularity is imposed in (roughly) the second half that brings the stasis to an end. Out of an irregular alternation in which B6 and D7 have no fixed, ordered, or even necessarily paired relationship, Varèse

Example 5.31: *Density 21.5*, mm. 46–50

establishes B6, D7 as the order by presenting the pair three times—with the D7, by virtue of its greater length, serving as conclusion each time—and by increasing, not only the length of each successive segment, but also the difference in length between the two pitches at each new occurrence.

Measures 50–61 (ex. 5.32)

Comparing now the immediate consequents of the two stases, we find more discontinuity in mm. 50–51 than in mm. 36–37. The groups (Ab–A–G)4 and C6–(F#–E#)5 (mm. 51–54) are placed at greater vertical distances from each other, and from the preceding material at m. 50, than their counterparts in mm. 36–41. Only gradually are the procedural links established between the two groups, and even then only as indirect connections. To begin, (Ab–A–G)4 replicates the chromatic group formed in mm. 43–44 (see ex. 5.27). The linear resemblance, reinforced by rhythmic similarity, to the succession (D–Eb–Db)5 in m. 38 is evident and continues the analogy to that previous passage. The group C6–(F#–E#)5, next to enter, has its clearest predecessor in the [1][6]: (D–Ab–A)4 that began the ascent in mm. 43–44. Thus the two spatially isolated trichords are related to the same region in the preceding music, although by different criteria.

The linear succession F5–C6–E4 in m. 53 implements the derivative [7][13] of derivative [6][7] in the constellation [1][6]. At the same time, the plunge from C6 to E4 and the subsequent articulation of (E–C#)4 recalls mm. 23–24, where no bridging trichordal form was read. By this point in the piece the pitches (E–C#)4 have powerful associations, and they draw after them now a series of details which together accomplish the third (and final) composing-out of this registral space. The linking of [7][13] (representing [6][7]) and constellation [3][10], a feature of mm. 24–28, is shown in example 5.32. Pitch D4 occurs as a member of [1][2], the original (y) group, now subdividing the lower [3] of the structure (C#–E–G)4. This bisected [6] is reconstructed, as (E–F#–G)4, the rotated projection of (E–D–C#)4, appears in mm. 54–55.[13] Notice the beautiful way in which the framework (C#–E–G)4 is articulated: (C#–E)4 is first filled in, then given as a single interval, and after that the same is done with (E–G)4. (Recall the projection of (G–A–Bb)4 to Bb4–(C–Db)5 in mm. 6–9 by the same technique.) In m. 56 the linear succession (Bb–E)4 acts as though gathering (C#–G)4 into a single interval by projection.

The entrance of A5 completes both a larger spatial relationship (contraction from previous boundaries) and the realization of the potential represented by

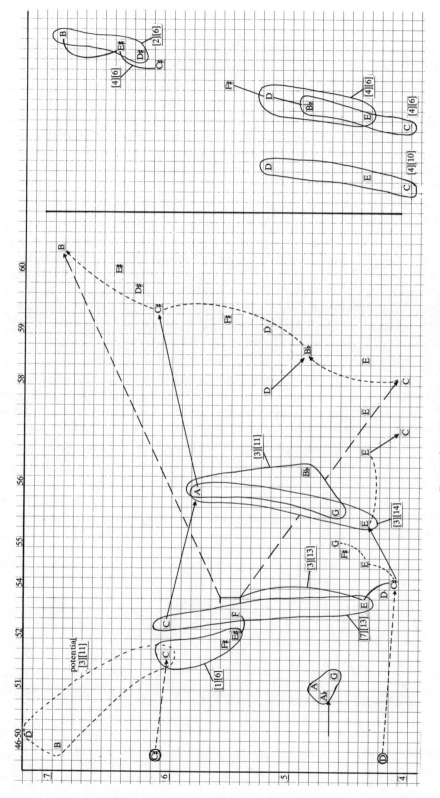

Example 5.32: *Density 21.5*, mm. 43–61

the earlier [3][11]: (C–B)6–D7. Further, as also shown in the graph of example 5.32, pitches E4 and A5 serve as the initiators of an expansion. It is also true that A5 divides C6–F♯5 (mm. 51–52) as [3][3], completing an analogy to (C♯–E–G)4 below. This is consistent with the contraction, since E4 and A5 in this scheme of bisected [6]s have parallel functions. Note incidentally that the span C♯4–C6 has already been defined by virtue of the projection from D4–C♯6 in mm. 43–45, a segment of the larger ascent to D7 distinguished by the lower boundary on one end and the highest nonstatic pitch in that ascent on the other. This interpretation gains in persuasive force from the explicit reiteration of D4 in m. 53—its only occurrence since m. 43—before the lower boundary shifts to C♯4 (next note, m. 54).

After B♭4 (m. 56), the very next pitch is C4, the lowest note on the instrument, which has not yet been used in the work. With this single new event the properties of internal structure change substantially. There can be no doubt that resemblances to what has gone before are intended: the collection (C–E)4–D5 is tantalizingly close to (C♯–E)4–D5 (m. 25), which as [3][10] constitutes a major structural force (ex. 5.33). And m. 25 is a partial condensation of mm. 1–11. Just as (C♯–E)4–D5 was abridged in m. 26 to a single interval of [13], so now (m. 58) is (C–E)4–D5 abridged to [14]. These resemblances, however, based as they are upon approximation, are fundamentally different from the types of reference by resemblance found earlier in *Density 21.5*. The advent of C4 seems to represent not just another step in the gradual evolution of new structures from old but a radical dissolution of all previous structures and their complete and abrupt replacement.

The new lattice, featuring adjacencies [2], [4], and [6], now grows inexorably upward to end the work. The trichordal forms [4][10], [4][6], and [2][6], circled in the extraction at the right of example 5.32, are common to a double constellation, [2][6] / [4][6]. One interval of [7] intrudes into this otherwise pure structure, and the graph shows its role. Without the intrusion, other spatial relationships (expansions, principally) would not be possible. Note also that the midsegment of the ascent in mm. 58–61 from C4 to B6 is B♭4–C♯6. This midsegment in the graph is placed under a single slur.

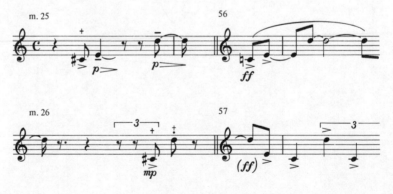

Example 5.33: *Density 21.5*

Why does *Density 21.5* end this way? Considered from one standpoint, the disjunction represented by the final measures is mysterious—and perhaps ultimately inexplicable. But looked at from another point of view, the analytical results obtained in the foregoing analysis should not appear so baffling. Certainly this major instance of discontinuity has been foreshadowed at various points in the work. A quick overview confirms this. Progress from the opening through m. 23 is smooth; then at m. 24 comes the first real break, one which however is eventually "explained"—that is, incorporated into the evolving spatial design. What follows m. 36 is also initially puzzling, for the trichordal characteristics previously developed seem to be abandoned here. Other forces enter the scheme to provide continuity, and the ascent to m. 46 presents a convincing analogy to the one in mm. 31–32. It is also significant that up to this point in the work, micro-structural continuity, which at the outset formed the core of musical motion and thereafter was split but left in control of outer boundaries, is still in evidence. However, the [2][3] unfoldings which must be invoked to explain the boundaries D4–D7 (mm. 43–46) and the oblique way in which these unfoldings are presented suggest that the power of the original material, expressed through its derivatives, has reached its limits, its influence become quite remote. In consequence, the break following m. 50 is more severe than any earlier one. The listener receives the initial impression of fragmentary echoes of earlier material, and this impression is never truly dispelled, for the internal details—a derivative of a derivative and a new constellation—signal fundamental structural realignments. As previously presented analyses have shown, in other works of Varèse the appearance of such new structures does not always represent discontinuity, or at least not to such a degree. But here, where the materials in use have been rigorously restricted throughout (only two constellations in all, plus two derivative-related micro-structures), the appearance of a third constellation—one which, unlike the first two, is not a natural outgrowth from previous points in the work—is a potentially disruptive event. The extent to which internal characteristics have shifted because of [3][11] becomes particularly evident after m. 54, where there occurs a clear reference to the rising motion of the opening passage. This reference is, even at the outset, highly modified with respect to the original, and after G4 (m. 55) also highly condensed. Once again, the sense of a fragmentary echo is conveyed in the pitches B♭4 and A5, which have individual correspondents in mm. 6–8 and m. 13, respectively, but certainly no direct connection to each other in that initial ascent.

The stage is thus set by m. 56 for the final act: the complete abandonment of resemblance to what has gone before and its supersession by the concluding ascent. That this final, decisive change is initiated by what is ostensibly a very modest move (C♯4 displaced by C4) should not distract us from the heart of the matter. This C4, saved for the end, represents yet a further expansion of space used in this piece, and this small step, taken after a great deal of preparation, leads to irrevocable and fundamental alteration. The fact that C4 happens to be the lowest pitch available on a flute not equipped with a B-foot is actually not particularly important—no more, really, than it is significant that the last note is not the highest available to the instrument. Like other Varèse endings, the purpose of this final ascent is not to close off by emphasizing the limits of the medium, not to reach a climax by neatly summing up, but to suggest the limitless possibilities of musical space. Varèse's phrase "open rather than bounded" is nowhere more appropriate. Like other musical compositions, *Density 21.5* must end somewhere, but the "journey into space" may go on, in however figurative a sense. This may be the real meaning of the repartitioning of registral space in mm. 56–61. One last point: the disappearance of micro-structural continuity after m. 50 in the form traced earlier can also be taken as a premonition of the final ascent. The more integral importance of micro-structure in *Density 21.5* than in other Varèse works may be a function of the narrower limits imposed upon registral space by a work for solo flute; in this sense (but only in this sense) is Wilkinson's allegation correct. What more striking way could be imagined of portraying a soar toward spatial freedom than to dissolve the micro-structural entities that have—if only symbolically—served as constraints upon that freedom throughout the work?

APPENDIX A
INDEX OF MUSICAL EXAMPLES

Amériques

3.30 (m. 8); 4.3 (mm. 1–7)

Arcana

2.23 (mm. 361–377); 3.24 (mm. 180–198); 4.8 (mm. 418–426); 4.31 (mm. 32, 36, 39, 59); 4.32 (mm. 79, 215, 283–284); 4.3 (mm. 45–48, 53–55); 4.34 (mm. 92–96, 301–327, 403–409); 4.35 (mm. 410–411); 4.36 (mm. 104, 427)

Density 21.5

3.10a (mm. 31–32); 3.10b (mm. 44–46); 5.23–5.33 (mm. 1–61, entire work)

Déserts

2.3 (mm. 21–22); 2.6 (mm. 171–174); 2.7 (mm. 29–30); 2.10 (mm. 85–93); 2.12 (mm. 46–53); 2.13 (mm. 81–82); 2.16 (mm. 63–65); 2.21 (mm. 71–78); 2.22 (mm. 226–242); 3.4 (m. 166); 3.13 (mm. 21–36); 3.31 (mm. 240–246); 4.9 (mm. 124–132); 4.16 (mm. 1–20); 4.17 (mm. 244–263); 4.18 (mm. 312–325); 4.20 (m. 47); 4.21 (mm. 1–11); 4.22 (mm. 87–92); 4.23 (mm. 23–29); 4.29 (mm. 264–269); 4.30 (mm. 200–203)

Ecuatorial

2.17 (mm. 211–220); 3.29 (m. 23); 3.35 (m. 19); 3.56–3.62 (mm. 1–18); 4.15 (mm. 135–147)

Hyperprism

3.20 (mm. 45–46); 3.25 (mm. 18–23); 3.32 (m. 42); 4.19 (mm. 30–33); 5.1–5.22 (mm. 1–89, entire work)

Intégrales

2.3 (m. 36); 2.4 (m. 69); 2.5 (m. 78); 2.8 (mm. 177–185); 2.11 (mm. 151–154); 2.18 (mm. 80–102); 2.19 (mm. 126–135); 2.24 (mm. 1–154); 3.7 (mm. 105, 144); 3.12 (1–25); 3.16 (mm. 25–29); 3.26 (mm. 32–52, 44–45); 3.28 (mm. 71–78); 3.33 (mm. 80–83); 3.34 (mm. 101, 105, 106); 3.37 (mm. 53–70); 3.38–3.39 (mm. 53–69); 3.40–3.46 (mm. 62–69); 4.7 (mm. 32–52); 4.10 (mm. 80–92); 4.12 (mm. 135–143); 4.24 (mm. 1–25); 4.25 (mm. 32–36); 4.26 (mm. 79–93); 4.27 (mm. 105–117)

Ionisation

4.11 (mm. 38–42); 4.14 (mm. 44–50); 4.37 (mm. 1, 4, 9); 4.38 (mm. 13–14, 23–24)

Nocturnal

3.6 (mm. 53–60); 3.14 (mm. 1–41); 3.23 (mm. 88–93)

Octandre

2.14 (II, mm. 39–66); 3.8 (II, mm. 17–20); 3.11 (II, mm. 10–21); 3.15 (I, mm. 8–10); 3.17 (I, m. 11); 3.19a (III, mm. 43–44); 3.22 (III, mm. 18–23); 3.27 (I, mm. 1–6); 3.47–3.55 (I, mm. 1–12); 4.1 (I, mm. 1–5); 4.4 (II, mm. 1–11); 4.5 (II, mm. 50–65); 4.6 (III, mm. 24–39); 4.13 (II, mm. 17–36)

Offrandes

2.15 (II, mm. 40–43); 2.20 (I, mm. 32–35); 3.9 (II, mm. 6–12); 3.18 (II, mm. 4–8); 3.19b (I, m. 14); 3.21 (I, mm. 30–31); 3.36 (II, m. 21); 4.2 (I, mm. 6–14); 4.28 (II, mm. 4–7)

APPENDIX B
ANNOTATED LIST OF WORKS

I. PUBLISHED WORKS (IN ORDER OF COMPLETION)

Un grand sommeil noir

For voice (unspecified)[1] and piano. The text is a short poem by Paul Verlaine. Date of composition unknown. The score is dedicated to Léon Claude Mercerot. First published by Senart, 1906; no evidence of any public performance at that time seems to have survived. Currently available in an edition reprinted from the original (Editions Salabert, Paris, 1976).

Amériques

For orchestra. Composed 1918–1921. The score is dedicated, according to Louise Varèse, "to my unknown friends of 1921." Premiered April 9, 1926, by the Philadelphia Orchestra, conducted by Leopold Stokowski, at the Academy of Music in Philadelphia. Revised 1927. Revision premiered May 30, 1929 by the Orchestre des Concerts Poulet, conducted by Gaston Poulet, at the Maison Gaveau in Paris. First version published by J. Curwen and Sons Ltd., London, 1925; revised version published by Max Eschig, Paris, 1929. The score published by Colfranc in 1973 is a new edition by Chou Wen-chung of the revised version based upon comparison of the manuscript with copies of previous publications of both versions. For further details, see Chou Wen-chung's perface to the Colfranc edition.

Offrandes

For soprano and chamber orchestra with percussion. Composed 1921. *Offrandes* consists of two songs, the first ("Chanson de là-haut") a setting of an extract from Vicente Huidobro's poem "Tour Eiffel," the second ("La croix du sud") of José Juan Tablada's poem of the same title. (See the notes on the texts under Huidobro and Tablada in section III of the bibliography.) The two songs are dedicated, respectively, "à Louise" and "à Carlos Salzedo." Originally entitled *Dédications*. Premiered April 23, 1922, at an International Composers' Guild concert at the Greenwich Village Theater, conducted by Carlos Salzedo and with Nina Koshetz as the soloist. First published by C. C. Birchard & Co., Boston, 1927; the score currently available from Colfranc is a reprint of the Birchard edition with a few minor corrections.

Hyperprism

For small orchestra with percussion. Composed 1922–1923. The score is dedicated to José Juan and Nena Tablada. Premiered March 4, 1923 at an International Composers' Guild concert at the Klaw Theater in New York, conducted by Varèse. First published by Curwen, 1924; the score currently available from Colfranc, dated 1966, is a reprint of the edition brought out by Ricordi in 1956.

Octandre

For flute/piccolo, oboe, clarinet/E-flat clarinet, bassoon, trumpet, horn, trombone, and double bass. Composed 1923. In three untitled movements. The score is dedicated to E. Robert Schmitz. Premiered January 13, 1924, at an International Composers' Guild concert at the Vanderbilt Theatre, New York, conducted by Schmitz. First published by Curwen, 1924; a reprint with a few corrections by Varèse was brought out by Ricordi in 1956. The currently available score (Colfranc, 1980) is a new edition by Chou Wen-chung, which includes a preface by the editor explaining the differences between this edition and its predecessor.

Intégrales

For chamber ensemble with percussion. Composed 1924–1925. The score is dedicated to Mrs. Juliana Force. Premiered March 1, 1925 at an International Composers' Guild Concert, Leopold Stokowski conducting, at Aeolian Hall in New York. First published by Curwen, 1926; a reprint with a few corrections by Varèse was brought out by Ricordi in 1956. The currently available score (Colfranc, 1980) is a new edition by Chou Wen-chung which, like the new editions of Amériques and Octandre, includes a preface by the editor.

Arcana

For orchestra. Composed 1925–February 1927. The score is dedicated to Leopold Stokowski. Premiered April 8, 1927, by the Philadelphia Orchestra, conducted by Stokowski, at the Academy of Music in Philadelphia. Varèse undertook some minor revisions in 1960 that he completed early in 1961, evidently in preparation for the recording made by Robert Craft and the Columbia Symphony for Columbia Records. First published by Eschig, 1931; the score currently available from Colfranc is a reprint of the edition brought out by Franco Colombo, New York, 1964.

Ionisation

For an ensemble of percussion instruments played by thirteen executants. Composed 1930–1931. The score is dedicated to Nicolas Slonimsky. Premiered March 6, 1933, at a concert conducted by Slonimsky at Carnegie Hall, New York. First published by Eschig, 1934; reprinted the same year by New Music Orchestra Series, San Francisco. This edition bears the legend "Paris, November 13, 1931" at the bottom of the last page. The score currently available (Colfranc, 1967) is a reprint of the edition brought out by Ricordi in 1956.

Ecuatorial

For solo bass voice, four trumpets, four trombones, piano, organ, two Theremins, and percussion. Composed 1933–1934. The text is taken from the Popul Vuh, the sacred book of the Maya Quiché, translated into Spanish by Father Jimines and included in Miguel Asturias's Leyendas de Guatemala (see bibliography, section III). The score is dedicated to Louise Varèse. Premiered April 15, 1934, at a Pan-American Association concert, conducted by Nicolas Slonimsky with Chase Baromeo as the soloist, at Town Hall, New York. In this first performance the bass was amplified with a hand-held megaphone, apparently with indifferent results. For the second performance (1961) Varèse replaced the single voice with a chorus of basses and the Theremins with two Ondes Martenot. First published by Ricordi in 1961, and reprinted currently by Colfranc; this edition reflects the changes made for the 1961 performance.

Density 21.5

For solo flute. Composed January, 1936. Commissioned by Georges Barrère, who also premiered the work in a recital on February 16, 1936, at Carnegie Hall, New York, at which he inaugurated his platinum flute. Revised April 1946 prior to publication by *New Music Quarterly*, July 1946. The score currently available (Colfranc, 1966) is a reprint of the edition brought out by Ricordi in 1956.

Déserts

For chamber ensemble with percussion and two-channel magnetic tape. In seven sections, four played by the live instruments alone in alternation with three of "organized sound" on the tape alone; the live instruments begin and end the work. The instrumental sections were composed between summer 1950 and late 1952. The raw material for the sections on tape was gathered between 1953 and 1954 "in the ironworks, sawmills, and various factories of Philadelphia" (Ouellette, p. 175). The actual composition of the taped sections began in October 1954, when Varèse arrived at the O.R.T.F. studios in Paris. The score is dedicated to Red Heller. Premiered December 2, 1954, by members of the Orchestre de la Radio-Télévision Française, conducted by Hermann Scherchen, at the Théâtre des Champs-Elysées in Paris. The taped interpolations were revised and re-recorded in 1961 with the technical assistance of Bulent Arel. First published by Ricordi, 1959 (only the instrumental sections are notated); the score currently available from Colfranc is a reprint of that edition.

Le Poème électronique

For magnetic tape (duration: 480 seconds). Composed between September 1957 and April 1958 at Philips Laboratories, Eindhoven, The Netherlands. Premiered at the Philips Pavilion, Brussels World's Fair, which opened in May 1958. No score, in any exactly representational sense, ever existed for *Poème*, only the charts which Varèse used to plan and execute the work. Originally composed for a tape with three synchronized tracks, which were used separately and in combination to create numerous "sound paths" through the Pavilion using ten amplifiers and 150 loudspeakers, *Poème* is now available only in a conventional two-channel stereo version, issued by Columbia Records on MG–31078 and MS–6146.

Nocturnal

For chamber orchestra with piano, chorus of basses, and solo soprano. Composed 1959–1961; unfinished. The text is composed of words and phrases taken from Anaïs Nin's *House of Incest* (see bibliography, section III), interspersed with vocal syllables supplied by Varèse himself. Premiered May 1, 1961, at a Composers' Showcase Concert, Town Hall, New York, conducted by Robert Craft and with Donna Precht as the soprano soloist. *Nocturnal* was edited and completed after Varèse's death from the composer's notes and sketches by Chou Wen-chung. The edition published by Colfranc in 1969 is of the completed version; a dotted line on p. 16 of the score shows where the work as it existed at the time of the premiere originally ended. Also included is a preface by Chou. Some of the material incorporated into both the incomplete and the complete versions was known at one time or another by other titles; see IIB below.

II. UNPUBLISHED WORKS

A. Complete

Etude pour Espace

For chorus, two pianos, and percussion. Premiered April 20, 1947,[2] by the New Music Society at the New School, West Twelfth Street, New York, conducted by Varèse. Exact dates of composition unknown. By 1947, material for Varèse's great work *Espace,* planned to be of monumental proportions but never finished, had been composed and repeatedly reworked for nearly two decades. The *Etude* appears to be what its title implies: a presentation, for much reduced forces, of some of the material originally intended to comprise *Espace.* It is thus only nominally a "complete work." the *Etude* now exists in no definitive form; according to Chou there are three copies among the materials of the Varèse legacy, each with a different set of revisions indicated in Varèse's hand. (*New Worlds,* p. 89.)

Dance for Burgess

For chamber orchestra with percussion. The score is dated December 30, 1949, on its last page. A reproduction of the hand-copied score (the hand probably Varèse's) is in the Library of Congress. According to Chou (telephone conversation with the author, August 2, 1983), this was written for a show done by Burgess Meredith on Broadway and is "not a real Varèse work"—in other words, it was probably not written with the same serious intent as were his other works. There certainly are grounds for this assertion; a glance at the score reveals that the harmonic and rhythmic characteristics of the *Dance* are quite different from those of any of Varèse's other music—for the most part much simpler, even to the point (possibly) of frivolity. It would be interesting to know, although perhaps by now impossible to discover, whether anyone other than Varèse had a hand in determining the final form of this work.

La Procession de Vergès

For magnetic tape (duration: 2 minutes, 47 seconds). Created for a sequence in Thomas Bouchard's film, *Around and about Miró* (New York: Bouchard Productions). The film was first shown at the Fogg Museum of Art, Cambridge, Mass., on December 7, 1955.[3] At least one copy of the film is presumed still to exist, but its whereabouts are unknown; in any case, it is not available for distribution.

B. Unfinished

Only extremely vague information, if any at all, is available about these works; at this writing no one—even Chou himself, the curator of the Varèse legacy—seems to be able to say to what extent these works actually exist *as* works (as opposed to disconnected fragments or sketches). Below are given titles of compositions that Varèse was known to be working on at one time or another, together with the approximate dates at which the work apparently took place.

Métal. 1930s?

Trinum. For orchestra; during the 1950s, following *Déserts.*

Dans la nuit; Nocturnal II; Nuit. These are not really distinct and separate compositions but rather alternative titles that Varèse used for the work that he was doing during the late 1950s (after *Le poème électronique*) and early 1960s. This work includes *Nocturnal;* in fact, *Dans la nuit* was the original title for *Nocturnal.* Chou has stated that "From the last years the titles *Dans la nuit, Nuit, Nocturnal,* and *Nocturnal II* were all references to the same work."[4] The titles which seem to date from after the premiere of the incomplete *Nocturnal* represented further attempts to complete this work, none successful.

Espace. What came to be known as *Espace* in the 1930s was actually the outgrowth of ideas that Varèse had had since the late 1920s (after *Arcana*). According to his biographers, his first plan had been for a work to be called *The One All Alone, a Miracle,* based upon American Indian myths. Gradually this was supplanted by *Astronome,* a work to be set in A.D.

2000 with a plot involving interstellar communication and the visitation of universal disaster upon the earth. Robert Desnos and Alejo Carpentier were engaged in 1929 or so to write the scenario, but this collaboration produced, by all accounts, not much of anything.[5] Subsequently, around 1932, Varèse approached Antonin Artaud with similar ideas. Artaud did eventually write four parts of a planned five-part scenario (see section III of the bibliography), but this was published only posthumously, and whether he ever actually showed it to Varèse is not clear. In any case, by the mid-1930s Varèse's interests had shifted toward a work of a more general, even abstract character. By 1936 he was publicizing his plans for a fifteen-minute piece to be called *Espace* (see "Varèse Envisions 'Space' Symphonies" and "The 'Red Symphony' Is Due to Explode," bibliography, section ID). Also in print is Varèse's own description of the work as he projected it (see under Dorothy Norman, bibliography, section ID). Work on the score apparently continued throughout the 1940s, but exactly how close *Espace* was brought to completion is not known and may never be, since many of the relevant materials were thrown away.[6] It does not seem likely, however, that the original conception came close to realization, since the success of the work as Varèse had imagined it depended upon technological developments in sound production that he believed were imminent at the time, but which proved not to be.

III. WORKS DESTROYED OR LOST

All of the following were apparently written for large forces: orchestra with or without choral augmentation and/or vocal soloists. All, except where noted, were destroyed in a warehouse fire in Berlin around the end of World War I; they had been stored there when the outbreak of war in 1914 necessitated Varèse's abrupt return to France. None, again except where noted, ever received a public performance. The titles are no doubt approximate in some cases and may overlap (for instance, if the *Trois pièces* had individual titles, then they may be represented elsewhere on this list). Most are given in Chou's "A Varèse Chronology"; a few not found there are mentioned in Louise Varèse and/or Ouellette.

A. Circa 1905–1907

Trois pièces
La chanson des jeunes hommes
Rhapsodie romane
Colloque au bord de la fontaine
Apothéose de l'océan
Dans le parc
Poème des brumes
Souvenir
Le Prélude à la fin d'un jour. Manuscript entrusted to Léon Deubel, whose poem "La fin d'un jour" inspired the musical composition; lost after Deubel's suicide (1913).

B. Circa 1908–1914

Mehr Licht
Les cycles du nord
Oedipus und die Sphynx (incomplete; opera with libretto by Hugo von Hofmannsthal)
Gargantua (incomplete)
Bourgogne. For orchestra. Premiered December 15, 1910, by the Blüthner Orchestra, conducted by Josef Stransky, in Berlin. Never published; manuscript destroyed by Varèse about 1962.

NOTES

INTRODUCTION

1. The two principal biographies are Fernand Ouellette, *Edgard Varèse* (Paris: Seghers, 1966; English translation by Derek Coltman, New York: Orion, 1968); Louise Varèse, *Varèse: A Looking-Glass Diary*, vol. 1: 1883–1928 (New York: Norton, 1972; remaining volumes yet to be published) (bibl. IIA). Two other books that qualify nominally as biographies, by Hilda Jolivet and Odile Vivier, are quite short and of limited interest (see bibl. IIA).

2. The reader would find it helpful to be familiar with at least the following works: *Hyperprism, Octandre, Intégrales, Density 21.5, Déserts.* Of the others, *Arcana* and *Offrandes* are fairly often cited, although not nearly so often as the first five. It would also be useful to know *Ionisation* well, even though it is not extensively excerpted in the present book.

3. All of the sketches and almost all of the manuscripts are under the direct control of the Varèse estate, for which Chou Wen-chung serves as executor. He has ruled out the possibility of anyone else's gaining access to this material until he has finished his long-planned study of Varèse's music (conversation with the author, March 14, 1976). In recent years he has seemed to be on the verge of relaxing this ban, and has spoken of putting the material into a condition in which it may be used by others, either at his home (formerly Varèse's, and now shared by Louise Varèse and the Chou family) or in a library. However, to date this task has apparently not been accomplished.

4. Chou Wen-chung, in *The New Worlds of Edgard Varèse*, ed. Sherman Van Solkema (Brooklyn: Institute for Studies in American Music, 1979), pp. 88–89 (bibl. IIB).

5. Most of these lost works were consumed in a warehouse fire in Berlin at the end of World War I. The surviving piece, *Un grand sommeil noir*, originally published in 1906, seems without question a juvenile work. Owing to this, and to its extreme brevity and economy of means, it remains a frustrating hint of Varèse's early career—one that cannot tell us much now, despite attempts to attribute greater significance to it (see Larry Stempel, "Not Even Varèse Can Be an Orphan," *Musical Quarterly* 60 [1974]: 46–60) (bibl. IIB). The manuscript of the one work which received a public performance before 1920, *Bourgogne*, remained in Varèse's possession until about 1962, when he destroyed it.

6. This is not to say, of course, that these works had nothing unusual or original about them. Eduard Steuermann, in conversation with Gunther Schuller, recalled hearing the premiere (and only performance) of *Bourgogne* in Berlin in 1910, and mentioned one passage that had stuck in his memory "for terrifically divisi strings—I don't know how many individual parts—that made a tremendous forest of string sound." At the time, this certainly must have been startling (Schuller, "Conversation with Steuermann," in *Perspectives on American Composers*, ed. Benjamin Boretz and Edward T. Cone [New York: Norton, 1971], p. 210) (bibl. III).

7. Milton Babbitt, "Edgard Varèse: A Few Observations of His Music," in *Perspectives on American Composers*, p. 41.

8. Wilkinson, in Dallapiccola et al., "In Memoriam: Edgard Varèse (1883–1965)," *Perspectives of New Music* 4/2 (1966): 12 (bibl. ID).

9. Feldman, in "In Memoriam," p. 12.

10. Babbitt, in "For Edgard Varèse on the Celebration of His 80th Year," Carnegie Hall program, March 31, 1965, p. 14 (bibl. IIC). The year 1965 was actually Varèse's eighty-second, but no one, apparently including Varèse, knew this at the time. Only after his death did someone check the record of his birth, in the tenth arrondissement in Paris, and discover that his actual year of birth was 1883, not 1885.

11. Gunther Schuller, "Conversation with Varèse," in *Perspectives on American Composers*, p. 38 (bibl. IB).

12. *Etude pour Espace*, however, was given its first (and to date only) performance in 1947. See appendix B for more information about this work and *Espace* itself.

13. Michael Sperling, "Varèse and Contemporary Music," *Trend* 2/3 (1934): 124–128 (bibl. ID). Varèse saw Europe as the chief source of neoclassic influence, and he frequently advised aspiring students of composition in the United States to remain at home for their education rather than travel to France or Germany to learn "a lot of old-maidish mannerisms" or "clever Parisian tricks." Interviewed in Berlin, where he had gone in 1922 to establish a branch of the International Composers' Guild, Varèse said to the press, "Music students do not need to come to Europe to get the best training today. They will find at home higher efficiency and more progressive instructors than in Europe" (letter to José Rodriguez, Paris, March 1, 1933, printed in *Letters of Composers: An Anthology, 1603–1945*, ed. Gertrude Norman and Miriam Lubell Shrifte [New York: Knopf, 1946], p. 360 [bibl. IC]; Sperling, p. 127; "Best Teachers of Music Here, Is the Word from Berlin," *New York Herald*, November 12, 1922, section 7, p. 8 [bibl. ID]).

14. Schuller, p. 35; Igor Stravinsky and Robert Craft, "Some Composers," *Musical America* 82/6 (June 1962): 11; reprinted in Stravinsky and Craft, *Dialogues* (Berkeley: University of California Press, 1982), p. 109 (bibl. ID).

15. Ouellette, p. 222.

16. Schuller, p. 34.

17. Varèse, "Jérôm' s'en va-t'en guerre," *The Sackbut* 4 (1923): 147 (bibl. IA).

18. "Edgard Varèse and Alexei Haieff Questioned by Eight Composers/Answers by Edgard Varèse," *Possibilities* 1 (Winter 1947–48): 96–97 (bibl. IB).

19. José André, "Edgar Varèse y la música de Vanguardía," *La Nación*, Paris, March 1930, trans. and quoted by David R. Bloch in "The Music of Edgard Varèse" (Ph.D. diss., University of Washington, 1973), p. 260 (bibl. IIB); Sperling, p. 127.

20. We note only in passing that at the time and for many years afterward the theoretical foundations of Schoenberg's method were widely misunderstood—the idea that all twelve notes of the row are equal at all times being a prominent example of such misunderstanding.

21. Varèse, letter to Dallapiccola, December 7, 1952; quoted in Ouellette, p. 173.

22. Varèse, quoted in Ouellette, p. 183.

23. Georges Charbonnier, *Entretiens avec Edgard Varèse* (Paris: Pierre Belfond, 1970), p. 25 (bibl. IB).

24. Varèse, "Le Destin de la musique est de conquérir la liberté," *Liberté* 5 (1959): 276 (bibl. IA). "Je devins même le phénomène de la classe à cause de mon aisance et de ma prestesse à jongler avec les subtilités de contrepoint. . . ."

25. Elliott Carter, "On Edgard Varèse," in Van Solkema, *The New Worlds of Edgar Varèse*, p. 7 (bibl. IIB).

26. "Varèse Answers *Amériques* Critics," *Evening Bulletin*, Philadelphia, April 12, 1926, p. 3 (bibl. ID).

27. "The 'Red Symphony' Is Due to Explode," *New York Times*, March 4, 1937, section 1, p. 25 (bibl. ID).

28. Anaïs Nin, *The Diary of Anaïs Nin*, vol. 3: 1939–1944, ed. Gunther Stuhlmann (New York: Harcourt Brace Jovanovich, 1969), pp. 155–156 (bibl. III). Presumably Nin saw the studio and its contents on several different occasions; other details suggest that this description, although it bears a specific date, may actually be an amalgamation of several visits. For example, immediately after the passage quoted above Nin mentions seeing a tape recorder, which could not possibly have been there in 1941.

29. Van Solkema, *The New Worlds of Edgard Varèse*, p. 88.

30. Stravinsky and Craft, *Dialogues*, p. 109.

31. This practice of borrowing is also related to the apparent reuse of material within the same composition, a phenomenon which is treated in detail in chapter 2.

32. Conversation with the author, New York, March 14, 1976.

33. Varèse, "Puff Balls," *New Mexico Sentinel,* September 21, 1937; quoted in Ouellette, p. 142.

34. The most important omissions are the electronic works and passages: *Poème électronique* and the music for a short sequence in Thomas Bouchard's film *Around and about Miró,* "La Procession de Vergès," together with the three interpolations of "organized sound" in *Déserts.* Unfortunately, without exact notation to work from, no meaningful analysis is possible, given the techniques that are now available. Perhaps some form of spectral analysis of the sort that Robert Cogan has been working on recently will eventually make these works accessible to theorists. (See Robert Cogan, *New Images of Musical Sound* [Cambridge: Harvard University Press, 1984; bibl. IIB], which contains "sound pictures" of passages from various compositions, including Varèse's *Hyperprism.*)

Among the earliest works, *Un grand sommeil noir* has been passed over for reasons explained earlier. Unlike all the pieces for conventional instruments from *Offrandes* on, *Amériques* has proved extremely problematic when approached with the methods developed in this book, suggesting that it has some aspects of a transitional work (parts of it were written as early as 1918). *Offrandes,* by contrast, begun three years later, is much more amenable. Therefore, only a few relatively brief examples from *Amériques* have been included.

The choice of pitch (in alliance with register) as primary domain simply does not engage the content of *Ionisation,* Varèse's only work exclusively for percussion instruments of indefinite pitch. (Piano, glockenspiel, and chimes do enter in the final measures, but they are used in the manner of indefinitely pitched instruments: their initial pitch configurations remain absolutely fixed until the end of the work.) Discussion of *Ionisation* is thus confined to chapter 4, although a fair amount is said about it there. The reader may wish to consult Chou's splendid analysis of this work, which adopts a timbrally based approach (Chou Wen-chung, "*Ionisation:* The Function of Timbre in Its Formal and Temporal Organization," in Van Solkema, *The New Worlds of Edgard Varèse,* pp. 26–74; bibl. IIB). Chou's assertion that "to analyze *Ionisation* . . . is to pave the way for understanding all of Varèse's music" is, however, difficult if not impossible to accept. The work is, as Chou himself notes, unique in Varèse's oeuvre in that it does without definite pitch, and is more appropriately regarded as a special case, in which unusual conditions reign, than as a key to the real nature of all the other works.

Finally, concerning the incomplete and/or unpublished pieces: first, the "performance" version of *Nocturnal* completed by Chou, although produced through painstaking and meticulous work and informed by an intimate knowledge of Varèse's methods and habits, cannot be regarded as authentic, except for the first ninety-three measures, which Varèse did complete himself; second, *Etude pour Espace,* unedited and unpublished, has remained inaccessible; third, *Dance for Burgess* (1949), although complete, has also never been published. None of Varèse's biographers mentions the piece, and only one article among all that have appeared on Varèse draws from it. It is really an occasional work, written in a somewhat frivolous spirit upon special request. For the purposes of this book it seemed best ignored (see appendix B for more information).

35. Stravinsky and Craft, *Dialogues,* p. 110.

36. Dallapiccola et al., "In Memoriam," p. 12.

37. Van Solkema, *The New Worlds of Edgard Varèse,* p. 84.

38. Henry Cowell, "The Music of Edgar Varèse," *Modern Music* 5/2 (1928): 9–18 (bibl. IIB).

39. The quotations are, in reverse order: Varèse in Schuller, p. 38; Varèse quoting Hoenë Wronsky's definition of music. Varèse had probably seen this quoted in Durutte's *Technie Harmonique* (1876), and he cited the phrase from Wronsky many times in his own lectures. For example, see "Music as an Art-Science" (1939), a lecture excerpt collected in "The Liberation of Sound," in *Contemporary Composers on Contemporary Music,* ed. Elliott Schwartz and Barney Childs (New York: Holt, Rinehart, and Winston, 1967), p. 199 (bibl. IA).

CHAPTER 1. VARESE'S AESTHETIC BACKGROUND

1. Edgard Varèse, in Charbonnier, p. 18.

2. "Edgard Varèse on Music and Art: A Conversation between Varèse and Alcopley," *Leonardo* 1 (1968): 189 (bibl. IB). The conversation actually took place in 1963.

3. Charbonnier, p. 25. Also see Louise Varèse, pp. 53–54.

4. Louise Varèse, pp. 52–56.

5. Ibid, pp. 54–55, 104, 108–110.

6. Louise Norton first met her future husband in 1917, after he had arrived in the United States.

7. Louise Varèse, pp. 124–125; William Innes Homer, *Alfred Stieglitz and the American Avant-Garde* (Boston: New York Graphic Society, 1977), pp. 181–182 (bibl. III).

8. See note 5 to the introduction.

9. Bram Dijkstra, *Cubism, Stieglitz, and the Early Poetry of William Carlos Williams* (Princeton: Princeton University Press, 1969), p. x (bibl. III).

10. Dijkstra, pp. ix–x.

11. Louise Varèse, p. 106.

12. Both Dijkstra and Christopher Gray, in *Cubist Aesthetic Theories* (Baltimore: Johns Hopkins University Press, 1953; bibl. III), have deliberately excluded later writings for similar reasons.

13. Of course the progression to cubism was not so sudden as that. For one thing, not everyone was converted at once; for another, many artists and critics recognized precedents in earlier work by others.

14. Varèse, "Jérôm' s'en va-t'en guerre," p. 145. The authors of the two quotations cited are Laurent Tailhade and Rémy de Gourmont.

15. Guillaume Apollinaire, "Georges Braque" (1908), in Edward F. Fry, *Cubism* (New York and Toronto: Oxford University Press, 1966), p. 49 (bibl. III).

16. Dijkstra, p. 55.

17. Louise Varèse, p. 45; Varèse, "Le Destin de la musique," p. 278. The Busoni quotation is taken from *Sketch of a New Aesthetic of Music*, in *Three Classics in the Aesthetic of Music* (New York: Dover, 1962), p. 88 (bibl. III).

18. Varèse, quoted in Henry Cowell, "Current Chronicle" [review of the premiere of *Déserts*], *Musical Quarterly* 41 (1955): 372 (bibl. ID).

19. Albert Gleizes and Jean Metzinger, *Cubism* (1912), in *Modern Artists on Art: Ten Unabridged Essays*, ed. Robert L. Herbert (Englewood Cliffs, N.J.: Prentice-Hall, 1964), p. 18 (bibl. III).

20. "Jérôm' s'en va-t'en guerre," p. 147, quoted above, p. xix.

21. Picasso, "Statement of 1935" (to Christian Zervos), in *Picasso on Art: A Selection of Views*, ed. Dore Ashton (New York: Viking, 1972), p. 11 (bibl. III).

22. Roger Allard, "The Signs of Renewal in Painting" (1912), in Fry, p. 72.

23. Max Kozloff, *Cubism/Futurism* (New York: Harper and Row, 1973), p. 9 (bibl. III).

24. Louise Varèse, p. 126; Varèse, in the *New York Telegraph*, March 1916, quoted in J. H. Klarén, *Edgar Varèse, Pioneer of New Music in America* (Boston: C. C. Birchard, 1928), p. 8 (bibl. ID).

25. Varèse, "The Liberation of Sound," p. 198; Varèse, "Les Instruments de musique et la machine électronique," *L'Age Nouveau* 92 (May 1955): 29–30 (bibl. IA); and other places.

26. Léonce Rosenberg, "Tradition and Cubism" (1919), in Fry, p. 150.

27. Gleizes and Metzinger, p. 3.

28. Varèse, quoted in Winthrop P. Tryon, "A New Edifice from Mr. Varèse," *Christian Science Monitor*, August 28, 1926, p. 8 (bibl. ID).

29. Louise Varèse, pp. 227–228. It is interesting that Varèse should have emulated—even if unconsciously—the visual artists in this respect, for one notices from time to time in their writings a certain envy for the composer's lot. In music, as they saw it, the issue of representation of objects did not even arise; musical composition was already an abstract art. Roger Allard, for example, asked pointedly: "Is it not remarkable how hard it is for our present-day critics and art-lovers to admit that painters and sculptors are justified in transmuting the vision of nature into an exact and abstract world of forms, when in other domains—in music and poetry—they already take a similar abstraction for granted?" (Allard, "Renewal," p. 71). Francis Picabia, too, according to the critic Arthur Jerome Eddy (*Cubism and Post-Impressionism* [Chicago: A.C. McClurg & Co., 1914], p. 62; bibl. III), was fond of making analogies to music.

30. "The Liberation of Sound," p. 203.

31. Pierre Reverdy, "On Cubism" (1917), in Fry, p. 145.

32. The epigraph to this section is from Roland Penrose, in *Picasso on Art*, p. 62, paraphrasing Picasso on the early days of cubism.

33. Daniel-Henry Kahnweiler, *The Rise of Cubism* (1915), trans. Henry Aronson (New York: Wittenborn, Schultz, 1949), p. 12 (bibl. III).

34. Maurice Raynal, "Preface to a Catalogue" (1912), in Fry, p. 92.

35. "The Liberation of Sound," p. 204.

36. Ibid., p. 197.

37. Ibid., pp. 198, 201.

38. Varèse, interviewed by Fred Grunfeld, radio station WQXR, December 13, 1953; quoted in Frederic Waldman, "Edgard Varèse: An Appreciation," *Juilliard Review* 1/3 (1954): 9 (bibl. ID). The same explanation was quoted in Fred Grunfeld, "The Well-Tempered Ionizer," *High Fidelity* 4 (1954): 106–107 (bibl. ID).

39. Waldman, p. 9.

40. See introduction, p. xxii.

41. "Varèse Envisions 'Space' Symphonies," *New York Times,* December 6, 1936, section 2, p. 7 (bibl. ID).

42. "The Liberation of Sound," pp. 205, 207. Le Corbusier has claimed that there were only 150 loudspeakers in all, of which 25 were for low notes and "special sounds." See Charles-Edouard Jeanneret-Gris [Le Corbusier], *Le Poème électronique Le Corbusier* (Paris: Minuit, 1958), p. 203.

43. Gleizes and Metzinger, p. 12.

44. Varèse paraphrased in André, "Edgar Varèse y la música de Vanguardía," trans. and quoted in Bloch, p. 61*n.*

45. "The Liberation of Sound," p. 197.

46. Gleizes and Metzinger, p. 12.

47. Ibid., pp. 9, 11–12.

48. Apollinaire, *The Cubist Painters: Aesthetic Meditations* (1913), trans. Lionel Abel (New York: George Wittenborn, 1970), p. 12 (bibl. III).

49. Schuller, p. 36.

50. Winthrop P. Tryon, "New Instruments in Orchestra Are Needed, Says Mr. Varèse," *Christian Science Monitor,* July 8, 1922, p. 18 (bibl. ID). The words quoted are Tryon's paraphrase.

51. "The Liberation of Sound," p. 202.

52. Jean Metzinger, "Cubism and Tradition" (1911), in Fry, p. 67.

53. Kahnweiler, *Cubism,* p. 7.

54. Apollinaire, *The Cubist Painters,* p. 17.

55. Gleizes and Metzinger, p. 8.

56. Jacques Rivière, "Present Tendencies in Painting" (1912), in Fry, p. 76.

57. Ibid., pp. 77–78.

58. Fernand Léger, "Contemporary Achievements in Painting" (1914), in Fry, p. 138.

59. *Picasso on Art,* p. 60.

60. Allard, "On Certain Painters" (1911), in Fry, p. 64. Italics in original.

61. "The Liberation of Sound," p. 197. Varèse spoke in the conditional tense because he was discussing, at this juncture, the future employment of new technical means which would enhance the structural function of timbre.

62. Tryon, "New Instruments in Orchestra Are Needed, Says Mr. Varese."

63. Varèse, quoted in Sperling, "Varèse and Contemporary Music," p. 128. We have it on the authority of Louise Varèse that Varèse composed at the piano at least some of the time (pp. 150, 216), but apparently he never began composing by writing out a piano score.

64. Gleizes and Metzinger, p. 15.

65. Metzinger, "Cubism and Tradition," pp. 66–67.

66. Raynal, "Conception and Vision" (1912), in Fry, p. 95. Similar expositions of this idea occur in Kahnweiler (*Cubism,* p. 11), in Rivière (Fry, p. 77), and in remarks attributed to Pierre Dumont by Eddy (in *Cubism and Post-Impressionism,* p. 180).

67. Fry, p. 32.

68. Apollinaire, *The Cubist Painters,* p. 22.

69. Louise Varèse, pp. 104–105.

70. Robert Delaunay, letter to August Macke (1912), in Herschel B. Chipp, ed., *Theories of Modern Art: A Source Book by Artists and Critics* (Berkeley: University of California Press, 1968), p. 317 (bibl. III).

71. However, Léger may have arrived at his ideas by another route, for Delaunay cited M. E. Chevreul's *De la loi du contraste simultané des couleurs* (1839) as the source of his terminology.

72. Delaunay, "Light" (1912), in Chipp, p. 319. In this and all of the following quotations from Delaunay, the italics are in the original.

73. Delaunay, letter to Franz Marc (1912), in Robert and Sonia Delaunay, *The New Art of Color: The Writings of Robert and Sonia Delaunay,* ed. Arthur A. Cohen, trans. David Shapiro and Arthur A. Cohen (New York: Viking, 1978), p. 116 (bibl. III).

74. "Light," p. 320.

75. Apollinaire, "Through the Salon des Indépendants" (1913), in *Apollinaire on Art: Essays and Reviews, 1902–1918,* ed. LeRoy C. Breunig, trans. Susan Suleiman (New York: Viking, 1972), p. 291 (bibl. III).

76. Robert and Sonia Delaunay, p. 50.

77. Louise Varèse, p. 55.

78. Allan Reginald Brown, "Orchestral Poetry," in *L'Art orphique,* ed. Henri Barzun, vol. 1, *Renaissance 1930* (Paris: Albert Morancé, 1930), p. 12 (bibl. III).

79. Ibid., pp. 12–13.

80. Fernand Divoire, "L'Art poétique orchestral/Simultanéisme = un mode d'expression qui permettra peut-être de grandes choses," in *L'Art orphique,* p. 44. (Reprinted from *La Meuse,* Liège, February 2, 1923.) "A cela, il n'y a qu'une seule objection à faire: Entend-on? Distingue-t-on, dans ces masses vocales, le sens des paroles? Cela, c'est une question de doigté, de 'métier,' si l'on veut. Et il faut bien avouer que le simultanéisme est un piège à apprentis, aussi bien que la composition musicale. L'expérience a montré que, lorsque l'instrument est bien manié, *on entend.*"

81. Quoted in Ouellette, p. 131. This material also appears, in various different formats and abridgments, in several other places: Henry Miller, *The Air-Conditioned Nightmare,* "With Edgar Varèse in the Gobi Desert" (New York: New Directions, 1945), pp. 163–164 (bibl. ID); Dorothy Norman, "Ionisation—Espace," *Twice a Year* 7 (1941): 259–260 (bibl. ID); "Que le monde s'éveille," Jeanneret-Gris, *Le Poème électronique Le Corbusier,* pp. 188–189 (bibl. IA); and "Déserts" ["Que le monde s'éveille"], and *Liberté* 5 (1959): 273 (bibl. IA).

82. "Edgard Varèse on Music and Art" (Alcopley interview), p. 192.

83. Schuller, p. 36.

84. Massimo Zanotti Bianco, "Edgar Varèse and the Geometry of Sound," *The Arts* 7 (1925): 35–36 (bibl. IIC).

85. "The Liberation of Sound," p. 203.

86. Amédée Ozenfant and Charles-Edouard Jeanneret, "Towards the Crystal" (1925), in Fry, pp. 170–171.

87. Apollinaire, *The Cubist Painters,* p. 13.

88. Kandinsky, "On the Question of Form" (1911), in *The Blaue Reiter Almanac,* ed. Wassily Kandinsky and Franz Marc; new documentary edition, ed. Klaus Lankheit, trans. Henning Falkenstein (New York: Viking, 1974), pp. 178–180 (bibl. III).

89. Gleizes and Metzinger, pp. 8–9.

90. Kahnweiler, *Cubism,* p. 13.

91. Apollinaire, *The Cubist Painters,* pp. 13–14; Varèse, "The Liberation of Sound," p. 197.

92. "Varèse Envisions 'Space' Symphonies." In a later interview (1955), Varèse told the same anecdote in which he had referred to a third dimension, but on this occasion he called it "une quatrième dimension" (Charbonnier, p. 74).

93. As his chroniclers have observed, the man's very personality frustrates attempts to find consistency in his opinions. See Ashton's introduction to *Picasso on Art,* particularly pp. xvii–xxi.

94. Discussion of Picasso's statements about his own art and about art in general has been reserved, for the most part, until now because, although his cubist phase is one of the most important in his oeuvre, his career continued for more than half a century beyond 1920, and most of the statements attributed to him either date from these later years or cannot be definitively dated at all.

95. Picasso, "Statement of 1923" (to Marius De Zayas), in *Picasso on Art,* p. 4.

96. "The Liberation of Sound," p. 202. That the phrase "alive in the present" may also owe something to Busoni is clear from a much earlier, more militantly worded statement: "In art there is only that which has existed sooner or later. There are no modern nor ancient works but only those which live in the present" ("Jérôm' s'en va-t'en guerre," p. 146). This corresponds to the following, from Busoni's *Sketch of a New Aesthetic of Music* (pp. 75–76): "There is nothing properly modern—only things which have come into being earlier or later; longer in bloom, or sooner withered. The Modern and the Old have always been."

97. Dijkstra, p. 55.

98. "Statement of 1935," p. 12.

99. "The Liberation of Sound," pp. 202, 201.

100. "Statement of 1923," p. 5.

101. Varèse, letter to John Edmunds, May 3, 1957. Quoted by Chou Wen-chung in "Varèse:

December 22, 1883—November 6, 1965," *Current Musicology* 2 (Fall 1965): 172 (bibl. ID); and in "Varèse: A Sketch of the Man and His Music," *Musical Quarterly* 52 (1966): 163 (bibl. IIB).

102. "Statement of 1923," p. 3.

103. "Statement of 1923," pp. 5–6; "Statement of 1935," p. 8.

104. "Statement of 1935," p. 8.

105. "The Liberation of Sound," p. 204; Schuller, p. 38.

106. "Statement of 1935," p. 8.

107. *Picasso on Art*, p. 16. (Here Picasso is quoted by Jaime Sabartés, Picasso's boyhood friend and personal secretary for many years.)

108. "Le Destin de la musique," p. 280; translated in "Autobiographical Remarks," a lecture given by Varèse at Princeton in 1959 (bibl. IA). A copy is in the clipping file on Varèse in the New York Public Library. The article to which Varèse refers is "Jérôm' s'en va-t'en guerre," which first appeared in *The Sackbut* and was reprinted in *The Aeolian Review* (later renamed *Eolus*) 3/2 (February 1924): 10–15.

109. Tryon, "New Instruments in Orchestra Are Needed, Says Mr. Varèse."

110. The painter Juan Gris, for example, noted that "starting from a general type" he sought to "make something particular and individual," and that this general type had its origins in "the elements of the intellect" and imagination. Further, his declaration that "I never know in advance the appearance of the object represented" suggests the same gradual obliteration of the original idea that both Picasso and Varèse discussed, and as well the same ranking in importance of process over result. (Gris, "Statement," in *L'Esprit Nouveau*, 1921; "Notes on My Painting," in *Der Querschnitt*, 1923; both reprinted in Daniel-Henry Kahnweiler, *Juan Gris: His Life and Work*, rev. ed., trans. Douglas Cooper [New York: Henry N. Abrams, Inc., 1968], pp. 193–194 [bibl. III.]

111. "The Liberation of Sound," p. 203.

112. In recollection by Hélène Parmelin (1966), in *Picasso on Art*, p. 83.

113. "Statement of 1935," p. 9.

114. Varèse quoted in David Ewen, *American Composers Today* (New York: H.W. Wilson, 1949), p. 250 (bibl. ID).

115. Varèse quoted by Stravinsky in "Some Composers," p. 11; reprinted in Stravinsky and Craft, *Dialogues*, p. 109.

116. Stein (1933), in *Picasso on Art*, p. 51.

117. Ewen, p. 250.

118. Louise Varèse, p. 108. The one other trace I have been able to find of this attitude is in an interview quotation: "The basis of music is sound, just as light is the basis of the painter's art" ("Edgar Varèse Interviewed: Shocks for Mus. Docs.," *Musical News and Herald* [London] 66, no. 1682 [June 21, 1924]: 584 [bibl. ID]).

119. Kahnweiler, *Cubism*, p. 3.

120. Delaunay, letter to Kandinsky (1912), in Chipp, p. 318. Delaunay was not alone in these sentiments. Stanton MacDonald Wright, in his "Statement on Synchromism" (1916)—a title which suggests an interest in color simultaneity something like Delaunay's—advocated the use of color as an abstract medium to avoid its superficial application as decoration, and spoke of "color-form" (Chipp, pp. 320–321). And Juan Gris, according to his statements about his work, was proceeding along similar lines: "I compose with abstractions (colors) and make my adjustments when these colors have assumed the form of objects" (in *L'Esprit Nouveau*, Paris, 1921; reprinted in Kahnweiler, *Juan Gris*, p. 193).

121. Delaunay, "Light," p. 319.

122. Lecture at Columbia University, 1948; quoted in Chou, "Varèse: A Sketch," p. 156.

123. Schuller, p. 35.

124. "Varèse Defies Hissers; Says He Won't Change Note of *Amériques*," *Philadelphia Public Ledger*, April 12, 1926, p. 3 (bibl. ID).

125. Varèse, interview in the *Morning Telegraph* (New York), March 1916. Quoted by Klarén in *Edgar Varèse*, p. 8.

126. Luigi Russolo, *The Art of Noises* (1913), in *Futurist Manifestos*, ed. Umbro Apollonio, trans. Robert Brain, R. W. Flint, J. C. Higgitt, and Caroline Tisdall (New York: Viking, 1973), p. 86 (bibl. III).

127. Varèse, "Que la musique sonne," in *391* 5 (June 1917); translated by Louise Varèse and printed as the epigraph to "The Liberation of Sound."

128. Cowell, "Current Chronicle," p. 371.

129. Varèse, letter to the editor dated July 26, 1955, in the *Musical Quarterly* 41 (October, 1955): 574 (bibl. IC). Unfortunately, this misperception of Varèse is so firmly established in some quarters that

it may never be completely extirpated. See for example Hans Richter, *Dada: Art and Anti-Art,* trans. David Britt (New York and Toronto: Oxford University Press, 1965), pp. 19, 98 (bibl. III).

130. Varèse, "Les Instruments de musique et la machine électronique," p. 28 ("La richesse des sons industriels, les bruits de nos rues, de nos ports . . . ont certainement changé et développé nos perceptions auditives"); Varèse, "Organized Sound for the Sound Film," *The Commonweal* 33/8 (December 13, 1940): 205 (bibl. IA); Cowell, "Current Chronicle," p. 371; Alcopley, "Edgard Varèse on Music and Art," p. 195.

131. Varèse, in "La Mécanisation de la musique: Conversation sténographiée à Bifur" [panel discussion with Alejo Carpentier, Robert Desnos, Ribemont-Dessaignes, Vicente Huidobro, Arthur Lourié, and Ungaretti], in *Bifur* 5 (1930): 122–23 (bibl. IB). "Ce qui nous manque, je le répète, ce sont les moyens de notre époque . . . ces moyens ne doivent pas conduire à une spéculation de reproductions des sons déjà existant mais au contraire permettre d'apporter de nouvelles réalisations suivant de nouvelles conceptions."

132. Louise Varèse, pp. 105–106.

133. Umberto Boccioni, "Absolute Motion + Relative Motion = Dynamism" (1914), in Apollonio, p. 150.

134. Louise Varèse, p. 107; F. T. Marinetti, "Let's Murder the Moonshine" (1909), in *Marinetti: Selected Writings,* ed. R. W. Flint (New York: Farrar, Straus and Giroux, 1972), pp. 45–54 (bibl. III).

135. Boccioni, Carlo Carrà, Russolo, Giacomo Balla, and Gino Severini, "The Exhibitors to the Public" (1912), in Apollonio, p. 49.

136. Varèse, "Le Destin de la musique," p. 278. "Je devins un sort de Parsifal diabolique, à la recherche non pas du Saint Graal mais de la bombe qui ferait exploser le monde musical et y laisserait entrer tous les sons par la brèche, sons qu'à l'époque—et parfois même aujourd'hui—on appelait bruits."

137. Marinetti, "Let's Murder the Moonshine," p. 45.

138. Carrà, "The Painting of Sounds, Noises, and Smells" (1913), in Apollonio, p. 113.

139. Carrà, "Plastic Planes as Spherical Expansions in Space" (1913), in Apollonio, p. 91.

140. Boccioni, "Technical Manifesto of Futurist Sculpture" (1912), in Apollonio, p. 63.

141. Boccioni, "Preface, First Exhibition of Futurist Sculpture" (1913), in Herbert, p. 49.

142. Ibid.

143. Boccioni, "Futurist Painting and Sculpture" (1914), in Apollonio, p. 178.

144. Boccioni, Carrà, Russolo, Balla, and Severini, "Manifesto of the Futurist Painters" (1910), in Apollonio, p. 25.

145. Varèse's enthusiasm for the developments that his era had brought into the world, however, was hardly unqualified. Louise Varèse, for instance, has pointed out that Varèse would never have agreed with Marinetti's assertion comparing the automobile favorably with a piece of classical sculpture (see Marinetti, "The Founding and Manifesto of Futurism," in *Selected Writings,* p. 41), for "Varèse thought automobiles hideous though at times convenient" (Louise Varèse, p. 107). Probably more significant is a quotation attributed to Varèse in a magazine article of the early 1920s: "Today music is the ideal form of expression, since we are living in a mechanical age. Melody [apparently a misprint for "music"], being formless, alone of the arts immaterial, is the antidote to materialism" ("Russia's Music, Surviving Turmoil, Is Still Supreme, Says Edgar Varèse," *Musical America,* December 23, 1922, p. 23 [bibl. ID]).

146. Tryon, "New Instruments in Orchestra Are Needed, Says Mr. Varèse."

147. Varèse, "Freedom for Music" (1939), in *The American Composer Speaks,* ed. Gilbert Chase (Baton Rouge: Louisiana State University Press, 1966), p. 190 (bibl.IA).

148. Varèse, "Musik auf neuen Wegen," *Stimmen* 15 (1949): 401, 403 (bibl. IA). "Der Kunstler, der auf sein Zeitalter abgestimmt ist, begreift, kristallisiert, und projiziert dessen besonderen Charakter. . . . Ganze Symphonien von neuen Tönen sind in der neuen industriellen Welt aufgekommen und bilden unser ganzes Leben lang einen Teil unseres täglichen Bewusstseins. Es erscheint unmöglich, dass ein Mensch, der sich ausschliesslich mit den Ton beschäftigt, durch sie unverändert bleiben kann."

149. Boccioni, "Plastic Dynamism" (1913), in Apollonio, p. 93.

150. Boccioni, "The Plastic Foundations of Futurist Sculpture and Painting" (1913), in Apollonio, p. 90.

151. Ibid., p. 89.

152. Boccioni, "Preface, First Exhibition of Futurist Sculpture," p. 48.

153. Anton Giulio Bragaglia, "Futurist Photodynamism" (1911), in Apollonio, p. 43.

154. Ibid., p. 40. At eight frames per second, cinematography in 1911 gave far less convincing an illusion of continuous movement than it does today.

155. "The Liberation of Sound," pp. 204–205. This suggests that Varèse's search for a way to produce continuous curves of sound may even predate the efforts of the futurists, although the year 1903 (Varèse's twentieth) should not be taken as an exact date. His experiments could have occurred at any time before his emigration to the United States in 1916.

156. Boccioni, "Preface, First Exhibition of Futurist Sculpture," p. 48.

157. Ibid.

158. "The Exhibitors to the Public," p. 48.

159. Boccioni, "Futurist Painting and Sculpture," p. 176.

160. Boccioni, "The Plastic Foundations of Futurist Sculpture and Painting," p. 89.

161. Eddy, p. 183. Emphasis in the original.

162. "The Exhibitors to the Public," p. 48.

163. Boccioni, "Technical Manifesto of Futurist Sculpture," in Herbert, p. 56.

164. "The Liberation of Sound," p. 197.

165. Boccioni, "Plastic Dynamism," p. 93.

166. Varèse quoted in Alfred Frankenstein, "Varèse, Worker in Intensities," *San Francisco Chronicle*, November 28, 1937, "This World" section, p. 13 (bibl. ID).

167. Severini, "The Plastic Analogies of Dynamism—Futurist Manifesto" (1913), in Apollonio, p. 124. The phrase "centrifugal and centripetal" has to do with a dual notion of movement, akin to ideas put forth by the cubists (see in particular Rivière), in which elements of the painting would both radiate out from and be drawn toward a center or centers simultaneously.

168. Carrà, "From Cézanne to Us, the Futurists" (1913), in Chipp, p. 308.

169. Boccioni, "Futurist Painting and Sculpture," p. 177.

170. Schuller, p. 38.

171. Boccioni, "Preface, First Exhibition of Futurist Sculpture," pp. 47–48.

172. Boccioni, "Plastic Dynamism," p. 92.

173. "The Exhibitors to the Public," p. 46. (This was the group manifesto printed on the occasion of the futurists' first London show, at the Sackville Gallery in March 1912.)

174. Boccioni, "Futurist Painting and Sculpture," p. 176.

175. Ibid., pp. 172–173.

176. Ibid., p. 177.

177. It would not be wise to overstate these "present-day distinctions," for the views of art historians cannot really be packaged as neatly as that. R. W. Flint, for instance, in his introduction to *Marinetti: Selected Writings*, summarizes current opinion about futurism as "a distinct moment in the transition from earliest Analytic Cubism to later Synthetic Cubism, Orphism, and their descendants" (p. 13).

178. Wassily Kandinsky, "Reminiscences," in Herbert, p. 35.

179. Kandinsky, "On the Question of Form," in *The Blaue Reiter Almanac*, p. 170.

180. Kandinsky, *Concerning the Spiritual in Art*, p. 77.

181. "Reminiscences," p. 40n.

182. *Concerning the Spiritual in Art*, p. 47; "On the Question of Form," p. 149.

183. "The Liberation of Sound," p. 203.

184. "On the Question of Form," p. 167.

185. "Reminiscences," pp. 31–32.

186. That is, if we are to believe certain later critics. See Stanley William Hayter, "The Language of Kandinsky" (1945), included as a preface to *Concerning the Spiritual in Art*, pp. 15–18. "In the year 1911 . . . Kandinsky, a forty-five-year-old ex-economist turned painter, was making improvisations in which dependence on the immediate visual image, even as a point of departure, had been abandoned" (p. 15).

187. Kandinsky, letter to Arthur Jerome Eddy [no date], in Eddy, p. 136.

188. *Concerning the Spiritual in Art*, p. 54.

189. The nature of the inner content (or meaning) for Kandinsky and others is approached more closely by the concept of *element*, which in combination with other elements produced forms, hence the external appearance of the composition. That *element* was not the same as *object* should be clear from the following, quoted from Paul Klee's "Creative Credo" (1920): "I have mentioned the elements of linear expression which are among the visual components of the picture. This does not mean that a given

work must consist of nothing but such elements. Rather, the elements must produce forms, but without being sacrificed in the process. They should be preserved. In most cases, a combination of several elements will be required to produce forms" (Chipp, p. 184).

190. "Reminiscences," p. 31.

191. Kandinsky, *Point and Line to Plane,* trans. Howard Dearstyne and Hilla Rebay (New York: Guggenheim Museum, 1947; reprint ed., New York: Dover, 1979), pp. 117–118 (bibl. III).

192. Hayter, p. 17.

193. *Point and Line to Plane,* p. 124.

194. Ibid., p. 92.

195. Ibid., p. 21.

196. Ibid., p. 33.

197. Ibid., p. 37. Kandinsky used the word "sound" (*Klang*) to denote the specific characteristics of an element or its function in a given location.

198. Ibid., p. 40.

199. Ibid., p. 145*n*.

200. Ibid., pp. 34–35. In Kandinsky as in the cubists we find an appreciation for the innately abstract character of music. For example: "A painter who finds no satisfaction in mere representation, however artistic, in his longing to express his internal life, cannot but envy the ease with which music, the least material of the arts today, achieves this end. He naturally seeks to apply the means of music to his own art. And from this results that modern desire for rhythm in painting, for mathematical, abstract construction, for repeated notes of color, for setting color in motion, and so on" (*Concerning the Spiritual in Art,* p. 40).

201. *Concerning the Spiritual in Art,* pp. 48–49.

202. "On the Question of Form," p. 150.

203. Kandinsky, letter to Eddy, p. 136.

204. *Concerning the Spiritual in Art,* p. 49.

205. Ibid., p. 51.

206. Ibid.

207. "The Liberation of Sound," p. 202.

208. *Concerning the Spiritual in Art,* p. 73.

209. Ibid., p. 46.

210. *Point and Line to Plane,* p. 53.

211. Ibid., p. 144.

212. *Concerning the Spiritual in Art,* p. 47.

213. *Point and Line to Plane,* p. 97.

214. Ibid. Klee, too, identified the "unification of visual oppositions" or "the simultaneous existence of the masculine principle (evil, stimulating, passionate) and the feminine principle (good, growing, calm)" as the way to achieve "self-contained stability," and even cited Robert Delaunay's "use of contrasts of divided color" as an example of how this could be done ("Creative Credo," pp. 185–186).

215. *Point and Line to Plane,* p. 103.

216. "The Liberation of Sound," p. 200.

217. *Concerning the Spiritual in Art,* p. 35.

218. "The Liberation of Sound," p. 201.

219. "Reminiscences," p. 39.

220. Ibid.

221. Alcopley, "Edgard Varèse on Music and Art," p. 189.

CHAPTER 2. THE SPATIAL ENVIRONMENT: PROCESS, PITCH/REGISTER, AND SYMMETRY

1. Complete information for the most important of these can be found in bibl. IIB. I have reviewed in detail the Wilkinson, Babbitt, Chou *Musical Quarterly,* Gümbel, and Nattiez publications in "A Theory of Pitch and Register for the Music of Edgard Varèse" (Ph.D. dissertation, Yale University, 1977; bibl. IIB), and the articles by Morgan and Chou in *The New Worlds of Edgard Varèse* in *Journal of Music Theory* 24 (1980): 277–283 (bibl. IIB). See also my article, "On *Density 21.5:* A Response to Nattiez," *Music Analysis* 5 (1986) (bibl. IIB).

2. The most prominent examples of this tendency are the work of Martin Gümbel, Robert Erickson, and John Strawn (bibl. IIB). See also Richard Swift's perceptive criticism of Erickson's approach in *Perspectives of New Music* 14/1 (1975): 148–158 (bibl. IIB).

3. See the articles by András Wilheim and by Larry Stempel ("Varèse's 'Awkwardness' . . ."). The distinction between pitch and pitch class is important and will be treated in detail later in this chapter.

4. Stempel, for example, with reference to a passage that he analyzes, says: "Something akin to the *tonal* frame therefore seems to be operating here, for the twelve-tone criteria do not apply" ("Varèse's 'Awkwardness,'" p. 164). In fact, alternative interpretations of this period have begun to surface in critical writing, although not yet in great numbers. One recent example of this trend is Robert Morgan's thought-provoking article, "Rewriting Music History: Second Thoughts on Ives and Varèse," *Musical Newsletter* 3/1 (January 1973): 3–12; and 3/2 (April 1973): 15–23+ (bibl. IIC).

5. Babbitt, "Edgard Varèse," p. 17.

6. Again, see bibl. IIB.

7. "The Liberation of Sound," p. 197.

8. Varèse cited in Louise Varèse, p. 211. She gives the source as the *New York Times* of December 22, 1923, but apparently this is an error. The real source might be a long-defunct publication called the *New York Review*, but no copies of the relevant issue seem to have survived.

9. Paul Rosenfeld was particularly fond of such images. See, for example, the chapter on Varèse in *An Hour with American Music* (Philadelphia: J. B. Lippincott, 1929), pp. 160–179 (bibl. IIC). The phrase "the geometry of sound," in its application to Varèse's music, comes from the title of Zanotti Bianco's article, "Edgar Varèse and the Geometry of Sound."

10. Winthrop P. Tryon, "Edgar Varèse's New Orchestral Work, 'Amériques,'" *Christian Science Monitor,* July 7, 1923, p. 16 (bibl. ID).

11. Varèse, in "La Mécanisation de la musique: Conversation sténographiée à Bifur," p. 126. "Prenant en masse les éléments sonores, il y a des possibilités de subdivision par rapport à cette masse: celle-ci se divisant en d'autres masses, en d'autres volumes, en d'autres plans, . . ."

12. Varèse, "The Liberation of Sound," p. 197; Varèse, "Le Destin de la musique," p. 13.

13. Schuller, p. 39.

14. Ibid., p. 36.

15. Ibid., p. 34.

16. Varèse quoted in Ouellette, p. 183.

17. Varèse quoted in Henry Cowell, "Current Chronicle" (review of the premiere of *Déserts*), p. 372.

18. "The Liberation of Sound," p. 203.

19. See George Perle, *Serial Composition and Atonality,* 5th ed. (Berkeley: University of California Press, 1981) (bibl. III).

20. "The Liberation of Sound," p. 203.

21. Ibid.

22. Schuller, p. 39.

23. The cubists' dislike for exact repetition is also relevant here.

24. Varèse quoted by André, "Edgar Varèse y la música de Vanguardía"; translated in Bloch, p. 260.

25. While the idea of octave equivalence may seem beyond challenge as a musical "fact," and while hardly anyone at the time seems to have been inclined to question it, nevertheless there apparently were a few doubters, even as early as the 1920s. The composer and critic Dane Rudhyar, for example, in an article entitled "What Is an Octave?" (*Aeolian Review* 2/1 [December 1922]: 8–12; bibl. III), proposed that octave equivalence, long viewed as an axiom, might have outlived its usefulness: "We see that the ratio of frequency between a note and its higher twelfth is 1:3, which ratio is certainly as simple as the ratio of the octave 1:2. Does it not mean that, after all, when you say C' is the octave of C (meaning that these two notes are in some way identical), you merely conform yourself to a convention, which convention appears self-evident only by virtue of a musical education which took this convention as an axiom? Then if it is a convention, may we not change it or, at least, may it not be in time susceptible to modification as all conventions are when a new civilization is constituted?" (p. 10). Rudhyar was a fervent advocate of Varèse's music and made it the subject of a number of pieces which he published during the 1920s. Varèse certainly knew of Rudhyar and could conceivably have come across the article on the octave, both for this reason and because the *Aeolian Review* was founded and edited by Carlos Salzedo, a close friend and musical associate of his; Varèse himself also contributed a piece to this

periodical about a year later. More important, however, is the likelihood that such ideas were abroad already, at least among those who regarded themselves as musical free-thinkers.

26. The term "pitch-class set" or "pc set," here and elsewhere in this book, refers to the definition of pitch groups in Allen Forte, *The Structure of Atonal Music* (New Haven: Yale University Press, 1973) (bibl. III). The label "3–2" used in this instance refers to the three-note group which in its "prime form," or closest possible spacing, consists of a semitone adjacent to a whole tone. Pitch-class sets, of course, are defined through octave and inversional equivalence, and although the theory of pitch-class sets has demonstrable relevance for much twentieth-century music, it does not seem to be the proper tool for analysis of Varèse's work.

27. Varèse, in fact, had no particular attachment to the tempered system, and one of his hopes for the future of music was that new means of sound production would not only provide more extensive timbral possibilities but would also free the composer from the "arbitrary rules" resulting from the inflexible division of sound space into semitones. He also speculated about the possibility of extending the available frequency range to the limits of human perception, adding perhaps two octaves above the highest pitch obtainable with conventional instruments. ("La Mécanisation de la musique: Conversation sténographiée à Bifur," pp. 123, 126.) Here the implication is clearly that a larger sound space, in the vertical sense, allows greater freedom to the composer.

28. See preface for explanation of the analytical symbols and terminology.

29. "The Liberation of Sound," p. 197.

30. Ibid. No analytical definition of projection would encompass all the various shades of meaning that Varèse intended for it. For instance, he also used the term to refer to enormous crescendi of single chords; thus it is clear that projection need not involve motion from one chord to another, although even here there is the implication that such crescendi might end by producing such motion.

31. See the preface for an explanation of the graphic notation used in many of the examples.

32. In the recent Colfranc edition of *Octandre* (revised and edited by Chou Wen-chung, 1980), the measures of the second movement have been numbered beginning with the piccolo entrance as m. 1. Even though the measure before this entrance is empty, it is written as a full measure and thus presumably should be numbered. In this book, all references by measure number to this movement reflect the correction.

33. The difference between the presence and the absence of explicitly delineated octave spans is dealt with later in this chapter and in chapter 3.

34. See Bernard, "Pitch/Register in the Music of Edgard Varèse," *Music Theory Spectrum* 3 (1981): 1–25 (bibl. IIB), example 16, pp. 14–15, for another interesting example of combined processes.

35. Ibid., example 18, p. 18, presents another passage involving penetration.

36. The interval [27] figures significantly in the immediately preceding measures, 30–31 (see ex. 3.21).

37. Tryon, "Edgar Varèse's New Orchestral Work, 'Amériques.'"

38. The implications of octave doubling for internal structure are numerous and interesting but are not within the province of this chapter. They are taken up in chapter 3, where additional analytical tools are developed to explore this problematic aspect of the spatial environment.

39. This is true to a somewhat lesser extent in *Ecuatorial*, where the doubling is largely the result of organ registration, than in the other two works.

40. Since in the case of the earlier passage (from *Déserts*) the two projected spans are of the same size and identical internally under rotation, the progression could be analyzed as an exchange, without rotation, just as plausibly.

41. Several examples in this and the next chapter provide much of this local evidence. See example 3.12, mm. 1–25; example 3.16, mm. 25–29; example 3.26, mm. 32–52; examples 3.37 through 3.46, mm. 53–69; example 3.28, mm. 71–78. See also examples 2.18 and 2.19, mm. 80–102 and 126–135 respectively; example 2.11, mm. 151–154 (and back to m. 144).

CHAPTER 3. THE SPATIAL ENVIRONMENT: INTERNAL STRUCTURE

1 Varèse quoted in Ewen, p. 250.

2. Different, that is, in the sense that no pair of pitches among the three forms a unison.

3. The term *derivative* used alone means first-order derivative unless otherwise stated.

4. Unless, of course, the trichord derived from infolding consists of two intervals of equal size.

5. See appendix 2 (pp. 306–308) of Bernard, "A Theory of Pitch and Register," for an exposition of tetrachordal forms.

6. Varèse, "The Liberation of Sound," p. 197. In the same passage, Varèse likened this journey to projection, which he defined as "that feeling that sound is leaving us with no hope of being reflected back."

7. That is, the first macro-structure. The group (E–F–G♭)5 in the piccolo is a micro-structure (see below under "Extensions of the Trichordal System").

8. See chapter 1, note 83, above.

9. Varèse, "The Liberation of Sound," p. 197. See also the discussion of near-repetition in chapter 2.

10. "The Liberation of Sound," p. 204. For another straightforward example of unit relationships, see "A Theory of Pitch and Register," chap. 2, ex. 17 (p. 83). The passage under discussion there is *Intégrales*, mm. 187–189.

11. There are [1][9]: E5–(D♭–D)6 and (D♭–D–B)6, and [6][7]: F♯–(D♭–G)6. Contributing too to overall symmetry are the two [13]-chains at the outer edges, A1–B♭2–B3 and F♯5–G6–G♯7.

12. G1–A♯3, in fact, is a linear succession: successive lowest notes attacked in m. 30.

13. *Nocturnal* is published with the notation: "Edited and completed by Chou Wen-chung" (former pupil of Varèse and his friend for many years). A dotted line on p. 16 of the score shows where Varèse's manuscript ends.

14. This symmetry does not include the octave "doublings" above. The various effects of octave equivalence upon the trichordal forms is taken up later in this chapter (see below under "Some Problems of the Trichordal System").

15. As in example 2.5, note that space between timbrally defined groups may be used, or not, to define segmental sizes.

16. The graph in example 3.30 does not purport to be a complete trichordal analysis of this passage, only a demonstration of the connections involving the doubled notes.

17. *Déserts* consists of seven sections, four scored for conventional instruments and played in alternation with three sections of "organized sound" on two-channel magnetic tape. The work, however, may also be performed without the interpolations.

18. See example 2.17.

19. These are: [5][6], [3][8], [6][7], [3][10], [4][7], and the double constellation [1][7] / [1][8].

20 Note-against-note textures are relatively rarely encountered in Varèse's music; they are not confined to any single period in his oeuvre, although there are more problematic ones in the earlier works (*Intégrales* and before) than in the later.

21. Recall the phrase "blocks of sound" and other similar expressions coined by critics of the 1920s, mentioned in chapter 2.

22. Relatively narrow registral boundaries are common to passages of rapid motion in general. See also *Intégrales*, mm. 121–126; *Hyperprism*, mm. 40–42 (discussed in chapter 5).

23. In examples 3.38 and 3.39 trichordal forms are identified only by the basic form of the constellation to which they belong.

24. Example 3.45 also shows that the momentum of spans [13] and [16] and the constellation [3][10] spills over into the next passage (mm. 71–78).

25. [3][11] is an unfolded derivative of [3][8]. From here on, the fact that a derivative relationship exists between two trichords will not be stated explicitly unless potential for confusion exists in a particular case.

26. The span A4–G6, in turn, eventually expands to the outer boundaries of m. 10: E♭4–C♯7.

27. This seems to be another, somewhat concealed use of octave equivalence. Although the projective distances are crucial and would mean something else entirely if they were shifted in octave location, still the dyadic connection from oboe to flute to horn/bassoon relies partly upon the fact that all three dyads are C–B.

28. [10][11] is finally articulated as a real form in m. 13, as shown in example 3.17.

CHAPTER 4. RHYTHM AND DURATION

1. Picasso, "Statement of 1935," p. 8.

2. Stockhausen, "Electronic and Instrumental Music," in *Die Reihe* 5 (*Reports, Analyses*), ed. Herbert Eimert and Karlheinz Stockhausen (Bryn Mawr: Theodore Presser, 1961), p. 61 (bibl. III).

3. Varèse, "The Liberation of Sound," p. 198.

4. Ibid., p. 202.

5. Recall from chapter 1 Kandinsky's words about Schoenberg.

6. Varèse, "By the Dozen," *Eolus* 11 (April 1932); quoted in Ouellette, p. 141.

7. As mentioned, for Varèse the term "rhythm" clearly embraces the traditional meanings of both rhythm and duration. However, in the interests of clarity, I have not suppressed the word "duration." Sometimes, as in the expression "the duration of this passage," the word "rhythm" is not an acceptable substitute; at other points the use of both words clarifies the distinction between small- and large-scale structure, "duration" usually connoting the latter.

8. Pierre Boulez, *Notes of an Apprenticeship,* pp. 61–62, 72–145.

9. Extensive studies of resultant rhythms in these highly complex situations have led me to conclude that no discernible patterning occurs at that level. See appendix 4 of "A Theory of Pitch and Register."

10. Robert P. Morgan, "Notes on Varèse's Rhythm," in *The New Worlds of Edgard Varèse,* p. 9.

11. See my review of *The New Worlds of Edgard Varèse,* cited in chapter 2, note 1.

12. Jean Metzinger, "Cubism and Tradition" (1911), in Fry, *Cubism,* p. 67 (cited in chapter 1).

13. See chapter 3, examples 3.37 through 3.46, for an extensive analysis of this passage.

14. The reader may find it of interest to compare mm. 125–132 with mm. 85–93 (see ex. 2.10).

15. On another level, the trombone interjections mentioned above divide the passage as a whole in the beat pattern 8–21–8.5: exactitude of durational relationships disrupted, in other words, by fractional amounts. This segmentation relies upon counting everything in the trombone interjection up to but not including the moment of release—the last, short chord—within the duration of the previous segment. It might be argued, on the other hand, that the trombones should be taken as the *initiation* of a segment, in which case the overall progression short-long-short through mm. 80–92 would remain intact, but the proportions involved would become much more approximate.

16. The durations of certain rests are counted in whole-beat values, a strategy which seems sensible in light of particular rhythmic features focused on here.

17. I have discussed the order of pitch/registral events in this passage in "Pitch/Register" (ex. 18, p. 18).

18. I offer the following as a brief, subsidiary commentary upon the segmentation within the three sections of level (a), since it is not directly relevant to the main point of example 4.16. Section I poses no difficulties except at the division between the segments of six and five beats' duration. Here F4–G5 has been taken, for the time being, as the controlling element in the stasis, but a case could be made for the overriding importance of the entrance of D2–E3. Taking this entrance as a point of division would obviously reverse the durational scheme, turning 6, 5 into 5, 6. The segmentation of section II is particularly problematic, for except at the end there are no long, uninterrupted durations as in section I, and there seems no good reason to hear the activity of either F4–(C–G)5 or (D–A)2–E3 as dominant or controlling. Thus the division in m. 12 may appear arbitrary, and these two segments would perhaps be better interpreted as one undivided segment of fifteen beats. In section III, control might be assigned instead to the C♯4 attacks, which as initiators of segments would produce the durations 6, 7.5, and 6.

19. Here the prominent timbral change affecting C5 at the downbeat of m. 14 is interpreted as part of the new development introducing B♭1 and B2; thus the first beat of m. 14 is counted as part of the third segment.

20. *Déserts* is usually performed with the taped interpolations, but a note at the head of the score specifically allows for the possibility of omitting them.

21. It must be admitted that there is hardly any use of stasis in *Nocturnal,* either in the portion completed by Varèse or in Chou's reconstruction from the sketches, and none at all in a terminating role. Without any knowledge of how much sketch material from the 1950s and the 1960s—for *Nocturnal* and for other works—remains unincorporated, one cannot proceed further. (See Chou's preface to the published score of *Nocturnal* [New York: Colfranc, 1969, pp. iii–v] and the "Discussion" in *The New Worlds of Edgard Varèse,* pp. 88–89.)

22. Varèse does not seem to have regretted this lack of standardization; in fact, he evinced great fascination for the limitless variety of sounds obtainable from percussion instruments. Visitors to his studio were often shown a bell or a gong, for instance, that he had just found and which he treasured for its unique sonorous qualities.

23. "River Sirens, Lion Roars, All Music to Varèse," *Santa Fe New Mexican,* August 21, 1936, p. 2 (bibl. ID).

24. Ibid.

25. Despite the inaccuracy of the term "unpitched," it will be used as shorthand for "indefinitely pitched," which is cumbersome.

26. This succession is repeated, with an altered durational structure, in mm. 34–37. For a discussion of the passage in context, see chapter 5.

27. The sound of the suspended cymbal is richer in high harmonics than that of the high gong and therefore sounds higher.

28. The two Chinese blocks and the three wood drums are all counted individually for these purposes, since they all have distinctly different pitch levels.

29. With one exception: the suspended cymbal is absent from m. 38.

30. The last two instruments are assigned to one player and are analogous in this passage to the Chinese blocks.

31. The truncation at m. 117 is combined with overlap, as the A material continues to sound until m. 119. This qualifies as a gradual dispersal of tension, a process in fact already begun before m. 117 but not consummated until new pitched material arrives.

32. José Juan Tablada, "La croix du sud," in *Obras,* vol. 1: *Poesia,* ed. and comp. Hector Valdés (Universidad Nacional Autónoma de México, Centro de Estudios Literarios, 1971), p. 588 (bibl. III). Varèse was responding, perhaps, to the nearly impenetrable mystery of such lines as "The monkeys at the pole are albinos, / Amber and snow, and frisk / Dressed in the aurora borealis" and "It is time to stride over the dusk / Like a zebra toward the isle of long ago / Where the murdered women wake" (Les singes du pôle sont albinos ambre et neige / et sautent vêtus d'aurore boréale;" "C'est l'heure d'enjamber le crépuscule comme un zèbre vers l'île de jadis / où se réveillent les femmes assassinées").

33. Refer to the published score throughout the following discussion.

34. This instrument can be either real twigs or a wire brush, struck against the bass drum shell.

35. These are not specifically labeled low and high, as are the maracas in *Ionisation,* but probably no two maracas of any kind would sound precisely alike.

36. The last sixteenth note of the drum part and the notes on the same line in m. 203 are indicated for "sn. dr.," but this is probably a misprint for "sd. dr"; otherwise there would be no point in explicitly changing the designation of the line above it from susp. cymb. to sn. dr. in the middle of the measure.

37. This is unlikely to have any serial significance; the avoidance of octaves simply ensures that spatial (vertical) distances are heard literally, without any of the collapsing or expanding effect usually associated with octaves in Varèse.

38. Arnold Whittall, "Varèse and Organic Athematicism," *Music Review* 28 (1967): 311–315 (bibl. IIB).

39. Eric Salzman, "Edgard Varèse," *Stereo Review* 26/6 (June 1971): 68 (bibl. IIC).

40. "Jérôm' s'en va-t'en guerre," p. 148.

41. The reader may wish to consult Chou Wen-chung's full-length analysis of this work in *The New Worlds of Edgard Varèse.*

42. Nicolas Slonimsky, "Analysis," included as a one-page preface to the published score of *Ionisation* (New York: Colfranc, 1966).

CHAPTER 5. ANALYSES

1. See example 3.25 for the details of segmentation which give rise to this multiple interpretation.

2. One might disagree that the pair of cymbals really sounds higher than the single crash, but the overall direction is clearly downwards.

3. This segmentation can also be defended on dynamic grounds. The pitch left out, E3, is the only one of the five sounding at *f;* all the others are at *ff.*

4. The tempo is not constant throughout this passage, but I have assumed here that, since metronome markings are not specified, the exact relative durations are not important and the beat retains its integral status as time-marker. The faster tempo in mm. 48–49 and 51–54 may be primarily a means of distinguishing the solo percussion passages from the pitched material.

5. In the published score, the treble clef in the horn 2 part beginning at m. 59 is a misprint for bass clef.

6. Wilheim, "The Genesis of a Specific Twelve-Tone System," pp. 213–214.

7. Jean-Jacques Nattiez, however, fills about 100 pages in his study. Other full-length analyses of *Density 21.5* are by Marc Wilkinson, Martin Gümbel, and James Tenney. See citations in bibl. IIB.

8. See chapter 1 of "A Theory of Pitch and Register."

9. Wilkinson says that the work is "somewhat limited by the fact that it is for solo flute" (p. 17).

10. The score of *Density 21.5* fills only two pages, but for copyright reasons it has not proved feasible to reproduce the entire work here. The reader is therefore advised to acquire a copy of the score and keep it at hand while following the analysis.

11. Both Wilkinson, in his analysis, and Harvey Sollberger, in his recording (*Twentieth-Century Flute Music*, Nonesuch Records HB–73028), interpret the last gesture in m. 23 as B♯5–C♯6–B5, as if the accidental applied to the grace note did not also apply to the real-value notes within the same measure. This apparent willingness to suspend normal notational rules for the sake of a conceit—in this case, that m. 23 is meant as an "inversion" of "the motive"—is astounding.

12. These words appear as a note in the published score (New York: Colfranc, 1966).

13. The connection provided by G4 in m. 51 is both spatial (a projection of [3]) and procedural (a member of the chromatic group).

APPENDIX B: ANNOTATED LIST OF WORKS

1. Range as written: B♭3–G5.

2. Ouellette erroneously gives February 23, 1947 as the date of the premiere.

3. The source of this date is the Fogg Museum Archives. Ouellette gives early October 1955 as the premiere date; Chou, in "A Varèse Chronology" (*Perspectives of New Music* 5/1 (1966): 7–10; bibl. IIA), states that Varèse completed his music for the film in 1956; Jacques Dupin, in *Joan Miró: Life and Work* (New York: Abrams, n.d., p. 585; bibl. III), identifies the producer and the place and date of production as "New York: Bouchard Productions, 1956." It would appear that all three of these authorities are wrong, unless there was a revised cut made of the film after its premiere in which Varèse's music was included for the first time. In that case, both Chou and Dupin might be right. However, there is no independent evidence to suggest that any such revision was ever made.

4. *The New Worlds of Edgard Varèse*, p. 88.

5. Carpentier discusses this project in his article "Edgar Varèse vivant" (bibl. ID) and mentions both earlier titles. He also names Georges Ribemont-Dessaignes as an additional collaborator and describes a plot that seems to represent a transitional phase between *The One All Alone* and *Astronome*.

6. See the "Discussion" in *The New Worlds of Edgard Varèse*, pp. 88–89.

BIBLIOGRAPHY

Here are listed the sources consulted for this work. Readers in search of further information are referred to the bibliographies in the Ouellette biography, the Bloch and Parks dissertations, and the Metzger-Riehn anthology, all included below.

The following plan of organization has been adopted:

I.   Sources of Varèse Quotations
   A. Varèse's Articles and Lectures
   B. Interviews
   C. Letters
   D. Miscellaneous
II. Works about Varèse
   A. Primarily Biographical
   B. Primarily Theoretical
   C. General Criticism
III. Other Sources

A Note on Varèse's First Name and Date of Birth

Varèse was christened Edgard; his name appears in this spelling on his birth certificate (reproduced in Ouellette, pl. 3, after p. 114) even though, as Ouellette notes (p. 221), the name is customarily spelled without a final *d* in French. From the time of his arrival in the United States (1916) he seems to have been known consistently as Edgar; this is borne out by his signature and by his name in print in concert programs, in published scores of his works, on the stationery of the International Composers' Guild, and on his personal stationery after 1925, when he purchased his home at 188 Sullivan Street in New York. By the late 1940s the original spelling had reappeared—the change reflected again in his signature and in his personal stationery—but with what consistency it is difficult to determine. Certainly toward the end of his life he was using "Edgard" exclusively, but even at this late date the spelling of his name in print was still not standardized, no doubt because many who had always known him as Edgar continued from force of habit to spell his name that way. Since Varèse's death (1965), "Edgard" has become the standard spelling, but for the purposes of citation of titles in which Varèse's first name appears it would seem the most accurate policy to preserve whichever spelling was actually used. This decision is reflected throughout this book.

Varèse's date of birth, also confirmed by his birth certificate, is December 22, 1883, but

257

as late as the year of his death it was believed to be 1885 even by Varèse himself (see also introduction, note 10). The date is wrong in a number of widely used standard sources.

I. SOURCES OF VARESE QUOTATIONS

Varèse's Articles and Lectures

Not every item under this heading is distinctly different from every other. Particularly from the mid-1950s on, when Varèse first gained general recognition as a major figure and began to receive frequent requests to speak and write about his music, a great deal of borrowing is in evidence. Sometimes Varèse quotes himself explicitly, citing the earlier text; more often whole passages are lifted, either verbatim or paraphrased only slightly, and presented as if they were brand new. Part of the reason for this—perhaps a large part—no doubt is pragmatic, but Varèse's practice also bespeaks a certain honesty. As noted in the introduction, although every Varèse piece is an entirely new work of art, his ideas about composition as reflected in these pieces seem to have changed very little after the maturation of his technique in the early 1920s. Perhaps it is small wonder, then, that Varèse saw no reason to find new words every time he was called upon to explain his music. Once he had found a good way of making a particular point, he was apparently quite willing to use it again.

"Autobiographical Remarks." Lecture, Princeton University, September 4, 1959. A copy is in the Varèse clipping file at the New York Public Library. A version in French appears as "Le Destin de la musique est de conquérir la liberté"; the same material in abridged and slightly altered form is included under "Rhythm, Form, and Content" in "The Liberation of Sound" (see below).

"Le Destin de la musique est de conquérir la liberté." Liberté 5 (1959): 276–283.

Ecrits. Textes réunis et présentés par Louise Hirbour. Traduction de l'anglais par Christiane Léaud. Paris: Christian Bourgois, 1983. A compilation from Varèse's articles, lectures, interviews, and letters. With a few minor exceptions, all of this material was previously published, much of it in English. Despite the convenience of having these texts together in one volume, the collection is of dubious value, since for some of the less easily available items, and for all of the unpublished correspondence, the editor has relied upon biographers' quotations rather than consulting the sources themselves. There are also numerous errors of citation.

"Electronic Music." Lecture, New York, November 9, 1958. Presented at "A Sunday Afternoon of Contemporary Music." Reprinted by Wolcott & Associates, New York. A copy is in the Varèse clipping file at the New York Public Library.

"Erinnerungen und Gedanken." Darmstädter Beiträge zur neuen Musik 3 (1960): 65–71. Closely related to Varèse's Princeton and Sarah Lawrence lectures of 1959. One interesting detail: Varèse quotes himself on Intégrales, reproducing a text which is also quoted in Grunfeld and in Waldman (bibl. ID). Waldman cites a radio interview of 1953 as the original source of Varèse's description, but Varèse claims that it dates back to his Santa Fe lecture of 1936. Since "New Instruments and New Music" in "The Liberation of Sound" is probably only an excerpt from the 1936 lecture, neither possible source can be ruled out.

"Ferruccio Busoni: A Reminiscence." Columbia University Forum 9/2 (Spring 1966): 20.

"Freedom for Music." In The American Composer Speaks, ed. Gilbert Chase. Baton Rouge: Louisiana State University Press, 1966, pp. 184–192. This is the most complete text available of Varèse's 1939 lecture at the University of Southern California. Abridgments appear below under "The Liberation of Sound" and "Music as an Art-Science."

"Les Instruments de musique et la machine électronique." L'Age Nouveau 92 (May 1955): 28–30.

"Jérôm' s'en va-t'en guerre." Translated by Louise Varèse. *The Sackbut* 4 (December 1923): 144–148. Reprinted in *Aeolian Review* 3/2 (February 1924): 10–15.

"The Liberation of Sound." In *Contemporary Composers on Contemporary Music,* ed. Elliott Schwartz and Barney Childs (New York: Holt, Rinehart, and Winston, 1967), pp. 195–208. Excerpts from Varèse's lectures, compiled and annotated by Chou Wen-chung. In the list below, the title given by Chou to each excerpt is matched with the place and date of the lecture from which it is taken. All citations of "The Liberation of Sound" in the present volume refer to this edition.

"New Instruments and New Music" (Santa Fe, 1936)
"Music as an Art-Science" (University of Southern California, 1939)
"Rhythm, Form, and Content" (Princeton University, 1959)
"Spatial Music" (Sarah Lawrence College, 1959)
"The Electronic Medium" (Yale University, 1962)

"The Liberation of Sound." *Perspectives of New Music* 5/1 (1966): 11–19. Reprinted in Boretz and Cone, eds., *Perspectives on American Composers,* pp. 25–33 (bibl. III). Excerpts from Varèse's lectures, compiled and edited by Chou Wen-chung. This is a considerable abridgment of "The Liberation of Sound" in the Schwartz and Childs anthology. "Spatial Music" has been cut entirely.

"Music as an Art-Science." *Bennington College Alumnae Quarterly* 7/1 (1955): 24–25.

"The Music of Tomorrow." *Musical Standard,* London, July 12, 1924 (New Illustrated Series), p. 14.

"Musik auf neuen Wegen." *Stimmen* 15 (1949): 401–404. Some material from the University of Southern California lecture of 1939 is included.

"Oblation" [poem]. *391,* vol. 5 (June 1917), p. 4; reprinted in Sanouillet, *391: Revue publiée de 1917 à 1924 par Francis Picabia,* vol. 1, p. 44 (bibl. ID).

"Organized Sound for the Sound Film." *Commonweal* 33 (December 13, 1940): 204–205.

"Déserts" ["Que le monde s'éveille . . ."]. *Liberté* 5 (1959): 273.

"Que le monde s'éveille . . ." In Charles Edouard Jeanneret-Gris, *Le Poème électronique Le Corbusier,* pp. 188–189 (bibl. III). The two versions of "Que le monde s'éveille" differ only in minor details. Both are translations and abridgments of a version in English which appeared in print earlier; see entries for Dorothy Norman and Henry Miller in bibl. ID.

"Que la musique sonne." *391,* vol. 5 (June 1917), p. 2; reprinted in Sanouillet, *391,* vol. 1, p. 42 (bibl. ID).

"Statements by Edgard Varèse," assembled with comments by Louise Varèse, *Soundings* (Berkeley) 10 (1976): [6–9]. Miscellaneous quotations from lectures, letters, and other sources. Some of what Louise Varèse describes as "never published to my knowledge" has appeared elsewhere.

"Tout jeune homme j'habitais Berlin. . . ." In Jeanneret-Gris, *Le Poème électronique Le Corbusier,* pp. 191–193 (bibl. III). A short autobiographical statement which has a great deal in common with the 1959 lectures at Princeton and Sarah Lawrence (see "The Liberation of Sound" and "Autobiographical Remarks," above).

"Verbe." *391,* vol. 5 (June 1917), p. 2; reprinted in Sanouillet, *391,* vol. 1, p. 42 (bibl. ID).

B. Interviews

Under this heading are listed only those items which are explicitly in interview format. Other sources of direct quotations can be found in bibl. ID.

Alcopley, L. "Edgard Varèse on Music and Art: A Conversation between Varèse and Alcopley." *Leonardo* 1 (1968): 187–195. The conversation took place in 1963. Several reproductions of paintings and drawings by Varèse are included.

Charbonnier, Georges. *Entretiens avec Edgard Varèse.* Paris: Pierre Belfond, 1970. The series of interviews on which this volume is based took place in 1955. Not all the material printed here, however, appears to represent a faithful transcription of actual "conversation." Some of it can be found nearly word for word in "The Liberation of Sound" and other related sources. The last section, "Son organisé—Art-science," is, with the exception of Charbonnier's interjections, a translation of Varèse's 1940 article, "Organized Sound and the Sound Film" (bibl. IA).

Schuller, Gunther. "Conversation with Varèse." *Perspectives of New Music* 3/2 (1965): 32–37. Reprinted in Boretz and Cone, eds., *Perspectives on American Composers,* pp. 34–39 (bibl. III).

Varèse, Edgard. "Edgard Varèse and Alexei Haieff Questioned by Eight Composers/Answers by Edgard Varèse." *Possibilities* 1 (Winter 1947–48): 96–97. The eight composers are Robert Palmer, Adolph Weiss, Milton Babbitt, Henry Cowell, Harold Shapero, Kurt List, Jacques de Menasce, and John Cage.

———. "Performer's Choice: A Symposium." *Listen* 8/6 (June 1946): 4–5. Answers by Varèse to questions prepared by the editors.

Varèse, Edgar; and Ribemont Dessaignes [sic], Vincent [sic] Huidobro, Ungaretti, Alejo Carpentier, Robert Desnos, and Arthur Lourié. "La Mécanisation de la musique: Conversation sténographiée à Bifur." *Bifur* 5 (1930): 121–129.

C. Letters

Only published items are listed here, in chronological order. Excerpts and quotations from unpublished correspondence may be found in the Jolivet and Ouellette biographies (bibl. IIA) and in Chou's article, "Varèse: A Sketch of the Man and His Music" (bibl. IIB).

"A League of Art. A Free Exchange to Make the Nations Acquainted." Letter to the *New York Times,* dated March 20, 1919. *New York Times,* March 23, 1919, section 3, p. 1.

Two letters to Béla Bartók, dated August 20, 1924, and October 19, 1931. In Denis Dille, ed., *Documenta Bartókiana,* vol. 3. Mainz: Schott, 1968, pp. 120–121, 164–165.

Letter to the Editor. *Eolus* 7/1 (January 1928): 31–32.

Letter to José Rodriguez, dated March 1, 1933. In *Letters of Composers: An Anthology, 1603–1945.* Edited by Gertrude Norman and Miriam Lubell Shrifte. New York: Knopf, 1946, p. 360.

Letter to the Editor, dated July 26, 1955. *Musical Quarterly* 41 (1955): 574.

D. Miscellaneous

Apollinaire, Guillaume. *Anecdotiques.* Paris: Gallimard, 1955. A personal communication from Varèse (1913) concerning his acquaintance with the poet Léon Deubel is quoted (pp. 126–127). This originally was published in Apollinaire's column "La Vie anecdotique" in the *Mercure de France* of November 1, 1913.

"Benefit Concert Contributes $325 for Community Piano." *Santa Fe New Mexican,* September 30, 1937, p. 3.

"Best Teachers of Music Here, Is The Word From Berlin/Higher Efficiency and More Progressive Instructors at Home, Says Varèse." *New York Herald,* November 12, 1922, section 7, p. 8.

Carpentier, Alejo. "Edgar Varèse vivant." *Nouveau Commerce* 10 (Fall–Winter 1967): 15–28.

Chou Wen-chung. "Varèse: December 22, 1883–November 6, 1965." *Current Musicology* 2 (Fall 1965): 169–174. Most of the contents of this article are incorporated into the author's later "Varèse: A Sketch of the Man and His Music" (bibl. IIB).

Cowell, Henry. "Current Chronicle" [review of the premiere of *Déserts*]. *Musical Quarterly* 41 (1955): 370–373. Cowell quotes at length from Varèse's program notes for *Déserts*.

Dallapiccola, Luigi; and Elliott Carter, Anaïs Nin, Arthur Szathmary, Morton Feldman, and Marc Wilkinson. "In Memoriam Edgard Varèse." *Perspectives of New Music* 4/2 (1966): 1–13. Dallapiccola's contribution is entitled "Encounters with Edgard Varèse (Pages from a Diary)" and covers the years 1951–1965.

Downes, Olin. "Music in the Future: Edgar Varèse Attacks Neo-Classicism and Suggests Electronics." *New York Times,* July 25, 1948, section 2, p. 5.

Edgar Varèse Interviewed: Shocks for Mus. Docs." *Musical News and Herald* (London) 66 (June 21, 1924): 584–585.

"Edgar Varèse Is True Modernist." *New York Telegraph,* April 20, 1919, section 4, p. 4. A copy is in the Varèse clipping file at the New York Public Library.

Ewen, David. *American Composers Today.* New York: H. W. Wilson, 1949. "Edgar Varèse," pp. 249–251.

Frankenstein, Alfred. "Varèse, Worker in Intensities." *San Francisco Chronicle,* November 28, 1937, "This World" section, p. 13.

Grunfeld, Frederic. "The Well-Tempered Ionizer." *High Fidelity* 4 (1954): 39–41+.

Klarén, J. H. *Edgar Varèse: Pioneer of New Music in America.* Boston: C. C. Birchard, [1928].

Miller, Henry. *The Air-Conditioned Nightmare.* New York: New Directions, 1945. "With Edgar Varèse in the Gobi Desert," pp. 163–178, quotes Varèse's description of *Espace* (pp. 163–164).

Norman, Dorothy. "Ionisation—Espace." *Twice a Year* 7 (1941): 259–260. Varèse's description of *Espace,* quoted here, is the same as in Miller, with a few differences in punctuation. See also the two sources of "Que le monde s'éveille," the abridgment in French cited in bibl. IA.

"Où Edgar Varèse nous parle de Berlioz." *Pour la victoire,* New York, March 10, 1945, p. 7.

Pobers, Michel. "De passage à Paris/Edgar Varèse maître de la musique *préparée:* 'Je veux élargir mon horizon musical.'" *Arts; Lettres-Spectacles,* July 30–August 5, 1958, p. 6.

"The 'Red Symphony' Is Due to Explode." *New York Times,* March 4, 1937, section 1, p. 25.

Rich, Alan. "Varèse Is Waiting for the Audience." *New York Herald Tribune,* March 28, 1965, magazine supplement, p. 35.

"River Sirens, Lion Roars, All Music to Varèse." *Santa Fe New Mexican,* August 21, 1936, p. 2.

"Russia's Music, Surviving Turmoil, Is Still Supreme, Says Edgar Varèse." *Musical America* 37 (December 23, 1922): 23.

Sanouillet, Michel, ed. *391: Revue publiée de 1917 à 1924 par Francis Picabia.* Réédition intégrale présentée par Michel Sanouillet. Vol. 1, facsimile; vol. 2, commentary. Paris: Le Terrain Vague, 1960. Includes Varèse's "Verbe," "Que la musique sonne," and "Oblation" (see separate entries in bibl. IA).

Schonberg, Harold C. "Art—from the Shoulders Up." *Musical Digest* 27/4 (March–April 1946): 10+.

"Simple Explanation of Music Given by Varèse." *Santa Fe New Mexican,* August 25, 1937, p. 3.

Skulsky, Abraham. "Varèse Set to Launch Electronic Music Age." *New York Herald Tribune,* January 24, 1954, section 4, p. 5.

Sperling, Michael. "Varèse and Contemporary Music." *Trend* 2/3 (1934): 124–128.

Stravinsky, Igor, and Robert Craft. "Some Composers." *Musical America* 82/6 (June 1962): 8–11. Reprinted in Stravinsky and Craft, *Dialogues* (Berkeley: University of California Press, 1982), pp. 99–112.

Tryon, Winthrop P. "Edgar Varèse's New Orchestral Work, *Amériques.*" *Christian Science Monitor,* July 7, 1923, p. 16.

———. "A New Edifice from Mr. Varèse." *Christian Science Monitor,* August 28, 1926, p. 8.

———. "New Instruments in Orchestra Are Needed, Says Mr. Varèse." *Christian Science Monitor,* July 8, 1922, p. 18.

"Varèse Answers *Amériques* Critics." *Evening Bulletin,* Philadelphia, April 12, 1926, p. 3.

"Varèse Defies Hissers, Says He Won't Change Note of *Amériques.*" *Philadelphia Public Ledger,* April 12, 1926, p. 3.

"Varèse Envisions 'Space' Symphonies." *New York Times,* December 6, 1936, section 2, p. 7.

"Viewpoint of Artist Summed Up by Varèse." *Santa Fe New Mexican,* September 1, 1937, p. 3.

Waldman, Frederic. "Edgard Varèse: An Appreciation." *Juilliard Review* 1/3 (Fall 1954): 3–10.

II. WORKS ABOUT VARESE

A. Primarily Biographical

Chou Wen-chung. "Open Rather Than Bounded." *Perspectives of New Music* 5/1 (1966): 1–6. Reprinted in Boretz and Cone, eds., *Perspectives on American Composers,* pp. 49–54 (bibl. III).

———. "A Varèse Chronology." *Perspectives of New Music* 5/1 (1966): 7–10. Reprinted in Boretz and Cone, eds., *Perspectives on American Composers,* pp. 55–58 (bibl. III).

Jolivet, Hilda. *Varèse.* [Paris]: Hachette, 1973. Includes some personal correspondence.

Julius, Ruth. "Edgard Varèse: An Oral History Project, Some Preliminary Conclusions." *Current Musicology* 25 (1978): 39–49.

Lott, R. Allen. " 'New Music for New Ears': The International Composers' Guild." *Journal of the American Musicological Society* 36 (1983): 266–286. Includes a complete and accurate list of concert programs given by the guild during the years of its existence (1922–1927).

Ouellette, Fernard. *Edgard Varèse.* Translated by Derek Coltman. New York: Orion, 1968. For lack of anything more comprehensive or more definitive, this is the standard biography of Varèse. It could also be called the "authorized biography," since the author enjoyed Varèse's full cooperation. The book suffers from the fact that Ouellette, a French-Canadian poet, knows very little about music; on the other hand, the writing, which reflects a deeply felt love for Varèse's music, is occasionally quite moving. Considered strictly from the point of view of historical/chronological accuracy, Ouellette is mostly reliable. The bibliography (pp. 239–262) is extensive and obviously the product of a great deal of research, but the incomplete format of many citations, not to mention the frequent typographical errors and the inclusion of some (apparently) nonexistent sources, make this feature of the book extremely trying to use. *Caveat lector.*

Roy, Jean. *Présence contemporaines: Musique française.* Paris: Nouvelles Editions Debresse, 1962. "Edgard Varèse," pp. 123–143.

Varèse, Louise. *Varèse: A Looking-Glass Diary.* Vol. 1, 1883–1928. New York: Norton, 1972. The material is largely anecdotal, but the author's obviously unique perspective makes this book indispensable to the study of Varèse's life and work. The fact that Mrs. Varèse is neither musician nor scholar does impose some limitations on the usefulness of her work from a documentary standpoint; furthermore, it should be kept in mind that all of her information about Varèse before 1917 has been obtained at second hand. In the end, however, the various inaccuracies probably matter less than the fact that Varèse's personality is vividly portrayed here as nowhere else. The sequel, if it ever sees print, should be even more valuable. According to Chou Wen-chung (telephone conversation, August 2, 1983), Mrs. Varèse has reached the early 1950s, and the manuscript has already grown to such extensive proportions that two further volumes will probably be required.

————. "Varèse—Artaud." *Soundings* (Berkeley) 10 (1976): [10–11]. Excerpts from letters from Louise Varèse to the editor (Peter Garland) concerning the aborted collaboration between Varèse and Artaud (see also under Artaud in III).

Vivier, Odile. "Edgard Varèse: Esquisses et oeuvres détruites." *Revue musicale* 265–266 (1968): 31–36.

————. *Varèse.* Paris: Seuil, [1973]. Varèse is quoted at some length on pp. 20–21, 24, 36, and 166.

Wehmeyer, Grete. *Edgard Varèse.* Mit gezeichneten Aufnahmen von seiner Musik von L. Alcopley. Regensburg: Gustav Bosse, 1977.

B. Primarily Theoretical

Babbitt, Milton. "Edgard Varèse: A Few Observations of His Music." *Perspectives of New Music* 4/2 (1966): 14–22. Reprinted in Boretz and Cone, eds., *Perspectives on American Composers,* pp. 40–48 (bibl. III).

Bernard, Jonathan W. "On *Density 21.5:* A Response to Nattiez." *Music Analysis* 5 (1986). (See Nattiez's essay on *Density 21.5* below.)

————. "Pitch/Register in the Music of Edgard Varèse." *Music Theory Spectrum* 3 (1981): 1–25.

————. "A Theory of Pitch and Register for the Music of Edgard Varèse." Ph.D. dissertation, Yale University, 1977. University Microfilms order no. 77–27, 059.

Bloch, David Reed. "The Music of Edgard Varèse." Ph.D. dissertation, University of Washington, 1973. University Microfilms order no 73–13, 794. Particularly useful for the "Anthology of Technical Statements by Varèse" (pp. 247–266) and the bibliography (pp. 267–277).

Carter, Elliott. "On Edgard Varèse." In Van Solkema, *The New Worlds of Edgard Varèse,* pp. 1–7.

Chou Wen-chung. "*Ionisation:* The Function of Timbre in Its Formal and Temporal Organization." In Van Solkema, *The New Worlds of Edgard Varèse,* pp. 26–74.

————. "Varèse: A Sketch of the Man and His Music." *Musical Quarterly* 52 (1966): 151–170.

Cogan, Robert. *New Images of Musical Sound.* Cambridge: Harvard University Press, 1984. Analysis of *Hyperprism,* pp. 96–102.

Cowell, Henry. "The Music of Edgar Varèse." *Modern Music* 5/2 (1928): 9–18.

Erickson, Robert. *Sound Structure in Music.* Berkeley: University of California Press, 1975. "Fused Ensemble Timbres and the Sound-Masses of Edgard Varèse," pp. 47–57. Reviewed by Richard Swift in *Perspectives of New Music* 14/1 (1975): 148–158.

Gümbel, Martin. "Versuch an Varèse *Density 21.5.*" *Zeitschrift für Musiktheorie* 1/1 (1970): 31–38.

Morgan, Robert P. "Notes on Varèse's Rhythm." In Van Solkema, *The New Worlds of Edgard Varèse,* pp. 9–25.

Nattiez, Jean-Jacques. "*Densité 21.5* de Varèse: Essai d'analyse sémiologique. Université de Montréal: Groupe de recherches en sémiologie musicale, 1975.

————. "Varèse's *Density 21.5:* A Study in Semiological Analysis." Revised by the author. Translated by Anna Barry. *Music Analysis* 1 (1982): 243–340.

Parks, Florence Anne. "Freedom, Form, and Process in Varèse." Ph.D. dissertation, Cornell University, 1974. University Microfilms order no. 74–17,668. The bibliography (pp. 448–463) is extensive and is organized in an intelligent and useful way. Unfortunately, it is also riddled with errors of citation; numbers signifying dates and pagination are frequently wrong.

Post, Nora. "Varèse, Wolpe, and the Oboe." *Perspectives of New Music* 20 (1981–1982): 135–148.

Stempel, Larry. "Not Even Varèse Can Be an Orphan." *Musical Quarterly* 60 (1974): 46–60.
———. "Varèse's 'Awkwardness' and the Symmetry in the 'Frame of 12 Tones': An Analytic Approach." *Musical Quarterly* 65 (1979): 148–166.
Strawn, John. "The *Intégrales* of Edgard Varèse: Space, Mass, Element, and Form." *Perspectives of New Music* 17/1 (1978): 138–160.
Tenney, James, with Larry Polansky. "Temporal Gestalt Perception in Music." *Journal of Music Theory* 24 (1980): 205–241. Includes an analysis of *Density 21.5* (pp. 221–230).
Van Solkema, Sherman, ed. *The New Worlds of Edgard Varèse: A Symposium.* I.S.A.M. Monographs, no. 11. Brooklyn: Institute for Studies in American Music, 1979. Reviewed by Jonathan W. Bernard in *Journal of Music Theory* 24 (1980): 277–283.
Whittall, Arnold. "Varèse and Organic Athematicism." *Music Review* 28 (1967): 311–315.
Wilheim, András. "The Genesis of a Specific Twelve-Tone System in the Works of Varèse." *Studia Musicologica* 19 (1977): 203–226.
Wilkinson, Marc. "An Introduction to the Music of Edgar Varèse." *The Score and I.M.A. Magazine* 19 (1957): 5–18.

C. General Criticism

Barzun, Jacques. "To Praise Varèse." *Columbia University Forum* 9/2 (1966): 16–20.
Boehmer, Konrad. "Über Edgard Varèse." In Dahlhaus, *Bericht,* pp. 307–313.
Boulez, Pierre. *Points de repère.* Edited by Jean-Jacques Nattiez. Paris: Seuil, 1981. "Varèse: *Hyperprisme, Octandre, Intégrales,*" pp. 365–367; "Arcanes Varèse," pp. 536–537.
Brinkmann, Reinhold. "Anmerkungen zu Varèse." In Dahlhaus, *Bericht,* pp. 313–316.
Dahlhaus, Carl, et al., ed. *Bericht über den internationalen musikwissenschaftlichen Kongress* (Bonn, 1970). Kassel: Bärenreiter, 1971.
"Edgard Varèse, Composer, Dead." *New York Times,* November 7, 1965, p. 89.
"For Edgard Varèse on the Celebration of His 80th [sic] Year." A selection of short tributes from various musicians, printed in the Carnegie Hall program of March 31, 1965, p. 14. A copy is in the Varèse clipping file at the New York Public Library.
Helm, Everett. "Aussenseiter Varèse." *Melos* 32 (1965): 433–437.
Metzger, Heinz-Klaus. "Hommage à Edgard Varèse." *Darmstädter Beiträge zur neuen Musik* 2 (1959): 54–66.
Metzger, Heinz-Klaus, and Rainer Riehn, eds. *Edgard Varèse: Rückblick auf die Zukunft.* Musik-Konzepte, no. 6. Munich: Editions text+kritik, 1978. Bibliography, pp. 106–116.
Morgan, Robert P. "Rewriting Music History: Second Thoughts on Ives and Varèse." *Musical Newsletter* 3/1 (January 1973): 3–12; 3/2 (April 1973): 15–23+.
Rosenfeld, Paul. *An Hour with American Music.* Philadelphia: J. B. Lippincott, 1929. "Edgar Varèse," pp. 160–179.
———. "Musical Chronicle." *The Dial* 76 (1924): 298–300.
———. *Musical Impressions: Selections from Paul Rosenfeld's Criticism.* Edited and with an introduction by Herbert A. Leibowitz. New York: Hill and Wang, 1969. "Edgard Varèse," pp. 269–285.
———. "We Want Varèse." *Twice a Year* 7 (1941): 252–258.
Rudhyar, Dane. "Future Music of America and Varèse as Its Pioneer." *Christian Science Monitor,* March 10, 1923, p. 16.
———. "The Music of Fire." *New Pearson's Magazine* 49 (April 1923): 45–47.
Salzman, Eric. "Edgard Varèse." *Stereo Review* 26/6 (June 1971): 56–68.
Steinhardt, Heinrich. "Varèse, unbegriffener Prophet einer kosmischen Schallwelt." *Melos* 38 (1971): 293–297.
Tryon, Winthrop P. "*Amériques,* Repartitioned." *Christian Science Monitor,* January 19, 1929, p. 10.

———. "Fall Flights." *Christian Science Monitor*, October 4, 1928, p. 8.

Vivier, Odile. "Innovations instrumentales d'Edgar Varèse." *Revue musicale* 226 (1955): 188–197.

Zanotti Bianco, Massimo. "Edgar Varèse and the Geometry of Sound." *The Arts* 7 (1925): 35–36.

III. OTHER SOURCES

Allard, Roger. "On Certain Painters" (1911). In Fry, *Cubism*, pp. 63–64.

———. "The Signs of Renewal in Painting" (1912). In Fry, *Cubism*, pp. 70–73.

Apollinaire, Guillaume. *Apollinaire on Art: Essays and Reviews, 1902–1918*. Edited by LeRoy C. Breunig. Translated by Susan Suleiman. New York: Viking, 1972.

———. *The Cubist Painters: Aesthetic Meditations* (1913). Translated by Lionel Abel. New York: George Wittenborn, 1970.

———. "George Braque" (1908). In Fry, *Cubism*, p. 49.

Apollonio, Umbro, ed. *Futurist Manifestos*. Translated by Robert Brain, R. W. Flint, J. C. Higgitt, and Caroline Tisdall. New York: Viking, 1973.

Artaud, Antonin. *Oeuvres complètes*. Vol. 2. Paris: Gallimard, 1961. "Il n'y a plus de firmament" (pp. 91–110) is the scenario Artaud produced in response to Varèse's request (ca. 1932) that he collaborate on *Espace*.

Ashton, Dore, ed. *Picasso on Art: A Selection of Views*. New York: Viking, 1972.

Asturias, Miguel Angel. *Leyendas de Guatemala*. Buenos Aires: Losada, 1957. With a preface by Paul Valéry. "Ahora que me acuerdo," pp. 21–26. From this section Varèse extracted a portion (pp. 22–23) which, with numerous ellipses and slight changes of wording, forms the text of *Ecuatorial*.

Balla, Giacomo. "The Late Balla—Futurist Balla" (1915). In Apollonio, *Futurist Manifestos*, p. 206.

Barzun, Henri, ed. *L'Art orphique*. Vol. 1: *Renaissance 1930*. Paris: Albert Morancé, [1930].

———. "L'Universel Poème, troisième épisode: Terre des pionniers." In Barzun, *L'Art orphique*, pp. 16–31.

Boccioni, Umberto. "Absolute Motion + Relative Motion = Dynamism" (1914). In Apollonio, *Futurist Manifestos*, pp. 150–154.

———. "Futurist Painting and Sculpture" (1914). In Apollonio, *Futurist Manifestos*, pp. 172–181.

———. "Plastic Dynamism" (1913). In Apollonio, *Futurist Manifestos*, pp. 92–95.

———. "The Plastic Foundations of Futurist Sculpture and Painting" (1913). In Apollonio, *Futurist Manifestos*, pp. 88–90.

———. "Preface, First Exhibition of Futurist Sculpture" (1913). In Herbert, *Modern Artists on Modern Art*, pp. 47–50.

———. "Technical Manifesto of Futurist Sculpture" (1912). In Apollonio, *Futurist Manifestos*, pp. 51–65; and in Herbert, *Modern Artists on Modern Art*, pp. 50–57.

Boccioni, Umberto; and Carlo Carrà, Luigi Russolo, Giacomo Balla, and Gino Severini. "The Exhibitors to the Public" (1912). In Apollonio, *Futurist Manifestos*, pp. 45–50.

———. "Futurist Painting: Technical Manifesto" (1910). In Apollonio, *Futurist Manifestos*, pp. 27–31.

———. "Manifesto of the Futurist Painters" (1910). In Apollonio, *Futurist Manifestos*, pp. 24–27.

Boretz, Benjamin, and Edward T. Cone, eds. *Perspectives on American Composers*. New York: Norton, 1971.

Boulez, Pierre. *Notes of an Apprenticeship*. Translated by Herbert Weinstock. New York: Knopf, 1968. "Toward a Technology," pp. 61–62; "Stravinsky Remains," pp. 72–145.

Bragaglia, Anton Giulio. "Futurist Photodynamism" (1911). In Apollonio, *Futurist Man-ifestos,* pp. 38–45.

Braque, Georges. "Personal Statement" (1908). In Fry, *Cubism,* p. 53.

Brown, Reginald Allan. "Orchestral Poetry." In Barzun, *L'Art orphique,* pp. 12–13.

Busoni, Ferruccio. *Sketch of a New Aesthetic of Music* (1906). Translated by T. Baker. New York: G. Schirmer, 1911. Reprinted in *Three Classics in the Aesthetic of Music,* New York: Dover, 1962, pp. 73–102.

Carrà, Carlo. "The Painting of Sounds, Noises, and Smells" (1913). In Apollonio, *Futurist Manifestos,* pp. 111–115.

———. "From Cézanne to Us, the Futurists" (1913). In Chipp, *Theories of Modern Art,* pp. 304–308.

———. "Plastic Planes as Spherical Expansions in Space" (1913). In Apollonio, *Futurist Manifestos,* pp. 91–92.

Chipp, Herschel B., ed. *Theories of Modern Art: A Source Book by Artists and Critics.* With contributions by Peter Selz and Joshua C. Taylor. Berkeley: University of California Press, 1968.

Delaunay, Robert. Letter to Wassily Kandinsky (1912). In Chipp, *Theories of Modern Art,* pp. 318–319.

———. Letter to August Macke (1912). In Chipp, *Theories of Modern Art,* pp. 317–318.

———. "Light" (1912). In Chipp, *Theories of Modern Art,* pp. 319–320.

Delaunay, Robert, and Sonia Delaunay. *The New Art of Color: The Writings of Robert and Sonia Delaunay.* Edited by Arthur A. Cohen. Translated by David Shapiro and Arthur A. Cohen. New York: Viking, 1978.

Dijkstra, Bram. *Cubism, Stieglitz, and the Early Poetry of William Carlos Williams: The Hiero-glyphics of a New Speech.* Princeton: Princeton University Press, 1969.

Divoire, Fernand. "L'Art poétique orchestral/simultanisme = un mode d'expression qui permettra peut-être de grandes choses." In Barzun, *L'Art orphique,* pp. 43–44.

Dupin, Jacques. *Joan Miró: Life and Work.* New York: Abrams, n.d.

Eddy, Arthur Jerome. *Cubists and Post-Impressionism.* Chicago: A. C. McClurg, 1914.

Forte, Allen. *The Structure of Atonal Music.* New Haven: Yale University Press, 1973.

Fry, Edward F. *Cubism.* With excerpts from documentary texts. New York and Toronto: Oxford University Press, 1966.

Gleizes, Albert, and Jean Metzinger. "Cubism" (1912). In Herbert, *Modern Artists on Modern Art,* pp. 1–18.

Gray, Christopher. *Cubist Aesthetic Theories.* Baltimore: Johns Hopkins University Press, 1953.

Green, Jonathan, ed. *Camera Work: A Critical Anthology.* Millerton, N.Y.: Aperture, 1973.

Gris, Juan. "Notes on My Painting" (1923). In Kahnweiler, *Juan Gris,* pp. 193–194.

———. "Statement" (1921). In Kahnweiler, *Juan Gris,* p. 193.

Henderson, Linda Dalrymple. "A New Facet of Cubism: 'The Fourth Dimension' and 'Non-Euclidean Geometry' Reinterpreted." *Art Quarterly* 34 (1971): 410–433.

Herbert, Robert L., ed. *Modern Artists on Modern Art: Ten Unabridged Essays.* Englewood Cliffs, N.J.: Prentice-Hall, 1964.

Homer, William Innes. *Alfred Stieglitz and the American Avant-Garde.* Boston: New York Graphic Society, 1977.

Huidobro, Vicente. *Le Citoyen de l'oubli.* Edited and translated by Fernand Verhesen. [Paris]: Saint-Germain-des-Près, 1974. The text of *Tour Eiffel,* "écrit directement en français" according to the editor, is cited in full on pp. 22–25. From this poem Varèse extracted a section (p. 24) which, with a few minor changes and ellipses, forms the text of "Chanson de là-haut," the first movement of *Offrandes.* Varèse's title is apparently inspired by the lines of Huidobro's poem immediately preceding the extract: "Jacqueline / Fille de France / Qu'est-ce que tu vois là-haut."

Jeanneret-Gris, Charles Edouard [Le Corbusier]. *Le Poème électronique Le Corbusier*. Paris: Minuit, 1958.

Kahnweiler, Daniel-Henry. *Juan Gris: His Life and Work*. Rev. ed. Translated by Douglas Cooper. New York: Henry N. Abrams, 1968.

———. *The Rise of Cubism* (1915). Translated by Henry Aronson. New York: Wittenborn, Schultz, 1949.

Kandinsky, Wassily. *Concerning the Spiritual in Art, and Painting in Particular* (1912). Translated by Michael Sadleir. Edited by Francis Golffing, Michael Harrison, and Ferdinand Ostertag. New York: Wittenborn, Schultz, 1947. With an introductory essay by Stanley William Hayter, "The Language of Kandinsky," pp. 15–18.

———. "On the Question of Form" (1911). In *The Blaue Reiter Almanac*, edited by Wassily Kandinsky and Franz Marc. New documentary edition, edited and with an introduction by Klaus Lankheit. Translated by Henning Falkenstein. New York: Viking, 1974, pp. 147–187.

———. *Point and Line to Plane* (1926). Translated by Howard Dearstyne and Hilla Rebay. New York: Guggenheim Museum, 1947. Reprint ed., New York: Dover, 1979.

———. "Reminiscences" (1913). In Herbert, *Modern Artists on Modern Art*, pp. 19–44.

Klee, Paul. "Creative Credo" (1920). In Chipp, *Theories of Modern Art*, pp. 182–186.

Kozloff, Max. *Cubism/Futurism*. New York: Harper and Row, 1973.

Léger, Fernand. "Contemporary Achievements in Painting" (1914). In Fry, *Cubism*, pp. 135–139.

Marinetti, Filippo Tommaso. *Marinetti: Selected Writings*. Edited and with an introduction by R. W. Flint. Translated by R. W. Flint and Arthur A. Coppotelli. New York: Farrar, Straus and Giroux, 1972.

Martin, Marianne W. *Futurist Art and Theory, 1909–1915*. Oxford: Clarendon, 1968. Reprint ed., New York: Hacker Art Books, 1978.

Metzinger, Jean. "Cubism and Tradition" (1911). In Fry, *Cubism*, pp. 66–67.

Nin, Anaïs. *The Diary of Anaïs Nin*. Vol. 3: 1939–1944. Edited by Gunther Stuhlmann. New York: Harcourt Brace Jovanovich, 1969.

———. *House of Incest*. Photomontages by Val Telberg. Chicago: Swallow, 1958. From this work, which might be called a prose poem, Varèse extracted isolated words and phrases and assembled them, in an order which bears no particular relationship to the original and interspersed with vocal syllables of his own devising, for the text of *Nocturnal*.

Olivier-Hourcade. "The Tendency of Contemporary Painting" (1912). In Fry, *Cubism*, pp. 74–75.

Ozenfant, Amédée, and Jeanneret, Charles-Edouard. "Towards the Crystal" (1925). In Fry, *Cubism*, pp. 170–171.

Perle, George. *Serial Composition and Atonality*. 5th ed. Berkeley: University of California Press, 1981.

Raynal, Maurice. "Conception and Vision" (1912). In Fry, *Cubism*, pp. 94–96.

———. "Preface to a Catalogue" (1912). In Fry, *Cubism*, pp. 91–93.

Reverdy, Pierre. "On Cubism" (1917). In Fry, *Cubism*, pp. 143–146.

Richter, Hans. *Dada: Art and Anti-Art*. Translated by David Britt. New York and Toronto: Oxford University Press, 1965.

Rivière, Jacques. "Present Tendencies in Painting" (1912). In Fry, *Cubism*, pp. 75–80.

Rosenberg, Léonce. "Tradition and Cubism" (1919). In Fry, *Cubism*, pp. 38–39.

Rudhyar, Dane. "What Is an Octave?" *Aeolian Review* 2/1 (December 1922): 8–12.

Russolo, Luigi. "The Art of Noises" (1913). In Apollonio, *Futurist Manifestos*, pp. 74–88.

Saint'Elia, Antonio. "Manifesto of Futurist Architecture" (1914). In Apollonio, *Futurist Manifestos*, pp. 160–172.

Salmon, André. "Anecdotal History of Cubism" (1912). In Fry, *Cubism*, pp. 81–90.

Schuller, Gunther. "Conversation with Steuermann." *Perspectives of New Music* 3/1 (1964):

22–35. Reprinted in Boretz and Cone, eds., *Perspectives on American Composers*, pp. 199–212.

Severini, Gino. "The Plastic Analogies of Dynamism—Futurist Manifesto" (1913). In Apollonio, *Futurist Manifestos*, pp. 118–125.

Shattuck, Roger. *The Banquet Years: The Origins of the Avant Garde in France, 1885 to World War I*. Rev. ed. New York: Vintage, 1968.

Stockhausen, Karlheinz. "Electronic and Instrumental Music." In *Die Reihe* 5 (*Reports, Analyses*), ed. Herbert Eimert and Karlheinz Stockhausen. Bryn Mawr: Theodore Presser, 1961, pp. 59–67.

Tablada, José Juan. *Obras*. Vol. 1: *Poesía*. Edited and compiled by Hector Valdés. Universidad Nacional Autónoma de México: Centro de Estudios Literarios, 1977. "La croix du sud," p. 588. This poem was written originally in French and is used in its entirety, unaltered, as the text for "La croix du sud," the second movement of *Offrandes*.

Tisdall, Caroline, and Bozzola, Angelo. *Futurism*. New York and Toronto: Oxford University Press, 1978.

Weber, Max. "The Fourth Dimension from a Plastic Point of View" (1910). In Green, *Camera Work*, pp. 202–203.

Wright, Stanton MacDonald. "Statement on Synchromism" (1916). In Chipp, *Theories of Modern Art*, pp. 320–321.

Yudice, George. "Cubist Aesthetics in Painting and Poetry." *Semiotica* 36 (1981): 107–133.

INDEX